THE UNLIKELY SPY

DANIEL SILVA

VILLARD BOOKS / NEW YORK

Library of Congress Cataloging-in-Publication Data

Silva, Daniel.
The unlikely spy / Daniel Silva.
p.   cm.
ISBN 0-679-45562-0
1. World War, 1939–1945—England—London—Fiction. I. Title.
PR6069.I362U54   1997
823′.914—dc20   96-27961

Random House website address: http://www.randomhouse.com/

Printed in the United States of America on acid-free paper
24689753

First U.S. Edition

FOR MY WIFE, JAMIE, WHOSE LOVE, SUPPORT,
AND CONSTANT ENCOURAGEMENT MADE THIS WORK
POSSIBLE, AND FOR MY CHILDREN,
LILY AND NICHOLAS

PREFACE

In April 1944, six weeks before the Allied invasion of France, the Nazi propagandist William Joyce—better known as Lord Haw-Haw—made a chilling radio broadcast directed at Britain.

According to Joyce, Germany knew the Allies were at work on large concrete structures in the south of England. Germany also knew those structures were to be towed across the English Channel during the coming invasion and sunk off the coast of France. Joyce declared, "Well, we are going to help you boys. When you come to get them under way, we're going to sink them for you."

Alarm klaxons sounded inside British Intelligence and the Allied high command. The concrete structures referred to by Joyce were actually components of a giant artificial harbor complex bound for Normandy codenamed Operation Mulberry. If Hitler's spies truly understood the purpose of Mulberry, they might very well know the most important secret of the war—the time and place of the Allied invasion of France.

Several anxious days later those fears were put to rest, when U.S. intelligence intercepted a coded message from Japan's ambassador to Berlin, Lieutenant General Hiroshi Baron Oshima, to his superiors in Tokyo. Oshima received regular briefings from his German allies on preparations for the looming invasion. According to the intercepted message, German intelligence believed the concrete structures were part of a massive antiaircraft complex—not an artificial harbor.

But how did German intelligence make such a crucial miscalculation? Did it simply misread its own intelligence? Or had it been deceived?

This project is so vital that it might be described as the crux of the whole operation.
—Admiralty memo

Considering the thousands of workers who at one time or another were involved, it was remarkable that the enemy had no inkling of what was afoot.
—Guy Hartcup,
Force Mulberry

In wartime, truth is so precious that she should always be attended by a bodyguard of lies.
—Winston Churchill

PART
ONE

❖

CHAPTER ONE

SUFFOLK, ENGLAND: NOVEMBER 1938

Beatrice Pymm died because she missed the last bus to Ipswich.

Twenty minutes before her death she stood at the dreary bus stop and read the timetable in the dim light of the village's single street lamp. In a few months the lamp would be extinguished to conform with the blackout regulations. Beatrice Pymm would never know of the blackout.

For now, the lamp burned just brightly enough for Beatrice to read the faded timetable. To see it better she stood on tiptoe and ran down the numbers with the end of a paint-smudged forefinger. Her late mother always complained bitterly about the paint. She thought it unladylike for one's hand to be forever soiled. She had wanted Beatrice to take up a neater hobby—music, volunteer work, even writing, though Beatrice's mother didn't hold with writers.

"Damn," Beatrice muttered, forefinger still glued to the timetable. Normally she was punctual to a fault. In a life without financial responsibility, without friends, without family, she had erected a rigorous personal schedule. Today, she had strayed from it—painted too long, started back too late.

She removed her hand from the timetable and brought it to her cheek, squeezing her face into a look of worry. Your father's face, her mother had always said with despair—a broad flat forehead, a large noble nose, a receding chin. At just thirty, hair prematurely shot with gray.

She worried about what to do. Her home in Ipswich was at least five miles away, too far to walk. In the early evening there might still be light traffic on the road. Perhaps someone would give her a lift.

She let out a long frustrated sigh. Her breath froze, hovered before her face, then drifted away on a cold wind from the marsh. The clouds shattered and a bright moon shone through. Beatrice looked up and saw a halo of ice floating around it. She shivered, feeling the cold for the first time.

She picked up her things: a leather rucksack, a canvas, a battered easel. She had spent the day painting along the estuary of the River Orwell. Painting was her only love and the landscape of East Anglia her only subject matter. It did lead to a certain repetitiveness in her work. Her mother liked to see *people* in art—street scenes, crowded cafés. Once she even suggested Beatrice spend some time in France to pursue her painting. Beatrice refused. She loved the marshlands and the dikes, the estuaries and the broads, the fen land north of Cambridge, the rolling pastures of Suffolk.

She reluctantly set out toward home, pounding along the side of the road at a good pace despite the weight of her things. She wore a mannish cotton shirt, smudged like her fingers, a heavy sweater that made her feel like a toy bear, a reefer coat too long in the sleeves, trousers tucked inside Wellington boots. She moved beyond the sphere of yellow lamplight; the darkness swallowed her. She felt no apprehension about walking through the dark in the countryside. Her mother, fearful of her long trips alone, warned incessantly of rapists. Beatrice always dismissed the threat as unlikely.

She shivered with the cold. She thought of home, a large cottage on the edge of Ipswich left to her by her mother. Behind the cottage, at the end of the garden walk, she had built a light-splashed studio, where she spent most of her time. It was not uncommon for her to go days without speaking to another human being.

All this, and more, her killer knew.

After five minutes of walking she heard the rattle of an engine behind her. A commercial vehicle, she thought. An old one, judging by the ragged engine note. Beatrice watched the glow of the headlamps spread like sunrise across the grass on either side of the roadway. She heard the engine lose power and begin to coast. She felt a gust of wind as the vehicle swept by. She choked on the stink of the exhaust.

Then she watched as it pulled to the side of the road and stopped.

The hand, visible in the bright moonlight, struck Beatrice as odd. It poked from the driver's-side window seconds after the van had stopped and beckoned her forward. A thick leather glove, Beatrice noted, the kind used by workmen who carry heavy things. A workman's overall—dark blue, maybe.

The hand beckoned once more. There it was again—something about the way it moved wasn't quite right. She was an artist, and artists know about motion and flow. And there was something else. When the hand moved it exposed the skin between the end of the sleeve and the base of the glove. Even in the poor light Beatrice could see the skin was pale and hairless—not like the wrist of any workman she had ever seen—and uncommonly slender.

Still, she felt no alarm. She quickened her pace and reached the passenger door in a few steps. She pulled open the door and set her things on the floor in front of the seat. Then she looked up into the van for the first time and noticed the driver was gone.

Beatrice Pymm, in the final conscious seconds of her life, wondered why anyone would use a van to carry a motorcycle. It was there, resting on its side in the back, two jerry cans of petrol next to it.

Still standing next to the van, she closed the door and called out. There was no answer.

Seconds later she heard the sound of a leather boot on gravel.

She heard the sound again, closer.

She turned her head and saw the driver standing there. She looked to the face and saw only a black woolen mask. Two pools of pale blue stared coldly behind the eyeholes. Feminine-looking lips, parted slightly, glistened behind the slit for the mouth.

Beatrice opened her mouth to scream. She managed only a brief gasp before the driver rammed a gloved hand into her mouth. The fingers dug into the soft flesh of her throat. The glove tasted horribly of dust, petrol, and dirty motor oil. Beatrice gagged, then vomited the remains of her picnic lunch—roast chicken, Stilton cheese, red wine.

Then she felt the other hand probing around her left breast. For an instant Beatrice thought her mother's fears about rape had finally been proved correct. But the hand touching her breast was not the hand of a molester or a rapist. The hand was skilled, like a doctor's, and curiously gentle. It moved from her breast to her ribs, pressing hard. Beatrice jerked, gasped, and bit down harder. The driver seemed not to feel it through the thick glove.

The hand reached the bottom of her ribs and probed the soft flesh at the top of her abdomen. It went no farther. One finger remained pressed against the spot. Beatrice heard a sharp click.

An instant of excruciating pain, a burst of brilliant white light.

Then, a benevolent darkness.

The killer had trained endlessly for this night, but it was the first time. The killer removed the gloved hand from the victim's mouth, turned, and was violently sick. There was no time for sentiment. The killer was a soldier— a major in the secret service—and Beatrice Pymm soon would be the enemy. Her death, while unfortunate, was necessary.

The killer wiped away the vomit from the lips of the mask and set to work, taking hold of the stiletto and pulling. The wound sucked hard but the killer pulled harder, and the stiletto slipped out.

An excellent kill, clean, very little blood.

Vogel would be proud.

The killer wiped the blood from the stiletto, snapped the blade back into place, and put it in the pocket of the overall. Then the killer grasped the body beneath the arms, dragged it to the rear of the van, and dumped it on the crumbling edge of the tarmac.

The killer opened the rear doors. The body convulsed.

It was a struggle to lift the body into the back of the van, but after a moment it was done. The engine hesitated, then fired. Then the van was on the move again, flashing through the darkened village and turning onto the deserted roadway.

The killer, composed despite the presence of the body, quietly sang a song from childhood to help pass the time. It was a long drive, four hours at least. During the preparation the killer had driven the route by motorcycle, the same bike that now lay beside Beatrice Pymm. The drive would take much longer in the van. The engine had little power, the brakes were bad, and it pulled hard to the right.

The killer vowed to steal a better one next time.

Stab wounds to the heart, as a rule, do not kill instantly. Even if the weapon penetrates a chamber, the heart usually continues to beat for some time until the victim bleeds to death.

As the van clattered along the roadway, Beatrice Pymm's chest cavity rapidly filled with blood. Her mind approached something close to a coma. She had some sense she was about to die.

She remembered her mother's warnings about being alone late at night.

She felt the wet stickiness of her own blood seeping out of her body into her shirt. She wondered if her painting had been damaged.

She heard singing. Beautiful singing. It took some time, but she finally discerned that the driver was not singing in English. The song was German, the voice a woman's.

Then Beatrice Pymm died.

First stop, ten minutes later, the bank of the River Orwell, the same spot where Beatrice Pymm had been painting that day. The killer left the van's engine running and climbed out. She walked to the passenger side of the van, opened the door, and removed the easel, the canvas, and the rucksack.

The easel was erected very near the slow-moving water, the canvas placed on it. The killer opened the rucksack, removed the paints and palette, and laid them on the damp ground. She glanced at the unfinished painting and thought it was rather good. A shame she couldn't have killed someone with less talent.

Next, she removed the half-empty bottle of claret, poured the remainder of the wine into the river, and dropped the bottle at the legs of the easel. Poor Beatrice. Too much wine, a careless step, a plunge into frigid water, a slow journey to the open sea.

Cause of death: presumed drowned, presumed accidental.

Case closed.

Six hours later, the van passed through the West Midlands village of Whitchurch and turned onto a rough track skirting the edge of a barley field. The grave had been dug the previous night—deep enough to conceal a corpse but not so deep that it might never be found.

She dragged Beatrice Pymm's body from the back of the van and stripped away the bloody clothing. She took hold of the naked corpse by the feet and dragged it closer to the grave. Then the killer walked back to the van and removed three items: an iron mallet, a red brick, and a small spade.

This was the part she dreaded most, for some reason worse than the murder itself. She dropped the three items next to the body and steadied herself. Fighting off another wave of nausea she took the mallet in her gloved hand, raised it, and crushed Beatrice Pymm's nose.

When it was over she could barely look at what was left of Beatrice Pymm's face. Using first the mallet, then the brick, she had pounded it into a mass of blood, tissue, smashed bone, and shattered teeth.

She had achieved the intended effect—the features had been erased, the face rendered unrecognizable.

She had done everything they had ordered her to do. She was to be different. She had trained at a special camp for many months, much longer than the other agents. She would be planted deeper. That was why she had to kill Beatrice Pymm. She wouldn't waste her time doing what other, less gifted agents could do: counting troops, monitoring railways, assessing bomb damage. That was easy. She would be saved for bigger and better things. She would be a time bomb, ticking inside England, waiting to be activated, waiting to go off.

She put a boot against the ribs and pushed. The corpse tumbled into the grave. She covered the body with earth. She collected the bloodstained clothing and tossed it into the back of the van. From the front seat she took a small handbag containing a Dutch passport and a wallet. The wallet held identification papers, an Amsterdam driver's permit, and photographs of a fat, smiling Dutch family.

All of it had been forged by the Abwehr in Berlin.

She threw the bag into the trees at the edge of the barley field, a few yards from the grave. If everything went according to plan, the badly decomposed and mutilated body would be found in a few months, along with the handbag. The police would believe the dead woman to be Christa Kunst, a Dutch tourist who entered the country in October 1938 and whose holiday came to an unfortunate and violent end.

Before leaving, she took a last look at the grave. She felt a pang of sadness for Beatrice Pymm. In death she had been robbed of her face and her name.

Someting else: the killer had just lost her own identity. For six months she had lived in Holland, for Dutch was one of her languages. She had carefully constructed a past, voted in a local Amsterdam election, even permitted herself a young lover, a boy of nineteen with a huge appetite and a willingness to learn new things. Now Christa Kunst lay in a shallow grave on the edge of an English barley field.

The killer would assume a new identity in the morning.

But tonight she was no one.

She refueled the van and drove for twenty minutes. The village of Alderton, like Beatrice Pymm, had been carefully chosen—a place where a van burning at the roadside in the middle of the night would not be noticed immediately.

She pulled the motorbike out of the van along a heavy plank of wood, difficult work even for a strong man. She struggled with the bike and gave up when it was three feet from the road. It crashed down with a loud bang, the one mistake she had made all night.

She lifted the bike and rolled it, engine dead, fifty yards down the road. Then she returned to the van. One of the jerry cans still contained some petrol. She doused the inside of the van, dumping most of the fuel on Beatrice Pymm's blood-soaked clothing.

By the time the van went up in a fireball she had kicked the bike into life. She watched the van burn for a few seconds, the orange light dancing on the barren field and the line of trees beyond.

Then she turned the bike south and headed for London.

CHAPTER TWO

OYSTER BAY, NEW YORK: AUGUST 1939

Dorothy Lauterbach considered her stately fieldstone mansion the most beautiful on the North Shore. Most of her friends agreed, because she was richer and they wanted invitations to the two parties the Lauterbachs threw each summer—a raucous, drunken affair in June and a more reflective occasion in late August, when the summer season ground to a melancholy conclusion.

The back of the house looked out over the Sound. There was a pleasant beach of white sand brought by truck from Massachusetts. From the beach a well-fertilized lawn raced toward the back of the house, pausing now and again to skirt the exquisite gardens, the red clay tennis court, the royal blue swimming pool.

The servants had risen early to prepare for the family's well-deserved day of inactivity, erecting a croquet set and a badminton net that would never be touched, removing the canvas cover from a wooden motorboat that would never be untied from the dock. Once a servant courageously pointed out to Mrs. Lauterbach the folly of this daily ritual. Mrs. Lauterbach had snapped at him, and the practice was never again questioned. The toys were raised each and every morning, only to stand with the sadness of Christmas decorations in May until they were ceremoniously removed at sundown and put away for the night.

The bottom floor of the house sprawled along the water from sunroom to sitting room, to dining room, and finally to the Florida room, though none of the other Lauterbachs understood why Dorothy insisted on calling it a Florida room when the summer sun on the North Shore could be just as warm.

The house had been purchased thirty years earlier when the young Lauterbachs assumed they would produce a small army of offspring. Instead they
had just two daughters who didn't care much for each other's company—
Margaret, a beautiful and immensely popular socialite, and Jane. And so the
house became a peaceful place of warm sunshine and soft colors, where most
of the noise was made by white curtains snapping in watery breezes and
Dorothy Lauterbach's restless pursuit of perfection in all things.

On that morning—the morning after the Lauterbachs' final party—the
curtains hung still and straight in the open windows, waiting for a breeze
that would never come. The sun blazed and a shimmering haze hung over
the bay. The air was itchy and thick.

Upstairs in her bedroom, Margaret Lauterbach Jordan pulled off her
nightgown and sat in front of her dressing table. She quickly brushed her
hair. It was ash blond, streaked by the sun and unfashionably short. But it
was comfortable and easy to manage. Besides, she liked the way it framed
her face and showed off the long graceful line of her neck.

She looked at her body in the mirror. She had finally lost the last few stubborn pounds she had gained while pregnant with their first child. The stretch
marks had faded and her stomach was tanned a rich brown. Bare midriffs
were *in* that summer, and she liked the way everyone on the North Shore
had been surprised by how trim she looked. Only her breasts were
different—they were larger, fine with Margaret because she had always
been self-conscious about their size. The new bras that summer were
smaller and stiffer, designed to achieve a high-bossomed effect. Margaret
liked them because Peter liked the way they made her look.

She pulled on a pair of white cotton slacks, a sleeveless blouse, knotted
beneath her breasts, and a pair of flat sandals. She looked at her reflection
one last time. She was beautiful—she knew that—but not in an audacious
way that turned heads on the streets of Manhattan. Margaret's beauty was
timeless and understated, perfect for the layer of society into which she had
been born.

She thought, And soon you're going to be a fat cow again!

She turned from the mirror and drew open the curtains. Harsh sunlight
spilled into the room. The lawn was in chaos. The tent was being lowered,
the caterers were packing away the tables and chairs, the dance floor was
being lifted panel by panel and carted away. The grass, once green and lush,
had been trampled flat. She opened the windows and smelled the sickly
sweet scent of spilled champagne. Something about it depressed her. "Hitler

may be preparing to conquer Poland, but a glittering time was had by all who attended Bratton and Dorothy Lauterbach's annual August gala Saturday night. . . ." Margaret could almost write the society columns herself by now.

She switched on the radio on her nightstand and tuned it to WNYC. "I'll Never Smile Again" played softly. Peter stirred, still asleep. In the brilliant sunlight his porcelain skin was barely distinguishable from the white satin sheets. Once she thought all engineers were men with flat-top haircuts, thick black glasses, and lots of pencils in their shirt pockets. Peter was not like that—strong cheekbones, a sharp jawline, soft green eyes, nearly black hair. Lying in bed now, his upper body exposed, he looked, Margaret thought, like a tumbled Michelangelo. He stood out on the North Shore, stood out from the fair-haired boys who had been born to extraordinary wealth and planned to live life from a deck chair. Peter was sharp and ambitious and brisk. He could run circles around the whole crowd. Margaret liked that.

She glanced at the hazy sky and frowned. Peter detested August weather like this. He would be irritable and cranky all day. There would probably be a thunderstorm to ruin the drive back into the city.

She thought, Perhaps I should wait to tell him the news.

"Get up, Peter, or we'll never hear the end of it," Margaret said, poking him with her toe.

"Five more minutes."

"We don't have five minutes, darling."

Peter didn't move. "Coffee," he pleaded.

The maids had left coffee outside the bedroom door. It was a practice Dorothy Lauterbach loathed; she thought it made the upstairs hallway look like the Plaza Hotel. But it was allowed if it meant that the children would abide by her single rule on weekends—that they come downstairs for breakfast promptly at nine o'clock.

Margaret poured a cup of coffee and handed it to him.

Peter rolled onto his elbow and drank some. Then he sat up in bed and looked at Margaret. "How do you manage to look so beautiful two minutes after getting out of bed?"

Margaret was relieved. "You're certainly in a good mood. I was afraid you'd have a hangover and be perfectly beastly all day."

"I do have a hangover. Benny Goodman is playing in my head, and my tongue feels like it could use a shave. But I have no intention of acting—" He paused. "What was the word you used?"

"Beastly." She sat down on the edge of the bed. "There's something we need to discuss, and this seems as fine a time as any."

"Hmm. Sounds serious, Margaret."

"That depends." She held him in her playful gaze, then feigned a look of irritation. "But get up and get dressed. Or aren't you capable of dressing and listening at the same time."

"I'm a highly trained, highly regarded engineer." Peter forced himself out of bed, groaning at the effort. "I can probably manage it."

"It's about the phone call yesterday afternoon."

"The one you were so evasive about?"

"Yes, that one. It was from Dr. Shipman."

Peter stopped dressing.

"I'm pregnant again. We're going to have another baby." Margaret looked down and toyed with the knot of her blouse. "I didn't plan for this to happen. It just did. My body has finally recovered from having Billy and— well, nature took its course." She looked up at him. "I've suspected it for some time but I was afraid to tell you."

"Why on earth would you be afraid to tell me?"

But Peter knew the answer to his own question. He had told Margaret he didn't want more children until he had realized his life's dream: starting his own engineering firm. At just thirty-three he had earned a reputation as one of the top engineers in the country. After graduating first in his class from the prestigious Rensselaer Polytechnic Institute, he went to work for the Northeast Bridge Company, the largest bridge construction firm on the East Coast. Five years later he was named chief engineer, made partner, and given a staff of one hundred. The American Society of Civil Engineers named him its engineer of the year for 1938 for his innovative work on a bridge spanning the Hudson River in upstate New York. *Scientific American* published a profile on Peter describing his as "the most promising engineering mind of his generation." But he wanted more—he wanted his own firm. Bratton Lauterbach had promised to bankroll Peter's company when the time was right, possibly next year. But the threat of war had put a damper on all that. If the United States was dragged into a war, all money for major public works projects would dry up overnight. Peter's new firm would go under before it had a chance to get off the ground.

He said, "How far along are you?"

"Almost two months."

Peter's face broke into a smile.

Margaret said, "You're not angry with me?"

"Of course not!"

"What about your firm and everything you said about waiting to have more children?"

He kissed her. "It doesn't matter. None of it matters."

"Ambition is a wonderful thing, but not too much ambition. You have to relax and enjoy yourself sometimes, Peter. Life isn't a dress rehearsal."

Peter stood and finished dressing. "When are you planning on telling your mother?"

"In my own good time. You remember how she was when I was pregnant with Billy. She drove me crazy. I have plenty of time to tell her."

Peter sat down beside her on the bed. "Let's make love before breakfast."

"Peter, we can't. Mother will kill us if we don't get downstairs."

He kissed her neck. "What was that you were saying about life not being a dress rehearsal?"

She closed her eyes, her head rolled back. "That's not fair. You're twisting my words."

"No, I'm not, I'm kissing you."

"Yes—"

"Margaret!" Dorothy Lauterbach's voice echoed up the stairs.

"We're coming, Mother."

"I wish," Peter muttered, and followed her downstairs to breakfast.

Walker Hardegen joined them for lunch by the swimming pool. They sat beneath an umbrella: Bratton and Dorothy, Margaret and Peter, Jane and Hardegen. A damp, fickle breeze blew from the Sound. Hardegen was Bratton Lauterbach's top lieutenant at the bank. He was tall and thick through the chest and shoulders, and most women thought he looked like Tyrone Power. He was a Harvard man, and during his senior year he had scored a touchdown in the Yale game. His football days had left him with a ruined knee and a slight limp that somehow made him even more attractive. He had a lazy New England accent and smiled easily.

A short time after Hardegen came to the bank he asked Margaret out and they dated several times. Hardegen wanted the relationship to continue but Margaret did not. She quietly terminated it but still saw Walker regularly at parties and they remained friends. Six months later she met Peter and fell in love. Hardegen was beside himself. One evening at the Copacabana, a little drunk and very jealous, he cornered Margaret and begged her to see him again. When she refused he grabbed her too roughly by the shoulder and shook her. By the icy look on her face, Margaret made it clear she would destroy his career if he did not end his childish behavior.

The incident remained their secret. Even Peter didn't know. Hardegen rose quickly through the ranks and became Bratton's most trusted senior officer. Margaret sensed there was an unspoken tension between Hardegen and Peter, a natural competitiveness. Both were young, handsome, intelligent, and successful. The situation had worsened earlier that summer, when Peter discovered Hardegen was opposed to lending the money for his engineering firm.

"I'm not one who usually goes in for Wagner, especially in the current climate," Hardegen said, pausing to sip his chilled white wine while everyone chuckled at his remark. "But you really must see Herbert Janssen in *Tannhäuser* at the Metropolitan. It's marvelous."

"I've heard such good things about it," Dorothy said.

She loved to discuss the opera, theater, and new books and films. Hardegen, who managed to see and read everything despite an immense workload at the bank, indulged her. The arts were safe topics, unlike family matters and gossip, which Dorothy deplored.

"We did see Ethel Merman in the new Cole Porter musical," Dorothy said, as the first course, a cold shrimp salad, was served. "The title slips my mind."

"Dubarry Was a Lady," Hardegen put in. "I loved it."

Hardegen continued talking. He had gone to Forest Hills yesterday afternoon and watched Bobby Riggs win his match. He thought Riggs was a sure thing to win the Open this year. Margaret watched her mother, who was watching Hardegen. Dorothy adored Hardegen, practically treating him like a member of the family. She had made it clear that she preferred Hardegen to Peter. Hardegen was from a wealthy, conservative family in Maine, not as rich as the Lauterbachs but close enough for comfort. Peter came from a lower-middle-class Irish family and grew up on the West Side of Manhattan. He might be a brilliant engineer, but he would never be *one of us*. The dispute threatened to destroy Margaret's relationship with her mother. It was ended by Bratton, who would tolerate no objections to his daughter's choice of a husband. Margaret had married Peter in a storybook wedding at St. James's Episcopal Church in June 1935. Hardegen was among the six hundred invited guests. He danced with Margaret during the reception and behaved like a perfect gentleman. He even stayed to see the couple off on their two-month honeymoon in Europe. It was as if the incident at the Copa never happened.

The servants brought the main course—chilled poached salmon—and the conversation inevitably shifted to the looming war in Europe.

Bratton said, "Is there any way of stopping Hitler now, or is Poland about to become the easternmost province of the Third Reich?"

Hardegen, a lawyer as well as a shrewd investor, had been placed in charge of disentangling the bank from its German and other risky European investments. Inside the bank he was affectionately referred to as Our In-House Nazi because of his name, his perfect German, and his frequent trips to Berlin. He also maintained a network of excellent contacts in Washington and served as the bank's chief intelligence officer.

"I spoke to a friend of mine this morning—he's on Henry Stimson's staff at the War Department," Hardegen said. "When Roosevelt returned to Washington from his cruise on the *Tuscaloosa,* Stimson met him at Union Station and rode with him to the White House. When Roosevelt asked him about the situation in Europe, Stimson replied that the days of peace could now be counted on the fingers of both hands."

"Roosevelt returned to Washington a week ago," Margaret said.

"That's right. Do the math yourself. And I think Stimson was being optimistic. I think war could be hours away."

"But what about this communication I read about this morning in the *Times?*" Peter asked. Hitler had sent a message to Britain the previous night, and the *Times* suggested it might pave the way for a negotiated settlement of the Polish crisis.

"I think he's stalling," Hardegen said. "The Germans have sixty divisions along the Polish border waiting for the word to move."

"So what's Hitler waiting for?" Margaret asked.

"An excuse."

"Certainly the Poles aren't going to give him an excuse to invade."

"No, of course not. But that won't stop Hitler."

"What are you suggesting, Walker?" Bratton asked.

"Hitler will invent a reason to attack, a provocation that will allow him to invade without a declaration of war."

"What about the British and the French?" Peter asked. "Will they live up to their commitments to declare war on Germany if Poland is attacked?"

"I believe so."

"They didn't stop Hitler at the Rhineland, or Austria, or Czechoslovakia," Peter said.

"Yes, but Poland is different. Britain and France now realize Hitler must be dealt with."

"What about us?" Margaret asked. "Can we stay out?"

"Roosevelt insists he wants to stay on the sidelines," Bratton said, "but I don't trust him. If the whole of Europe slides into war, I doubt if we'll be able to stay out of it for long."

"And the bank?" Margaret asked.

"We're terminating all our deals with German interests," Hardegen replied. "If there is a war there will be plenty of other opportunities for investment. This war may be just what we need to finally pull the country out of the Depression."

"Ah, nothing like earning a profit from death and destruction," Jane said.

Margaret frowned at her younger sister and thought, Typical Jane. She liked to portray herself as an iconoclast, a dark, brooding intellectual, critical of her class and everything it represented. At the same time she socialized relentlessly and spent her father's money as if the well were about to run dry. At thirty, she had no means of support and no prospects for marriage.

"Oh, Jane, have you been reading Marx again?" Margaret asked playfully.

"Margaret, please," Dorothy said.

"Jane spent time in England a few years ago," Margaret continued, as though she had not heard her mother's plea for peace. "She became quite a Communist then, didn't you, Jane?"

"I'm entitled to an opinion, Margaret!" Jane snapped. "Hitler's not running this house."

"I think I'd like to become a Communist too," Margaret said. "The summer has been rather dull, with all this talk of war. Converting to communism would be a nice change of pace. The Huttons are throwing a costume party next weekend. We could go as Lenin and Stalin. After the party we'll go out to the North Fork and collectivize all the farms. It will be great fun."

Bratton, Peter, and Hardegen burst into laughter.

"Thank you, Margaret," Dorothy said sternly. "You've entertained us all quite enough for one day."

The talk of war had gone on long enough. Dorothy reached out and touched Hardegen's arm.

"Walker, I'm so sorry you couldn't come to our party last night. It was wonderful. Let me tell you *all* about it."

The lavish apartment on Fifth Avenue overlooking Central Park had been a wedding present from Bratton Lauterbach. At seven o'clock that evening,

Peter Jordan stood at the window. A thunderstorm had moved in over the city. Lightning flashed over the deep green treetops of the park. The wind drove rain against the glass. Peter had driven back into the city alone because Dorothy had insisted that Margaret attend a garden party at Edith Blakemore's. Margaret was being driven back into the city by Wiggins, the Lauterbachs' chauffeur. And now they were going to be caught in the bad weather.

Peter shoved out his arm and glanced at his watch for the fifth time in five minutes. He was supposed to meet the head of the Pennsylvania road and bridge commission at the Stork Club for dinner at seven-thirty. Pennsylvania was accepting bids and design proposals for a new bridge over the Allegheny River. Peter's boss wanted him to lock up the deal tonight. He was often called on to entertain clients. He was young and smart, and his beautiful wife was the daughter of one of the most powerful bankers in the country. They were an impressive couple.

He thought, Where the hell is she?

He telephoned the Oyster Bay house and spoke to Dorothy.

"I don't know what to say to you, Peter. She left in plenty of time. Perhaps Wiggins was delayed by the weather. You know Wiggins—one sign of rain and he slows to a crawl."

"I'll give her another fifteen minutes. Then I have to leave."

Peter knew Dorothy wouldn't apologize, so he hung up before there could be an awkward moment of silence. He made himself a gin and tonic and drank it very fast while he waited. At seven-fifteen he took the elevator downstairs and stood in the lobby while the doorman went out into the rain and flagged down a taxi.

"When my wife arrives, ask her to come directly to the Stork Club."

"Yes, sir, Mr. Jordan."

The dinner went well, despite the fact that Peter left the table three times to telephone the apartment and the Oyster Bay house. By eight-thirty he was no longer annoyed, he was worried sick.

At 8:45 P.M. Paul Delano, the headwaiter, presented himself at Peter's table.

"You have a telephone call at the bar, sir."

"Thanks, Paul."

Peter excused himself. At the bar he had to raise his voice above the clinking glasses and the din of conversation.

"Peter, it's Jane."

Peter heard her voice tremble. "What's wrong?"

"I'm afraid there's been an accident."

"Where are you?"

"I'm with the Nassau County Police."

"What happened?"

"A car pulled in front of them on the highway. Wiggins couldn't see it in the rain. By the time he did it was too late."

"Oh, God!"

"Wiggins is in very bad shape. The doctors aren't holding out much hope for him."

"What about Margaret, dammit!"

Lauterbachs did not cry at funerals; grieving was done in private. It was held at St. James's Episcopal Church, the same church where Peter and Margaret had been married four years earlier. President Roosevelt sent a note of condolence and expressed his disappointment that he could not attend. Most of New York society *did* attend. So did most of the financial world, even though the markets were in turmoil. Germany had invaded Poland, and the world was waiting for the other shoe to drop.

Billy stood next to Peter during the service. He wore short pants and a little blazer and tie. As the family filed out of the church, he reached up and tugged on the hem of his Aunt Jane's black dress.

"Will Mommy ever come home?"

"No, Billy, she won't. She's left us."

Edith Blakemore overheard the child's question and burst into tears.

"What a tragedy," she gasped, sobbing. "What a needless tragedy!"

Margaret was buried under brilliant skies in the family plot on Long Island. During the Reverend Pugh's final words a murmur passed through the graveside mourners, then died away.

When it was over Peter walked back to the limousines with his best friend, Shepherd Ramsey. Shepherd had introduced Peter to Margaret. Even in his somber dark suit, he looked as though he'd just stepped off the deck of his sailboat.

"What was everyone talking about?" Peter asked. "It was damned rude."

"Someone arrived late, and they'd been listening to a bulletin on the car radio," Shepherd said. "The British and French just declared war on Germany."

CHAPTER THREE

LONDON: MAY 1940

Professor Alfred Vicary vanished without explanation from University College on the third Friday of May 1940. A secretary named Lillian Walford was the last member of the staff to see him before his abrupt departure. In a rare indiscretion, she revealed to the other professors that Vicary's last telephone call had been from the new prime minister. In fact, she had spoken to Mr. Churchill personally.

"Same thing happened to Masterman and Cheney at Oxford," Tom Perrington, an Egyptologist, said as he gazed at the entry in the telephone log. "Mysterious calls, men in dark suits. I suspect our dear friend Alfred has slipped behind the veil." Then he added, sotto voce, "Into the secret Acropolis."

Perrington's languid smile did little to hide his disappointment, Miss Walford would remark later. Too bad Britain wasn't at war with the ancient Egyptians—perhaps Perrington would have been chosen too.

Vicary spent his last hours in the cramped disorderly office overlooking Gordon Square putting the final touches on an article for *The Sunday Times*. The current crisis might have been avoided, it suggested, if Britain and France had attacked Germany in 1939 while Hitler still was preoccupied with Poland. He knew it would be roundly criticized given the current climate; his last piece had been denounced as "Churchillian warmongering" by a publication of the pro-Nazi extreme right. Vicary secretly hoped his new article would be similarly received.

It was a glorious late-spring day, bright sunshine but deceptively chilly.

Vicary, an accomplished if reluctant chess player, appreciated deception. He rose, put on a cardigan sweater, and resumed his work.

The fine weather painted a false picture. Britain was a nation under siege—defenseless, frightened, reeling in utter confusion. Plans were drawn up to evacuate the Royal Family to Canada. The government asked that Britain's other national treasure, its children, be sent into the country-side where they would be safe from the Luftwaffe's bombers.

Through the use of skilled propaganda the government had made the general public extremely aware of the threat posed by spies and Fifth Columnists. It was now reaping the consequences. Constabularies were being buried by reports of strangers, odd-looking fellows, or German-looking gentlemen. Citizens were eavesdropping on conversations in pubs, hearing what they liked, then telling the police. They reported smoke signals, winking shore lights, and parachuting spies. A rumor swept the country that German agents posed as nuns during the invasion of the Low Countries; suddenly, nuns were suspect. Most left the walled sanctuary of their convents only when absolutely necessary.

One million men too young, too old, or too feeble to get into the armed forces rushed to join the Home Guard. There were no extra rifles for the Guard so they armed themselves with whatever they could: shotguns, swords, broom handles, medieval bludgeons, Gurkha knives, even golf clubs. Those who somehow couldn't find a suitable weapon were instructed to carry pepper to toss into the eyes of marauding German soldiers.

Vicary, a noted historian, watched his nation's jittery preparations for war with a mixture of enormous pride and quiet depression. Throughout the thirties his periodic newspaper articles and lectures had warned that Hitler posed a serious threat to England and the rest of the world. But Britain, exhausted from the last war with the Germans, had been in no mood to hear about another. Now the German army was driving across France with the ease of a weekend motor outing. Soon Adolf Hitler would stand atop an empire stretching from the Arctic Circle to the Mediterranean. And Britain, poorly armed and ill prepared, stood alone against him.

Vicary finished the article, set down his pencil, and read it from the beginning. Outside, the sun was setting into a sea of orange over London. The smell of the crocuses and daffodils in the gardens of Gordon Square drifted in his window. The afternoon had turned colder; the flowers were likely to set off a sneezing fit. But the breeze felt wonderful on his face and somehow made the tea taste better. He left the window open and enjoyed it.

The war—it was making him think and act differently. It was making him look more fondly upon his countrymen, whom he usually viewed with something approaching despair. He marveled at how they made jokes while filing into the shelter of the underground and at the way they sang in pubs to hide their fear. It took Vicary some time to recognize his feelings for what they were: patriotism. During his lifetime of study he had concluded it was the most destructive force on the planet. But now he felt the stirring of patriotism in his own chest and did not feel ashamed. We are good and they are evil. Our nationalism is justified.

Vicary had decided he wanted to contribute. He wanted to do something instead of watching the world through his well-guarded window.

At six o'clock Lillian Walford entered without knocking. She was tall with a shot-putter's legs and round glasses that magnified an unfaltering gaze. She began straightening papers and closing books with the quiet efficiency of a night nurse.

Nominally, Miss Walford was assigned to all the professors in the department. But she believed that God, in his infinite wisdom, entrusted each of us with one soul to look after. And if any poor soul needed looking after, it was Professor Vicary. For ten years she had overseen the details of Vicary's uncomplicated life with military precision. She made certain there was food at his house in Draycott Place in Chelsea. She saw that his shirts were delivered and contained the right amount of starch—not too much or it would irritate the soft skin of his neck. She saw to his bills and lectured him regularly about the state of his poorly managed bank account. She hired new maids with seasonal regularity because his fits of bad temper drove away the old ones. Despite the closeness of their working relationship they never referred to each other by their Christian names. She was Miss Walford and he was Professor Vicary. She preferred to be called a personal assistant and, uncharacteristically, Vicary indulged her.

Miss Walford brushed past Vicary and closed the window, casting him a scolding look. "If you don't mind, Professor Vicary, I'll be going home for the evening."

"Of course, Miss Walford."

He looked up at her. He was a fussy, bookish little man, bald on top except for a few uncontrollable strands of gray hair. His long-suffering half-moon reading glasses rested on the end of his nose. They were smudged with fingerprints because of his habit of taking them on and off whenever he was nervous. He wore a weather-beaten tweed coat and a carelessly selected tie stained with tea. His walk was something of a joke around the university; without his knowledge some of his students had learned to imitate it perfectly. A shattered knee during the last war had left him with a stiff-jointed, mechanized limp—a toy soldier no longer in good working order, Miss Walford thought. His head tended to tilt down so he could see over his reading glasses, and he seemed forever rushing somewhere he'd rather not be.

"Mr. Ashworth delivered two nice lamb chops to your house a short time ago," Miss Walford said, frowning at a messy stack of papers as though it were an unruly child. "He said it may be the last lamb he gets for some time."

"I should think so," said Vicary. "There hasn't been meat on the menu at the Connaught in weeks."

"It's getting a little absurd, don't you think, Professor Vicary? Today, the government decreed the tops of London's buses should be painted battleship gray," Miss Walford said. "They think it will make it more difficult for the Luftwaffe to bomb them."

"The Germans are ruthless, Miss Walford, but even they won't waste their time trying to bomb passenger buses."

"They've also decreed that we should not shoot carrier pigeons. Would you please explain to me how I'm supposed to tell a carrier pigeon from a real one?"

"I can't tell you how often I'm tempted to shoot pigeons," Vicary said.

"By the way, I took the liberty of ordering you some mint sauce as well," Miss Walford said. "I know how eating lamb chops without mint sauce can destroy your week."

"Thank you, Miss Walford."

"Your publisher rang to say the proofs of the new book are ready for you to examine."

"And only four weeks late. A record for Cagley. Remind me to find a new publisher, Miss Walford."

"Yes, Professor Vicary. Miss Simpson telephoned to say she'll be unable to have dinner with you tonight. Her mother has taken ill. She asked me to tell you it's nothing serious."

"Damn," Vicary muttered. He had been looking forward to the date with Alice Simpson. It was the most serious he had been about a woman in a very long time.

"Is that all?"

"No—the prime minister telephoned."

"What! Why on earth didn't you tell me?"

"You left strict instructions not to be disturbed. When I told this to Mr. Churchill he was quite understanding. He says nothing upsets him more than being interrupted when he's writing."

Vicary frowned. "From now on, Miss Walford, you have my explicit permission to interrupt me when Mr. Churchill telephones."

"Yes, Professor Vicary," she replied, undeterred in her belief that she had acted properly.

"What did the prime minister say?"

"You're expected for lunch tomorrow at Chartwell."

Vicary varied his walks home according to his mood. Sometimes he preferred to jostle along a busy shopping street or through the buzzing crowds of Soho. Other nights he left the main thoroughfares and roamed the quiet residential streets, now pausing to gaze at a splendidly lit example of Georgian architecture, now slowing to listen to the sounds of music, laughter, and clinking glass drifting from a happy cocktail party.

Tonight he floated along a quiet street through the dying twilight.

Before the war he had spent most nights doing research at the library, wandering the stacks like a ghost late into the evening. Some nights he fell asleep. Miss Walford issued instructions to the night janitors: When they found him he was to be awakened, tucked into his mackintosh, and sent home for the night.

The blackout had changed that. Each night the city plunged into pitch darkness. Native Londoners lost their way along streets they had walked for years. For Vicary, who suffered from night blindness, the blackout made navigation next to impossible. He imagined this is what it must have been like two millennia ago, when London was a clump of log huts along the swampy banks of the River Thames. Time had dissolved, the centuries retreated, man's undeniable progress brought to a halt by the threat of Göring's bombers. Each afternoon Vicary fled the college and rushed home before becoming stranded on the darkened side streets of Chelsea. Once safely inside his home he drank his statutory two glasses of burgundy and consumed the plate of chop and peas his maid left for him in a warm oven. Had they not prepared his meals he might have starved, for he still was grappling with the complexities of the modern English kitchen.

After dinner, some music, a play on the wireless, even a detective novel, a private obsession he shared with no one. Vicary liked mysteries; he liked riddles. He liked to use his powers of reasoning and deduction to solve the cases long before the author did it for him. He also liked the character studies in mysteries and often found parallels to his own work—why good people sometimes did wicked things.

Sleep was a progressive affair. It began in his favorite chair, reading lamp still burning. Then he would move to the couch. Then, usually in the hours just before dawn, he would march upstairs to his bedroom. Sometimes the concentration required to remove his clothes would leave him too alert to fall back to sleep, so he would lie awake and think and wait for the gray dawn and the snicker of the old magpie that splashed about each morning in the birdbath outside in the garden.

He doubted he would sleep much tonight—not after the summons from Churchill.

It was not unusual for Churchill to ring him at the office, it was just the timing. Vicary and Churchill had been friends since the autumn of 1935, when Vicary attended a lecture delivered by Churchill in London. Churchill, confined to the wilderness of the backbench, was one of the few voices in Britain warning of the threat posed by the Nazis. That night he claimed Germany was rearming herself at a feverish pace, that Hitler intended to fight as soon as he was capable. England must rearm at once, he argued, or face enslavement by the Nazis. The audience thought Churchill had lost his mind and heckled him mercilessly. Churchill had cut short his remarks and returned to Chartwell, mortified.

Vicary stood at the back of the lecture hall that night, watching the spectacle. He too had been observing Germany carefully since Hitler's rise to power. He had quietly predicted to his colleagues that England and Germany would soon be at war, perhaps before the end of the decade. No one listened. Many people thought Hitler was a fine counterbalance to the Soviet Union and should be supported. Vicary thought that utter nonsense. Like the rest of the country he considered Churchill a bit of an adventurer, a bit too bellicose. But when it came to the Nazis, Vicary believed Churchill was dead on target.

Returning home, Vicary sat at his desk and jotted him a one-sentence note: *I attended your lecture in London and agree with every word you uttered.* Five days later a note from Churchill arrived at Vicary's home: *My God, I am not alone after all. The great Vicary is at my side! Please do me the honor of coming to Chartwell for lunch this Sunday.*

Their first meeting was a success. Vicary was immediately absorbed into the ring of academics, journalists, civil servants, and military officers who would give Churchill advice and intelligence on Germany for the rest of the decade. Winston forced Vicary to listen while he paced the ancient wooden floor of his library and explained his theories about German intentions. Sometimes Vicary disagreed, forcing Churchill to clarify his positions. Sometimes Churchill lost his temper and refused to back down. Vicary would hold his ground. Their friendship was cemented in this manner.

Now, walking through the gathering dusk, Vicary thought of Churchill's summons to Chartwell. It certainly wasn't just to have a friendly chat.

Vicary turned into a street lined with white Georgian terraces, painted rose by the last minutes of the spring twilight. He walked slowly, as if lost, one hand clutching his leaden briefcase, the other rammed into his mackintosh pocket. An attractive woman, roughly his age, emerged from a doorway. A handsome man with a bored face followed her. Even from a distance— even with his dreadful eyesight—he could see it was Helen. He would recognize her anywhere: the erect carriage, the long neck, the disdainful walk, as if she were always about to step into something disagreeable. Vicary watched them climb into the back of the chauffeur-driven car. It drew away from the curb and headed in his direction. *Turn away, you damned fool! Don't look at her!* But he was incapable of heeding his own advice. As the car passed he turned his head and looked into the rear seat. She saw him—just for an instant—but it was long enough. Embarrassed, she looked quickly down. Vicary, through the rear window of the car, watched her turn and murmur something to her husband that made his head snap back with laughter.

Idiot! Bloody damned idiot!

Vicary started walking again. He looked up and watched the car vanish around a corner. He wondered where they were headed—off to another party, the theater maybe. *Why can't I just let her go? It's been twenty-five years, for God's sake!* And then he thought, *And why is your heart beating like it was the first time you saw her face?*

He walked as fast as he could until he grew tired and out of breath. He thought of anything that came into his mind—anything but her. He came to a playground and stood at the wrought-iron gate, staring through the bars at the children. They were overdressed for May, bumping around like tiny plump penguins. Any German spy lurking about would surely realize many Londoners had discounted the government's warning and kept their children with them in the city. Vicary, normally indifferent to children, stood at the gate and listened, mesmerized, thinking there was nothing quite so comforting as the sound of little ones at play.

❖

Churchill's car was waiting for him at the station. It sped, top down, through the rolling green countryside of southeast England. The day was cool and breezy, and it seemed everything was in bloom. Vicary sat in back, one hand holding his coat closed, the other pressing his hat to his head. Wind blew over the open car like a gale over the prow of a ship. He debated whether he should ask the driver to stop and put up the top. Then the inevitable sneezing fit began—at first like sporadic sniper fire, then progressing into a full-fledged barrage. Vicary couldn't decide which hand to free to cover his mouth. He repeatedly pivoted his head and sneezed so the little puffs of moisture and germs were carried away by the wind.

The driver saw Vicary's gyrations in the mirror and became alarmed. "Would you like me to stop the car, Professor Vicary?" he asked, easing off the throttle.

The sneezing attack subsided and Vicary was actually able to enjoy the ride. He didn't care for the countryside as a rule. He was a Londoner. He liked the crowds and the noise and the traffic and tended to get disoriented in open spaces. He also hated the quiet of the nights. His mind wandered and he became convinced there were stalkers roaming in the darkness. But now he sat back in the car and marveled at England's natural beauty.

The car turned into the drive at Chartwell. Vicary's pulse quickened as he stepped from the car. As he approached the door, it opened and Churchill's man Inches stood there to greet him.

"Good morning, Professor Vicary. The prime minister has been awaiting your arrival most eagerly."

Vicary handed over his coat and his hat and stepped inside. About a dozen men and a couple of young girls were at work in the drawing room, some in uniform, some like Vicary in civilian clothes. They spoke in hushed, confessional tones, as though all the news was bad. A telephone rattled, then another. Each was answered after one ring.

"I hope you had a pleasant trip," Inches was saying.

"Marvelous," Vicary replied, lying politely.

"As usual, Mr. Churchill is running late this morning," Inches said. Then he added confidingly, "He sets an unattainable schedule, and we all spend the rest of the day trying to catch up with it."

"I understand, Inches. Where would you like me to wait?"

"Actually, the prime minister is quite eager to see you this morning. He asked that you be shown upstairs immediately upon your arrival."

"Upstairs?"

Inches knocked gently and pushed open the bathroom door. Churchill lay in his tub, a cigar in one hand, the day's second glass of whisky resting on a small table within easy reach. Inches announced Vicary and withdrew. "Vicary, my dear man," Churchill said. He put his mouth at the waterline and blew bubbles. "How good of you to come."

Vicary found the warm temperature of the bathroom oppressive. He also found it hard not to laugh at the enormous pink man splashing about in his bath like a child. He removed his tweed jacket and, reluctantly, sat down on the toilet.

"I wanted a word with you in private—that's why I've invited you here to my lair." Churchill pursed his lips. "Vicary, I must admit from the outset that I am angry with you."

Vicary stiffened.

Churchill opened his mouth to continue, then stopped himself. A perplexed, defeated look dawned over his face.

"Inches!" he bellowed.

Inches drifted in. "Yes, Mr. Churchill?"

"Inches, I believe my bathwater has dropped below one hundred four degrees. Would you check the thermometer?"

Rolling up his sleeve, Inches retrieved the thermometer. He studied it like an archaeologist examining an ancient bone fragment. "Ah, you're right, sir. The temperature of your bath has plummeted to one hundred two degrees. Shall I warm it?"

"Of course."

Inches opened the hot water tap and let it run for a moment. Churchill smiled as his bathwater attained its proper temperature. "Much better, Inches."

Churchill rolled onto his side. Water cascaded over the side of the tub, soaking the leg of Vicary's trousers.

"You were saying, Prime Minister?"

"Ah, yes, I was saying, Vicary, that I was angry with you. You never told me that in your younger days you were quite good at chess. Beat all comers at Cambridge, so I'm told."

Vicary, thoroughly confused, said, "I apologize, Prime Minister, but the subject of chess never arose during any of our conversations."

"Brilliant, ruthless, gambling—that's how people have described your play to me." Churchill paused. "You also served in the Intelligence Corps in the First War."

"I was only in the Motorcycle Unit. I was a courier, nothing more."

Churchill turned his gaze from Vicary and stared at the ceiling. "In 1250

B.C. the Lord told Moses to send agents to spy out the land of Canaan. The Lord was good enough to give Moses some advice on how to recruit his spies. Only the best and the brightest men were capable of such an important task, the Lord said, and Moses took his words to heart."

"This is true, Prime Minister," Vicary said. "But it is also true that the intelligence gathered by the spies of Moses was poorly utilized. As a result the Israelites spent another forty years wandering the desert."

Churchill smiled. "I should have learned long ago never to argue with you, Alfred. You have a nimble mind. I've always admired that."

"What is it you want me to do?"

"I want you to take a job in Military Intelligence."

"But, Prime Minister, I'm not qualified for that sort of—"

"Nobody over there knows what they're doing," Churchill said, cutting Vicary off. "Especially the professional officers."

"But what about my students? My research?"

"Your students will be in the service soon, fighting for their lives. And as for your research, it can wait." Churchill paused. "Do you know John Masterman and Christopher Cheney from Oxford?"

"Don't tell me they've been pulled in."

"Indeed—and don't expect to find a mathematician worth his salt at any of the universities," Churchill said. "They've all been snatched up and bundled off to Bletchley Park."

"What on earth are they doing there?"

"Trying to crack German ciphers."

Vicary made a brief show of thought. "I suppose I accept."

"Good." Churchill thumped his fist on the side of the tub. "You're to report first thing Monday to Brigadier Sir Basil Boothby. He is the head of the division to which you will be assigned. He is also the complete English ass. He'd thwart me if he could, but he's too stupid for that. Man could fuck up a steel ball."

"Sounds charming."

"He knows you and I are friends and therefore he will oppose you. Don't allow yourself to be bullied by him. Understood?"

"Yes, Prime Minister."

"I need someone I can trust inside that department. It's time to put the *intelligence* back in Military Intelligence. Besides, this will be good for you, Alfred. It's time you emerged from your dusty library and rejoined the living."

Vicary was caught off guard by Churchill's sudden intimacy. He thought of the previous evening, of his walk home, of staring into Helen's passing car.

"Yes, Prime Minister, I believe it *is* time. Just what will I do for Military Intelligence?"

But Churchill had vanished below the waterline.

CHAPTER FOUR

RASTENBURG, GERMANY: JANUARY 1944

Rear Admiral Wilhelm Franz Canaris was a small, nervous man who spoke with a slight lisp and possessed a sarcastic wit on those rare occasions when he chose to display it. White-haired, with piercing blue eyes, he was seated in the back of a staff Mercedes as it rumbled from the Rastenburg airfield to Hitler's secret bunker nine miles away. Usually, Canaris shunned uniforms and martial trappings of any kind, preferring a dark business suit instead. But since he was about to meet with Adolf Hitler and the most senior military officers in Germany, he was wearing his Kriegsmarine uniform beneath his formal greatcoat.

Known as the Old Fox by friends and detractors alike, Canaris's detached, aloof personality suited him perfectly to the ruthless world of espionage. He cared more about his two dachshunds—sleeping now on the floor at his feet—than anyone except his wife, Erika, and his daughters. When work mandated overnight travel, he booked a separate room with double beds so the dogs could sleep in comfort. When it was necessary to leave them behind in Berlin, Canaris checked in with his aides constantly to make certain the animals had eaten and had proper bowel movements. Abwehr staff who dared to speak ill of the dogs faced the very real threat of having their careers destroyed if word of their treachery ever reached Canaris's ears.

Raised in a walled villa in the Dortmund suburb of Aplerbeck as a member of the German elite so detested by Adolf Hitler, Wilhelm Canaris was the son of a chimney baron and descendant of Italians who emigrated to Germany in the sixteenth century. He spoke the languages of Germany's friends as well as her enemies—Italian, Spanish, English, French, and Russian—and regularly presided over recitals of chamber music in the salon of his stately

Berlin home. In 1933 he was serving as commander of a naval depot on the Baltic Sea at Swinemünde when Hitler unexpectedly chose him to head the Abwehr, the intelligence and counterespionage service. Hitler commanded his new spymaster to create a secret service on the British model—"an order, doing its work with passion"—and Canaris formally took control of the spy agency on New Year's Day 1934, his forty-seventh birthday.

The decision would prove to be one of Hitler's worst. Since taking command of the Abwehr, Wilhelm Canaris had been engaged in an extraordinary high-wire act—providing the German General Staff with the intelligence it needed to conquer most of Europe while at the same time using the service as a tool to rid Germany of Hitler. He was a leader of the resistance movement dubbed the Black Orchestra—*Schwarze Kapelle*—by the Gestapo. A tightly knit group of German military officers, government officials, and civic leaders, the Black Orchestra had tried unsuccessfully to overthrow the Führer and negotiate a peace settlement with the Allies. Canaris had engaged in other treasonous activities as well. In 1939, after learning of Hitler's plans to invade Poland, he warned the British in a futile attempt to spur them into action. He did the same in 1940 when Hitler announced plans to invade the Low Countries and France.

Canaris turned and peered out the window, watching as the forest swept past—dark, silent, heavily wooded, like the setting of a fairy tale by the brothers Grimm. Lost in the quiet of the snow-covered trees, he thought of the most recent attempt on the Führer's life. Two months earlier, in November, a young captain named Axel von dem Bussche volunteered to assassinate Hitler during an inspection of a new Wehrmacht greatcoat. Bussche planned to conceal several grenades beneath the coat, then detonate them during the demonstration, killing himself and the Führer. But one day before the assassination attempt, Allied bombers destroyed the building where the coats were housed. The demonstration was canceled, never to be rescheduled.

Canaris knew there would be more attempts—more brave Germans willing to sacrifice their own lives in order to rid Germany of Hitler—but he also knew time was running out. The Anglo-American invasion of Europe was a certainty. Roosevelt had made it clear he would accept nothing short of unconditional surrender. Germany would be destroyed, just as Canaris feared back in 1933 when Hitler's messianic ambitions became clear to him. He also realized his tenuous grip on the Abwehr was growing weaker by the day. Several members of Canaris's executive staff at Abwehr headquarters in Berlin had been arrested by the Gestapo and charged with treason. His enemies were plotting to seize control of the spy agency and put his neck in a noose of piano wire. He understood his days were numbered—that his long and dangerous high-wire act was nearing an end.

The staff car passed through a myriad of gates and checkpoints, then turned into the compound at Hitler's *Wolfschanze*—the Wolf's Lair. The dachshunds awakened, whimpering nervously, and jumped onto his lap. The conference was to be held in the frigid, airless map room in the underground bunker. Canaris climbed out of the car and walked morosely across the compound. At the bottom of the stairs a burly SS bodyguard stood with hand out to relieve Canaris of any weapons he might be carrying. Canaris, who shunned firearms and detested violence, shook his head and brushed past.

"In November, I issued Führer Directive Number Fifty-one," Hitler began without preamble, pacing the room violently, hands clasped behind his back. He wore a dove-gray tunic, black trousers, and resplendent knee-length jackboots. On his left breast pocket he wore the Iron Cross he earned at Ypres while serving as an infantryman in the List Regiment in the First War. "Directive Number Fifty-one stated my belief that the Anglo-Saxons will attempt to invade northwest France no later than the spring, perhaps earlier. During the last two months, I have seen nothing to change my opinion."

Canaris, seated at the conference table, watched the Führer prancing around the room. Hitler's pronounced stoop, caused by a kyphotic spine, seemed to have worsened. Canaris wondered if he was finally feeling the pressure. He should be. What was it Frederick the Great had said? *He who defends everything defends nothing.* Hitler should have heeded the advice of his spiritual guide, for Germany was in the same position she had been in during the Great War. She had conquered far more territory than she could possibly defend.

It was Hitler's own fault, the damned fool! Canaris glanced up at the map. In the East, German troops were fighting along a 2,000-kilometer front. Any hope of a military victory over the Russians had been crushed the previous July at Kursk, where the Red Army had decimated a Wehrmacht offensive and inflicted staggering casualties. Now the German army was attempting to hold a line stretching from Leningrad to the Black Sea. Along the Mediterranean, Germany was defending 3,000 kilometers of coastline. And in the West—My God! Canaris thought—6,000 kilometers of territory stretching from the Netherlands to the southern tip of the Bay of Biscay. Hitler's *Festung Europa*—Fortress Europe—was far-flung and vulnerable on all sides.

Canaris looked around the table at the men seated with him: Field Marshal Gerd von Rundstedt, commander in chief of all German forces in the West; Field Marshal Erwin Rommel, commander of Army Group B in northwest France; Reichsführer Heinrich Himmler, head of the SS and chief of the German police. A half dozen of Himmler's most loyal and ruthless men stood watch, just in case any of the top brass of the Third Reich decided to make an attempt on the Führer's life.

Hitler stopped pacing. "Directive Fifty-one also stated my belief that we can no longer justify reducing our troop levels in the West in order to support our forces battling the Bolsheviks. In the East, the vastness of space will, as a last resort, permit us to give up vast amounts of territory before the enemy threatens the German homeland. Not so in the West. If the Anglo-Saxon invasion succeeds, the consequences will be disastrous. So it is here, in northwest France, where the most decisive battle of the war will be fought."

Hitler paused, allowing his words to sink in. "The invasion will be met with the full fury of our might and destroyed at the high-water mark. If that is not possible, and if the Anglo-Saxons succeed in securing a temporary beachhead, we must be prepared to rapidly redeploy our forces, stage a massive counterattack, and hurl the invaders back into the sea." Hitler crossed his arms. "But to achieve that goal, we must know the enemy's order of battle. We must know when he intends to strike. And, more importantly, where. Herr Generalfeldmarshal?"

Field Marshal Gerd von Rundstedt rose and wearily moved to the map, right hand clutching the jeweled field marshal's baton he carried at all times. Known as "the last of the German knights," Rundstedt had been dismissed and recalled to duty by Adolf Hitler more times than Canaris or even his own staff could remember. Detesting the fanatical world of the Nazis, it was Rundstedt who had derisively christened Hitler "the little Bohemian corporal." The strain of five long years of war was beginning to show on the narrow aristocratic features of his face. Gone were the stiff precise mannerisms that characterized the General Staff officers of the imperial days. Canaris knew Rundstedt drank more champagne than he should and needed large quantities of whisky to sleep at night. He regularly rose at the thoroughly unmilitary hour of ten o'clock in the morning; the staff at his headquarters at Saint-Germain-en-Laye rarely scheduled meetings before noon.

Despite his advancing years and moral decline, Rundstedt was still Germany's finest soldier—a brilliant tactician and strategic thinker—as he demonstrated to the Poles in 1939 and to the French and British in 1940. Canaris did not envy Rundstedt's situation. On paper he presided over a large and powerful force in the West: one and a half million men, including 350,000 crack Waffen-SS troops, ten panzer divisions, and two elite *Fallschirmjäger* paratroop divisions. If deployed quickly and correctly, Rundstedt's armies were still capable of dealing the Allies a devastating defeat. But if the old Teutonic knight guessed wrong—if he deployed his forces incorrectly or made tactical blunders once the battle had begun—the Allies would establish their precious foothold on the Continent and the war in the West would be lost.

"In my opinion the equation is simple," Rundstedt began. "East of the Seine at the Pas de Calais or west of the Seine at Normandy. Each has its advantages and disadvantages."

"Go on, Herr Generalfeldmarshal."

Rundstedt continued in a dull monotone. "Calais is the strategic linchpin of the Channel coast. If the enemy secures a beachhead at Calais, he can turn to the east and be a few days' march from the *Ruhrgebiet,* our industrial heartland. The Americans want the war to be over by Christmas. If they succeed in a landing at Calais, they might get their wish." Rundstedt paused to allow his warning to sink in, then resumed his briefing. "There is another reason why Calais makes sense militarily—the Channel is the narrowest there. The enemy will be able to pour men and matériel into Calais four times faster than he would at Normandy or Brittany. Remember, the clock is ticking for the enemy the moment the invasion begins. He must build up troops, weapons, and supplies at an extremely rapid rate. There are three excellent deepwater ports in the Pas de Calais area"—Rundstedt tapped each with the tip of his baton, moving up the coastline—"Boulogne, Calais, and Dunkirk. The enemy needs ports. It is my belief that the first goal of the invaders will be to seize a major port and reopen it as quickly as possible, for without a major port the enemy cannot supply his troops. If he cannot supply his troops, he is dead."

"Impressive, Herr Generalfeldmarshal," Hitler said. "But why not Normandy?"

"Normandy presents the enemy with many problems. The distance across the Channel is much greater. At some points, high cliffs stand between the beaches and the mainland. The closest harbor is Cherbourg, at the tip of a heavily defended peninsula. It might be days before the enemy could take

Cherbourg from us. And even if he did, he knows we would render it useless before surrendering it. But the most logical argument against a strike at Normandy, in my opinion, is its geographic location. It is too far to the west. Even if the enemy succeeds in landing at Normandy, he runs the risk of being pinned down and strategically isolated. He must fight us all the way across France before even reaching German soil."

"Your opinion, Herr Generalfeldmarshal?" Hitler snapped.

"Perhaps the Allies will engage in some trickery," Rundstedt said cautiously, fingers working over the baton. "A diversionary landing, perhaps, as you yourself have suggested, my Führer. But the real strike will come here." He jabbed at the map. "At Calais."

"Admiral Canaris?" Hitler asked. "What kind of intelligence do you have to support that theory?"

Canaris, not one for formal displays at the map, remained seated. He reached into the breast pocket of his coat, where he kept a pack of cigarettes. The SS men flinched nervously. Canaris, shaking his head, slowly withdrew the cigarettes and displayed them. He laboriously lit one and blew a stream of smoke toward Himmler, knowing full well the Reichsführer's pet peeve about tobacco. Himmler glared at him through the swirling pall of blue smoke, eyes betraying no emotion, the side of his face twitching nervously.

Canaris explained that the Abwehr was collecting and analyzing three types of intelligence connected with the invasion preparations: aerial photographs of enemy troops in southern England; enemy wireless communications monitored by the *Funkabwehr,* the agency's listening service; and reports from agents operating inside Britain.

"And what is that intelligence telling you, Herr Admiral?" Hitler snapped.

"Our initial intelligence tends to support the field marshal's assessment— that the Allies intend to strike at Calais. According to our agents there has been increased enemy activity in southeast England, directly across the Channel from the Pas de Calais. We have monitored wireless transmissions referring to a new force called the First United States Army Group. We have also been analyzing the enemy's air activity over northwest France. He is spending far more time over Calais—for the purposes of bombing and reconnaissance—than over Normandy or Brittany. I have one other piece of new information to report, my Führer. One of our agents in England has a source inside the Allied high command. Last night, the agent transmitted a report. General Eisenhower has arrived in London. The Americans and British intend to keep his presence secret for the time being."

Hitler seemed impressed by the agent's report. If only Hitler knew the truth, Canaris thought: that now, just months before the most important battle of the war, the Abwehr's intelligence networks in England were very likely in tatters. Canaris blamed Hitler. During the preparations for Operation Seelöwe—the aborted invasion of Britain—Canaris and his staff recklessly poured spies into England. All caution was thrown to the wind because of the desperate need for intelligence on coastal defenses and British troop positions. Agents were hastily recruited, poorly trained, and even more poorly equipped. Canaris suspected most walked straight into the arms of MI5, inflicting permanent damage on networks that took years of painstaking work to build. He could not admit that now; to do so would be to sign his own death warrant.

Adolf Hitler was pacing again Canaris knew Hitler did not fear the coming invasion Quite the opposite, he welcomed it. He had ten million Germans under arms and an armaments industry that, despite relentless Allied bombing and shortages of labor and raw material, continued to produce staggering amounts of weapons and supplies. He remained confident of his ability to repel the invasion and hand the Allies a cataclysmic defeat. Like Rundstedt, he believed a landing at the Pas de Calais made strategic sense, and it was there that his *Atlantikwall* most resembled his vision of an impregnable fortress. In effect, Hitler had tried to force the Allies to invade at Calais by ordering the launching sites for his V-1 and V-2 rockets to be placed there. Yet Hitler was also aware the British and Americans had engaged in deception throughout the war and would do so again as a prelude to the invasion of France.

"Let us reverse the roles," Hitler finally said. "If I were going to invade France from England, what would I do? Would I come by the obvious route, the route my enemy expects me to take? Would I stage a frontal assault on the most heavily defended portion of the coastline? Or would I take another route and attempt to surprise my enemy? Would I broadcast false wireless messages and send false reports through spies? Would I make misleading statements to the press? The answer to all these questions is yes. We must expect the British to engage in deception and even a major diversionary landing. As much as I would wish them to attempt a landing at Calais, we must be prepared for the possibility of an invasion at Normandy or Brittany. Therefore, our panzers must remain safely back from the coast until the enemy's intentions are clear. Then we will concentrate our armor at the main point of the attack and hurl them back into the sea."

"There is one other thing to take into account that might support your argument," Field Marshal Erwin Rommel said.

Hitler spun on his heel to face him. "Go on, Herr Generalfeldmarshal."

Rommel gestured at the large floor-to-ceiling map behind Hitler. "If you would permit a demonstration, my Führer."

"Of course."

Rommel reached inside his briefcase, removed a pair of calipers, and walked to the map. In December, Hitler had ordered him to assume command of Army Group B along the Channel coast. Army Group B included the 7th Army in the Normandy area, the 15th Army between the Seine estuary and the Zuider Zee, and the Army of the Netherlands. Physically and psychologically recovered from his disastrous defeats in North Africa, the famed Desert Fox had thrown himself into his new assignment with an incredible display of energy, dashing about the French coast in his Mercedes 230 cabriolet at all hours, inspecting his coastal defenses and the disposition of his troops and armor. He had promised to turn the French coastline into a "Devil's garden"—a landscape of artillery, minefields, concrete fortifications, and barbed wire from which the enemy would never emerge. Yet privately, Rommel believed any fortification devised by man could be defeated by man.

Standing before the map, Rommel pulled open the calipers. "This represents the range of the enemy's Spitfire and Mustang fighter planes. These are the locations of major fighter bases in the south of England." He placed one end of the calipers on each of the sites and drew a series of arcs on the map. "As you can see, my Führer, both Normandy and Calais are well within range of the enemy's fighters. Therefore, we must regard both areas as possible sites for the invasion."

Hitler nodded, impressed by Rommel's display. "Place yourself in the enemy's position for a moment, Herr Generalfeldmarshal. If you were attempting to invade France from England, where would you strike?"

Rommel made a brief show of thought, then said, "I must admit, my Führer, that all signs point to an invasion at the Pas de Calais. But I cannot rid myself of the belief that the enemy would never attempt a frontal assault on our strongest concentration of forces. I am also tainted by the experience of Africa. The British engaged in deception before the battle of Alamein, and they will do so again before an invasion of France."

"And the Westwall, Herr Generalfeldmarshal? How is the work proceeding?"

"Much to be done, my Führer. But we are making good progress."

"Will it be done before spring?"

"I believe so. But coastal fortifications alone cannot stop the enemy. We need to have our armor arrayed properly. And for that I'm afraid we need to know where they plan to strike. Nothing short of that will be of any use. If the enemy succeeds, the war may be lost."

"Nonsense," Heinrich Himmler said. "Under the Führer, Germany's ultimate victory is beyond question. The beaches of France will be a graveyard for the British and the Americans."

"No," Hitler said, waving his hand, "Rommel is correct. If the enemy is able to secure a beachhead, the war is lost. But if we destroy the invasion before it ever gets started"—Hitler's head tilted back, eyes blazing—"it would take months to organize another attempt. The enemy would never try again. Roosevelt would never be reelected. He might even end up in jail somewhere! British morale would collapse overnight. Churchill, that sick fat old man, would be destroyed! With the Americans and the British paralyzed, licking their wounds, we can take men and matériel from the west and pour them into the east. Stalin will be at our mercy. He will sue for peace. Of this, I am certain."

Hitler paused, allowing his words to sink in.

"But if the enemy is to be stopped we must know the location of the invasion," he said. "My generals think it will be Calais. I'm skeptical." He spun on his heel and glared at Canaris. "Herr Admiral, I want you to settle the argument."

"That may not be possible," Canaris said carefully.

"Is it not the task of the Abwehr to provide military intelligence?"

"Of course, my Führer."

"You have spies operating inside Britain—this report about General Eisenhower's arrival in London is proof of that."

"Obviously, my Führer."

"Then I suggest you get to work, Herr Admiral. I want *proof* of the enemy's intentions. I want you to bring me the secret of the invasion—and quickly. Let me assure you, you don't have much time."

Hitler paled visibly and seemed suddenly exhausted.

"Now, unless you gentlemen have any more bad news for me, I'm going to get a few hours of sleep. It's been a very long night."

They all rose as Hitler walked up the stairs.

CHAPTER FIVE

NORTHERN SPAIN: AUGUST 1936

He is standing before the doors, open to the warm night, holding a bottle of icy white wine. He pours himself another glass without offering to refill hers. She is lying on the bed, smoking, listening to his voice. Listening to the warm wind stirring the trees off the veranda. Heat lightning is flickering silently over the valley. His valley, as he always says. My fucking valley. And if the mother-fucking Loyalists ever try to take it from me I'll cut off their fucking balls and feed them to the dogs.

"Who taught you to shoot like that?" he demands. They went hunting in the morning and she has taken four pheasant to his one.

"My father."

"You shoot better than me."

"So I've noticed."

The lightning is quietly in the room again and she can see Emilio clearly for a few seconds. He is thirty years older, yet she thinks he is beautiful. His hair is gray-blond, the sun has made his face the color of oiled saddle leather. His nose is long and sharp, an ax blade. She wanted to be kissed by his lips but he wanted her very fast and rough the first time, and Emilio always gets what he fucking wants, darling.

"You speak English very well," he informs her, as if she is hearing this for the first time. "Your accent is perfect. I could never lose mine, no matter how hard I tried."

"My mother was English."

"Where is she now?"

"She died a long time ago."

"You have French as well?"

"Yes," she answers.

"Italian?"

"Yes, I have Italian."

"Your Spanish is not so good, though."

"Good enough," she says.

He is fingering his cock while he speaks. He loves it like he loves his money and his land. He speaks of it as though it is one of his finest horses. In bed it is like a third person.

"You lie with Maria by the stream; then at night you let me come to your bed and fuck you," he says.

"That's one way of putting it," she answers. "Do you want me to stop with Maria?"

"You make her happy," he says, as if happiness is grounds for anything.

"She makes me happy."

"I've never known a woman like you before." He sticks a cigarette into the corner of his mouth and lights it, hands cupped against the evening breeze. "You fuck me and my daughter on the same day without blinking an eye."

"I don't believe in forming attachments."

He laughs his quiet, controlled laugh.

"That's wonderful," he says, and laughs quietly again. "You don't believe in forming attachments. That's marvelous. I pity the poor bastard who makes the mistake of falling in love with you."

"So do I."

"Do you have any feelings?"

"No, not really."

"Do you love anyone or anything?"

"I love my father," she says. "And I love lying by the stream with Maria."

Maria is the only woman she has ever met whose beauty is a threat to her. She neutralizes that threat by pillaging Maria's beauty for herself. Her mane of brown curly hair. Her flawless olive skin. The perfect breasts that are like summer pears in her mouth. The lips that are the softest things she has ever touched. "Come to Spain for the summer and live with me at my family's estancia," Maria says one rainy afternoon in Paris, where they are both studying at the Sorbonne. Father will be disappointed, but the idea of spending the summer in Germany watching the fucking Nazis parading around the streets holds nothing for her. She did not know she would be walking straight into a civil war instead.

But the war does not intrude on Emilio's insolent enclave of paradise in the foothills of the Pyrenees. It is the most wonderful summer of her life. In the morning the three of them hunt or run the dogs, and in the afternoon she and Maria ride up to the stream, swim in the icy deep pools, sun themselves on the warm rocks. Maria likes it best when they are outside. She likes the sensation of the sun on her breasts and Anna between her legs. "My father wants you too, you know," Maria announces one afternoon as they lie in the shade of a eucalyptus tree. "You can have him. Just don't fall in love with him. Everyone is in love with him."

Emilio is talking again.

"When you return to Paris next month there's someone I want you to meet. Will you do that for me?"

"That depends."

"On what?"

"On who it is."

"He will contact you. When I tell him about you he will be very interested."

"I'm not going to sleep with him."

"He won't be interested in sleeping with you. He's a family man. Like me," he adds, and laughs his laugh again.

"What's his name?"

"Names are not important to him."

"Tell me his name."

"I'm not sure which name he's using these days."

"What does your friend do?"

"He deals in information."

He comes back to the bed. Their conversation has aroused him. His cock is hard and he wants her again right away. He is pushing her legs apart and trying to find his way inside her. She takes him in her hands to help him, then digs her nails into him.

"Ahhhh! Anna, my God! Not so hard!"

"Tell me his name."

"It's against the rules—I can't!"

"Tell me," she says, and squeezes him harder.

"Vogel," he mutters. "His name is Kurt Vogel. Jesus Christ."

BERLIN: JANUARY 1944

The Abwehr had two primary kinds of spies operating against Britain. The S-Chain consisted of agents who entered the country, settled under assumed identities, and engaged in espionage. R-Chain agents were mainly third-country nationals who periodically entered Britain legally, collected intelligence, and reported back to their masters in Berlin. There was a third, a smaller and highly secretive network of spies, referred to as the V-Chain—a handful of exceptionally trained sleeper agents who burrowed deeply into English society and waited, sometimes for years, to be activated. It was named for its creator and single control officer, Kurt Vogel.

Vogel's modest empire consisted of two rooms on the fourth floor of Abwehr headquarters, located in a pair of dour gray stone town houses at 74–76 Tirpitz Ufer. The windows overlooked the Tiergarten, the 630-acre park in the heart of Berlin. Once it had been a spectacular view, but months of Allied bombing had left panzer-sized craters in the bridle paths and reduced most of the chestnut and lime trees to blackened stumps. Much of Vogel's office was consumed by a row of locked steel cabinets and a heavy safe. He suspected the clerks in the Abwehr's central registry had been turned by the Gestapo and refused to keep files there. His only assistant—a decorated Wehrmacht lieutenant named Werner Ulbricht who was maimed fighting the Russians—worked in the anteroom. He kept a pair of Lugers in the top drawer of his desk and had been instructed by Vogel to shoot anyone who entered without permission. Ulbricht had nightmares about mistakenly killing Wilhelm Canaris.

Vogel officially held the rank of captain in the Kriegsmarine, but it was only a formality designed to give him the rank necessary to operate in certain quarters. Like his mentor Canaris, he rarely wore a uniform. His wardrobe varied little: an undertaker's charcoal suit, a white shirt, a dark tie. He had iron-gray hair that looked as though he had cut it himself and the intense gaze of a coffeehouse revolutionary. His voice was like a rusty hinge; after nearly a decade of clandestine conversations in cafés, hotel rooms, and bugged offices, it rarely rose above a chapel murmur. Ulbricht, deaf in one ear, constantly struggled to hear him.

Vogel's passion for anonymity ran to the absurd. His office contained only one personal item, a portrait of his wife, Gertrude, and his twin girls. He banished them to Gertrude's mother's home in Bavaria when the bombing started and saw them infrequently. Whenever he left the office, even for a few moments, he removed the portrait from the desktop and locked it away in a drawer. Even his identification badge was a riddle. It contained no picture—he had refused to be photographed for years—and the name was false. He kept a small flat near the office, reached by a pleasant walk along the leafy banks of the Landwehr Canal, for those rare nights when he permitted himself to escape. His landlady believed he was a college professor with a lot of girlfriends.

Even inside the Abwehr little else was known of him.

Kurt Vogel was born in Düsseldorf. His father was the principal of a local school, his mother a part-time music teacher who gave up a promising career as a concert pianist to marry and raise a family. Vogel earned a doctorate of law from Leipzig University, where he studied civil and political law under two of the greatest legal minds in Germany, Herman Heller and Leo Rosenberg. He was a brilliant student—the top of his class—and his professors quietly predicted Vogel would one day sit on the Reichsgericht, Germany's supreme court.

Hitler changed all that. Hitler believed in the rule of men, not the rule of law. Within months of taking power he turned Germany's entire judicial system upside down. *Führergewalt*—Führer power—became the absolute law of the land, and Hitler's every maniacal whim was immediately translated into codes and regulations. Vogel remembered some of the ridiculous maxims coined by the architects of Hitler's legal overhaul of Germany: *Law is what is useful to the German people! Law must be interpreted through healthy folk emotions!* When the normal judiciary stood in their way the Nazis established their own courts—*Volksgerichtshof,* the People's Courts. In Vogel's opinion the darkest day in the history of German jurisprudence came in October 1933, when ten thousand lawyers stood on the steps of the Reichsgericht in Leipzig, arms raised in a Nazi salute, and swore to "follow the course of the Führer to the end of our days." Vogel had been among them. That night he went home to the small flat he shared with Gertrude, burned his law books in the stove, and drank himself sick.

Several months later, in the winter of 1934, he was approached by a small dour man with a pair of dachshunds—Wilhelm Canaris, the new head of the Abwehr. Canaris asked Vogel if he would be willing to go to work for him. Vogel accepted on one condition—that he not be forced to join the Nazi party—and the following week he vanished into the world of German military intelligence. Officially, he served as Canaris's in-house legal counsel. Unofficially, he was given the task of preparing for the war with Britain that Canaris thought was inevitable.

Now Vogel sat at his desk, hunched over a memo, knuckles pressed to his temples. He struggled to concentrate over the noise: the rattle of the old lift as it struggled up and down the well just beyond his wall, the splatter of freezing rain against the windows, the cacophony of car horns that accompanied the Berlin evening rush. He moved his hands from his temples to his ears and pressed until there was silence.

The memo had been given to him by Canaris earlier that day, a few hours after the Old Fox returned from a meeting with Hitler at Rastenburg. Canaris thought it looked promising, and Vogel had to agree. "Hitler wants results, Kurt," Canaris had said, sitting behind his battered antique desk like an impervious old don, eyes wandering the overflowing bookshelves as though searching for a treasured but long-lost volume. "He wants proof it's Calais or Normandy. Perhaps it's time we brought your little nest of spies into the game."

Vogel had read it once quickly. Now he read it more carefully a second time. Actually it was more than promising, it was perfect—the opportunity he had been waiting for. When he finished he looked up and murmured Ulbricht's name several times as if he were speaking directly into his ear. Finally, receiving no reply, he rose and walked into the anteroom. Ulbricht was cleaning his Lugers.

"Werner, I've been calling you for five minutes," Vogel said, his voice nearly inaudible.

"I'm sorry, Captain, I didn't hear you."

"I want to see Müller first thing in the morning. Make me an appointment."

"Yes, sir."

"And Werner, do something about your damned cars. I was shouting at the top of my lungs in there."

The bombers came at midnight as Vogel dozed fitfully in his office on a stiff camp bed. He swung his legs to the floor, rose, and walked to the window as the aircraft droned overhead. Berlin shuddered as the first fires erupted in the districts of Pankow and Weissensee. Vogel wondered how much more punishment the city could absorb. Vast sections of the capital of the thousand-year Reich had already been reduced to rubble. Many of the city's most famous neighborhoods resembled canyons of crushed brick and twisted steel. The lime trees of the Unter den Linden had been scorched, as had many of the once-glittering shops and banks lining the broad boulevard. The renowned clock at the Kaiser Wilhelm Memorial Church had been stilled at seven-thirty since November, when Allied bombers laid waste to one thousand acres of Berlin on a single night.

The memo ran around in his head while he watched the night raid.

ABWEHR/BERLIN XFU0465848261

TO: CANARIS

FROM: MULLER

DATE: 2 NOV 43

    ON 21 OCTOBER CAPTAIN DIETRICH OF ASCUNCION STATION DEBRIEFED AMERI-CAN ASSET SCORPIO IN PANAMA CITY. AS YOU KNOW SCORPIO IS ONE OF OUR MOST IMPORTANT AGENTS IN AMERICA. HE IS HIGHLY PLACED IN NEW YORK FINANCIAL CIRCLES AND IS WELL CONNECTED IN WASHINGTON. HE IS PERSONAL FRIENDS WITH MANY SENIOR OFFICERS AT BOTH THE DEPARTMENTS OF WAR AND STATE. HE HAS MET PERSONALLY WITH ROOSEVELT. THROUGHOUT THE WAR HIS INFORMATION HAS BEEN TIMELY AND HIGHLY ACCURATE. I REMIND YOU ABOUT THE INTELLIGENCE HE SUPPLIED TO US ON THE AMERICAN ARMS SHIPMENTS TO THE BRITISH.

    ACCORDING TO SCORPIO, A RENOWNED AMERICAN ENGINEER NAMED PETER JORDAN WAS RECRUITED BY THE AMERICAN NAVY LAST MONTH AND DISPATCHED TO LONDON TO WORK ON A HIGHLY SECRET CONSTRUCTION PROJECT. JORDAN HAS NO PREVIOUS MILITARY EXPERIENCE. SCORPIO KNOWS JORDAN PERSONALLY AND SPOKE WITH HIM BEFORE HIS DEPARTURE FOR LONDON. SCORPIO SAYS THE PROJECT IS DEFINITELY CONNECTED TO THE ENEMY'S PLAN TO INVADE FRANCE.

    JORDAN IS RESPECTED FOR HIS WORK ON SEVERAL MAJOR AMERICAN BRIDGE PROJECTS. JORDAN IS A WIDOWER. HIS WIFE, THE DAUGHTER OF AMERICAN BANKER BRATTON LAUTERBACH, WAS KILLED IN AN AUTOMOBILE ACCIDENT IN AU-GUST 1939. SCORPIO BELIEVES JORDAN IS HIGHLY VULNERABLE TO APPROACH BY A FEMALE ASSET.

    JORDAN IS NOW LIVING ALONE IN THE SECTION OF LONDON KNOWN AS KEN-SINGTON. SCORPIO HAS PROVIDED THE ADDRESS OF THE HOUSE AS WELL AS THE COMBINATION OF THE SAFE INSIDE THE STUDY.

    SUGGEST ACTION.

Vogel noticed a wedge of light from the doorway and heard the scrape of Ulbricht's wooden leg against the floor. The bombing disturbed Ulbricht in a way he could not put into words and Vogel could never understand. Vogel removed his key ring from the desk drawer and went to one of the steel cabinets. The file was inside an unmarked black folder. Returning to his desk, he poured himself a large cognac and opened the cover. It was all there: the photographs, the background material, the performance reports. He didn't need to read it. He had written it himself and, like the subject, he had the curse of a flawless memory.

He turned a few more pages and found the notes he had made after their first meeting in Paris. Beneath it was a copy of the cable sent to him by the man who discovered her—Emilio Romero, a wealthy Spanish landowner, a Fascist, a talent spotter for the Abwehr.

SHE IS EVERYTHING YOU ARE LOOKING FOR. I'D LIKE TO KEEP HER FOR MYSELF BUT BECAUSE I AM A FRIEND I WILL GIVE HER TO YOU. AT A REASONABLE PRICE OF COURSE.

The room felt suddenly bone-chillingly cold. He lay down on his army cot and covered himself in a blanket.

Hitler wants results, Kurt. Perhaps it's time we brought your little nest of spies into the game.

Sometimes he imagined leaving her in place until it was all over, then finding some way of getting her out. But she was perfect for it, of course. She was beautiful, she was intelligent, and her English and her knowledge of British society were faultless. He turned and looked at the photograph of Gertrude and the children. To think that he fantasized giving them up for her. He had been such a fool. He switched off the light. The air raid had ended. The night was a symphony of sirens. He tried to sleep but it was no good. She was under his skin again.

Poor Vogel. I've made a shambles of your heart, haven't I.

The eyes in the photograph of his family were boring into him. It was obscene, looking at them, remembering her. He stood up, went to his desk, and locked the picture away in his drawer.

"For God's sake, Kurt!" Müller exclaimed as Vogel entered his office the following morning. "Who's cutting your hair these days, my friend? Let me give you the name of the woman who does mine. Maybe she can help you."

Vogel, exhausted from a night of little sleep, sat down and silently regarded the figure before him. Paul Müller was in charge of the Abwehr's intelligence networks in the United States. He was short, tubby, and impeccably dressed in a shiny French suit. His thin hair was oiled and combed straight back from his cherubic face. His tiny mouth was sumptuous and red, like that of a child who has just eaten cherry candy.

"Imagine this, the great Kurt Vogel, here in my office," Müller said through a smirk. "To what do I owe this privilege?"

Vogel was used to the professional jealousy of the other senior staff. Because of the special status of his V-Chain network, he was given more money and assets than the other case officers. He was also allowed to poke his nose into their affairs, which made him extremely unpopular within the agency.

Vogel removed his copy of Müller's memo from the breast pocket of his jacket and waved it in front of him. "Tell me about Scorpio," he said.

"So the Old Man finally circulated my note. Look at the date on the goddamned thing. I gave it to him two months ago. It's been sitting on his desk gathering dust. That information is like gold. But it goes into the Fox's Lair and never comes out again." Müller paused, lit a cigarette, and blew a stream of smoke at the ceiling. "You know, Kurt, sometimes I wonder whose side Canaris is on."

The remark was not unusual these days. Since the arrest of several members of the Abwehr's executive staff on charges of treason, morale at Tirpitz Ufer had sunk to a new low. Vogel sensed that Germany's military intelligence agency was dangerously adrift. He had heard rumors that Canaris had fallen out of favor with Hitler. There were even rumors among the staff that Himmler was plotting to bring down Canaris and place the Abwehr under the control of the SS.

"Tell me about Scorpio," Vogel repeated.

"I had dinner with him at the home of an American diplomat." Müller threw back his round head and stared at the ceiling. "Before the war, 1937 I believe it was. I'll check his file to make certain. The fellow's German was better than mine. Thought the Nazis were a wonderful bunch of fellows doing great things for Germany. Only thing he hated worse than the Jews was the Bolsheviks. It was like an audition. I recruited him myself the next day. Easiest snare of my career."

"What's his background?"

Müller smiled. "Investment banking. Ivy League, good contacts in industry, friends with half of Washington. His information on war production has been excellent."

Vogel was folding the memo and putting it back in his pocket. "His name?"

"Come on, Kurt. He's one of my best agents."

"I want his name."

"This place is like a sieve, you know that. I tell you, everybody knows."

"I want a copy of his file on my desk in an hour," Vogel said, his underpowered voice barely a whisper. "And I want everything you have on the engineer."

"You can have the information on Jordan."

"I want it all, and if I have to go to Canaris I'll do it."

"Oh, for Christ's sake, Kurt. You're not going to go running to Uncle Willy, are you?"

Vogel stood and buttoned his jacket. "I want his name and I want his file." He turned and walked out of the office.

"Kurt, come back here," Müller called out. "Let's work this out. Jesus Christ."

"If you want to talk, I'll be in the Old Man's office," Vogel said as he walked down the narrow hallway.

"All right, you win." Müller's doughy hands were digging in a cabinet. "Here's the fucking file. You don't have to run to Uncle Willy again. Jesus Christ, you're worse than the fucking Nazis sometimes."

Vogel spent the rest of the morning reading about Peter Jordan. When he finished he removed a pair of files from one of his cabinets, returned to his desk, and read them carefully.

The first file contained information on an Irishman who had worked as a spy for a short time but was cut loose because his information was poor. Vogel had taken possession of his dossier and placed him on the V-Chain payroll. Vogel was not concerned with the bad reviews the spy had received in the past—he was not looking for a spy. There were other qualities about the agent Vogel found attractive. He worked a small farm on an isolated stretch of Britain's Norfolk coast. It was a perfect safe house—close enough to London to make the journey by train in three hours, far enough away so the place wasn't crawling with MI5 officers.

The second file contained the dossier of a former Wehrmacht paratrooper who had been barred from jumping because of a head wound. The man had all the qualities Vogel liked: perfect English, an eye for detail, a cool intelligence. Ulbricht had found him at an Abwehr wireless listening post in northern France. Vogel placed him on the V-Chain payroll and tucked him away for the right assignment.

Vogel pushed the files aside and drafted two messages. He added the ciphers to be used, the frequencies at which the messages were to be sent, and the transmission schedule. Then he looked up and called for Ulbricht.

"Yes, Herr Captain," Ulbricht said. He entered the office, limping heavily on his wooden leg. Vogel looked at Ulbricht an instant before speaking, wondering if the man was up to the demands of an operation like the one he was about to launch. Ulbricht was twenty-seven years old but looked at least forty. His close-cropped black hair was flecked with gray. Pain lines ran like tributaries from the edge of his one good eye. The second eye had been lost in the explosion; the empty socket was hidden behind a neat black patch. A

Knight's Cross dangled at his throat. The top button of Ulbricht's tunic was undone because the exertion of the most simple movements caused him to become overheated and perspire. In all the time they had worked together, Vogel had never once heard Ulbricht complain.

"I want you to go to Hamburg tomorrow night." He handed Ulbricht the transcripts of the messages. "Stand over the radio operator while he sends these. Make certain there are no mistakes. See that the acknowledgments from the agents are in order. If there is anything out of the ordinary I want to know about it. Understood?"

"Yes, sir."

"Before you go, I want you to track down Horst Neumann."

"He's in Berlin, I believe."

"Where is he staying?"

"I'm not certain," Ulbricht said, "but I believe there is a woman involved."

"There usually is." Vogel walked to the window and looked out. "Contact the staff at the Dahlem farm. Tell them to expect us tonight. I want you to join us there when you return from Hamburg tomorrow. Tell them we'll be there for a week. We have a lot to go over. And tell them to rig the jump platform in the barn. It's been a long time since Neumann jumped from an airplane. He'll need practice."

"Yes, sir."

Ulbricht went out, leaving Vogel alone in the office. He stood at the window for a long time, thinking it through once more. The most closely guarded secret of the war and he planned to steal it with a woman, a cripple, a grounded paratrooper, and a British traitor. Quite a team you've assembled, Kurt, old man. If his own ass wasn't on the line he might have found the whole thing funny. Instead, he just stood there like a statue, watching snow drifting silently over Berlin, worrying himself to death.

CHAPTER SIX

LONDON

The Imperial Security Intelligence Service—better known by its military intelligence designation, MI5—was headquartered in a small cramped office building at 58 St. James's Street. MI5's task was counterintelligence. In the lexicon of espionage, counterintelligence means protecting one's secrets—and, when necessary, catching spies. For much of its forty-year existence, the Security Service toiled in the shadow of its more glamorous cousin, the Secret Intelligence Service, or MI6. Such internecine rivalries did not matter much to Professor Alfred Vicary. It was MI5 that Vicary joined in May 1940 and where, on a dismal rainy evening five days after Hitler's secret conference at Rastenburg, he could still be found.

The top floor was the preserve of the senior staff: the director-general's office, his secretariat, the assistant directors and division heads. Brigadier Sir Basil Boothby's office was there, hidden behind a pair of intimidating oaken doors. A pair of lights glared down from over the doors, a red one signifying the room was too insecure to permit access, a green one meaning enter at your own risk. Vicary, as always, hesitated before pressing the buzzer.

Vicary had received his summons at nine o'clock, while he was locking away his things in his gunmetal gray cabinet and tidying up his hutch, as he referred to his small office. When MI5 exploded in size at the beginning of the war, space became a precious commodity. Vicary was relegated to a windowless cell the size of a broom closet, with worn bureaucratic green carpet and a sturdy little headmasterly desk. Vicary's partner, a former Metropolitan Police officer named Harry Dalton, sat with the other junior men in a common area at the center of the floor. The place had a newsroom rowdiness about it, and Vicary ventured there only when absolutely necessary.

Officially, Vicary held the rank of a major in the Intelligence Corps, though military rank meant next to nothing inside the department. Much of the staff routinely referred to him as Professor, and he had worn his uniform just twice. Vicary's manner of dress had changed, though. He had forsaken the tweedy clothes of the university, dressing instead in sharp gray suits he purchased before clothing, like almost everything else, was rationed. Occasionally, he bumped into an acquaintance or old colleague from University College. Despite incessant warnings by the government about the dangers of loose talk, they inevitably asked Vicary exactly *what* he was doing. He usually smiled wearily, shrugged his shoulders, and gave the prescribed response: he was working in a very dull department of the War Office.

Sometimes it was dull, but not often. Churchill had been right—it had been time for him to rejoin the living. His arrival at MI5 in May 1940 had been his rebirth. He thrived on the atmosphere of wartime intelligence: the long hours, the crises, the dismal tea in the canteen. He had even taken up cigarette smoking again, which he had sworn off his last year at Cambridge. He loved being an actor in the theater of the real. He seriously doubted whether he could be satisfied again in the sanctuary of academia.

Surely the hours and the tension were talking a toll on him, but he had never felt better. He could work longer and needed less sleep. When he did go to bed he dropped off immediately. Like the other officers, he spent many nights at MI5 headquarters, sleeping on a small camp bed he kept folded next to his desk.

Only the ill treatment of his half-moon reading glasses survived Vicary's catharsis—still smudged and battered and something of a joke inside the department. In moments of distress, he still absently beat his pockets for them and thrust them onto his face for comfort.

Which he did now, as the light over Boothby's office suddenly shone green. Vicary pressed the buzzer with the reflective air of a man about to attend the funeral of a boyhood friend. It purred softly, the door opened, and Vicary stepped inside.

Boothby's office was big and long, with fine paintings, a gas fireplace, rich Persian carpets, and a magnificent view through the tall windows. Sir Basil kept Vicary waiting the statutory ten minutes before finally entering the room through a second doorway connecting his office to the director-general's secretariat.

Brigadier Sir Basil Boothby had classic English size and scale—tall, angular, still showing signs of the physical agility that made him a star athlete at school. It was there in the easy way his strong hand held his drink, in the square shoulders and thick neck, in the narrow hips where his trousers, waistcoat, and jacket converged in graceful perfection. He had the sturdy good looks that a certain type of younger woman finds attractive. His gray-blond hair and eyebrows were so lush the department wits referred to him as the bottle brush from the fifth floor.

Officially, little was known about Boothby's career—only that he had served in Britain's intelligence and security organizations his entire professional life. Vicary thought the gossip and rumor surrounding a man often said more about him than his résumé. Speculation about Boothby had spawned a veritable cottage industry within the department. According to the rumor mill, Boothby ran a spy network during the First War that penetrated the German General Staff. In Delhi, he personally executed an Indian accused of murdering a British citizen. In Ireland, he beat a man to death with his pistol butt for refusing to divulge the location of an arms cache. He was an expert in the martial arts and used his spare time to keep his skills sharp. He was ambidextrous and could write, smoke, drink his gin and bitters, or break your neck with either hand. His tennis was so good he could have won Wimbledon. *Deceptive* was the word used most often to describe his play, and his ability to switch hands mid-match still confounded his opponents. His sex life was much talked about and much debated: a relentless womanizer who had bedded half the typists and the girls from Registry; a homosexual.

In Vicary's opinion, Sir Basil Boothby symbolized all that was wrong with British Intelligence between the wars—the wellborn Englishman educated at Eton and Oxford who believed the secret exercise of power was as much a birthright as his family fortune and his centuries-old Hampshire mansion: rigid, lazy, orthodox, a cop in handmade shoes and a Savile Row suit. Boothby had been eclipsed intellectually by the new recruits drawn into MI5 at the outset of the war: the top brains from the universities, the best barristers from London's most prestigious houses. Now he was in an unenviable position—supervising men who were more clever than he and at the same time attempting to claim bureaucratic credit for their accomplishments.

"Sorry to keep you waiting, Alfred. A meeting in the Underground War Rooms with Churchill, the director-general, Menzies, and Ismay. I'm afraid we've got a bit of a crisis on our hands. I'm drinking brandy and soda. What will you have?"

"Whisky," Vicary said, watching Boothby. Despite the fact that he was one of the most senior officers in MI5, Boothby still took a childlike pride in dropping the names of the powerful people with whom he met on a regular basis. The group of men who had just gathered in the prime minister's underground fortress were the elite of Britain's wartime intelligence community: the director-general of MI5, Sir David Petrie; the director-general of MI6, Sir Stewart Menzies; and Churchill's personal chief of staff, General Sir Hastings Ismay. Boothby pressed a button on his desk and asked his secretary to bring Vicary's drink. He walked to the window, lifted the blackout shade, and looked out.

"I hope to God they don't come again tonight, bloody Luftwaffe. It was different in 1940. It was all new and exciting in a strange kind of way. Carrying your steel helmet beneath your arm to dinner. Running for the shelters. Fire-watching from the rooftops. But I don't think London could endure another winter of a full-fledged blitz. Everyone's too tired. Tired and hungry and ill-clothed and sick of the petty humiliations that go with being at war. I'm not sure how much more this nation can take."

Boothby's secretary brought Vicary's drink. It was on the center of a silver tray, resting atop a white paper napkin. Boothby had a fetish about water marks on the furniture of his office. He sat down in a chair next to Vicary and crossed his long legs, pointing the polished toe of his shoe at Vicary's kneecap like a loaded gun.

"We have a new assignment for you, Alfred. And in order for you to truly understand its importance, we've decided it's necessary to lift the veil a little higher and show you a little more than you've been allowed to see previously. Do you understand what I'm saying to you?"

"I believe so, Sir Basil."

"You're the historian. Know much about Sun-tzu?"

"Fourth century B.C. China is not exactly my field, Sir Basil, but I've read him."

"Know what Sun-tzu wrote about military deception?"

"Sun-tzu wrote that all warfare is based on deception. He preached that every battle is won or lost *before* it's ever fought. His advice was simple: Attack the enemy where he is unprepared and appear where you are not expected. He said it was vital to undermine the enemy, subvert and corrupt him, sow internal discord among his leaders, and destroy him without fighting him."

"Very good," Boothby said, visibly impressed. "Unfortunately, we'll never be able to destroy Hitler without fighting him. And in order to have any chance at all of beating him in a fight, we have to deceive him first. We have to heed those wise words of Sun-tzu. We need to appear where we are not expected."

Boothby rose, went to his desk, and brought back a secure briefcase. It was made of metal—the color of polished silver—with a set of handcuffs attached to the grip.

"You're about to be BIGOT-ed, Alfred," Boothby said, opening the briefcase.

"I beg your pardon?"

"BIGOT-ed—it's a supersecret classification developed specifically to cover the invasion. It takes its name from a stamp we placed on documents carried by British officers to Gibraltar for the invasion of North Africa. TO GIB—to Gibraltar. We just reversed the characters. TO GIB became BIGOT."

"I see," Vicary said. Four years after coming to MI5, Vicary still found many of the code names and security classifications ridiculous.

"BIGOT now refers to anyone who is privy to the most important secret of Overlord, the time and place of the invasion of France. If you know the secret, you're a BIGOT. Any documents pertaining to the invasion get a BIGOT stamp."

Boothby unlocked the briefcase, reached inside, and withdrew a beige folder. He laid it carefully on the coffee table. Vicary looked at the cover, then at Boothby. It was emblazoned with the sword and shield of SHAEF—the Supreme Headquarters Allied Expeditionary Force—and stamped BIGOT. Below were the words Plan Bodyguard, followed by Boothby's name and a distribution number.

"It is a very small fraternity you're about to enter—just a few hundred officers," Boothby resumed. "And there are those of us who think even that's too many. I should also tell you that your personal and professional background has been thoroughly investigated. No stone has been left unturned, as they say. I'm happy to report you're not a known member of any Fascist or Communist organization, you don't drink to excess, at least not in public, you don't put yourself about with loose women, and you aren't a homosexual or any other type of sexual deviant."

"That's good to know."

"I should also tell you that you are subject to further security checks and surveillance at any time. None of us are immune from it, not even General Eisenhower."

"I understand, Sir Basil."

"Good. First, I'd like to ask you a question or two. Your work has dealt with the invasion. Your caseload has given you a window on some of the preparations. Where do you think we're planning to strike?"

"Based on the little I know, I'd say we're going to hit them at Normandy."

"And how would you assess the chances of success for a landing at Normandy?"

"Amphibious assaults by their nature are the most complicated of all military operations," Vicary said. "Especially when they involve the English Channel. Julius Caesar and William the Conqueror managed to pull it off. Napoleon and the Spaniards failed. Hitler finally gave up on the idea in 1940. I'd say the chances of a successful invasion are no better than fifty-fifty."

Boothby snorted. "If that, Alfred, if that." He stood and paced the length of his office. "We've managed to pull off three successful amphibious operations so far: North Africa, Sicily, and Salerno. But none of those landings involved a fortified coast."

Boothby stopped pacing and looked at Vicary.

"You're right, by the way. It *is* Normandy. And it's scheduled for the late spring. And if we are going to have even your fifty-fifty chance of success, Hitler and his generals need to think we're going to attack somewhere else." Boothby sat down and picked up the folder. "That's why we've developed this—it's called Plan Bodyguard. Being a historian, you'll have a special appreciation for Bodyguard. It is a *ruse de guerre* of a scale and ambition never before attempted."

The code name meant nothing to Vicary. Boothby sailed on with his indoctrination lecture.

"Bodyguard used to be called Plan Jael, by the way. It was renamed out of respect for a rather eloquent remark the prime minister made to Stalin at Teheran. Churchill said, 'In wartime, truth is so precious that she should always be attended by a bodyguard of lies.' The Old Man has a certain way with words, I'll grant him that. Bodyguard is not an operation in itself. It is the code name for all the strategic cover and deception operations, to be carried out on a global scale, designed to mislead Hitler and the General Staff about our intentions on D-Day."

Boothby picked up the folder and flipped violently through it.

"The most important component of Bodyguard is Operation Fortitude. It is the goal of Fortitude to delay the Wehrmacht's reaction to the invasion for as long as possible by leading them to believe that other parts of north-western Europe are also under the direct threat of attack—specifically Norway and the Pas de Calais.

"The Norwegian deception is code-named Fortitude North. Its goal is to force Hitler to leave twenty-seven divisions in Scandinavia by convincing him we're planning to attack Norway, before or even after D-Day."

Boothby turned to another page in the folder and drew a deep breath.

"Fortitude South is the more critical and, I daresay, more dangerous of the two deceptions. The goal of Fortitude South is to slowly convince Hitler, his generals, and his intelligence officers that we intend to stage not one invasion of France but two. The first strike, according to Fortitude South, is to be a diversionary strike across the Baie de la Seine at Normandy. The second strike, the main thrust, will take place three days later across the Strait of Dover at Calais. From Calais, our invading armies can turn directly to the east and be inside Germany within a few weeks." Boothby paused to sip his brandy and soda and allow his words to sink in. "Fortitude says that the goal of the first assault is to force Rommel and von Rundstedt to hurl their crack panzer units of the German Fifteenth Army at Normandy, thus leaving Calais undefended when the *real* invasion occurs. Obviously, we want the opposite to take place. We want the panzers of the Fifteenth Army to remain at Calais, waiting for the real invasion, paralyzed by indecision, while we come ashore at Normandy."

"Brilliant in its simplicity."

"Quite," Boothby said. "But with one glaring weakness. We don't have enough men to pull it off. By late spring there will be just thirty-seven divisions in Britain—American, British, and Canadian—barely enough to stage one strike against France, let alone two. If Fortitude is to have any chance of succeeding, we must convince Hitler and his generals that we have the divisions necessary to stage two invasions."

"How in heaven's name are we going to do that?"

"Why, we're simply going to create an army of a million men. Conjure it up, I'm afraid, completely out of thin air."

Vicary sipped his drink, staring at Boothby, disbelief on his face. "You can't be serious."

"Yes, we can, Alfred—we're deadly serious. In order for the invasion to have that one-in-two chance of succeeding, we have to convince Hitler, Rommel, and von Rundstedt that we have a massive and powerful force coiled behind the cliffs of Dover, waiting to lash out across the Channel at Calais. We won't, of course. But by the time we're finished, the Germans are going to believe they're confronted with a living, breathing force of some thirty divisions. If they don't believe this force exists—if we fail and they see through our deception—there is a very good chance the return to Europe, as Churchill calls it, will end in a bloody and cataclysmic failure."

"Does this phantom army have a name?" Vicary asked.

"Indeed—the First United States Army Group. FUSAG for short. It even has a commander, Patton himself. The Germans believe General Patton is our finest battlefield commander and think we would be fools to launch any invasion without his playing a major role. At his disposal Patton will have some one million men, made up primarily of nine divisions from the U.S. Third Army and two divisions of the Canadian First Army. FUSAG even has its own London headquarters in Bryanston Square."

Vicary blinked rapidly, trying to digest the extraordinary information he was being given. Imagine creating an army of a million men, completely out of thin air. Boothby was right—it was a *ruse de guerre* of unimaginable proportions. It made the Trojan horse of Odysseus look like a college escapade.

"Hitler's no fool, and neither are his generals," he said. "They're well schooled in the lessons of Clausewitz, and Clausewitz offered valuable advice about wartime intelligence: 'A great part of the information obtained in war is contradictory, a still greater part is false, and by far the greatest part is doubtful.' The Germans aren't going to believe there's an army of a million men camped in the Kent countryside just because we tell them it's so."

Boothby smiled, reached into the briefcase, and withdrew another folder. "True, Alfred. Which is why we came up with this: Quicksilver. The goal of Quicksilver is to put flesh and bones on our little army of ghosts. In the coming weeks, as the phantom forces of FUSAG begin arriving in Britain, we're going to flood the airwaves with wireless traffic—some of it in codes we know the Germans have already broken, some of it *en clair*. Everything has to be perfect, just the way it would be if we were putting a real army of a million men in Kent. Quartermasters complaining about the lack of tents. Mess units griping about shortages of food and silver. Radio chatter during exercises. Between now and the invasion, we're going to bombard their listening posts in northern France with close to a million messages. Some of those messages will provide the Germans a small clue, a tidbit of information about the location of the forces or their disposition. Obviously, we want the Germans to find those clues and latch onto them."

"A million wireless messages? How is that possible?"

"The U.S. 3103 Signals Service Battalion. They're bringing quite a crew with them—Broadway actors, radio stars, voice specialists. Men who can imitate the accent of a Jew from Brooklyn one minute and the bloody awful drawl of a Texas farmhand the next. They'll record the false messages in a studio on sixteen-inch records and then broadcast them from trucks circulating through the Kent countryside."

"Unbelievable," Vicary said, beneath his breath.

"Yes, quite. And that's only a small part of it. Quicksilver accounts for what the Germans will hear *over* the air. But we also have to take into account what they'll see *from* the air. We have to make it look as though a massive army is staging a slow and methodical buildup in the southeast corner of the country. Enough tents to house a force of a million men, a massive armada of aircraft, tanks, landing craft. We're going to widen the roads. We're even going to build a bloody oil depot in Dover."

Vicary said, "But surely, Sir Basil, we don't have enough planes, tanks, and landing craft to waste on a deception."

"Of course not. We're going to build models out of plywood and canvas. From the ground, they'll look like what they are—crude, hastily prepared fakes. But from the air, through the lens of a Luftwaffe surveillance camera, they'll look like the real thing."

"How do we know the surveillance planes will get through?"

Boothby smiled broadly, finished the rest of his drink, and deliberately lit a cigarette. "Now you're getting it, Alfred. We know they're going to get through because we're going to let them through. Not all of them, of course. They'd smell a rat if we did that. RAF and American aircraft will constantly patrol the skies over our phantom FUSAG, and they'll chase away most of the intruders. But some of them—only those flying over thirty thousand feet, I should add—will be allowed through. If all goes according to the script, Hitler's aerial surveillance analysts will tell him the same thing his eavesdroppers in northern France are telling him: that there is a massive Allied force poised off the Pas de Calais."

Vicary was shaking his head. "Wireless signals, aerial photographs—two of the ways the Germans can gather intelligence about our intentions. The third way, of course, is through spies."

But were there really any spies left? In September 1939, the day war broke out, MI5 and Scotland Yard engaged in a massive roundup. All suspected spies were jailed, turned into double agents, or hanged. In May 1940, when Vicary arrived, MI5 was in the process of capturing the new spies Canaris was sending to England to collect intelligence for the coming invasion. Those new spies suffered the same fate as the previous wave.

Spycatcher was not an appropriate word to describe what Vicary did at

MI5. He was technically a Double Cross officer. It was his job to make sure the Abwehr believed its spies were still in place, still gathering intelligence, and still sending it back to their case officers in Berlin. Keeping the agents alive in the minds of the Abwehr had obvious advantages. MI5 had been able to manipulate the Germans from the very outset of the war by controlling the flow of intelligence from the British Isles. It also kept the Abwehr from sending new agents into Britain because Canaris and his control officers believed most of their spies were still on the job.

"Exactly, Alfred. Hitler's third source of intelligence about the invasion is his spies. Canaris's spies, I should say. And we know how effective they are. The German agents under our control will make a vital contribution to Bodyguard by confirming for Hitler much of what he can see from the skies and hear over the airwaves. In fact, one of our doubles, Tate, has already been brought into the game."

Tate earned his code name because of his uncanny resemblance to the popular music hall comedian Harry Tate. His real name was Wulf Schmidt, an Abwehr agent who parachuted from a Heinkel 111 into the Cambridgeshire countryside on the night of September 19, 1940. Vicary, though not assigned to the Tate case, knew the basics. Having spent the night in the open, he buried his parachute and wireless and walked into a nearby village. His first stop was Wilfred Searle's barbershop, where he purchased a pocket watch to replace the wristwatch he smashed leaping from the Heinkel. Next he purchased a copy of *The Times* from Mrs. Field, the newsagent, washed his swollen ankle at the village pump, and took his breakfast in a small café. Finally, at 10 A.M., he was taken into custody by Private Tom Cousins of the local Home Guard. The following day he was driven to MI5's interrogation facility in Ham Common, Surrey, and there, after thirteen days of questioning, Tate agreed to work as a double agent and send Double Cross messages back to Hamburg over his wireless.

"Eisenhower is in London, by the way. Only a select few on our side have been made aware of that. Canaris knows it, however. And now, so does Hitler. In fact, the Germans knew Eisenhower was here before he settled down for his first night at Hayes Lodge. They knew he was here because Tate told them he was here. It was perfect, of course—a seemingly important yet completely harmless piece of intelligence. Now the Abwehr believes Tate has an important and credible source inside SHAEF. That source will be critical as the invasion draws nearer. Tate will be given an important lie to transmit. And with any luck, the Abwehr will believe that too.

"In the coming weeks, Canaris's spies will begin to see signs of a massive buildup of men and matériel in southeast England. They'll see American and Canadian troops. They'll see encampments and staging areas. They'll hear horror stories from the British public about the terrible inconvenience of having so many soldiers crammed in so small a place. They'll see General Patton careening through the villages of East Anglia with his polished boots and ivory-handled revolver. The good ones will even learn the names of this army's top commanders, and they'll send those names back to Berlin. Your own Double Cross network will play a critical role."

Boothby paused, crushed out his cigarette, and immediately lit another.

"But you're shaking your head, Alfred. I suspect you've spotted the Achilles' heel of the entire deception plan."

Vicary's lips curled into a careful smile. Knowing Vicary's love of Greek history and lore, Boothby realized he would automatically think of the Trojan War when being briefed on the details of Operation Fortitude. "May I?" Vicary said, gesturing toward Boothby's packet of Players cigarettes. "I'm afraid I've left mine downstairs."

"Of course," Boothby said, handing Vicary the cigarettes and holding up the flame of his lighter for him.

"Achilles died after being struck by an arrow in his one vulnerable spot—his heel," Vicary said. "The Achilles' heel of Fortitude is the fact that it can be undone by one genuine report from a source Hitler trusts. It requires total manipulation of every source of information Hitler and his intelligence officers possess. Each one of them has to be poisoned in order for Fortitude to work. Hitler must be enmeshed in a total web of lies. If one thread of truth slips through, the entire scheme could unravel." Vicary, pausing for a pull on his Players, could not resist making the historical parallel. "When Achilles was undone, his armor was awarded to Odysseus. Our armor, I'm afraid, will be awarded to Hitler."

Boothby picked up his empty glass and rolled it consciously in the palm of his large hand.

"That's the danger inherent to all military deception, isn't it, Alfred? It almost always points the way to the truth. General Morgan, the invasion planner, said it best. All it would take is one decent German spy to walk the south coast of England from Cornwall to Kent. If that happened, the entire thing would come crashing down, and with it the hopes of Europe. Which is why we've been holed up with the prime minister all evening and why you're here now."

Boothby stood and slowly paced the length of his office.

"As of this moment, we are acting under the reasonable certitude that we have in fact poisoned all Hitler's sources of intelligence. We are also acting under the reasonable certitude that we have accounted for all of Canaris's spies in Britain and that none of them are operating outside our control. We wouldn't be embarking on a stratagem such as Fortitude if that weren't the case. I use the words *reasonable certitude* because there is no way we can ever be truly certain of that fact. Two hundred and sixty spies—all arrested, turned, or hanged."

Boothby drifted from the weak lamplight and vanished into the dark corner of his office.

"Last week, Hitler staged a conference in Rastenburg. All the heavies were there: Rommel, von Rundstedt, Canaris, and Himmler. The subject was the invasion—specifically, the time and place of the invasion. Hitler put a gun to Canaris's head—figuratively, not literally—and ordered him to learn the truth or face some rather distressing consequences. Canaris in turn gave the job to a man on his staff named Vogel—Kurt Vogel. Until now, we've always believed Kurt Vogel was Canaris's personal legal adviser. Obviously, we were wrong. Your job is to make sure Kurt Vogel doesn't learn the truth. I haven't had a chance to read his file. I suspect Registry may have something on him."

"Right," Vicary said.

Boothby had drifted back into the dim light. He pulled a mild frown, as though he had overheard something unpleasant in the next room, then fell into a long speculative silence.

"Alfred, I want to be perfectly honest with you about something from the outset of this case. The prime minister insisted you be given the assignment over the strenuous objections of the director-general and myself."

Vicary held Boothby's gaze for a moment; then, embarrassed by the remark, he looked away and allowed his eyes to wander. Over the walls. Over the dozens of photographs of Sir Basil with famous people. Over the deep burnished-oak paneling. Over the old oar that hung on one wall, strangely out of place in the formal setting. Perhaps it was a reminder of happier, less complicated times, Vicary thought. A glassy river at sunrise. Oxford versus Cambridge. Train rides home on chilly autumn afternoons.

"Allow me to explain that remark, Alfred. You have done marvelous work. Your Becker network has been a stunning success. But both the director general and I feel a more senior man might be better suited to this case."

"I see," Vicary said. A more senior man was code for a career officer, not one of the new recruits Boothby so mistrusted.

"But obviously," Boothby resumed, "we were unable to convince the prime minister that you were not the best man for the case. So it's yours. Give me regular updates on your progress. And good luck, Alfred. I suspect you'll need it."

CHAPTER SEVEN

LONDON

By January 1944 the weather had resumed its rightful place as the primary obsession of the British public. The summer and autumn had been unusually dry and hot; the winter, when it came, unusually cold. Freezing fogs rose from the river, stalked Westminster and Belgravia, hovered like gunsmoke over the ruins of Battersea and Southwark. The blitz was little more than a distant memory. The children had returned. They filled the toy shops and department stores, mothers in tow, exchanging unwanted Christmas presents for more desirable items. On New Year's Eve, large crowds had jammed Piccadilly Circus. It all might have seemed normal if not for the fact that the celebration took place in the gloom of the blackout. But now the Luftwaffe, after a long and welcome absence, had returned to the skies over London.

At 8 P.M., Catherine Blake hurried across Westminster Bridge. Fires burned across the East End and the docks; tracer fire and searchlights crisscrossed the night sky. Catherine could hear the dull *thump-thump* of antiaircraft fire from the batteries in Hyde Park and along the Embankment and taste the acrid bite of smoke from the fires. She knew she was in for a long, busy night.

She turned into Lambeth Palace Road and was struck by an absurd thought—she was absolutely famished. Food was in shorter supply than ever. The dry autumn and bitter cold winter had combined to eliminate almost all green vegetables from the country. Potatoes and brussels sprouts were delicacies. Only turnips and swedes were in plentiful supply. She thought, If I have to eat one more turnip, I'll shoot myself. Still, she suspected things were much worse in Berlin.

A policeman—a short chubby man who looked too old to get into the army—stood watch at the entrance to Lambeth Palace Road. He raised his hand and, shouting over the wail of the air raid sirens, asked for her identification.

As always, Catherine's heart seemed to miss a beat.

She handed over a badge identifying her as a member of the Women's Voluntary Service. The policeman glanced at it, then at her face. She touched the policeman's shoulder and leaned close to his ear so that when she spoke he could feel her breath on his ear. It was a technique she had used to neutralize men for years.

Catherine said, "I'm a volunteer nurse at St. Thomas Hospital."

The police officer looked up. By the expression on his face Catherine could see he was no longer a threat to her. He was grinning stupidly, gazing at her as if he had just fallen in love. The reaction was nothing new to Catherine. She was strikingly beautiful, and she had used her looks as a weapon her entire life.

The policeman handed back her identification.

"How bad is it?" she asked.

"Bad. Be careful and keep your head down."

London's need for ambulances had far exceeded the supply. The authorities grabbed anything suitable they could lay their hands on—delivery vans, milk trucks—anything with four wheels, a motor, and room in the back for the injured and a medic. Catherine noticed a red cross painted over the faded name of a popular local bakery on one of the ambulances pouring into the hospital's emergency entrance.

She walked quickly now, trailing the ambulance, and stepped inside. It was bedlam. The emergency room was filled with wounded. They seemed to be everywhere—the floors, the hallways, even the nurses' station. A few cried. Others sat staring, too dazed to comprehend what had happened to them. Dozens of patients had yet to see a doctor or a nurse. More were arriving by the minute.

Catherine felt a hand on her shoulder.

"No time for standing round, Miss Blake."

Catherine turned and saw the stern face of Enid Pritt. Before the war, Enid had been a kind, sometimes confused woman accustomed to dealing with cases of influenza and, occasionally, the loser of a Saturday-night knife fight outside a pub. All that changed with the war. Now she stood ramrod straight and spoke in a clear parade-ground voice, never using more words than needed to make a point. She ran one of the busiest emergency wards in London without a hitch. A year earlier her husband of twenty-eight years had been killed in the blitz. Enid Pritt did not grieve—that could wait until after the Germans were beaten.

"Don't let them see what you're thinking, Miss Blake," Enid Pritt said briskly. "Frightens them even more. Off with your coat and get to work. At least a hundred and fifty wounded in this hospital alone, and the morgue's filling fast. Been told to expect more."

"I haven't seen it this bad since September 1940."

"That's why they need you. Now get to work, young lady, quick as you like."

Enid Pritt moved off across the emergency room like a commander crossing a battlefield. Catherine watched her take a young nurse to task over a sloppy dressing. Enid Pritt didn't play favorites—she was hard on nurses and volunteers alike. Catherine hung up her coat and started making her way down a hallway filled with injured. She began with a small girl clutching a scorched stuffed bear.

"Where does it hurt, little one?"

"My arm."

Catherine rolled up the sleeve of the girl's sweater, revealing an arm that was obviously broken. The child was in shock and unaware of the pain. Catherine kept her talking, trying to keep her mind off the wound.

"What's your name, sweetheart?"

"Ellen."

"Where do you live?"

"Stepney, but our house isn't there anymore." Her voice was calm, emotionless.

"Where are your parents? Are they here with you?"

"The fireman told me they're with God now."

Catherine said nothing, just held the girl's hand. "The doctor will be along to see you soon. Just sit still and try not to move your arm. All right, Ellen?"

"Yes," she said. "You're very pretty."

Catherine smiled. "Thank you. You know what?"

"What?"

"So are you."

Catherine moved up the hallway. An older man with a contusion across the top of his bald head looked up as Catherine examined the wound. "I'm just fine, young lady. There are a lot of people hurt worse than myself. See to them first."

She smoothed his rumpled ring of gray hair and did as he asked. It was a quality she had seen in the English time and time again. Berlin was foolish to resume the blitz. She wished she were allowed to tell them.

Catherine moved down the hall, tending to the wounded, listening to the stories while she worked.

"I was in the kitchen pourin' meself a cup of bleedin' tea when *boom!* A thousand-pound bomb lands right on me bleedin' doorstep. Next thing I know I'm lyin' flat on me back in what used to be me garden, lookin' up at a pile of rubble that used to be me bleedin' house."

"Watch your mouth, George, there's children present."

"That's not so bad, mate. House across the street from mine took a direct hit. Family of four, good people, wiped out."

A bomb landed nearby; the hospital shook.

A nun, badly injured, blessed herself and began leading the others in the Lord's Prayer.

"It's gonna take more than prayer to knock the Luftwaffe out of the sky tonight, Sister."

"Thy kingdom come, Thy will be done . . ."

"I lost my wife to the blitz in 1940. I think I may have lost my only daughter tonight."

". . . on Earth as it is in Heaven. . . ."

"What a war, Sister, what a bleedin' war."

". . . as we forgive those who trespass against us,   ."

"You know, Melvin, I get the impression Hitler doesn't much like us."

"I've noticed that too."

The emergency room erupted with laughter.

Ten minutes later, when the nun decided that prayer had run its course, the inevitable singing began.

"Roll out the barrel . . ."

Catherine shook her head.

"We'll have a barrel of fun. . . ."

But after a moment she found herself singing along with the others.

It was eight o'clock the next morning when she let herself into her flat. The morning's post had arrived. Her landlady, Mrs. Hodges, always slipped it beneath the door. Catherine bent down, picked up the letters, and immediately tossed three envelopes into the trash bin in the kitchen. She did not need to read them because she had written them herself and mailed them from different locations around London. Under normal circumstances,

Catherine would receive no personal letters, for she had no friends and no family in Britain. But it would be odd for a young, attractive, educated woman never to correspond with anyone—and Mrs. Hodges was a bit of a snoop—so Catherine engaged in an elaborate ruse to make sure she had a steady stream of personal mail.

She went into the bathroom and opened the taps above the tub. The pressure was low, the water trickled from the spigot in a thread, but at least it was hot today. Water was in short supply because of the dry summer and fall, and the government was threatening to ration that too. Filling the tub would take several minutes.

Catherine Blake had been in no position to make demands at the time of her recruitment, but she made one anyway—enough money to live comfortably. She had been raised in large town houses and sprawling country estates—both her parents had come from the upper classes—and spending the war in some hovel of a boardinghouse sharing a bathroom with six other people was out of the question. Her cover was a war widow from a middle-class family of respectable means and her flat matched it to perfection, a modest yet comfortable set of rooms in a Victorian terrace in Earl's Court.

The sitting room was cozy and modestly furnished, though a stranger might have been struck by the complete lack of anything personal. There were no photographs and no mementos. There was a separate bedroom with a comfortable double bed, a kitchen with all modern appliances, and her own bathroom with a large tub.

The flat had other qualities that a normal Englishwoman living alone might not demand. It was on the top floor, where her AFU suitcase radio could receive transmissions from Hamburg with little interference, and the Victorian bay window in the sitting room provided a clear view of the street below.

She went into the kitchen and placed a kettle of water on the stove. The volunteer work was time-consuming and exhausting but it was essential for her cover. Everyone was doing *something* to help. It wouldn't look right for a healthy young woman with no family to be doing nothing for the war effort. Signing up to work at a munitions factory was risky—her cover might not withstand much of a background check—and joining the Wrens was out of the question. The Women's Voluntary Service was the perfect compromise. They were desperate for people. When Catherine went to sign up in September 1940 she was put to work that same night. She cared for the injured at St. Thomas Hospital and handed out books and biscuits in the underground during the night raids. By all appearances she was the model young Englishwoman doing her bit.

Sometimes she had to laugh.

The kettle screamed. She returned to the kitchen and made tea. Like all Londoners she had become addicted to tea and cigarettes. It seemed the whole country was living on tannin and tobacco, and Catherine was no exception. She had used up her ration of powdered milk and sugar so she drank the tea plain. At moments like these she longed for the strong bitter coffee of home and a piece of sweet Berlin cake.

She finished the first cup and poured a second. She wanted to take a bath, crawl into bed, and sleep round the clock, but she had work to do, and she needed to stay awake. She would have been home an hour earlier if she moved around London like a normal woman. She would have taken the underground straight across London to Earl's Court. But Catherine did not move around London like a normal woman. She had taken a train, then a bus, then a taxi, then another bus. She had stepped off the bus early and walked the final quarter mile to her flat, constantly checking to make certain she was not being followed. When she finally arrived home she was soaked by the rain but confident she was alone. After more than five years, some agents might be tempted to become complacent. Catherine would never become complacent. It was one of the reasons she survived when others had been arrested and hanged.

She went into the bathroom and undressed in front of the mirror. She was tall and fit; years of heavy riding and hunting had made her much stronger than most women and many men. She was broad through the front of her shoulders, and her arms were smooth and firm as a statue's. Her breasts were rounded and heavy and perfectly shaped, her stomach hard and flat. Like almost everyone she was thinner than before the war. She undid the clasp that held her hair in a discreet nurse's bun, and it tumbled about her neck and shoulders, framing her face. Her eyes were ice blue—the color of a Prussian lake, her father had always said—and the cheekbones were wide and prominent, more German than English. The nose was long and graceful, the mouth generous, with a pair of sensuous lips.

She thought, All in all, you're still a very attractive woman, Catherine Blake.

She climbed into the tub, feeling suddenly very alone. Vogel had warned her about the loneliness. She never imagined it could be so intense. Sometimes it was actually worse than the fear. She thought it would be better if she were completely alone—isolated on a deserted island or mountaintop—than to be surrounded by people she could not touch.

She had not allowed herself a lover since the boy in Holland. She missed men and she missed sex but she could live without both. Desire, like all her emotions, was something she could turn on and off like a light switch. Besides, having a man was difficult in her line of work. Men tended to become obsessive about her. The last thing she needed now was a lovesick man looking into her past.

Catherine finished her bath and got out. She combed her wet hair quickly and put on her robe. She went to the kitchen and opened the door to the pantry. The shelves were barren. The suitcase radio was on the top shelf. She brought it down and took it into the sitting room near the window, where the reception was the best. She opened the lid and switched it on.

There was another reason why she had never been caught: Catherine stayed off the airwaves. Each week she switched on the radio for a period of ten minutes. If Berlin had orders for her they would send them then.

For five years there had been nothing, only the hiss of the atmosphere.

She had communicated with Berlin just once, the night after she murdered the woman in Suffolk and assumed her new identity. Beatrice Pymm. She thought of the woman now, feeling no remorse. Catherine was a soldier, and during wartime soldiers were forced to kill. Besides, the murder was not gratuitous. It was absolutely necessary.

There were two ways for an agent to slip into Britain: clandestinely, by parachute or small boat, or openly, by passenger ship or airplane. Each method had drawbacks. Attempting to slip into the country undetected from the air or by small boat was risky. The agent might be spotted or injured in the jump; simply learning how to parachute would have added months to Catherine's already interminable training. The second method—coming by legal means—carried its own danger. The agent would have to go through passport control. A record would be made of the date and port of entry. When war broke out, MI5 would surely rely on those records to help track down spies. If a foreigner entered the country and never left, MI5 could safely assume that person was a German agent. Vogel devised a solution: enter Britain safely by boat, then erase the record of the entry by erasing the actual person. Simple, except for one thing—it required a body. Beatrice Pymm, in death, became Christa Kunst. MI5 had never discovered Catherine because they had never looked. Christa Kunst's entry and departure were both accounted for. They had no hint Catherine ever existed.

Catherine poured another cup of tea, slipped on her earphones, and waited.

She nearly spilled it on herself when, five minutes later, the radio crackled into life.

The operator in Hamburg tapped out a burst of code.

German keyers had the reputation of being the most precise in the world. Also the fastest. Catherine struggled to keep up. When the Hamburg operator finished, she asked him to repeat the message.

He did, more slowly.

Catherine acknowledged and signed off.

It took several minutes to find her codebook and several more to decode the message. When she was finished she stared at it in disbelief.

EXECUTE RENDEZVOUS ALPHA.

Kurt Vogel finally wanted her to meet with another agent.

CHAPTER EIGHT

HAMPTON SANDS, NORFOLK

Rain drifted across the Norfolk coast as Sean Dogherty, done in by five pints of watery ale, tried to mount his bicycle outside the Hampton Arms. He succeeded on his third attempt and set out for home. Dogherty, cycling steadily, barely noticed the village: a dreary place really—a cluster of cottages along the single street, the village store, the Hampton Arms pub. The sign hadn't been painted since 1938; paint, like nearly everything else, was rationed. St. John's Church rose over the east end. The graveyard lay at the edge of the village. Dogherty unconsciously blessed himself as he passed the lych-gate and pedaled over the wooden bridge spanning the sea creek. A moment later the village disappeared behind him.

Darkness gathered; Dogherty struggled to keep the bicycle upright on the pitted lane. He was a small man of fifty, green eyes set too deeply in his skull, a derelict gray beard. His nose, twisted and off center, had been broken more times than he cared to remember, once during a brief career as a welterweight in Dublin and a few more times in drunken street fights. He wore an oilskin coat and a woolen cap. The cold air clawed at the exposed skin of his face: North Sea air, knife edged, scented with the arctic ice fields and Norwegian fjords it had passed before assaulting the Norfolk coast.

The curtain of rain parted and the terrain came into view—broad emerald fields, endless gray mudflats, salt marshes deep with reeds and grass. To his left a wide, seemingly endless beach ran down to the water's edge. To his right, in the middle distance, green hills blended into low cloud.

A pair of Brent geese—down from Siberia for the winter—rose out of the marsh and banked out over the water, wings pumping gently. A perfect habitat for many species of birds, the Norfolk coast once was a popular tourist destination. But the war had made bird-watching all but impossible.

Much of Norfolk was a restricted military zone, and petrol rationing left few citizens with the means to travel to such an isolated corner of the country. If they had, they would have found it difficult to find their way around. In the spring of 1940, with invasion fever running high, the government took down all the road signs.

Sean Dogherty, more than other residents of the Norfolk coast, took special note of such things. In 1940 he had been recruited to spy for the Abwehr and given the code name Emerald.

The cottage appeared in the distance, smoke lifting gently from the chimney only to be sliced off by the wind and carried across the broad meadow. It was a smallholding on rented land but it provided an adequate living: a small flock of sheep that gave them wool and meat, chickens, a small plot of root vegetables that fetched good prices these days at the market. Dogherty even owned a dilapidated old van and transported goods from neighboring farms to the market in King's Lynn. As a result he was given an agricultural ration of petrol, more than the standard civilian ration.

He turned into the drive, climbed off his bicycle, and pushed it along the pitted pathway toward the barn. Overhead, he heard the drone of Lancaster bombers setting out from their Norfolk bases. He remembered a time when the planes came from the other direction—the Luftwaffe's heavy Heinkels, sweeping in over the North Sea toward the industrial centers of Birmingham and Manchester. Now the Allies had established supremacy of the skies, and the Heinkels rarely ventured over Norfolk.

He looked up and saw the curtains of the kitchen window part slightly, saw the blurry image of Mary's face through the rain-streaked glass. Not tonight, Mary, he thought, eyes consciously averted. Please, not again tonight.

It had not been difficult for the Abwehr to convince Sean Dogherty to betray England and go to work for Nazi Germany. In 1921, his older brother, Daniel, was arrested and hanged by the British for leading an Irish Republican Army flying column.

Inside the barn Dogherty unlocked a tool cabinet and took down his Abwehr-issue suitcase transceiver, his cipher pad, a notebook, and a pencil. He switched on the radio and smoked a cigarette while he waited. His instructions were simple: turn on the radio once each week and stand by for any instructions from Hamburg. It had been more than three years since the Abwehr had asked him to do anything. Still, he dutifully switched on his radio at the instructed time and waited for ten minutes.

With two minutes remaining in the window, Dogherty placed the cipher pad and the notebook back in the cabinet. With one minute left, he reached for the power switch. He was about to shut off the radio when it suddenly came to life. He lunged for his pencil and wrote furiously until the radio went silent. He quickly tapped out an acknowledgment and signed off.

It took Dogherty several minutes to decode the message.

When he finished, he couldn't believe his eyes.

EXECUTE RECEPTION PROCEDURE ONE.

The Germans wanted him to take in an agent.

It had been fifteen minutes since Mary Dogherty, standing in the kitchen window, had seen her husband enter the barn. She wondered what was taking so long. Sean's dinner would go cold if he didn't come in soon. She wiped her hands on her apron and carried a mug of steaming tea to the front window. The rain was coming down harder now, wind whipping across the coastline from the North Sea.

She thought, Terrible night to be out in it, Sean Dogherty.

She cupped her hands around the chipped enamel mug, letting the rising steam warm her face. She knew what he was doing in the barn—he was on the radio with the Germans.

Spying for the Nazis, Mary had to admit, had rejuvenated Sean. In the spring of 1940 he reconnoitered huge sections of the Norfolk countryside. Mary watched in amazement as he seemed to come back to life under the assignment, pedaling several miles a day, looking for signs of military activity, taking photographs of coastal defenses. The information was passed to an Abwehr contact in London, who in turn passed it on to Berlin. Sean thought it was all very dangerous and loved every moment of it.

Mary hated it. She feared Sean would be caught. Everyone was on the lookout for spies; it was a national obsession. One slip, one mistake, and Sean would be arrested. The 1940 Treachery Act prescribed a single sentence for spying: execution. Mary had read about spies in the newspapers— the hangings at Wandsworth and Pentonville—and each one sent ice through her veins. One day, she feared, she would read of Sean's execution.

The rain fell harder now, and the wind beat so furiously against the side of the sturdy little cottage Mary feared it might come down. She thought of living alone on the broken-down old farm; it would be miserable. Shuddering, she drew away from the window and moved closer to the fire.

Perhaps it would have been different if she had been able to give him children. She pushed it from her mind; she had punished herself needlessly too long. No use dredging up things she could do nothing about. Sean was what he was and there was nothing she could do to change him.

Sean, Mary thought, what on earth has become of you?

The pounding at the door startled Mary, causing her to spill tea on her apron. It was not like Sean to lock himself out. She set down the mug in the window and hurried to the door, prepared to yell at him for leaving the cottage without his key. Instead, when she pulled back the door, she saw the figure of Jenny Colville, a girl who lived on the other side of the village. She stood in the rain, a shiny oilskin coat hanging over bony shoulders. She wore no hat and her shoulder-length hair lay plastered against her head, framing an awkward face that one day might be very pretty.

Mary could tell she had been crying.

"What happened, Jenny? Did your father hit you again? Has he been drinking?"

Jenny nodded and burst into tears.

"Come in out of the rain," Mary said. "You'll catch your death of cold out there on a night like this."

As Jenny came inside Mary looked in the front garden for her bicycle. It wasn't there; she had walked all the way from the Colville cottage, more than a mile away.

Mary closed the door. "Take off those clothes. They're soaking wet. I'll get you a robe to wear until they're dry."

Mary disappeared into the bedroom. Jenny did as she was told. Exhausted, she shed the oilskin, letting it fall from her shoulders onto the floor. Then she pulled off her heavy wool sweater and dropped it on the floor next to the oilskin.

Mary came back with the robe. "Get the rest of those clothes off, young lady," she said, gentle mock anger in her voice.

"But what about Sean?"

Mary lied. "He's out fixing a break in one of his blessed fences."

"In this weather?" Jenny sang in her heavy Norfolk accent, regaining some of her usual good humor. Mary marveled at her resiliency. "Is he daft, Mary?"

"I've always known you were a perceptive child. Now, off with the rest of those wet clothes."

Jenny stripped off her trousers and her undershirt. She tended to dress like a boy, even more so than other country girls. Her skin was milky white and covered with goose bumps. She would be very lucky not to come down with a heavy cold. Mary helped Jenny into the robe and wrapped it around her tightly.

"Now, isn't that better?"

"Yes, thank you, Mary." Jenny started to cry again. "I don't know what I'd do without you."

Mary drew Jenny to her. "You'll never be without me, Jenny. I promise."

Jenny climbed into an old chair next to the fire and covered herself with a musty blanket. She pulled her feet up under herself, and after a moment the shivering stopped and she felt warm and safe. Mary was at the stove, singing softly to herself.

After a few moments the stew bubbled, filling the cottage with a wonderful smell. Jenny closed her eyes, her tired mind leaping from one pleasant sensation to the next—the warm smell of the lamb stew, the heat of the fire, the thrilling sweetness of Mary's voice. The wind and rain lashed at the window next to her head. The storm made Jenny feel wonderful to be safely inside a peaceful home. She wished her life were always like this.

A few moments later Mary brought a tray with a bowl of stew, a lump of hard bread, and a steaming mug of tea. "Sit up, Jenny," she said, but there was no response. Mary set down the tray, covered the girl with another quilt, and let her sleep.

Mary was reading next to the fire when Dogherty let himself into the cottage. She regarded him silently as he came into the room. He pointed to the chair where Jenny slept and said, "Why is she here? Her father hit her again?"

"Shhhh!" Mary hissed. "You'll wake her."

Mary rose and led him into the kitchen. She set a place for him at the table. Dogherty poured himself a mug of tea and sat down.

"What Martin Colville needs is a bit of his own medicine. And I'm just the man to give it to him."

"Please, Sean—he's half your age and twice your size."

"And what's that supposed to mean, Mary?"

"It means you could get hurt. And the last thing we need is for you to attract the attention of the police by getting in some stupid fight. Now, finish your dinner and be quiet. You'll wake the girl."

Dogherty did as he was told and resumed eating. He took a spoonful of the stew and pulled a face. "Jesus, but this food is stone cold."

"If you'd come home at a decent hour it wouldn't be. Where have you been?"

Without lifting his head from his plate, Dogherty cast Mary an icy glance through his eyebrows. "I was in the barn," he said coldly.

"Were you on the wireless, waiting for instructions from Berlin?" Mary whispered sarcastically.

"Later, woman," Sean growled.

"Don't you realize you're wasting your time out there? And risking both our necks too?"

"I said later, woman!"

"Stupid old goat!"

"That's enough, Mary!"

"Maybe one day the boys in Berlin will give you a real assignment. Then you can get rid of all the hate that's inside you and we can get on with what's left of our lives." She rose and looked at him, shaking her head. "I'm tired, Sean. I'm going to bed. Put some more wood on the fire so Jenny will be warm enough. And don't do anything to wake her. She's had a rough time of it tonight."

Mary walked upstairs to their bedroom and quietly closed the door behind her. When she was gone, Dogherty went to the cupboard and took down a bottle of Bushmills. Whisky was like gold these days, but it was a special night so he poured himself a generous measure.

"Maybe the boys in Berlin will do just that, Mary Dogherty," he said, raising his glass in a quiet toast. "In fact, maybe they already have."

CHAPTER NINE

LONDON

Alfred Vicary had actually engaged in deception to get a job with military intelligence during the First War. He was twenty-one, nearing the end of his studies at Cambridge, and convinced England was foundering and in need of all the good men she could lay her hands on. He wanted nothing to do with the infantry. He knew enough of history to realize there was no glory in it, only boredom, misery, and very likely death or serious injury.

His best friend, a brilliant philosophy student named Brendan Evans, arrived at the perfect solution. Brendan had heard the army was starting up something called the Intelligence Corps. The only qualifications were fluent German and French, extensive travel throughout Europe, the ability to ride and repair a motorbike, and perfect eyesight. Brendan had contacted the War Office and made appointments for them the next morning.

Vicary was despondent; he did not meet the qualifications. He had fluent if uninspired German, passable French, and he had traveled broadly across Europe, including inside Germany. But he had no idea how to ride a motorbike—indeed, the contraption scared the daylights out of him—and his eyesight was atrocious.

Brendan Evans was everything Vicary was not: tall, fair, strikingly handsome, possessed of a boyish lust for adventure and more women than he knew what to do with. They had one trait in common, flawless memories.

Vicary conceived his plan.

That evening, in the cool twilight of August, Brendan taught him to ride a motorcycle on a deserted patch of road in the Fens. Vicary nearly killed them both several times, but by the end of the night he was roaring along the pathways, experiencing a thrill and a recklessness he had never before felt.

The following morning, during the train ride from Cambridge to London, Brendan drilled him relentlessly on the anatomy of motorbikes.

When they arrived in London, Brendan went into the War Office while Vicary waited outside in the warm sunshine. He emerged an hour later, grinning broadly. "I'm in," Brendan said. "Now, it's your turn. Listen carefully." He then proceeded to read back the entire eye chart used for the vision test, even the hopelessly tiny characters at the bottom.

Vicary removed his spectacles, handed them to Brendan, and walked like a blind man into the dark, forbidding building. He passed with flying colors—he made only one mistake, transposing a B for a D, but that was Brendan's fault, not his. Vicary was immediately commissioned as a second lieutenant in the motorcyclist section of the Intelligence Corps, given a warrant for his uniform and kit, and ordered to cut his hair, which had grown long and curly over the summer. The following day he was ordered to Euston Station to collect his motorbike, a shiny new Rudge model packed in a wooden crate. A week later Brendan and Vicary boarded a troopship along with their motorbikes and sailed for France.

It was all so simple then. Agents slipped behind enemy lines, counted troops, watched the railways. They even used carrier pigeons to deliver secret messages. Now it was more complex, a duel of wits over the wireless that required immense concentration and attention to detail.

Double Cross. . . .

Karl Becker was a perfect example. He was sent by Canaris to England during the heady days of 1940, when invasion seemed certain. Becker, posing as a Swiss businessman, set himself up in suitable style in Kensington and began collecting every questionable secret he could lay his hands on. It was Becker's use of counterfeit sterling that set Vicary onto him, and within a matter of weeks he had been spun into MI5's web. Vicary, with the help of the watchers, went everywhere Becker went: to the parties where he traded in gossip and drank himself stiff on black-market champagne; to his meetings with live agents; to his dead drops; to his bedroom, where he brought his women, his men, his children, and only God knew what else. After a month Vicary brought down the hammer. He arrested Becker—pulled him from the arms of a young girl he had kept locked away and drunk on champagne—and rolled up an entire network of German agents.

Next came the tricky part. Instead of hanging Becker, Vicary turned him—convinced him to go to work for MI5 as a double agent. The following night Becker, from his prison cell, turned on his radio and tapped out a coded recognition signal to the operator in Hamburg. The operator asked him to stay on the air for instructions from his Abwehr control officer in Berlin, who ordered Becker to determine the exact location and size of an RAF fighter base in Kent. Becker confirmed the message and signed off.

But it was Vicary who went to the airfield the next day. He could have called the RAF, obtained the coordinates for the base, and sent them to the Abwehr, but it wouldn't be so easy for a spy. To make the message appear authentic, Vicary went about reconnoitering the air base just the way a spy would do it. He took the train from London and, because of delays, didn't arrive in the area until dusk. A military policeman harassed him on a hillside outside the base and asked him for his identification. Vicary could see the air base on the flats below, the same perspective from which a spy might see it. He saw a cluster of Nissen huts and a few aircraft along the grassy runway. During his return to London, Vicary composed a brief report on what he had seen. He noted that the light had been poor because the trains were late and said he had been prevented from getting too close by an MP. That night Vicary forced Becker to send the report with his own hand, for each spy had his own distinctive keying style, known as a *fist,* that German radio operators could recognize. Hamburg congratulated him and signed off.

Vicary then contacted the RAF and explained the situation. The real Spitfires were removed to another field, the personnel evacuated, and several badly damaged fighters were fueled and placed along the runway. That night the Luftwaffe came. The dummy planes exploded into fireballs; certainly the crews of the Heinkel bombers thought they had scored a direct hit. The next day the Abwehr asked Becker to return to Kent to assess the damage. Again, it was Vicary who went, gathered a report on what he could see, and forced Becker to send it.

The Abwehr was ecstatic. Becker was a star, a superspy, and all it had cost the RAF was a day patching up the runway and carting off the charred skeletons of the Spitfires.

So impressed were Becker's controllers, they asked him to recruit more agents, which he did—actually, which Vicary did. By the end of 1940, Karl Becker had a ring of a dozen agents working for him, some reporting to him, some reporting directly to Hamburg. All were fictitious, products of Vicary's imagination. Vicary tended to every aspect of their lives: they fell in love, they had affairs, they complained about money, they lost houses and friends in the blitz. Vicary even allowed himself to arrest a couple of them; no network operating on enemy soil was foolproof, and the Abwehr would never believe none of their agents had been lost. It was mind-bending, tedious work, requiring attention to the most trivial detail; Vicary found it exhilarating and loved every minute of it.

The lift was on the blink again, so Vicary had to take the stairs from Boothby's lair down to Registry. Opening the door he was struck by the smell of the place: decaying paper, dust, tangy mildew from the damp creeping through the cellar walls. It reminded him of the library at the university. There were files on open shelves, files in the file cabinets, files stacked on the cold stone floor, piles of paper waiting to ripen into files. A trio of pretty girls—the shakedown night staff—moved quietly about, speaking a language of inventory Vicary could not understand. The girls— known as Registry Queens in the lexicon of the place—looked strangely out of place amid the paper and the gloom. He half expected to turn a corner and spot a pair of monks reading an ancient manuscript by candlelight.

He shivered. God, but the place was cold as a crypt. He wished he had worn a sweater or brought something warm to drink. It was all here—the entire secret history of the service. Vicary, wandering the stacks, was struck by the thought that long after he left MI5 there would be an eternal record of his every action. He wasn't certain if he found the thought comforting or sickening.

Vicary thought of Boothby's disparaging remarks about him, and a cold shiver of anger passed over him. Vicary was a damned good Double Cross officer, even Boothby couldn't deny that. He was convinced it was his training as a historian that suited him so perfectly to the work. Often, a historian must engage in conjecture—taking a series of small inconclusive clues and reaching a reasonable inference. Double Cross was very much like engaging in conjecture, only in reverse. It was the job of the Double Cross officer to provide the Germans with small inconclusive clues so they could arrive at desired conclusions. The officer had to be careful and meticulous in the clues he revealed. They had to be a careful blend of fact and fiction, of truth and painstakingly veiled lies. Vicary's bogus spies had to work very hard for their information. The intelligence had to be fed to the Germans in small, sometimes meaningless bites. It had to be consistent with the spy's cover identity. A lorry driver from Bristol, for example, could not be expected to come into possession of stolen documents in London. And no piece of intelligence could ever seem too good to be true, for information too easily obtained is easily discarded.

The files on Abwehr personnel were stored on open floor-to-ceiling shelves in a smaller room at the far end of the floor. The *V*'s started on a bottom shelf, then jumped to a top one. Vicary had to get down on all fours and tilt his neck sideways, as if he were looking for a lost valuable beneath a piece of furniture. Damn! The file was on the top shelf, of course. He struggled to his feet and, craning his neck, peered at the files over his half-moon reading glasses. Bloody hopeless. The files were six feet above him, too far to read the names—Boothby's revenge on all those who had not attained regulation department height.

One of the Registry Queens found him gazing upward and said she would bring him a library ladder. "Claymore tried to use a chair last week and nearly broke his neck," she sang, returning a moment later, dragging the ladder. She took another look at Vicary, smiled as if he were a daft uncle, and offered to get the file for him. Vicary assured her he could manage.

He climbed the ladder and, using his forefinger as a probe, picked through the files. He found a manila folder with a red tab: VOGEL, KURT— ABWEHR BERLIN. He pulled it down, opened it, and looked inside.

Vogel's file was empty.

A month after he arrived at MI5, Vicary had been surprised to find Nicholas Jago working there too. Jago had been head archivist at University College and was recruited by MI5 the same week as Vicary. He was assigned to Registry and ordered to impose some discipline on the sometimes fickle memory of the department. Jago, like Registry itself, was dusty and irritable and difficult to use. But once past the rough exterior he could be kind and generous, bubbling with valuable information. Jago had one other valuable skill: he knew how to lose a file as well as find one.

Despite the late hour, Vicary found Jago working at his desk in his cramped, glass-enclosed office. Unlike the file rooms it was a sanctuary of neatness and order. When Vicary rapped his knuckle against the windowed door, Jago looked up, smiled, and waved him in. Vicary noticed the smile did not extend to his eyes. He looked exhausted; Jago *lived* in this place. There was something else: in 1940 his wife had been killed in the blitz. Her death had left him shattered. He had taken a personal oath to defeat the Nazis—not with the gun, with organization and precision.

Vicary sat down and refused Jago's offer of tea—"real stuff I hoarded before the war," he said excitedly. Not like the atrocious wartime tobacco he was stuffing into the bowl of his pipe and setting ablaze with a match. The vile smoke smelled of burning leaves, and it hung between them in a pall while they swapped banalities about returning to the university when the job was done.

Vicary signaled he wanted to get down to business by gently clearing his throat. "I'm looking for a file on a rather obscure Abwehr officer," Vicary said. "I was surprised to find it's missing. The exterior cover is on the shelf, but the contents are gone."

"What's the name?" Jago asked.

"Kurt Vogel."

Jago's face darkened. "Christ! Let me take a look for it. Wait here, Alfred. I'll just be a moment."

"I'll come with you," Vicary said. "Maybe I can help."

"No, no," Jago insisted. "I wouldn't hear of it. I don't help you find spies, you don't help me find files." He laughed at his own joke. "Stay here, make yourself comfortable. I'll just be a moment."

That's the second time you've said that, Vicary thought: *I'll just be a moment.* Vicary knew that Jago had become obsessive about his files, but one missing dossier on an Abwehr officer was not cause for a departmental emergency. Files were misplaced and mistakenly discarded all the time. Once Boothby sounded a red alert after losing an entire briefcase filled with important files. Department legend said they had been found a week later at the flat of his mistress.

Jago rushed back into the office a moment later, a cloud of the vile pipe smoke floating behind him like steam from a locomotive. He handed Vicary the file and sat down behind his desk.

"Just as I thought," Jago said, absurdly proud of himself. "It was right there on the shelf. One of the girls must have placed it in the wrong folder. Happens all the time."

Vicary listened to the dubious excuse and frowned. "Interesting—never happened to me before."

"Well, maybe you're just lucky. We handle thousands of files a week down here. We could use more staff. I've taken it up with the director-general, but he says we've used up our allotment and we can't have any more."

Jago's pipe had gone dead and he was making a vast show of relighting it. Vicary's eyes teared as the little chamber of an office filled with smoke again. Nicholas Jago was a thoroughly good and honest man, but Vicary didn't believe a word of his story. He believed the file had been pulled by someone recently and hadn't made its way back to the shelf. And the someone who pulled it must have been someone damned important, judging by the look on Jago's face when Vicary had asked for it.

Vicary used the file to wave a clear patch in the cloud of smoke. "Who had Vogel's file last?"

"Come on, Alfred, you know I can't tell you that."

It was the truth. Mere mortals like Vicary had to sign out files. Records were kept on who pulled what files and when. Only the Registry staff and department heads had access to those records. A handful of very senior officers could get files without signing them out. Vicary suspected Vogel's file had been pulled by one of those officers.

"All I have to do is ask Boothby for a chit to see the access list and he'll give it to me," Vicary said. "Why don't you let me see it now and save me the time?"

"He might, he might not."

"What do you mean by that, Nicholas?"

"Listen, old man, the last thing I want to do is get between you and Boothby again." Jago was busying himself with the pipe again—stuffing the bowl, digging a match out of the matchbox. He stuck the thing between his clenched teeth so the bowl bounced while he spoke. "Talk to Boothby. If he says you can see the access list, it's all yours."

Vicary left him sitting in his smoky glass chamber, trying to set fire to his cheap tobacco, his match flaring with every drag on the pipe. Taking one last glance at him as he walked away with Vogel's file, he thought Jago looked like a lighthouse on a foggy point.

Vicary stopped at the canteen on the way back up to his office. He couldn't remember when he had last eaten. His hunger was a dull ache. He no longer craved fine food. Eating had become a practical undertaking, something to be done out of necessity, not pleasure. Like walking London at night—do it quickly, try not to get hurt. He remembered the afternoon in May 1940 when they had come for him. *Mr. Ashworth delivered two nice lamb chops to your house a short time ago. . . .* Such a waste of precious time.

It was late and the selection was worse than usual: a chunk of brown bread, some suspect cheese, a bubbling cauldron of brown liquid. Someone had crossed out the words *Beef broth* on the menu and written *Stone soup.* Vicary passed on the cheese and sniffed at the broth. It seemed harmless enough. He cautiously ladled himself out a bowl. The bread was as hard as the cutting board. Vicary hacked off a hunk with the dull knife. Using Vogel's file as a service tray, he picked his way through the tables and chairs. John Masterman sat stooped over a volume of Latin. A pair of famous lawyers sat at a corner table, rearguing an old courtroom duel. A popular writer of crime novels was scribbling in a battered notebook. Vicary shook his head. MI5 had recruited a remarkable array of talent.

He walked carefully up the stairs, the bowl of broth balanced precariously on the file. The last thing he needed was to soil the dossier. Jago had written countless irate memoranda imploring case officers to take better care of the files.

What's the name?

Kurt Vogel.

Christ! Let me take a look for it.

Something about it just wasn't right—that Vicary knew. Better not to force it. Better to set it aside and let his subconscious turn over the pieces.

He set the file and the soup down on his desk and switched on the lamp. He read the file through once while he sipped at the soup. It tasted like a boiled leather boot. Salt was one of the few spices the cooks had in plentiful supply, and they had used it generously. By the time he finished reading the file the second time, he had a desert thirst and his fingers were beginning to swell.

Vicary looked up and said, "Harry, I think we have a problem."

Harry Dalton, who had drifted off to sleep at his desk in the common area outside Vicary's office, got to his feet and came inside. They were a dubious pairing, jokingly referred to inside the department as Muscle & Brains, Ltd. Harry was tall and athletic, sharp-suited, with thickly brilliantined black hair, intelligent blue eyes, and a ready all-purpose smile. Before the war he was Detective-Inspector Harry Dalton of the Metropolitan Police Department's elite murder squad. He was born and raised in Battersea and still had a trace of working-class south London in his soft pleasant voice.

"He's got brains, that's for certain," Vicary said. "Look at this: doctorate of law from Leipzig University, studied under Heller and Rosenberg. Doesn't sound like your typical Nazi to me. The Nazis perverted the laws of Germany. Someone with an education like that couldn't be too thrilled about them. Then in 1935 he suddenly decides to forsake the law and go to work for Canaris as his personal attorney, a sort of in-house counsel for the Abwehr? I don't believe that. I think he's a spy, and this business about being Canaris's legal adviser is just another layer of cover."

Vicary was flipping through the file again.

"You have a theory?" Harry asked.

"Three theories, actually."

"Let's hear them."

"Number one, Canaris has lost faith in the British networks and has commissioned Vogel to undertake an investigation. A man with Vogel's background and training is the perfect officer to sift through all the files and all the agent reports to look for inconsistencies. We've been damned careful, Harry, but maintaining Double Cross is an enormously complex task. I bet we've made a couple of mistakes along the way. And if the right person were looking for them—an intelligent man like Kurt Vogel, for instance—he might be able to spot them."

"Theory two?"

"Theory two, Canaris has commissioned Vogel to construct a new network. It's very late in the game for something like that. Agents would have to be discovered, recruited, trained, and inserted into the country. That usually takes months to do the right way. I doubt that's what they're up to, but it can't be totally discounted."

"Theory three?"

"Theory three is that Kurt Vogel is the control officer of a network we don't know about."

"An entire network of agents that we haven't uncovered—is that possible?"

"We have to assume it is."

"Then all our doubles would be at risk."

"It's a house of cards, Harry. All it takes is one good agent, and the entire thing comes crashing down."

Vicary lit a cigarette. The tobacco took the aftertaste of the broth out of his mouth.

"Canaris must be under enormous pressure to deliver. He'd want the best to handle the operation."

"So that means Kurt Vogel is a man operating in a pressure cooker."

"Right."

"That could make him dangerous."

"It could also make him careless. He has to make a move. He has to use his radio or send an agent into the country. And when he does, we'll be on to him."

They sat in silence for a moment, Vicary smoking, Harry thumbing his way through Vogel's file. Then Vicary told him about what had happened in Registry.

"Lots of files go missing now and again, Alfred."

"Yes, but why *this* file? And more importantly, why *now*?"

"Good questions, but I suspect the answers are very simple. When you're in the middle of an investigation it's best to stay focused, not get sidetracked."

"I know, Harry," Vicary said, frowning. "But it's driving me to distraction."

Harry said, "I know one or two of the Registry Queens."

Vicary looked up. "I'm sure you do."

"I'll poke around, ask a few questions."

"Do it quietly."

"There's no other way to do it, Alfred."

"Jago's lying—he's hiding something."

"Why would he lie?"

"I don't know," Vicary said, crushing out his cigarette, "but I'm paid to think wicked thoughts."

CHAPTER TEN

BLETCHLEY PARK, ENGLAND

Officially it was called the Government Code and Cipher School. However, it was not a school at all. It looked as though it *might* be a school of some kind—a large ugly Victorian mansion surrounded by a high fence—but most people in the narrow-streeted railway town of Bletchley understood that something portentous was going on there. The great lawns were covered with dozens of makeshift huts. The remaining space had been trampled into pathways of frozen mud. The gardens were overgrown and shabby, like tiny jungles. The staff was an odd collection—the country's brightest mathematicians, chess champions, crossword-puzzle wizards—all assembled for one purpose: cracking German codes.

Even in the notoriously eccentric world of Bletchley Park, Denholm Saunders was considered an oddball. Before the war he had been a top mathematician at Cambridge. Now he was among the best cryptanalysts in the world. He also lived in a hamlet outside Bletchley with his mother and his Siamese cats, Plato and St. Thomas Aquinas.

It was late afternoon. Saunders was seated at his desk in the mansion, working over a pair of messages sent by the Abwehr in Hamburg to German agents inside Britain. The messages had been intercepted by the Radio Security Service, flagged as suspicious, and forwarded to Bletchley Park for decoding.

Saunders whistled tunelessly while his pencil scraped across his pad, a habit that irritated his colleagues no end. He worked in the hand cipher section of the park. His work space was crowded and cramped, but it was relatively warm. Better to be here than outside in one of the huts, where cryptanalysts slaved over German army and naval ciphers like Eskimos in an igloo.

Two hours later the scraping and the whistling stopped. Saunders was aware only of the sound of melting snow gurgling through the gutters of the old house. The work that afternoon had been far from challenging; the messages had been transmitted in a variation of a code Saunders unbuttoned himself in 1940.

"My goodness, but they are getting a bit boring, aren't they?" Saunders said, to no one in particular.

His superior was a Scot named Richardson. Saunders knocked, stepped inside, and laid the pair of decodes on the desk. Richardson read them and frowned. An officer at MI5 named Alfred Vicary had put out a red flag for this kind of thing just yesterday.

Richardson called for a motorcycle courier.

"There's one other thing," Saunders said.

"What's that?"

"The first message—the agent seemed to have some difficulty with the Morse. In fact he asked for the keyer to send it twice. They get testy about things like that. Could be nothing. There might have been some interference. But it might be a good idea to tell the boys at MI5 about it."

Richardson thought, Good idea indeed.

When Saunders was gone he typed out a brief memo describing how the agent *appeared* to struggle with the Morse. Five minutes later the decodes and Richardson's note were tucked inside a leather pouch for the forty-two-mile ride to London.

CHAPTER ELEVEN

SELSEY, ENGLAND

"It was the oddest thing I've ever seen," Arthur Barnes told his wife over breakfast that morning. Barnes, as he did every morning, had walked his beloved corgi Fionna along the waterfront. Part of it still was open to civilians; most of it had been sealed off and designated a restricted military zone. Everyone wondered what the military was doing there. No one talked about it. Dawn was late that morning—a gray overcast sky, rain now and again. Fionna was off her leash, scampering up and down the docks.

Fionna spotted the thing first, then Barnes did.

"A bloody giant concrete monster, Mabel. Like a block of flats lying on its side." Two tugs were pulling it out to sea. Barnes carried a pair of field glasses inside his coat—a friend once spotted the conning tower of a German U-boat and Barnes was dying to catch a glimpse of one too. He removed the glasses and raised them to his eyes.

The concrete monster had a boat attached to it with a broad, flat prow pushing through the choppy seas. Barnes scanned off its port side—"Hard to tell the port side from the starboard side, mind you"—and he spotted a small vessel with a bunch of military types on deck.

"I couldn't believe it, Mabel," he recounted, finishing the last of his toast. "They were clapping and cheering, giving each other hugs and pats on the back." He shook his head. "Imagine that. Hitler's got the world by the short hairs, and our boys get excited because they can make a giant hunk of concrete float."

The giant floating concrete structure spotted by Arthur Barnes that dreary January morning was code-named Phoenix. It was 200 feet long, 50 feet wide, and displaced more than 6,000 tons of water. More than two hundred were scheduled to be built. Its interior—invisible from Barnes's vantage point on the harbor front—was a labyrinth of hollow chambers and scuttling valves, for the Phoenix was not designed to remain on the surface for long. It was designed to be towed across the English Channel and sunk off the coast of Normandy. The Phoenixes were just one component of a massive Allied project to construct an artificial harbor in England and drag it to France on D-Day. The overall code name for the project was Operation Mulberry.

It was Dieppe that taught them their lesson, Dieppe and the amphibious landings in the Mediterranean. At Dieppe, site of the disastrous Allied raid on France in August 1942, the Germans denied the Allies use of a port for as long as possible. In the Mediterranean they destroyed ports before abandoning them, rendering them useless for long periods. The invasion planners determined that attempting to capture a port intact was hopeless. They decided the men and supplies would come ashore the same way—on the beaches of Normandy.

The problem was the weather. Studies of weather patterns along the French coast showed that periods of fair conditions could be expected to last no more than four consecutive days. Therefore, the invasion planners had to assume that supplies would have to be brought ashore in a storm.

In July 1943, Prime Minister Winston Churchill and a delegation of three hundred officials sailed for Canada aboard the *Queen Mary*. Churchill and Roosevelt were meeting in Quebec in August to approve plans for the Normandy invasion. During the journey, Professor J. D. Bernal, a distinguished physicist, gave a dramatic demonstration in one of the vessel's luxurious staterooms. He filled the bath with a few inches of water, the shallow end representing the Normandy beaches, the deep end the Baie de la Seine. Bernal placed twenty paper ships in the bath and used a back brush to simulate stormy conditions. The boats immediately sank. Bernal then inflated a Mae West life belt and laid it across the bath as a breakwater. The back brush was again used to create a storm, but this time the vessels survived. Bernal explained that the same thing would happen at Normandy. A storm would create havoc; an artificial harbor was needed.

At Quebec, the British and the Americans agreed to build two artificial harbors for the Normandy invasion, each with the capacity of the great port of Dover. Dover took seven years to build; the British and Americans had roughly eight months. It was a task of unimaginable proportions. Each Mulberry cost $96 million. The British economy, crippled by four years of war, would have to supply four million tons of concrete and steel. Hundreds of topflight engineers would be needed, as well as tens of thousands of skilled construction workers. To get the Mulberries from England to France on D-Day would require every available tug in Britain and on the eastern seaboard of the United States.

The only assignment equal to the task of building the Mulberries would be keeping them secret—proved by the fact that Arthur Barnes and his corgi Fionna were still standing on the waterfront when the coaster carrying the team of British and American Mulberry engineers nosed against the dock. The team disembarked and walked toward a waiting bus. One of the men broke away toward a staff car waiting to return him to London. The driver stepped out and crisply opened the rear door, and Commander Peter Jordan climbed inside.

NEW YORK CITY: OCTOBER 1943

They came for him on a Friday. He would always remember them as Laurel and Hardy: the thick, stubby American who smelled of bargain aftershave and his lunchtime beer and sausage; the thin smooth Englishman who shook Jordan's hand as though searching for a pulse. In reality their names were Leamann and Broome—or at least that's what it said on the identification cards they waved past him. Leamann said he was with the War Department; Broome, the angular Englishman, murmured something about being attached to the War Office. Neither man wore a uniform— Leamann a shabby brown suit that pulled across his corpulent stomach and rode up his crotch, Broome an elegantly cut suit of charcoal gray, a little too heavy for the American fall weather.

Jordan received them in his magnificent lower Manhattan office. Leamann suppressed little belches while admiring Jordan's spectacular view of the East River bridges: the Brooklyn Bridge, the Manhattan Bridge, the Williamsburg. Broome, who showed almost no interest in things man-made, commented on the weather—a perfect autumn day, a crystalline blue sky, brilliant orange sunshine. An afternoon to make you believe Manhattan is the most spectacular place on earth. They walked to the south window and chatted while watching freighters move in and out of New York harbor.

"Tell us about the work you're doing now, Mr. Jordan," Leamann said, a trace of South Boston in his voice.

It was a sore subject. He was still the chief engineer of the Northeast Bridge Company and it was still the largest bridge construction firm on the East Coast. But his dream of starting his own engineering firm had died with the war, just as he feared.

Leamann, it seemed, had memorized his résumé, and he recited it now as if Jordan had been nominated for an award. "First in your class at the Rensselaer Polytechnic Institute. Engineer of the Year in 1938. Scientific American *says you're the greatest thing since the guy who invented the wheel. You're hot stuff, Mr. Jordan."*

An enlarged version of the Scientific American *article hung on the wall in a neat black frame. The photograph taken of him then looked like another man. He was thinner now—some said more handsome—and even though he still was not yet forty, flecks of gray had appeared at his temples.*

Broome, the narrow Englishman, was wandering the office, scrutinizing the photographs and the models of bridges the company had designed and built.

"You have many Germans working here," Broome observed, as if it would be a news bulletin to Jordan. It was true—Germans among the engineering staff and Germans on the secretarial staff. Jordan's own secretary was a woman named Miss Hofer whose family came to America from Stuttgart when she was a girl. She still spoke English with a German accent. Then, as if to prove Broome's point, two mail boys walked past Jordan's door prattling in Berlin-accented German.

"What kind of security checks have you run on them?" It was Leamann talking again. Jordan could tell he was a cop of some sort—or at least he had been a cop in another life. It was written in the poor fit of his threadbare suit and the look of dogged determination on his face. For Leamann the world was filled with evil people, and he was the only thing standing between order and anarchy.

"We don't run security checks on them. We build bridges here, not bombs."

"How do you know they're not sympathetic to the other side?"

"Leamann. Is that a German name?"

Leamann's meaty face collapsed into a frown. "Irish, actually."

Broome broke off his inspection of the bridge models to chuckle at the exchange. Then he said, "Do you know a man named Walker Hardegen?"

Jordan had the uncomfortable feeling he had been investigated. "I think you already know the answer to that question. And yes, his family is German. He speaks the language and he knows the country. He's been invaluable to my father-in-law."

"You mean your former father-in-law?" Broome asked.

"We've remained very close since Margaret's death."

Broome was stooped over another model. "Is this a suspension bridge?"

"No, it's a cantilever design. You're not an engineer?"

Broome looked up and smiled as if he found the question somewhat offensive. "No, of course not."

Jordan sat down behind his desk. "All right, gentlemen, suppose you tell me what this is all about."

"It has to do with the invasion of Europe," Broome said. "We may need your help."

Jordan smiled. "You want me to build a bridge between England and France?"

"Something like that," Leamann said.

Broome was lighting a cigarette. He blew an elegant stream of smoke toward the river.

"Actually, Mr. Jordan, it's nothing like that at all."

CHAPTER TWELVE

LONDON

The skies erupted into a downpour as Alfred Vicary hurried across Parliament Square toward the Underground War Rooms, Winston Churchill's subterranean headquarters beneath the pavements of Westminster. The prime minister had personally telephoned Vicary and asked to see him straightaway. Vicary had quickly changed into his uniform and, in his haste, fled MI5 headquarters without an umbrella. Now, his only defense against the onslaught of freezing rain was to quicken his pace, one hand clutching the throat of his mackintosh, the other holding a batch of files over his head like a shield. He rushed past the contemplative statues of Lincoln and Beaconsfield and then, thoroughly wet, presented himself to the Royal Marine guard at the sandbagged doorway of No. 2 Great George Street.

MI5 was in a panic. The previous evening, a pair of decoded Abwehr signals had arrived by motorcycle courier from Bletchley Park. They confirmed Vicary's worst suspicions—at least two agents were operating inside Britain without MI5's knowledge, and it appeared the Germans planned to send in another. It was a disaster. Vicary, after reading the messages with a sinking heart, had telephoned Sir Basil at home and broken the news. Sir Basil had contacted the director-general and other senior officers involved in Double Cross. By midnight the lights were burning on the fifth floor. Vicary was now heading one of the most important cases of the war. He had slept less than an hour. His head ached, his eyes burned, his thoughts were coming and going in chaotic, turbulent flashes.

The guard glanced at Vicary's identification and waved him inside. Vicary descended the stairs and crossed the small lobby. Ironically, Neville Chamberlain had ordered construction to begin on the Underground War Rooms the day he returned from Munich declaring "peace in our time." Vicary would always think of the place as a subterranean monument to the failure of appeasement. Shielded by four feet of concrete reinforced with old London tram rails, the underground labyrinth was regarded as absolutely bombproof. Along with Churchill's personal command post, the most vital and secret arms of the British government were housed here.

Vicary moved down the corridor, ears filled with the clatter of typewriters and the rattle of a dozen unanswered telephones. The low ceiling was buttressed by the timbers of one of Nelson's ships of the line. A sign warned MIND YOUR HEAD. Vicary, barely five and a half feet tall, passed easily beneath it. The walls, once the color of Devonshire cream, had faded like old newspaper to a dull beige. The floors were covered in an ugly brown linoleum. Overhead, in a brace of drainage pipes, Vicary could hear the gurgle of sewage from the aboveground New Public Offices. Even though the air was filtered by a special ventilation system, it smelled of unwashed bodies and stale cigarette smoke. Vicary approached a doorway, where another Royal Marine guard stood at ease. The guard snapped to attention as Vicary passed, the crack of his heels deadened by a special rubber mat.

Vicary looked at the faces of the staff who worked, lived, ate, and slept belowground in the prime minister's subterranean fortress. The word *pale* did not do justice to the state of their complexions; they were pasty, waxen troglodytes, scampering about their underground warren. Suddenly, Vicary's windowless hutch in St. James's Street didn't seem so bad after all. At least it was above the ground. At least there was something approaching fresh air.

Churchill's private quarters were located in room 65A, next door to the map room and across the hall from the Transatlantic Telephone Room. An aide took Vicary immediately inside, earning him the icy stares of a band of bureaucrats who looked as though they had been waiting since the last war. It was a tiny space, much of it consumed by a small bed made up with gray army blankets. At the foot of the bed stood a table with a bottle and two glasses. The BBC had installed a permanent microphone so Churchill could make his radio broadcasts from the safety of his underground fortress. Vicary noticed a small, darkened sign that said QUIET—ON THE AIR. The room contained only one luxury item, a humidor for the prime minister's Romeo y Julieta cigars.

Churchill, cloaked in a green silk robe, the first cigar of the day between his fingers, sat at his small desk. He remained there as Vicary entered the room. Vicary sat on the edge of the bed and regarded the figure before him. He was not the same man Vicary had seen that afternoon in May 1940. Nor was he the jaunty, confident figure of newsreels and propaganda films. He was obviously a man who had worked too much and slept too little. He had just returned to Britain a few days earlier from North Africa, where he convalesced after suffering a mild heart attack and contracting pneumonia. His eyes were rimmed with red, his cheeks puffy and pale. He managed a weak smile for his old friend.

"Hello, Alfred, how have you been?" Churchill said, when the Royal Marine orderly closed the door.

"Fine, but I should be asking that of you. You're the one who's been through the mill."

"Never better," Churchill said. "Bring me up to date."

"We've intercepted two messages from Hamburg to German agents operating inside Britain." Vicary handed them across to Churchill. "As you know, we were acting on the assumption that we had arrested, hanged, or turned every German agent operating in Britain. This is obviously a major blow. If the agents transmit any information that contradicts material we've sent through Double Cross, they will suspect everything. We also believe they are planning to insert a new agent into the country."

"What are you doing to stop them?"

Vicary briefed Churchill on the steps they had taken thus far. "But unfortunately, Prime Minister, the chances of capturing the agent at the drop are not good. In the past—in the summer of 1940, for example, when they were sending in spies for the invasion—we were able to capture incoming spies because the Germans often told old agents operating in Britain precisely when, where, and how the new spies were coming."

"And those old agents were working for you as doubles."

"Or sitting in a prison cell, yes. But in this case, the message to the existing agent was very vague, a code phrase only: EXECUTE RECEPTION PROCEDURE ONE. We assume it tells the agent everything he needs to know. Unfortunately, it tells us nothing. We can only guess how the new spy is planning to get into the country. And unless we're very lucky, the chances of capturing him are slim at best."

"Damn!" Churchill swore, bringing his hand down on the arm of the chair. He rose and poured brandy for them both. He stared into his glass, mumbling to himself, as if he had forgotten Vicary was there.

"Do you remember the afternoon in 1940 when I asked you to come to work for the MI-Five?"

"Of course, Prime Minister."

"I was right, wasn't I?"

"How do you mean?"

"You've had the time of your life, haven't you. Look at you, Alfred, you're a completely different man. Good heavens, but I wish I looked as good as you."

"Thank you, Prime Minister."

"You've done marvelous work. But it will all mean nothing if these German spies find what they're looking for. Do you understand?"

Vicary exhaled heavily. "I understand the stakes involved, Prime Minister."

"I want them stopped, Alfred. I want them crushed."

Vicary blinked rapidly and, unconsciously, beat his breast pockets for his half-moon reading glasses. Churchill's cigar had gone dead in his hand. Relighting it, he indulged himself in a quiet moment of smoking.

"How's Boothby?" Churchill said finally.

Vicary sighed. "As ever, Prime Minister."

"Supportive?"

"He wants to be kept abreast of every move I make."

"In writing, I suppose. Boothby's a stickler for having things in writing. Man's office generates more bloody paper than *The Times*."

Vicary permitted himself a mild chuckle.

"I never told you this, Alfred, but I had my doubts about whether you could be successful. Whether you truly had what it took to operate in the world of military intelligence. Oh, I never doubted you had the brains, the intelligence. But I doubted whether you possessed the sort of low cunning necessary to be a good intelligence officer. I also doubted whether you could be ruthless enough."

Churchill's words stunned Vicary.

"Now why are you looking at me like that? You're one of the most decent men I've ever met. The men who usually succeed in your line of work are men like Boothby. He'd arrest his own mother if he thought it would further his career or stab the enemy in the back."

"But I have changed, Prime Minister. I've done things I've never thought I was capable of doing. I've also done things I'm ashamed of."

Churchill looked perplexed. "Ashamed?"

"'When one is employed to sweep chimneys one must black one's fingers,'" Vicary said. "Sir James Harris wrote those words while he was serving as minister to The Hague in 1785. He detested the fact that he was asked to pay bribes to spies and informers. Sometimes, I wish it were still that simple."

Vicary remembered a night in September 1940. He and his team had hidden in the heather on a clifftop overlooking a rocky Cornish beach, sheltered from the cold rain beneath a black oilskin tarp. Vicary knew the German would come that night; the Abwehr had asked Karl Becker to arrange a reception party for him. He was little more than a boy, Vicary remembered, and by the time he reached the shore in his inflatable raft he was half dead with cold. He fell into the arms of the Special Branch men, babbling in German, just happy to be alive. His papers were atrocious, his two hundred pounds of currency badly forged, his English limited to a few well-rehearsed pleasantries. It was so bad Vicary had to conduct the interrogation in German. The spy had been assigned to gather intelligence on coastal defenses and, when the invasion came, engage in sabotage. Vicary determined that he was useless. He wondered how many more Canaris had like him—poorly trained, poorly equipped and financed, with virtually no chance of succeeding. Maintaining MI5's elaborate deception required that they execute a few spies, so Vicary recommended hanging him. He attended the execution at Wandsworth Prison and would never forget the look in the spy's eyes as the hangman slipped the hood over his head.

"You must make a stone of your heart, Alfred," Churchill said in a hoarse whisper. "We don't have time for feelings like shame or compassion—none of us, not now. You must set aside whatever morals you still have, set aside whatever feelings of human kindness you still possess, and do whatever it takes to win. Is that clear?"

"It is, Prime Minister."

Churchill leaned closer and spoke in a confessional tone. "There is an unfortunate truth about war. While it is virtually impossible for one man to win a war, it is entirely possible for one man to lose one." Churchill paused. "For the sake of our friendship, Alfred, don't be that man."

Vicary, shaken by Churchill's admonition, gathered up his things and showed himself to the door. Opening it, he walked out into the corridor. On the wall the weather board, updated hourly, read RAINY. Behind him he heard Winston Churchill, alone in his underground chamber, muttering to himself. It took Vicary a moment to understand what the prime minister was saying. "Blasted English weather," Churchill murmured. "Blasted English weather."

Vicary, by instinct, looked for clues in the past. He read and reread decodes of messages sent by agents inside Britain to the radio operators in Hamburg.

Decodes of messages sent by Hamburg to the agents inside Britain. Case histories, even cases he had been involved with. He read the final report of one of the first cases he had handled, an incident that had ended in the north of Scotland at a place aptly named Cape Wrath. He read the letter of commendation that went into his file, grudgingly written by Sir Basil Boothby, division head, copy forwarded to Winston Churchill, prime minister. He felt the pride all over again.

Harry Dalton shuttled back and forth between Vicary's desk and Registry like some medieval outrider, bringing new documents in one direction, returning old ones in the other. Other officers, aware of the tension building in Vicary's office, drifted past his doorway in twos and threes like motorists passing a road accident—eyes averted, stealing quick frightened glances. When Vicary would finish with one batch of files, Harry would ask, "Anything?" Vicary would pull a fussy frown and say, "No, nothing, dammit."

By two o'clock that afternoon the walls were collapsing in on him. He had smoked too many cigarettes and drunk too many cups of murky gray tea.

"I need some fresh air, Harry."

"Get out of here for a couple of hours. Be good for you."

"I'm going to take a walk—have some lunch, perhaps."

"Want some company?"

"No, thanks."

A freezing drizzle, like the smoke of a nearby battle, drifted over Westminster as Vicary marched along the Embankment. A bitterly cold wind rose from the river, clattered the shabby temporary street signs, whistled through a pile of splintered timber and broken brick where once a splendid building stood. Vicary moved quickly with his stiff-jointed mechanical limp, head down, hands plunged into coat pockets. By the look on his face a passing stranger might have guessed he was late for an important meeting or fleeing an unpleasant one.

The Abwehr had just so many ways of inserting an agent into Britain. Many put ashore in small boats launched from submarines. Vicary had just read arrest reports of double agents code-named Mutt and Jeff; they waded ashore from an Arado seaplane near the herring fishing village of Macduff east of Spey Bay. Vicary already had asked the coastguards and Royal Navy to be especially vigilant. But the British coastline stretches many thousands of miles, impossible to cover entirely, and the chances of catching an agent on a darkened beach were slim.

The Abwehr had parachuted spies into Britain. It was impossible to account for every square inch of airspace, but Vicary had asked the RAF to be watchful of stray aircraft.

The Abwehr had dropped and landed agents in Eire and Ulster. To get to England they had to take the ferry. Vicary had asked the ferry operators in Liverpool to keep an eye out for strange passengers: anyone unfamiliar with the routine of ferry passage, uncomfortable with the language or currency. He couldn't give them a description because he didn't have one.

The brisk walk and cold weather made him hungry. He entered a pub near Victoria Station and ordered a vegetable pie and a half pint of beer.

You must make a stone of your heart, Churchill had said.

Unfortunately, he had done that a long time ago. Helen. . . . She was the spoiled, attractive daughter of a wealthy industrialist, and Vicary, against his better judgment, had fallen hopelessly in love with her. Their relationship began to crumble the afternoon they made love for the first time. Somehow, Helen's father had read the signs correctly: the way they held hands on the way back from the lake, the way Helen touched Vicary's already thinning hair. That evening he summoned Helen for a private chat. Under no circumstances would she be allowed to marry the son of a mid-level bank clerk who attended university on a scholarship. Helen was instructed to terminate the relationship as quickly and quietly as possible, and she did exactly as she was told. She was that kind of girl. Vicary never held it against her, and he loved her still. But something went out of him that day. He supposed it was his ability to trust. He wondered if he would ever get it back.

It is virtually impossible for one man to win a war. . . .

Vicary thought, Damn the Old Man for laying that on my shoulders.

The publican, a well-fed woman, appeared at the table. "That bad, dearie?"

Vicary looked down at his plate. The carrots and potatoes had been pushed to the side and he had been absently trailing the point of his knife through the gravy. He looked at the plate carefully and noticed he had traced an outline of Britain in the brown mess.

He thought, Where will that damned spy land?

"It was fine," Vicary said politely, handing the plate over. "I suppose I wasn't quite as hungry as I thought."

Outside Vicary turned up the collar of his overcoat and started back toward the office.

It is entirely possible for one man to lose one.

Dead leaves rattled across Vicary's path as he hurried along Birdcage Walk. The afternoon's last light retreated with little resistance. In the gathering darkness, Vicary could see the blackout curtains closing like eyelids in the windows overlooking St. James's Park. He imagined Helen standing in one of the windows, watching him hurry along the walkway below. He entertained a wild fantasy that by solving the case, arresting the spies, and winning the war he would prove himself worthy of her and she would have him back.

Don't be that man.

There was something else Churchill had said; he had been complaining about the ceaseless rain. The prime minister, safe in the shelter of his subterranean fortress, complaining about the weather. . . .

Vicary rushed past the guard at MI5 headquarters without showing his identification badge.

"Any inspiration?" Harry asked, when Vicary returned to his office.

"Perhaps. If you needed to get a spy into the country on short notice, Harry, which route would you use?"

"I suppose I'd come through the east: Kent, East Anglia, even eastern Scotland."

"My thoughts exactly."

"So?"

"If you were mustering an operation quickly, which mode of transportation would you choose?"

"That depends."

"Come on, Harry!"

"I suppose I'd chose an airplane."

"Why not a submarine—put the spy ashore in a raft?"

"Because it's easier to get a small plane on short notice than a precious submarine."

"Exactly, Harry. And what do you need to drop a spy into England by plane?"

"Decent weather, for one thing."

"Right again, Harry."

Vicary snatched up the telephone receiver and waited for the operator to come on the line. "This is Vicary. Connect me with the RAF meteorological service immediately."

A young woman picked up a moment later. "Hello."

"This is Vicary from the War Office. I need some information about the weather."

"Quite a nasty spell we're having, isn't it."

"Yes, yes," Vicary said impatiently. "When is it going to break in the east?"

"We expect the current system to move offshore sometime tomorrow afternoon."

"And we'll have clear skies?"

"Crystal."

"Damn!"

"But not for long. There's another front behind it, moving rapidly across the country in a southeasterly direction."

"How far behind it?"

"That's difficult to say. Probably twelve to eighteen hours."

"And after that?"

"The entire country will be in the soup for the next week—intermittent snow and rain."

"Thank you."

Vicary put down the phone and turned to Harry.

"If our theory holds, our agent will try to enter the country by parachute tomorrow night."

CHAPTER THIRTEEN

HAMPTON SANDS, NORFOLK

The bicycle ride down to the beach usually took about five minutes. Sean Dogherty, late that afternoon, timed it just to make certain. He pedaled at a careful, unhurried pace, head inclined into the freshening wind beating off the sea. He wished the bicycle were in better shape. Like wartime England itself, it was battered, kicked around, desperately in need of maintenance. It clattered and grated with every turn of the pedals. The chain needed oil, which was scarce, and the tires were so bald and patched Dogherty might as well have been riding on the rims.

The rain had tapered off at midday. Plump, broken clouds floated over Dogherty's head like barrage balloons adrift at their moorings. Behind him the sun lay on the horizon like a fireball. The marshes and hillsides burned with a fine orange light.

Dogherty felt an intense excitement rising in his chest. He had not felt anything like this since the first time he met his Abwehr contact in London early in the war.

The road ended in a grove of pines at the base of the dunes. A weathered sign warned of mines on the beach; Dogherty, like everyone else in Hampton Sands, knew there were none. In the bicycle's basket, Dogherty had placed a sealed quart jar of precious petrol. He removed the jar, pushed the bicycle into the grove, and leaned it carefully against a tree.

Dogherty checked his watch—five minutes exactly.

A footpath led through the trees. Dogherty followed it, sand and dry pine needles beneath his feet, and started through the dunes. The crash of breaking waves filled the air.

The sea opened before him. The tide had reached its high mark two hours ago. Now it was running out fast and hard. By midnight, when the drop was scheduled, there would be a wide strip of flat hard sand along the water's edge, perfect for landing an agent by parachute.

Dogherty had the beach to himself. He returned to the pine trees and spent the next five minutes gathering enough wood for three small signal fires. It took four trips to carry the wood to the beach. He checked the wind—from the northeast, about twenty miles per hour. Dogherty stacked the wood in piles twenty yards apart in a straight line indicating the direction of the wind.

The twilight was dying. Dogherty opened the jar of petrol and doused the wood. He was to wait by his radio tonight until he received a signal from Hamburg that the plane was approaching. Then he would ride down to the beach, light the signal fires, take in the agent. Simple, if everything went according to plan.

Dogherty started back across the beach. It was then he saw Mary standing atop the dunes, silhouetted by the last light of sunset, arms folded beneath her breasts. The wind tossed hair across her face. He had told her the previous night; told her that the Abwehr had asked him to take in an agent. He had asked her to leave Hampton Sands until it was over; they had friends and family in London she could stay with. Mary had refused to leave. She had not said a word to him since. They bumped around the cramped cottage in angry silence, eyes averted, Mary slamming pots onto the stove and breaking plates and cups because of her jangled nerves. It was as if she were staying to punish him with her presence.

By the time Dogherty reached the top of the dunes Mary was gone. He followed the path to the spot where he had left the bicycle. Mary had taken it. Dogherty thought, Another round in our silent war. He turned up his collar against the wind and walked back to the cottage.

Jenny Colville had discovered the spot when she was ten years old—a small depression in the pine trees, several hundred yards from the roadway, sheltered from the wind by a pair of large rocks. A perfect hiding place. She had constructed a crude camp stove by stacking stones in a circle and placing a small metal grill on top. Now she laid the makings of a fire—pine needles, dried dune grass, small lengths of fallen tree limbs—and touched a match to it. She blew on it gently, and a moment later the fire crackled into life.

She kept a small case hidden beneath the rocks, covered with a layer of pine needles. She brushed away the needles and pulled it out. Opening the lid, Jenny removed the contents: a worn woolen blanket, a small metal pot, a chipped enamel mug, and a tin of dry, dusty tea. Jenny unfolded the blanket and spread it next to the fire. She sat down and warmed her hands against the flames.

Two years ago a villager had found her things and concluded a tinker was living on the beach. It caused the most excitement in Hampton Sands since the fire at St. John's in 1912. For a time Jenny stayed away. But the scandal quickly calmed and she was able to return.

The flames died, leaving a bed of glowing red embers. Jenny filled the pot with water from a canteen she had carried from home. She set the pot on the grill and waited for it to boil, listening to the sound of the sea and the wind hissing through the pines.

As always, the place worked its magic.

She began to forget about her problems—her father.

Earlier that afternoon, when she arrived home from school, he had been sitting at the kitchen table, drunk. Soon he would become belligerent, then angry, then violent. He would take it out on the person nearest him; inevitably that would be Jenny. She decided to head off the beating before it could take place. She made him a plate of meager sandwiches and a pot of tea and set them on the table. He had said nothing—expressed no concern about where she was going—as Jenny put on her coat and slipped out the door.

The water boiled. Jenny added the tea, covered it, removed it from the fire. She thought of the other girls from the village. They would be home now, sitting down with their parents for supper, talking over the events of the day, not hiding in the trees near the beach with nothing but the sound of breaking waves and a cup of tea for company. It had made her different, older, more clever. She had been stripped of her childhood, her time of innocence, forced to confront the fact very early in life that the world could be an evil place.

God, why does he hate me so much? What have I ever done to hurt him?

Mary had done her best to explain Martin Colville's behavior. He loves you, Mary had said countless times, but he's just hurt and angry and unhappy, and he takes it out on the person he cares about most.

Jenny had tried to put herself in her father's place. She vaguely remembered the day her mother packed her things and left. She remembered her father begging and pleading with her to stay. She remembered the look on his face when she refused, remembered the sound of shattering glass, breaking dishes, the horrid things they said to each other. For many years she was not told where her mother had gone; it was simply not discussed. When Jenny asked her father, he would stalk off in a stormy silence. Mary was the one who finally told her. Her mother had fallen in love with a man from

Birmingham, had an affair with him, and was living with him there now. When Jenny asked why her mother had never tried to contact her, Mary could supply no answer. To make matters worse, Mary said Jenny had become her mirror image. Jenny had no proof of this—the last memory she had of her mother was of a desperate and angry woman, eyes swollen and red from crying—and her father had destroyed all photographs of her long ago.

Jenny poured tea, holding the enamel mug close for warmth. The wind gusted, stirring the canopy of pine trees over her head. The moon appeared, followed by the first stars. Jenny could tell it would be a very cold night. She wouldn't be able to stay too long. She laid two larger pieces of wood on the fire and watched the shadows dancing on the rocks. She finished her tea and curled up in a ball, pillowing her head on her hands.

She pictured herself somewhere else, anywhere but Hampton Sands. She wanted to do something great and never come back. She was sixteen years old. Some of the older girls from the surrounding villages had gone to London and other big cities to take over the jobs left behind by the men. She could find work in a factory, wait tables in a café, *anything.* . . .

She was beginning to drift off to sleep when she thought she heard a sound from somewhere near the water. For a moment she wondered if there really *were* tinkers living on the beach. Startled, Jenny got to her feet. The pine trees ended at the dunes. She walked carefully through the grove, for it had grown dark rapidly, and started up the slope of sand. She paused at the top, dune grass dancing in the wind at her feet, staring in the direction of the sound. She saw a figure dressed in an oilskin, sea boots, and a sou'wester.

Sean Dogherty.

He seemed to be stacking wood, pacing, calculating some distance. Maybe Mary was right. Maybe Sean was going crazy.

Then Jenny spotted another figure at the top of the dunes. It was Mary, just standing there in the wind, arms folded, gazing at Sean silently. Then Mary turned and quietly left without waiting for Sean.

When Sean was out of sight Jenny doused the embers, put away her things, and pedaled her bicycle home. The cottage was empty, cold, and dark when she arrived. Her father was gone, the fire long dead. There was no note explaining his whereabouts. She lay awake in bed for some time, listening to the wind, replaying the scene she had witnessed on the beach. There was something very wrong about it, she concluded. Something very wrong indeed.

❖

"Surely there's something else we could do, Harry," Vicary said, pacing his office.

"We've done everything we can do, Alfred."

"Perhaps we should check with the RAF again."

"I just checked with the RAF."

"Anything?"

"Nothing."

"Well, call the Royal Navy—"

"I just got off the telephone with the Citadel."

"And?"

"Nothing."

"Christ!"

"You've just got to be patient."

"I'm not endowed with natural patience, Harry."

"I've noticed."

"What about—"

"I've called the ferry in Liverpool."

"Well?"

"Shut down by rough seas."

"So they won't be coming from Ireland tonight."

"Not bloody likely."

"Perhaps we're just approaching this from the wrong direction, Harry."

"What do you mean?"

"Perhaps we should be focusing our attention on the two agents already in Britain."

"I'm listening."

"Let's go back to the passport and immigration records."

"Christ, Alfred, they haven't changed since 1940. We've rounded up everyone we thought was a spy and interned everyone we had doubts about."

"I know, Harry. But perhaps there's something we missed."

"Such as?"

"How the hell should I know!"

"I'll get the records. It can't hurt."

"Perhaps we've run out of luck."

"Alfred, I've known a lot of lucky cops in my day."

"Yes, Harry?"

"But I've never known a lucky *lazy* cop."

"What are you driving at?"

"I'll get the files and make a pot of tea."

Sean Dogherty let himself out the back door of the cottage and walked along the footpath toward the barn. He wore a heavy sweater and an oilskin coat and carried a kerosene lantern. The last clouds had moved off. The sky was a mat of deep blue, thick with stars, a bright three-quarter moon. The air was bitterly cold.

A ewe bleated as he pulled open the barn door and went inside. The animal had become entangled in the fencing earlier that day. In her struggle to get free she had managed to slash her leg and tear a hole in the fence at the same time. She lay now on a bed of hay in the corner of the barn.

Dogherty switched on his radio and started changing the dressing, humming quietly to calm both their nerves. He removed the bloodied gauze, replaced it, and taped it securely in place.

He was admiring his work when the radio crackled into life. Dogherty bolted across the barn and slipped on his earphones. The message was brief. He sent back an acknowledging signal and dashed outside.

The ride to the beach took less than three minutes.

Dogherty dismounted at the end of the road and pushed the bicycle into the trees. He climbed the dunes, scrambled down the other side, and ran across the beach. The signal fires were intact, ready to be lit. In the distance he could hear the low rumble of an airplane.

He thought, Good Lord, he's actually coming!

He lit the signal fires. In a few seconds the beach was ablaze with light.

Dogherty, crouching in the dune grass, waited for the plane to appear. It descended over the beach, and a moment later a black dot leapt from the back. The parachute snapped open as the plane banked and headed out to sea.

Dogherty rose from the dune grass and ran across the beach. The German made a perfect landing, rolled, and was gathering up his black parachute by the time Dogherty arrived.

"You must be Sean Dogherty," he said in perfect public school English.

"That's right," Sean replied, startled. "And you must be the German spy."

The man frowned. "Something like that. Listen, old sport, I can manage this. Why don't you put out those bloody fires before the whole world knows we're here."

PART
TWO

CHAPTER FOURTEEN

EAST PRUSSIA: DECEMBER 1925

The deer are starving this winter. They leave the woods and scratch about the meadows for food. The big buck is there, standing in the brilliant sunshine, nose pushing into the snow for a little frozen grass. They are behind a low hill, Anna on her belly, Papa crouching beside her. He is whispering instructions but she does not hear him. She needs no instruction. She has waited for this day. Imagined it. Prepared for it.

She is slipping the shells into the barrel of her rifle. It is new, the stock smooth, unscratched, and smelling of clean gun oil. It is her birthday present. Today she is fifteen.

The deer is her present too.

She had wanted to take a deer earlier but Papa had refused. "It is a very emotional thing, killing a deer," he had said, by way of explanation. "It's hard to describe. You have to experience it, and I won't let that happen until you are old enough to understand."

It is a difficult shot—one hundred and fifty meters, a brisk icy crosswind. Anna's face stings with the cold, her body is shuddering, her fingers have gone numb in her gloves. She choreographs the shot in her mind: squeeze the trigger gently, just like on the shooting range. Just like Papa taught her.

The wind gusts. She waits.

She rises onto one knee and swings the rifle into firing position. The deer, startled by the crunch of snow beneath her, raises its massive head and turns in the direction of the sound.

Quickly, she finds the buck's head in her sight, accounts for the crosswind, and fires. The bullet pierces the buck's eye, and it collapses onto the snowy meadow in a lifeless heap.

She lowers the gun, turns to Papa. She expects him to be beaming, cheering, to have his arms open to hold her and tell her how proud he is. Instead his face is a blank mask as he stares first at the dead buck, then at her.

"Your father always wanted a son, but I didn't give him one," Mother said as she lay dying of tuberculosis in the bedroom at the end of the hall. "Be what he wants you to be. Help him, Anna. Take care of him for me."

She has done everything Mother asked. She has learned to ride and shoot and do everything the boys do, only better. She has traveled with Papa to his diplomatic postings. On Monday, they sail for America, where Papa will be first consul.

Anna has heard about the gangsters in America, racing around the streets in their big black cars, shooting everyone in sight. If the gangsters try to hurt Papa, she'll shoot them through the eye with her new gun.

That night they lie together in Papa's great bed, a large wood fire burning brightly on the hearth. Outside it is a blizzard. The wind howls and the trees beat against the side of the house. Anna always believes they are trying to get inside because they are cold. The fire is crackling and the smoke smells warm and wonderful. She presses her face against Papa's cheek, lays her arm across his chest.

"It was hard for me the first time I took a deer," he says, as if admitting failure. "I almost put down my gun. Why wasn't it hard for you, Anna darling?"

"I don't know, Papa, it just wasn't."

"All I could see was the damn thing's eyes staring at me. Big brown eyes. Beautiful. Then I saw the life go out of them and I felt terrible. I couldn't get the damned thing out of my mind for a week afterward."

"I didn't see the eyes."

He turns to her in the dark. "What did you see?"

She hesitates. "I saw his face."

"Whose face, darling?" He is confused. "The deer's face?"

"No, Papa, not the deer."

"Anna, darling, what on earth are you talking about?"

She wants desperately to tell him, to tell someone. If Mother were still alive she might be able to tell her. But she cannot bring herself to tell Papa. He would go insane. It would not be fair to him.

"Nothing, Papa. I'm tired now." She kisses his cheek. "Good night, Papa. Sweet dreams."

LONDON: JANUARY 1944

It had been six days since Catherine Blake received the message from Hamburg. During that time she had thought long and hard about ignoring it.

Alpha was the code name of a rendezvous point in Hyde Park, a footpath through a grove of trees. She couldn't help but feel jittery about going forward with the meeting. MI5 had arrested dozens of spies since 1940. Surely some of those spies had spilled everything they knew before their appointments with the hangman.

Theoretically, this should make no difference in her case. Vogel had promised her she would be different. She would have different radio procedures, different rendezvous procedures, and different codes. Even if every other spy in England were arrested and hanged, they would have no way of getting at her.

Catherine wished she could share Vogel's confidence. He was hundreds of miles away, cut off from Britain by the Channel, flying blindly. The smallest mistake might get her arrested or killed. Like the rendezvous site, for example. It was a bitterly cold night; anyone loitering in Hyde Park would automatically come under suspicion. It was a silly mistake, so unlike Vogel. He must be under enormous pressure. It was understandable. There was an invasion coming; everyone knew it. The only question was when and where.

She was reluctant to make the rendezvous for another reason: she was frightened of being drawn into the game. She had grown comfortable—too comfortable, perhaps. Her life had assumed a structure and a routine. She had her warm flat, she had her volunteer work at the hospital, she had Vogel's money to support her. She was reluctant, at this late stage of the war, to put herself in danger. She did not regard herself as a German patriot by any means. Her cover seemed totally secure. She could wait out the war and then make her way back to Spain. Back to the grand *estancia* in the foothills. Back to Maria.

Catherine turned into Hyde Park. The evening traffic in Kensington Road faded to a pleasant hum.

She had two reasons for making the rendezvous.

The first was her father's safety. Catherine had not volunteered to work for the Abwehr as a spy, she had been forced to do it. Vogel's instrument of coercion was her father. He had made it clear her father would be harmed— arrested, thrown into a concentration camp, even killed—if she did not agree to go to Britain. If she refused to take an assignment now, her father's life would surely be in danger.

The second reason was more simple—she was desperately lonely. She had been cut off and isolated for six years. The normal agents were allowed to use their radios. They had *some* contact with Germany. She had been permitted almost no contact. She was curious; she wanted to talk to someone from her own side. She wanted to be able to drop her cover for just a few minutes, to shed the identity of Catherine Blake.

She thought, God, but I almost can't remember my real name.

She decided she would make the rendezvous.

She walked along the edge of the Serpentine, watching a fleet of ducks fishing the gaps in the ice. She followed the pathway toward the trees. The last light had faded; the sky was a mat of winking stars. One nice thing about the blackout, she thought: you could see the stars at night, even in the heart of the West End.

She reached inside her handbag and felt for the butt of her silenced pistol, a Mauser 6.35 automatic. It was there. If anything appeared out of the ordinary she would use it. She had made one vow—that she would never allow herself to be arrested. The thought of being locked up in some stinking British jail made her physically sick. She had nightmares about her own execution. She could see their laughing English faces before the hangman placed the black hood over her head and the rope around her neck. She would use her suicide pill or she would die fighting, but she would never let them touch her.

An American soldier passed in the other direction. A prostitute clung to his shoulder, was rubbing his cock and sticking her tongue in his ear. It was a common sight. The girls worked Piccadilly. Few wasted time or money on hotel rooms. Wall jobs, the soldiers called them. The girls just took their customers into alleyways or parks and raised their skirts. Some of the more naive girls thought fucking standing up would keep them from getting pregnant.

Catherine thought, Stupid English girls.

She entered the trees and waited for Vogel's agent to show.

The afternoon train from Hunstanton arrived at Liverpool Street Station a half hour late. Horst Neumann collected his small leather grip from the luggage rack and joined the line of passengers spilling onto the platform. The station was chaos. Knots of weary travelers wandered the terminus like victims of a natural disaster, faces blank, waiting for hopelessly delayed trains. Soldiers slept wherever they liked, heads pillowed on kit bags. A few uniformed railway policemen meandered about, trying to keep order. All the porters were women. Neumann stepped onto the platform. Small, agile, bright-eyed, he sliced his way through the dense crowd.

The men at the exit had AUTHORITY written all over them. They wore rumpled suits and bowler hats. He wondered if they were looking for him. There was no way they could have a description. Instinctively, he reached inside his jacket and felt for the butt of his pistol. It was there, tucked in the waistband of his trousers. He also felt for his billfold in his breast pocket. The name on his identity card read James Porter. His cover was a traveling pharmaceutical salesman. He brushed past the two men and joined the crowd jostling along Bishopsgate Road.

The journey, except for the inevitable delay, had gone smoothly. He had shared a compartment with a group of young soldiers. For a time they had eyed him malevolently while he read his newspapers. Neumann guessed any healthy-looking young man not in uniform would be subjected to a certain amount of contempt. He told them he had been wounded at Dunkirk and brought back to England half dead aboard an oceangoing tug—one of the "little ships." The soldiers asked Neumann to join them in a game of cards, and he beat the pants off them.

The street was pitch dark, the only light provided by the shaded headlamps of the evening traffic working its way along the road and the pale blackout torches carried by many of the pedestrians. He felt as if he were in the midst of a child's game, trying to perform a ridiculously simple task while blindfolded. Twice he smashed straight into a pedestrian coming in the opposite direction. Once he collided with something cold and hard and started to apologize before noticing it was a lamppost.

He had to laugh. London certainly had changed since his last visit.

He was born Nigel Fox in London in 1919 to a German mother and an English father. When his father died in 1927, his mother returned to Germany and settled in Düsseldorf. A year later she remarried—a wealthy manufacturer named Erich Neumann, a stern disciplinarian who wasn't about to have a stepson named Nigel who spoke German with an English accent. He immediately changed the boy's name to Horst, allowed him to take his family name, and enrolled him in one of the toughest military schools in the country. Horst was miserable. The other boys teased him because of his poor German. Small, easily bullied, he came home most weekends with blackened eyes and split lips. His mother grew worried; Horst had become quiet and withdrawn. Erich thought it was good for him.

But when Horst turned fourteen his life changed. At an all-comers track meet he entered the 1,500 meters in his school shorts and no shoes. He finished well under five minutes, stunning for a boy with no training. A coach from the national federation had watched the race. He encouraged Horst to train and convinced his school to make special provisions for the boy.

Horst came alive. Freed from the drudgery of the school's physical education classes, he spent afternoons running through the countryside and the mountains. He loved being alone, away from the other boys. He was never happier. He quickly became one of the best junior track athletes in the country and a source of pride for the school. He joined the Hitler *Jugend*—the Hitler Youth. Boys who had picked on him years earlier suddenly were vying for his attention. In 1936, he was invited to attend the Olympic Games in Berlin. He watched the American Jesse Owens stun the world by winning four gold medals. He met Adolf Hitler at a reception for Hitler Youth and even shook his hand. He was so excited he telephoned home to tell his mother. Erich was immensely proud. Sitting in the grandstand, Horst dreamed of 1944, when he would be old enough and fast enough to compete for Germany.

The war would change all that.

He joined the Wehrmacht early in 1939. His physical fitness and lone-wolf attitude brought him to the attention of the *Fallschirmjäger,* the paratroopers. He was sent to paratroop school at Stendhal and jumped into Poland on the first day of the war. France, Crete, and Russia followed. He had his Knight's Cross by the end of 1942.

Paris would end his jumping days. Late one evening he went into a small bar for a brandy. A group of SS officers had taken over the back room for a private party. Halfway through his drink, Neumann heard a scream from the back room. The Frenchman behind the bar froze, too terrified to go investigate. Neumann did it for him. When he pushed back the door he saw a French girl on the table, arms and legs pinned down by SS men. A major was raping her, another was beating her with a belt. Neumann went in on the run and delivered a brutal blow to the major's face. His head struck the corner of a table; he never regained consciousness.

The other SS men dragged him into an alley, beat him savagely, and left him for dead. He spent three months in a hospital recovering. His head injuries were so severe he was declared unfit to jump. Because of his fluent

English he was assigned to an army intelligence listening post in northern France, where he spent his days sitting before a radio receiver in a cramped, claustrophobic hut, monitoring wireless communications originating across the Channel in England. It was drudgery.

Then came the man from the Abwehr, Kurt Vogel. He was gaunt and tired, and under different circumstances Neumann might have thought he was an artist or an intellectual. He said he was looking for qualified men willing to go to Britain and conduct espionage. He said he would double Neumann's Wehrmacht pay. Neumann wasn't interested because of the money, he was bored out of his skull. He accepted on the spot. That night he left France and returned to Berlin with Vogel.

A week before coming to Britain, Neumann was taken to a farmhouse in the district of Dahlem just outside Berlin for a week of briefings and intense preparation. Mornings were spent in the barn, where Vogel had rigged a jump platform for Neumann to practice. A live jump was deemed out of the question for security reasons. He also brushed up his skills with a handgun, which were impressive to begin with, and silent killing. Afternoons were given over to the essence of field work: dead drops, rendezvous procedures, codes, and radio. At times the briefings were handled by Vogel alone. At other times he brought his assistant, Werner Ulbricht. Neumann playfully referred to him as Watson, and Ulbricht accepted it with an uncharacteristic relish. In the late afternoons, with the winter light dying over the gentle snowy landscape of the farm, Neumann was allowed forty-five minutes for running. For three days he was permitted to go alone. But on the fourth day, his head filling with Vogel's secrets, a jeep shadowed him from a distance.

Evenings were Vogel's private preserve. After a group supper in the farmhouse kitchen, Vogel would lead Neumann into the study and lecture him by the fire. He never used notes, for Vogel, Neumann could see, had the gift of memory. Vogel told him of Sean Dogherty and the drop procedure. He told him of an agent named Catherine Blake. He told him of an American officer named Peter Jordan.

Each night Vogel would cover old ground before adding another level of detail. Despite the informality of the country atmosphere, his wardrobe never changed: dark suit, white shirt, and dark tie. His voice was as annoying as a rusty hinge, yet it held Neumann with its intensity and singleness of purpose. On the sixth night, pleased with his pupil's progress, Vogel actually permitted himself a brief smile, which he quickly covered with his right hand, embarrassed by his dreadful teeth.

Enter Hyde Park from the north, Vogel had reminded him during their final meeting. From Bayswater Road. Which Neumann did now. Follow the pathway to the trees overlooking the lake. Make one pass to make certain the place is clean. Make your approach on the second pass. Let her decide whether it will continue. She will know if it is safe. She is very good.

The small man appeared on the pathway. He wore a wool overcoat and a brimmed hat. He walked briskly past without looking at her. She wondered if she was losing her power to attract men.

She stood in the trees, waiting. The rules for the rendezvous were specific. If the contact does not appear exactly on time, leave and come back the following day. She decided to wait another minute, then leave.

She heard the footsteps. It was the same man who had passed her a moment earlier. He nearly bumped into her in the dark.

"I say, I do seem to be a bit lost," he said, in an accent she couldn't quite place. "Can you point me in the direction of Park Lane?"

Catherine looked at him carefully. He wore an all-weather smile, his eyes burning bright blue beneath the brim of his hat.

She pointed west. "It's in that direction."

"Thank you." He started to walk away, then turned around. *"Who shall ascend into the hill of the Lord? or who shall stand in his holy place?"*

"He that hath clean hands, and a pure heart; who hath not lifted up his soul unto vanity, nor sworn deceitfully."

He smiled and said, "Catherine Blake, as I live and breathe. Why don't we go somewhere warm where we can talk."

Catherine reached inside her purse and removed her blackout torch.

"Do you have one of these?" she asked.

"Unfortunately, no."

"That's a stupid mistake. And stupid mistakes like that could get us both killed."

CHAPTER FIFTEEN

LONDON

While Harry Dalton was still on the Met he was considered a meticulous, shrewd, and relentless investigator who believed no lead, no matter how trivial, should be discarded. His big break came in 1936. Two young girls had vanished from an East End playground, and Harry was assigned to the crack team of officers investigating the case. After three sleepless days of digging, Harry arrested a drifter named Spencer Thomas. Harry handled the interrogation. At daybreak he led a search party to a secluded spot along the Thames Estuary, where Thomas had told him he would find the mutilated bodies of the girls. In the days that followed he also found the bodies of a prostitute in Gravesend, a waitress in Bristol, and a housewife in Sheffield. Spencer Thomas was locked up in an asylum for the criminally insane. Harry was promoted to detective-inspector.

Nothing in his professional experience had prepared him for a day as frustrating as this. He was looking for a German agent but he didn't have a single clue or lead. His only recourse was to telephone local police forces and ask for reports of anything out of the ordinary, any crime that might be committed by a spy on the move. He couldn't tell them he was looking for a spy; that would be a breach of security. He was fishing, and Harry Dalton hated fishing.

The conversation Harry had with a police officer in Evesham was typical.

"What did you say your name was?"

"Harry Dalton."

"Calling from where?"

"The War Office in London."

"I see. What would you be wanting with me?"

"I want to know whether you've had any reports of crimes that might be committed by someone on the run."

"Such as?"

"Such as stolen cars, stolen bicycles, stolen ration coupons, petrol. Use your imagination."

"I see."

"Well?"

"We did have a report of a stolen bicycle."

"Really! When?"

"This morning."

"That could be something."

"Bicycles are bloody valuable these days. I had an old wreck rusting in my shed. Took it out, cleaned it up a bit, sold it to a Yank corporal for ten quid. Ten quid! Can you believe it? That thing wasn't worth ten shillings!"

"That's interesting. What about the stolen bicycle?"

"Hold on a minute—what did you say your name was?"

"Harry."

"Harry. Hold on a minute, Harry. . . . George, did we hear anything more about that missing bicycle up on Sheep Street? Yeah, that one. . . . What do you mean he found it? Where the hell was it? . . . In the middle of the pasture? How the hell did it get there? . . . He did! Christ almighty! You with me, Harry?"

"I'm still here."

"Sorry, false alarm."

"That's all right. Thanks for looking into it."

"No problem."

"If you hear of anything—"

"You'll be the first to know, Harry."

"Cheers."

In the late afternoon he had fielded dozens of telephone calls from policemen in the countryside, one more bizarre then the next. An officer from Bridgewater called to report a broken window.

Harry said, "Look like a breaking and entering?"

"Not really."

"Why not?"

"Because it was the stained glass window at the church."

"Right. Keep your eyes open."

The police in Skegness reported someone trying to get into a pub after hours.

Harry said, "The man I'm looking for may not be familiar with English licensing laws."

"I'll look into it a little harder then."

"Good, keep in touch."

He called back twenty minutes later.

"It was just a local woman looking for her husband. Terrible drunk, I'm afraid."

"Damn!"

"Sorry, Harry, didn't mean to get your hopes up."

"You did—but thanks for checking it out."

Harry looked at his watch: four o'clock, shift change in Registry. Grace would be coming on duty. He thought, Maybe I can make something out of this day. He took the lift down to Registry and found her pushing a metal cart brimming with files. She had a shock of short, white-blond hair, and her cheap, bloodred wartime lipstick made her look as if she were tarted up for a man. She wore a schoolboy's gray woolen sweater and a black skirt that was a little too short. Her heavy stockings could not hide the shape of her long, athletic legs.

She spotted Harry and smiled warmly. Within the world of Registry, Grace was the exception. Vernon Kell, the founder of the Service, believed only members of the aristocracy or relatives of MI5 officers could be trusted for such sensitive work. As a result, Registry was always populated with a staff of rather beautiful debutantes. But Grace was a middle-class girl, the daughter of a schoolteacher. She spotted Harry and smiled warmly. Then, with only a sideways glance of her bright green eyes, she told him to meet her in one of the small side rooms. She joined him a moment later, closed the door, and kissed his cheek.

"Hello, Harry darling. How have you been?"

"Fine, Grace. Good to see you."

It started in 1940 during a night raid over London. They sheltered together in the underground and in the morning, when the all clear sounded, she had taken him to her flat and to her bed. She was attractive in an unconventional way and a passionate, uninhibited lover—a pleasant, convenient escape from the pressure of the office. For Grace, Harry was someone kind and gentle who would help pass the time until her husband came back from the army.

They could have carried on that way the entire war. But three months into the affair Harry was suddenly overwhelmed with guilt. *The poor sod is fighting for his life in North Africa, and I'm here in London bedding his wife.* The feelings provoked a deeper crisis for him. He was a young man; maybe he should be in the army risking his life instead of chasing relatively harmless spies around Britain. He told himself MI5's work was vital to the war effort—indispensable—but the nagging feelings of doubt persisted. *What would I do on the battlefield? Would I pick up my gun and fight or would I cower in a foxhole?* He told Grace about his feelings the next night when he broke off the affair. They made love one last time, her kisses salty with tears. Bloody war, she kept saying. Lousy, bloody, awful war.

"I need a favor, Grace," Harry said, voice low.

"Listen to you, Harry. You don't call, you don't write, you don't bring me flowers. Then you pop round and say you need a favor." She smiled and kissed him again. "All right, what do you need?"

"I need to see the access list on a file."

Her face darkened. "Come on, Harry. You know I can't do that."

"An Abwehr man named Vogel—Kurt Vogel."

A look of recognition flashed across her face, then dissipated.

"Grace, I don't need to tell you we're working a very important case."

"I know you're working on an important case, Harry. The whole department is buzzing about it."

"When Vicary came down to pull Vogel's file, it was missing. He went to see Jago, and two minutes later he had the bloody thing in his hand. Jago spun some yarn about it being mislaid."

She was angrily digging through the files on the cart. She grabbed a bunch and began replacing them on the shelves.

"I know all about it, Harry."

"How do *you* know?"

"Because he blamed it on *me*. He wrote a letter of reprimand and put it in my file, the bastard."

"Who blamed you?"

"Jago!" she hissed.

"Why?"

"To cover his arse, that's why."

She was digging through the files again. Harry reached out and took her hands in his to make her stop. "Grace, I need to see that access list."

"The access list won't tell you anything. The person who had that file before Vicary doesn't leave a trail."

"Grace, please. I'm begging."

"I like it when you beg, Harry."

"Yeah, I remember."

"Why don't you come over for some dinner one night?" She dragged the tip of her finger over the back of Harry's hand. It was black from sorting files. "I miss your company. We'll talk, have a few laughs, nothing else."

"I'd like that, Grace." It was the truth. He missed her very much.

"If you tell anyone where you got this, Harry, so help me God—"

"It stays between you and me."

"Not even Vicary," she insisted.

Harry put his hand over his heart. "Not even Vicary."

Grace picked up another handful of files, then looked up at him. With her bloodred lips she mouthed the initials *BB*.

"How is it possible you don't have a single lead?" Basil Boothby said as Vicary sank down into the deep overstuffed couch. Sir Basil had demanded nightly updates on the progress of the investigation. Vicary, knowing Boothby's passion for having things in writing, suggested a concise note, but Sir Basil wanted to be briefed in person.

Tonight, Boothby had an engagement. He had mumbled something about "the Americans" to explain the fact he was dressing in his formal wear when Vicary was shown into the office. While he spoke his big paw was engaged in an abortive effort to stuff a gold cuff link through the starched cuff of his shirt. Sir Basil had a valet to assist him with such tedious tasks at home.

Vicary's briefing was suspended a moment while Boothby summoned his pretty secretary to help him dress. It gave him a moment to process the information Harry had given him. It was Sir Basil who had pulled Vogel's file. He tried to remember their first conversation. What was it Boothby had said? *Registry may have something on him.*

Boothby's secretary slipped quietly out. Vicary resumed his briefing. They had men watching every rail station in London. Their hands were tied because they had no description of the agents they were supposed to be looking for. Harry Dalton had compiled a list of every known location used by German agents for rendezvous points. Vicary had men watching as many of those as he could.

"I'd give you more men, Alfred, but there aren't any," Boothby said. "The watchers are all pulling double and triple shifts. The head of the watchers is complaining to me that you're running them into the ground. The cold is killing them. Half of them have been struck down by the flu."

"I'm sympathetic to the plight of the watchers, Sir Basil. I'm using them as judiciously as possible."

Boothby lit a cigarette and sipped his gin and bitters while pacing the length of the room. "We have three German agents loose in the country outside our control. I don't need to tell you how serious this is. If one of those agents tries to contact one of our doubles, we're going to be in trouble. The whole Double Cross apparatus will be in jeopardy."

"My guess is they won't try to contact any other agents."

"Why not?"

"Because I think Vogel is running his own show. I think we're dealing with a separate network of agents we never knew about."

"That's just a hunch, Alfred. We need to deal with the facts."

"Ever read Vogel's file?" Vicary said, as carelessly as possible.

"No."

And you're a liar, Vicary thought. "Judging by the way this affair has unfolded, I'd say Vogel has kept a network of sleeper agents inside Britain, on ice, since before the beginning of the war. If I had to guess, the primary agent is operating in London, the subagent somewhere in the countryside, where he could take in an agent on short notice. The agent who arrived last night is almost certainly here to brief the lead agent on his assignment. For all we know, they're meeting right now as we speak. And we're falling further and further behind."

"Interesting, Alfred, but it's all based on guesswork."

"Educated guesswork, Sir Basil. In the absence of hard, provable facts, I'm afraid that's our only recourse." Vicary hesitated, aware of the response his next suggestion was likely to generate. "In the meantime, I think we should schedule a meeting with General Betts to brief him on developments."

Boothby's face sagged into an angry frown. Brigadier General Thomas Betts was the deputy chief of intelligence at SHAEF. Tall, bearlike, Betts had one of the most unenviable jobs in London—making sure none of the several hundred American and British officers who knew the secret of Overlord gave that secret, intentionally or unintentionally, to the enemy.

"That's premature, Alfred."

"Premature? You said it yourself, Sir Basil. We have three German spies on the loose."

"I've got to go down the hall and brief the director-general in a moment. If I suggest to him that we broadcast our failures to the Americans, he will fall on me from a very great height."

"I'm sure the DG won't be too hard on you, Sir Basil." Vicary knew that

Boothby had convinced the director-general that he was indispensable. "Besides, it's hardly a failure."

Boothby stopped pacing. "What would you call it?"

"A temporary setback."

Boothby snorted and crushed out his cigarette. "I will not permit you to tarnish the reputation of this department, Alfred. I won't have it."

"Perhaps there's something else you should consider besides the reputation of this department, Sir Basil."

"What's that?"

Vicary struggled out of the soft, deep couch. "If the spies succeed, we may very well lose the war."

"Well, then, *do* something, Alfred."

"Thank you, Sir Basil. That's certainly sound advice."

CHAPTER SIXTEEN

LONDON

From Hyde Park they took a taxi into Earl's Court. They paid off the driver a quarter mile from her flat. During the short walk they doubled back twice, and Catherine made a bogus call from a phone box. They were not being tailed. Her landlady, Mrs. Hodges, was in the hall as they arrived. Catherine threaded her arm through Neumann's. Mrs. Hodges shot her a glance of disapproval as they walked upstairs.

Catherine was reluctant to take him to her flat. She had jealously protected its whereabouts and refused to provide the address to Berlin. The last thing she needed was some agent on the run from MI5 to come pounding on her door in the middle of the night. But meeting in public was out of the question; they had much to discuss, and doing it in a café or a railway station was too dangerous.

She watched Neumann as he led himself on a tour of her flat. She could tell by the precise walk and economical gestures that he had been a soldier once. His English was flawless. Clearly, Vogel had chosen him carefully. At least he wasn't sending some rank amateur to brief her. He went to the drawing room window, parted the curtains, and gazed down into the street.

"Even if they're out there, you'll never spot them," Catherine said as she sat down.

"I know—but it makes me feel better to look." He came away from the window. "It's been a long day. I could use a cup of tea."

"Everything you need is in the kitchen. Help yourself."

Neumann set water on the stove to boil, then came back into the room.

"What's your name?" she asked him. "Your real name."

"Horst Neumann."

"You're a soldier. At least you used to be one. What's your rank?"

"I'm a lieutenant."

She smiled. "I outrank you, by the way."

"Yes, I know—*major*."

"What's your cover name?"

"James Porter."

"Let me see your identification."

He handed it across. She examined it carefully. It was an excellent forgery. She gave it back to him. "It's good," she said. "But show it only if it is absolutely necessary. What's your cover?"

"I was wounded at Dunkirk and invalided out of the army. I'm a traveling salesman now."

"Where are you staying?"

"The Norfolk coast—a village called Hampton Sands. Vogel has an agent there named Sean Dogherty. He's an IRA sympathizer who runs a small farm."

"How did you enter the country?"

"Parachute."

"Very impressive," she said genuinely. "And Dogherty took you in? He was waiting for you?"

"Yes."

"Vogel contacted him by radio?"

"I assume so, yes."

"That means MI-Five is looking for you."

"I think I spotted two of their men at Liverpool Street."

"It makes sense. They'd certainly be watching the stations." She lit a cigarette. "Your English is excellent. Where did you learn it?"

While he told her the story Catherine looked at him carefully for the first time. He was small and sparingly built; he might have been an athlete once, a tennis player or a runner. His hair was dark, his eyes a penetrating blue. He was obviously intelligent—not like some of the imbeciles she had seen at the Abwehr spy school in Berlin. She doubted he had been behind enemy lines before as an agent, yet he showed no sign of nerves. She had a few more questions before she would listen to what he had to say.

"How did you end up in this line of work?"

Neumann told her the story: that he had been a member of the *Fallschirm-jäger*, that he had seen action in more places than he could remember. He told her about Paris. About his transfer to the *Funkabwehr* eavesdropping unit in northern France. And about his eventual recruitment by Kurt Vogel.

"Our Kurt is very good at finding work for the restless," Catherine said, when he had finished. "So what does Vogel have in mind for *me?*"

"One assignment, then out. Back to Germany."

The kettle screamed. Neumann went into the kitchen and busied himself with the tea. *One assignment, then out. Back to Germany.* And with a highly capable former paratrooper to help her make her escape. She was impressed. She had always assumed the worst: when the war ended she would be abandoned in Britain and forced to fend for herself. The British and the Americans—when the inevitable victory came—would pore over captured Abwehr files. They would find her name, realize she had never been arrested, and come after her. That was the other reason she had withheld so much information from Vogel; she didn't want to leave a trail in Berlin for her enemies to follow. But Vogel obviously wanted her back in Germany, and he had taken steps to make sure that happened.

Neumann came back into the drawing room with a pot of tea and two mugs. He placed the things on a table and sat down again.

Catherine said, "What's your job, besides briefing me on my assignment?"

"Whatever you need, basically. I'm your courier, your support agent, and your radio operator. Vogel wants you to continue to stay off the air. He's convinced it's not safe. The only time you're to use your radio is if you need me. You contact Vogel with a prearranged signal, and Vogel will contact me."

She nodded, then said, "And when it's all over? How are we supposed to get out of Britain? And please don't say something heroic like steal a boat and sail back to France. Because it's not possible."

"Of course not. Vogel has arranged first-class passage for you aboard a U-boat."

"Which one?"

"U-509."

"Where?"

"The North Sea."

"It's big. Where in the North Sea?"

"Spurn Head, off the Lincolnshire coast."

"I've lived here for five years, Lieutenant Neumann. I know where Spurn Head is. How are we supposed to get to the U-boat?"

"Vogel has a boat and a skipper waiting at a dock along the River Humber. When it's time to leave I contact him and he takes us out to the submarine."

She thought, So Vogel has a built-in escape hatch he's never told me about.

Catherine sipped her tea, inspecting Neumann over the brim of the mug. It was remotely possible he was an MI5 man posing as a German agent. She could play silly games—like testing his German or asking him about some little-known Berlin café—but if he truly was MI5 he would be smart enough to avoid an obvious trap. He knew the patter, he knew a great deal about Vogel, and his story seemed credible. She decided to let it continue. As Neumann was about to resume speaking, the air raid sirens wailed.

"Do we need to take this seriously?" Neumann asked.

"Did you see the building behind this one?"

Neumann had seen it, a pile of broken brick and smashed timber. "Where's the nearest shelter?"

"Around the corner." She smiled at him. "Welcome back to London, Lieutenant Neumann."

It was early evening the following day when Neumann's train drew into Hunstanton Station. Sean Dogherty was smoking anxiously on the platform as he stepped off the train.

"How did it go?" Dogherty asked, as they walked to his truck.

"Went off without a hitch."

Dogherty drove uncomfortably fast over the rolling, crumbling, single-lane track. It was a rattletrap van, badly in need of an overhaul by the sound of it. Blackout shades shrouded the headlamps. A dribble of pale yellow light tried vainly to illuminate the roadway. Neumann had the sensation of walking through a strange darkened house with only a match for light. They passed through bleak darkened villages—Holme, Thornham, Titchwell—no lights burning, shops and cottages tightly shuttered, no sign of human habitation. Dogherty was telling him about his day, but Neumann gradually tuned him out, thinking about last night.

They had rushed to a tube station like everyone else and waited three hours on the dank platform for the all clear to sound. She slept for a time, allowing her head to fall against his shoulder. He wondered if it was the first time she had felt safe in six years. He stared at her in the darkness. A remarkably beautiful woman but there was a distant sadness—a childhood wound, perhaps, inflicted by a careless adult. She stirred in her sleep, troubled by dreams. He touched the pile of curls that lay spread across his shoulder. When the all clear sounded she awoke like all soldiers in enemy territory—quickly, eyes suddenly wide, hand reaching for the nearest weapon. In her case it was the handbag, where Neumann assumed she kept a gun or a knife.

They talked until dawn. Actually, *he* had talked and she had listened. She never spoke except to correct him when he had made a mistake or contradicted something he had said hours earlier. She obviously had a powerful mind, capable of storing immense amounts of information. No wonder Vogel had so much respect for her abilities.

A gray dawn was spreading over London when Neumann slipped out of her flat. He had moved like a man leaving his mistress, sneaking small glances over his shoulder, searching the faces of passersby for traces of suspicion. For three hours he weaved through London in a cold drizzle, making sudden course changes, getting on and off buses, looking at reflections in windows. He decided he was not being followed and started back to Liverpool Street station.

On the train he pillowed his head on his hands and tried to sleep. Don't fall under her spell, Vogel had playfully warned on their last day together at the farm. Keep to a safe distance. She has dark places where you don't want to go.

Neumann pictured her in her flat, listening in the faint light as he told her of Peter Jordan and what she was expected to do. It was the unnerving stillness about her that struck him most, the way the hands lay folded in the lap, the way the head and shoulders never seemed to move. Only the eyes, casting around the room, back and forth across his face, up and down his body. Like searchlights. For a moment he allowed himself to entertain a fantasy that she desired him. But now, as Hampton Sands vanished into the gloom behind them and the Dogherty cottage appeared before them, Neumann came to a disturbing conclusion. Catherine was not looking at him that way because she found him attractive, she was deciding how best to kill him if she ever needed to.

Neumann had given her the letter as he left that morning. She had placed it aside, too terrified to read it. Now she opened it, hands trembling, and read it as she lay in bed.

My dearest Anna,

I am relieved to hear you are well and safe. Since you have left me all light has gone from my life. I pray that this war will end soon so we can be together again. Good night, sweet dreams, little one.

Your adoring Father

When she finished reading it she carried the letter into the kitchen, touched it to the gas flame, and tossed it into the sink. It flared a moment, then quickly died away. She ran the tap and washed the black ashes down the drain. She suspected it was a forgery—that Vogel had concocted it in order to keep her in line. Her father, she feared, was dead. She went back to bed, lying awake in the soft gray light of morning, listening to the rain drumming against her window. Thinking of her father, thinking of Vogel.

CHAPTER SEVENTEEN

GLOUCESTERSHIRE, ENGLAND

"Congratulations, Alfred. Come inside. I'm sorry it had to happen this way, but you've just become a rather wealthy man." Edward Kenton thrust out his hand as if he were waiting for Vicary to impale himself on it. Vicary took the hand and shook it weakly before brushing past Kenton into the drawing room of his aunt's cottage. "Damned cold outside," Kenton was saying as Vicary surveyed the room. He hadn't been here since the war, but nothing had changed. "I hope you don't mind, but I've made a fire. The place was like an icebox when I arrived. There's tea as well. And *real* milk. I don't suppose you see much of that in London these days."

Vicary removed his coat while Kenton went into the kitchen. It wasn't really a cottage—that was what Matilda had insisted on calling it. It was a rather large home of Cotswold limestone, with spectacular gardens surrounded by a high wall. She died of a massive stroke the night Boothby assigned him the case. Vicary had planned to attend the funeral but he was summoned by Churchill that morning, after Bletchley Park decoded the German radio signals. He felt horrible about missing the services. Matilda had virtually raised Vicary after his own mother died when he was just twelve. They had remained the best of friends. She was the only person he had told about his assignment to MI5. *What do you do exactly, Alfred?* I catch German spies, Aunt Matilda. *Oh, good for you, Alfred!*

French doors overlooked the gardens, dead with winter. Sometimes I catch spies, Aunt Matilda, he thought. Sometimes they get the better of me.

That morning Bletchley Park had forwarded Vicary a decoded message from an agent in Britain. It said the rendezvous had been successful and the agent had accepted the assignment. Vicary was growing discouraged about his chances of catching the spies. Things had worsened that morning. Two men were observed meeting in Leicester Square and brought in for questioning. The older of the two turned out to be a senior Home Office clerk; the younger man was his lover. Boothby had blown a fuse.

"How was the drive?" Kenton asked from the kitchen over the tinkle of china and running water.

"Fine," Vicary said. Boothby had reluctantly permitted him to have a Rover and a driver from Transport.

"I can't remember the last time I took a relaxing drive through the country," Kenton said. "But I suppose petrol and motorcars are some of the fringe benefits of your new job."

Kenton came into the room with a tray of tea. He was tall—as tall as Boothby—but with none of the bulk or physical agility. He wore round spectacles, too small for his face, and a thin mustache that looked as though it had been put there with a woman's eyebrow pencil. He set the tea down on the table in front of the couch, poured milk into the cups as though it were liquid gold, then added the tea.

"My goodness, Alfred, how long has it been?"

Twenty-five years, Vicary thought. Edward Kenton had been friends with Helen. They had even dated a few times after Helen broke off the relationship with Vicary. By coincidence he became Matilda's solicitor ten years earlier. Vicary and Kenton had spoken by telephone several times over the past few years as Matilda grew too old to manage alone, but it was the first time they had seen each other face-to-face. Vicary wished he could conclude his dead aunt's affairs without the specter of Helen hanging over the proceedings.

Kenton said, "You've been assigned to the War Office, I hear."

"That's right," Vicary said and swallowed half his cup of tea. It was delicious—much better than the swill they served in the canteen.

"What do you do exactly?"

"Oh, I work for a very dull department doing this and that." Vicary sat down. "I'm sorry, Edward, I hate to rush things along, but I really have to be heading back to London."

Kenton sat down opposite Vicary and fished a batch of papers from his black leather briefcase. Licking the tip of his slender forefinger, he guardedly turned to a suitable page. "Ah, here we are. I drew up this will myself five years ago," he said. "She spread some money and other properties among your cousins, but she left the bulk of her estate to you."

"I had no idea."

"She's left you the house and quite a large amount of money. She was frugal. She spent carefully and invested wisely." Kenton turned the papers around so Vicary could read them. "Here's what's coming to you."

Vicary was stunned; he had no idea. Missing her funeral over a couple of German spies seemed even more obscene. Something must have shown on his face because Kenton said, "It's a shame you couldn't make it to the funeral, Alfred. It really was a lovely service. Half the county was there."

"I wanted to be here but something came up."

"I have a few papers for you to sign to take possession of the cottage and the money. If you'll give me an account number in London, I can move the money and close her bank accounts."

Vicary spent the next few minutes silently signing his name to a pile of legal and financial documents. At the last one Kenton looked up and said, "Done."

"Is the telephone still working?"

"Yes. I used it myself before you arrived."

The telephone was on Matilda's writing table in the drawing room. Vicary picked up the receiver and looked at Kenton. "Edward, if you wouldn't mind, it's official."

Kenton forced a smile. "Say no more. I'll clear away the dishes."

Something about the exchange warmed the vindictive corners of Vicary's heart. The operator came on the line, and he gave her the number of MI5 headquarters in London. It took a few moments to get through. A department operator answered and connected Vicary to Harry Dalton.

Harry answered, his mouth full of food.

"What's the fare today?" Vicary asked.

"They claim it's vegetable stew."

"Any news?"

"I think so, actually."

Vicary's heart leapt.

"I've been going over the immigration lists one more time, just to see if we missed anything." The immigration lists were the meat and potatoes of MI5's contest with Germany's spies. In September 1939, while Vicary was still on the faculty at University College, MI5 had used immigration and passport records as the primary tool in a massive roundup of spies and Nazi sympathizers. Aliens were classified in three categories: Category C aliens were allowed complete freedom; Category B aliens were subject to certain restrictions—some weren't allowed to own automobiles or boats and limits were placed on their movement within the country; Category A aliens, those deemed to be a threat to security, were interned. Anyone who had entered the country before the war and could not be accounted for was assumed to be a spy and hunted down. Germany's espionage networks were rolled up and smashed, virtually overnight.

"A Dutch woman named Christa Kunst entered the country in November 1938 at Dover," Harry continued. "A year later her body was discovered in a shallow grave in a field near a village called Whitchurch."

"What's unusual about that?"

"The thing just doesn't *feel* right to me. The body was badly decomposed when it was pulled out of the ground. The face and skull had been crushed. All the teeth were missing. They used the passport to make the identification; it was conveniently buried with the body. It sounds too neat to me."

"Where's the passport now?"

"The Home Office has it. I've sent a courier up to collect it. It has a photograph. They say it got roughed up a bit while it was in the ground, but it's probably worth looking at."

"Good, Harry. I'm not sure this woman's death has anything to do with the case, but at least it's a lead."

"Right. How did the meeting go with the lawyer, by the way?"

"Oh, just a few papers to sign," Vicary lied. He felt suddenly awkward about his newfound financial independence. "I'm leaving now. I should be back in the office late this afternoon."

Vicary rang off as Kenton came back into the drawing room. "Well, I think that about does it." He handed Vicary a large brown envelope. "All the papers are there as well as the keys. I've included the name of the gardener and his address. He'll be happy to serve as caretaker."

They put on their coats, locked up the cottage, and went outside. Vicary's car was in the drive.

"Can I drop you anywhere, Edward?"

Vicary was relieved when he declined the offer.

"I spoke to Helen the other day," Kenton said suddenly.

Vicary thought: Oh, good heavens.

"She says she sees you from time to time in Chelsea."

Vicary wondered whether Helen had told Kenton about the afternoon in 1940 when he had stared into her passing car like some silly schoolboy. Mortified, Vicary opened the door of the car, absently beating his pockets for his half-moon glasses.

"She asked me to say hello, so I'm saying it. *Hello.*"

"Thank you." Vicary got inside.

"She also says she'd like to see you sometime. Do some catching up."

"That would be lovely," Vicary said, lying.

"Well, marvelous. She's coming to London next week. She'd love to have lunch with you."

Vicary felt his stomach tighten.

"One o'clock at the Connaught, a week from tomorrow," Kenton said. "I'm supposed to speak with her later today. Shall I tell her you'll be there?"

The back of the Rover was cold as a meat locker. Vicary sat on the big leather seat, legs covered in a traveling rug, watching the countryside of Gloucestershire sweep past his window. A red fox crossed the road, then darted back into the hedge. Drowsy fat pheasants pulled at the cropped remains of a snowy cornfield, feather coats puffed out against the cold. Bare tree limbs scratched at the clear sky. A small valley opened before him. Fields stretched like a rumpled patchwork quilt into the distance. The sun was sinking into a sky splashed with watercolor shades of purple and orange.

He was angry with Helen. His spiteful half wanted to believe his job with British Intelligence somehow made him more interesting to her. His rational half told him he and Helen had managed to part as friends and a quiet lunch might be very pleasant. At the very least it would be a welcome diversion from the pressure of the case. He thought, What are you so afraid of? That you might remember you were actually happy for the two years she was part of your life?

He pushed Helen from his mind. Harry's news intrigued him. By instinct he attacked it like a problem of history. His area of expertise was nineteenth-century Europe—he won critical acclaim for his book on the collapse of the balance of power after the Congress of Vienna—but Vicary had a secret passion for the history and myth of ancient Greece. He was intrigued by the fact that much scholarship on the age had to be based on guesswork and conjecture; the immense passage of time and lack of a clear historical record made that necessary. Why, for example, did Pericles launch the Peloponnesian War with Sparta that eventually led to the destruction of Athens? Why not accept the demands of his more powerful rival and revoke the Megarian decree? Was he driven by fear of the superior armies of Sparta? Did he believe war was inevitable? Did he embark on a disastrous foreign adventure to relieve pressure at home?

Now Vicary asked similar questions about his rival in Berlin, Kurt Vogel.

What was Vogel's goal? Vicary believed Vogel's goal was to build a network of elite sleeper agents at the outset of the war and leave them in place until the climactic moment of the confrontation. In order to succeed, great care would have to be given to the way the agent was inserted into the country. Obviously, Vogel had done this; the mere fact that MI5 had no knowledge of the agent until now confirmed it. Vogel would have to assume immigration and passport-control records would be used to find his agents; Vicary would certainly assume that if the roles were reversed. But what if the person who entered the country was dead? There would be no search. It was brilliant. But there was one problem—it required a body. Was it possible they actually murdered someone to trade places with Christa Kunst?

Germany's spies, as a rule, were not killers. Most were money-grubbers, adventurers, and petty Fascists, poorly trained and financed. But if Kurt Vogel had established a network of elite agents, they would be better motivated, more disciplined, and almost certainly more ruthless. Was it possible one of those highly trained and ruthless agents was a woman? Vicary had handled only one case involving a woman—a young German girl who managed to get a job as a maid in the home of a British admiral.

"Stop in the next village," Vicary said to the Wren driving the car. "I need to use the telephone."

The next village was called Aston Magna—a hamlet really, no shops, just a clump of cottages bisected by a pair of narrow lanes. An old man was standing along the roadway with his dog.

Vicary wound down the window and said, "Hello."

"Hello." The man wore Wellington boots and a lumpy tweed coat that looked at least a hundred years old. The dog had three legs.

"Is there a telephone in the village?" Vicary asked.

The man shook his head. Vicary swore the dog was shaking its head too. "No one's bothered to get one yet."

The man's accent was so broad Vicary had trouble understanding him.

"Where's the nearest telephone?"

"That'll be in Moreton."

"And where's that?"

"Follow that road there past the barn. Go left at the manor house and follow the trees into the next village. That's Moreton."

"Thank you."

The dog barked as the car sped away.

Vicary used the telephone at a bakery. He munched a cheese sandwich while he waited for the operator to connect him with the office. He wanted to share a little of his newfound wealth, so he ordered two dozen scones for the typists and the girls in Registry.

Harry came on the line.

Vicary said, "I don't think it was Christa Kunst they dug out of that grave in Whitchurch."

"Then who was it?"

"That's your job, Harry. Get on the phone with Scotland Yard. See if a woman went missing about the same time. Start within a two-hour radius of Whitchurch; then go wider if you have to. When I get back to the office, I'll brief Boothby."

"What are you going to tell him?"

"That we're looking for a dead Dutch woman. He'll love that."

CHAPTER EIGHTEEN

EAST LONDON

Finding Peter Jordan would not be a problem. Finding him the right way would.

Vogel's information was good. Berlin knew Jordan worked at Grosvenor Square at the Supreme Headquarters Allied Expeditionary Force, better known as SHAEF. The square was heavily patrolled by military policemen, impenetrable to an outsider. Berlin had the address of Jordan's house in Kensington and had put together an extraordinary amount of information on Jordan's background. What was missing was a minute-by-minute account of his daily routine in London. Without it Catherine could only guess at how best to make her approach.

Following Jordan herself was out of the question for a number of reasons. The first dealt with her personal security. It would be very dangerous for her to trail an American officer through the West End of London. She could be spotted by military policemen or by Jordan himself. If the officers were feeling especially diligent they could bring her in for questioning. A little checking might reveal that the real Catherine Blake died thirty years ago at the age of eight months and that she was a German agent.

The second reason for not following Peter Jordan herself was purely practical. It was virtually impossible for her to do the job correctly alone. Even if Neumann helped it would be difficult. The first time Jordan stepped into a military staff car she would be completely helpless. She couldn't walk up to a taxi and say "Follow that American staff car." Cabbies were aware of the threat posed to Allied officers by spies. She might be driven straight to the nearest police station instead. She needed nondescript vehicles to tail him, nondescript men to walk with him, nondescript men to maintain a static post outside his home.

She needed help.

She needed Vernon Pope.

Vernon Pope was one of London's biggest and most successful under-world figures. Pope, along with his brother Robert, ran protection rackets, illegal gambling parlors, prostitution rings, and a thriving black market operation. Early in the war Vernon Pope had brought Robert to the emergency room at St. Thomas Hospital with a serious head wound suffered in the blitz. Catherine examined him quickly, saw that he was concussed, and suspected his skull might have been fractured. She made certain Robert was seen by a doctor straightaway. A grateful Vernon Pope had left a note for her. It said, *If there's ever anything I can do to repay you please don't hesitate to ask.*

Catherine kept the note. It was in her handbag.

Somehow, Vernon Pope's warehouse had survived the bombing. It stood intact, an arrogant island surrounded by seas of destruction. Catherine had not ventured to the East End in nearly four years. The devastation was shocking. It was difficult to make certain she was not being followed. There were few doorways left for shelter, no boxes for false telephone calls, no shops for a small purchase, just endless mountains of debris.

She watched the warehouse from across the street, a light cold rain falling. She wore trousers, sweater, and a leather coat. The doors of the warehouse were pulled back, and three heavy lorries rumbled out into the street. A pair of well-dressed men pulled them shut quickly, but not before Catherine caught a glimpse inside. It was a beehive of activity.

A knot of dockworkers walked past her, coming off the day shift. She dropped in a few paces behind them and walked toward the Pope warehouse.

There was a small gate with an electric buzzer for deliveries. She pressed it, received no answer, and pressed it again. Catherine felt she was being watched. Finally the gate drew back.

"What can we do for you, luv?" The pleasant Cockney voice did not match the figure before her. He stood well over six feet tall, with black hair cropped close to his skull and small spectacles. He wore an expensive gray suit with a white shirt and silver tie. The muscles of his upper arms filled out the sleeves of the jacket.

"I'd like to speak to Mr. Pope, please." Catherine handed the hulk the note. He read quickly, as though he had seen many of them before.

"I'll ask the boss if he has a minute to see you. Come inside."

Catherine stepped through the gate, and he closed it behind her.

"Hands above your head, darling, that's a good girl. Nothing personal. Mr. Pope requires it of everyone." Pope's man patted her down. It was brisk and not very professional. She cringed as he ran his hands over her breasts. She resisted an impulse to crush his nose with her elbow. He opened her handbag, glanced inside, and handed it back. She had expected this so she had come unarmed. She felt naked without a weapon, vulnerable. Next time she would bring a stiletto.

He led her through the warehouse. Men dressed in overalls were loading crates of goods into half a dozen vans. At the far end of the warehouse boxes stood floor to ceiling on wooden pallets: coffee, cigarettes, sugar, as well as barrels of petrol. There was a fleet of shining motorbikes parked in a neat row. Vernon Pope was obviously doing a brisk business.

"This way, luv," he said. "Name's Dicky, by the way."

He led her into a freight lift, pulled shut the doors, and pressed the button. Catherine reached into her purse for a cigarette and stuck it between her lips.

"Sorry, darling," said Dicky, waving a finger in disapproval. "The boss hates fags. Says one day we're going to find out they're killing us. Besides, there's enough petrol and ammunition in this place to blow us clear to Glasgow."

"That's some favor," Vernon Pope said. He rose from his comfortable leather sofa and roamed his office. It was not just an office but more like a small flat, with a seating area and a kitchen filled with modern appliances. There was a bedroom behind a pair of black teak doors. They parted briefly and Catherine spotted a drowsy blonde waiting impatiently for the meeting to conclude. Pope poured himself another whisky. He was tall and handsome, with pale skin, fair brilliantined hair, wintry gray eyes. His suit was carefully tailored and circumspect; it might have been worn by a successful executive or someone born to wealth.

"Can you imagine that, Robert? Catherine here actually wants us to spend three days chasing an American naval officer around the West End."

Robert Pope remained at the fringes, pacing like a skittish gray wolf.

"That's not really our line of work, Catherine darling," Vernon Pope said. "Besides, what if the Yank or British security boys catch on to our little game? The London police I deal with. MI-Five is another story."

Catherine withdrew a cigarette. "Do you mind?"

"If you must. Dicky, give her an ashtray."

Catherine lit the cigarette and smoked quietly for a moment. "I've seen the equipment you have downstairs in your warehouse. You could easily mount the kind of surveillance operation I'm talking about."

"And why in the world would a volunteer nurse from St. Thomas Hospital want to mount a surveillance operation on an Allied officer, Robert, I ask you?"

Robert Pope knew he was not expected to provide an answer. Vernon Pope moved to the window, drink cupped in his hand. The blackout curtains were raised, giving him a view of the boats working up and down the river. "Look at what the Germans have done to this place," he said finally. "Used to be the center of the world, the biggest port on the face of the earth. And now look at it: a bloody wasteland. Things will never be the same around here. You're not working for the Germans, are you, Catherine?"

"Of course not," she said calmly. "My reasons for following him are strictly personal."

"Good. I'm a thief but I'm still a patriot." He paused, then asked, "So why do you want him followed?"

"I'm offering you a job, Mr. Pope. Frankly, the reasons why are none of your business."

Pope turned around and faced her. "Very good, Catherine. You've got guts. I like that. Besides, you'd be a fool to tell me."

The bedroom doors parted and the blonde emerged, wearing a man's paisley silk robe. It was tied loosely at the waist, revealing a good pair of legs and small upturned breasts.

"Vivie, we're not finished yet," Pope said.

"I was thirsty." She glanced at Catherine while pouring herself a gin and tonic. "How much longer are you going to be, Vernon?"

"Not long. Business, darling. Back in the bedroom."

Vivie moved back to the bedroom, hips flowing beneath the gown. She threw another glance at Catherine over her shoulder before softly closing the door.

"Pretty girl," Catherine said. "You're a lucky man."

Vernon Pope laughed quietly and shook his head. "Sometimes I wish I could bestow some of my luck on another man."

There was a long silence while Pope paced the room. "I'm into a lot of shady things, Catherine, but I don't like this. I don't like it one little bit."

Catherine lit another cigarette. Maybe she had made a mistake by approaching Vernon Pope with the offer.

"But I'm going to do it. You helped my brother, and I made you a promise. I'm a man of my word." He paused, looking her up and down. "Besides, there's something about *you* I like. Very much."

"I'm glad we can do business together, Mr. Pope."

"It's going to cost you, luv. I've got a lot of overhead. I've got wages to pay. This kind of thing is going to take a good deal of my resources."

"That's why I came to you." Catherine reached inside her purse and withdrew an envelope. "How does two hundred pounds sound? One hundred now, one hundred on delivery of the information. I want Commander Jordan followed for seventy-two hours, twenty-four hours a day. I want a minute-by-minute accounting of his movements. I want to know where he eats, who he meets with, and what they talk about. I want to know if he's seeing any women. Can you manage that, Mr. Pope?"

"Of course."

"Good. Then I'll contact you on Saturday."

"How can I reach you?"

"Actually, you can't."

Catherine laid the envelope on the table and got to her feet.

Vernon Pope smiled pleasantly. "I thought you would say that. Dicky, show Catherine the way out. Put together a bag of groceries for her. Some coffee, some sugar, maybe a little tinned beef if that shipment came in. Something nice, Dicky."

"I have a bad feeling about this one, Vernon," Robert Pope said. "Maybe we should drop the whole thing."

Vernon Pope hated to be questioned by his younger brother. As far as Vernon was concerned, he made the business decisions and Robert handled the muscle.

"It's nothing we can't handle. Did you have her followed?"

"Dicky and the boys picked her up as she left the warehouse."

"Good. I want to know who that woman is and what she's playing at."

"Maybe we could turn this to our advantage. We could buy ourselves some goodwill with the police if we quietly tell them what she's up to."

"We'll do nothing of the kind. Is that clear?"

"Maybe you should think a little more about business and a little less about getting it wet."

Vernon turned on him and grabbed him by the throat. "What I do is none of your goddamned business. Besides, it's a helluva lot better than what you and Dicky do."

Robert visibly reddened.

"Why are you looking at me like that, Robert? You think I don't know what goes on?"

Vernon released his grip.

"Now get out on the street where you belong and make sure Dicky doesn't lose her."

Catherine spotted the tail two minutes after leaving the warehouse. She had expected it. Men like Vernon Pope don't stay in business long unless they are cautious and suspicious. But the tail was clumsy and amateurish. After all, Dicky had been the one who had greeted her, searched her, and taken her inside. She knew his face. Stupid of them to put him on the street to follow her. Losing him would be easy.

She ducked into an underground station, melting into the evening crowds. She crossed through the tunnel and emerged on the other side of the street. A bus was waiting. She boarded it and found a seat next to an elderly woman. Through the fogged window she watched Dicky charge up the stairs into the street, panic on his face.

She felt a little sorry for him. Poor Dicky was no match for a professional, and Vernon Pope would be furious. She would take no chances: a taxi ride, two or three more buses, a stroll through the West End before returning to her flat.

For now she settled into her seat and enjoyed the ride.

The bedroom was dark when Vernon Pope entered and quietly closed the doors. Vivie rose to her knees at the end of the bed. Vernon kissed her deeply. He was being rougher than usual. Vivie thought she knew why. She slid her hand down the front of his trousers. "Oh, my God, Vernon. Is this for me or that bitch?"

Vernon parted the silk robe and pushed it down over her shoulders. "A little of both, I'm afraid," he said, kissing her again.

"You wanted her right there in the office. I could see it on your face."

"You always were a perceptive little girl."

She kissed him again. "When is she coming back?"

"End of the week."

"What's her name?"

"Calls herself Catherine."

"Catherine," Vivie said. "What a lovely name. She's beautiful."

"Yes," Pope said distantly.

"What kind of business is she into?"

Pope told her about the meeting; there were no secrets between them.

"Sounds a bit touchy. I think we could bring a good bit of leverage to bear on her."

"You're a very smart girl."

"No, just a very nasty girl."

"Vivie, I can tell when your mind is working in evil ways."

She laughed wickedly. "I have three days to dream up all the wonderful things we can do to that woman when she comes back. Now, take off your pants so I can help ease your pain."

Vernon Pope did as he was told.

A moment later there was a soft knock at the door. Robert Pope stepped inside without waiting for an answer. A shaft of light partially illuminated the scene. Vivie looked up, unashamed, and smiled. Vernon exploded in anger.

"How many times have I told you not to come in here when the door is closed?"

"It's important. She got away from us."

"How in the hell did that happen?"

"Dicky swears she was there one minute and gone the next. She just vanished."

"For Christ's sake!"

"No one gets away from Dicky. She's obviously a professional. We ought to stay as far away from her as possible."

Vivie felt a stab of panic.

"Get out of here and close the door, Robert."

When Robert was gone, Vivie licked Vernon playfully.

"You're not going to take that little queer's advice, are you, Vernon?"

"Of course not."

"Good," she said. "Now, where were we?"

"Oh, my God," Vernon groaned.

CHAPTER NINETEEN

LONDON

Early the following morning, Robert Pope and Richard "Dicky" Dobbs made their unwitting debut in the world of wartime espionage with a hastily improvised surveillance of Commander Peter Jordan that would have made the watchers of MI5 a touch green with envy.

It began before the damp freezing dawn, when the pair arrived outside Jordan's Edwardian house in Kensington in a black paneled van, complete with boxes of tinned food in the back and the name of a West End grocer on the side. They waited there until shortly before eight o'clock, Pope dozing, Dicky nervously munching a soggy bun and drinking coffee from a paper cup. Vernon Pope had threatened him with grievous bodily harm over last night's foul-up with the woman. He was damned if he was going to lose Peter Jordan. Dicky, considered the finest wheel man in London's criminal underground, had secretly vowed to pursue Jordan across the lawns of Green Park if need be.

Such motoring heroics would not be necessary, for at seven fifty-five an American military staff car drew up outside Jordan's house and blew its horn. The door of the house opened and a man of medium height and build emerged. He wore a U.S. Navy uniform, a white cap, and a dark overcoat. A thin leather briefcase hung at the end of his arm. He vanished into the back of the car and closed the door. Dicky had been concentrating on Jordan so intently he forgot to start the engine. When he tried to do so it coughed once and died. He cursed it, threatened it, and cajoled it before trying again. This time the van roared into life, and their silent watch on Peter Jordan was under way.

Grosvenor Square would present them with their first challenge. It was crowded with taxis, staff cars, and Allied officers rushing in every direction.

Jordan's car passed through the square, entered an adjacent side street, and stopped outside a small unmarked building. Remaining on the street was impossible. Vehicles were parked on both sides with only one lane for traffic, and a white-helmeted MP was pacing up and down, lazily swinging his baton. Pope hopped out and walked back and forth along the street while Dicky circled. Ten minutes later Jordan emerged from the building, a heavy briefcase chained to his wrist.

Dicky collected Pope and headed back to Grosvenor Square, arriving in time to spot Jordan walking through the front entrance of SHAEF headquarters. He found a parking space in Grosvenor Street with a clear view and turned off the engine. A few minutes later they caught a glimpse of General Eisenhower flashing one of his famous smiles before disappearing through the entrance.

Pope, even if he had been trained by MI5 itself, could not have discharged his next moves any better. He determined that they could not cover the building with a static post alone; it was a huge complex, with many ways in and out. Using a public phone, he telephoned Vernon at the warehouse and demanded three men. When they arrived he posted one behind the building in Blackburn Street, another in Upper Brook Street, and the third in Upper Grosvenor Street. Two hours later Pope called the warehouse again and demanded three fresh faces—it wasn't safe for civilians to loiter around American installations. Vicary and Boothby, had they been able to hear the conversation, might have laughed at the irony, for like any good desk man and field agent, Vernon and Robert quarreled bitterly over resources. The stakes were different, though. Vernon needed a couple of good men to pick up a shipment of stolen coffee and to rough up a shopkeeper who had fallen behind with his protection payments.

They changed vehicles at midday. The grocer's van was replaced by an identical van with the name of a fictitious laundry service stenciled on the side. It was so quickly prepared that the word *laundry* was spelled *laundery* and the white clothes bags piled in the back were stuffed with crumpled old newspapers. At two o'clock they were brought a thermos flask of tea and a bag of sandwiches. An hour later, having finished eating and smoking a pair of cigarettes, Pope was growing nervous. Jordan had been inside nearly seven hours. It was getting late. Every side of the building was covered. But if Jordan left in the gloom of the blackout, it would be nearly impossible to spot him. But at four o'clock, the light almost gone, Jordan left the building by the main door on Grosvenor Square.

He repeated the same circuit as the morning, only in reverse. He walked across the square to the smaller building, the same heavy briefcase chained to his wrist, and went inside. He emerged a few moments later carrying the smaller briefcase he had had earlier that morning. The rain had stopped, and Jordan apparently decided a walk would do him good. He headed west, then turned south in Park Lane. Following him in the van would be impossible. Pope hopped out and shadowed Jordan along the pavement, staying several yards behind him.

It was more difficult than Pope imagined. The large Grosvenor House hotel in Park Lane had been taken over by the Americans as a billet for officers. Dozens of people jammed the pavement outside. Pope moved closer to Jordan to make certain he didn't mistake him for one of the other men. A military policeman glanced at Pope as he sliced through the crowd after Jordan. On some streets in the West End, Englishmen stuck out the same way they would in Topeka, Kansas. Pope tensed. Then he realized he wasn't doing anything wrong. He was simply walking down the street in his own country. He relaxed and the MP looked away. Jordan walked past Grosvenor House. Pope moved carefully behind him.

Pope lost him at Hyde Park Corner.

Jordan had vanished into a crowd of soldiers and British civilians waiting to cross the street. When the light changed Pope followed an American naval officer roughly Jordan's height along Grosvenor Place. Then he looked down and realized the officer wasn't carrying a briefcase. He stopped and looked behind him, hoping Jordan would be there. He was gone.

Pope heard a horn blast in the street and looked up. It was Dicky.

"He's in Knightsbridge," Dicky said. "Get in."

Dicky executed a perfect U-turn through the buzzing evening traffic. Pope spotted Jordan a moment later and breathed a sigh of relief. Dicky pulled over and Pope jumped out. Determined not to lose his man again, Pope closed to within a few feet of him.

The Vandyke Club was a club for American officers in Kensington, off limits to British civilians. Jordan went inside. Pope walked a few feet past the doorway, then doubled back. Dicky had pulled to the curb across the street. Pope, winded and chilled, climbed inside and closed the door. He lit a cigarette and finished the dregs of tea in the thermos. Then he said, "Next time Commander Jordan decides to walk halfway across London, you get out and walk with him, Dicky."

Jordan came out forty-five minutes later.

Pope thought, Please God, not another forced march.

Jordan stepped to the curb and flagged down a taxi.

Dicky dropped the van into gear and eased carefully out into the traffic. Following the taxi was easier. It headed east, past Trafalgar Square and into the Strand; then, after traveling a short distance, it turned right.

Pope said, "Now this is more like it."

They watched as Jordan paid off his taxi and stepped inside the Savoy Hotel.

The vast majority of British civilians survived the war on subsistence levels of food, a few ounces of meat and cheese each week, a few ounces of milk, one egg if they were lucky, delicacies like tinned peaches and tomatoes once in a great while. No one was starving, but few people put on weight. But there was another London, the London of fine restaurants and lavish hotels, which secured a steady supply of meat, fish, vegetables, wine, and coffee on the black market, then charged their customers exorbitant prices for the privilege of dining there. The Savoy Hotel was one of those establishments.

The doorman wore a green greatcoat, trimmed in silver, and a stovepipe hat. Pope brushed past him and went inside. He crossed the lobby and entered the salon. There were rich businessmen, reclining in the comfortable easy chairs, beautiful women in fashionable wartime evening clothes, dozens of American and British officers in uniform, tweedy landed gentry up from the country for a few days in the city. Pope, following Jordan through the crowd, had a mixed reaction to the opulent scene. The West End rich were living the high life while the underprivileged East Enders were hungry and suffering the most from the blitz. But then, he and his brother had made a fortune in the black market. He dismissed the disparity as an unfortunate consequence of war.

Pope followed Jordan into the Grill bar. Jordan stood alone among the throng, trying vainly to get the bartender's attention to order a drink. Pope stood a few feet from him. He caught the bartender's eye and ordered a whisky. When he turned around, Jordan had been joined by a tall American naval officer with a red face and a good-natured smile. Pope took a step closer so he could hear their conversation.

The tall man said, "Hitler should come here and try to get a drink on a Friday night. I'm sure he'd have second thoughts about wanting to invade this country."

"You want to try our luck at Grosvenor House?" Jordan asked.

"Willow Run? Are you out of your mind? The French chef quit the other day. They ordered him to make the meals out of C-rations and he refused."

"Sounds like the last sane man in London."

"I'll say."

"What do you have to do to get a drink around this place?"

"This usually works: Two martinis, for Christ's sake!"

The bartender looked up, grinned, and reached for a bottle of Beefeaters. "Hello, Mr. Ramsey."

"Hello, William."

Pope made a mental note. Jordan's friend was named Ramsey.

"Well done, Shepherd."

Pope thought, *Shepherd Ramsey.*

"It helps to be a foot taller than anyone else."

"Did you make a reservation? There's no way we're going to get in the Grill tonight without one."

"Of course I did, old sport. Where the hell have you been anyway? I tried calling you last week. Let the telephone at your house ring off the hook: no answer. Rang your office as well. They said you couldn't come to the phone. Rang back the next day, same story. What the hell were you doing that you couldn't come to the phone for two days?"

"None of your business."

"Ah, still working on that project of yours, are you?"

"Drop it, Shepherd, or I'll knock you on your ass right here in this bar."

"In your dreams, old sport. Besides, if you make a scene in here, where the hell will we do our drinking? No decent establishment would have your kind."

"Good point."

"So when are you going to tell me what you've been working on?"

"When the war is over."

"That important, huh?"

"Yeah."

"Well, at least one of us is doing something important." Shepherd Ramsey downed his drink. "William, two more, please."

"Are we going to get drunk before dinner tonight?"

"I just want you to loosen up, that's all."

"This is about as loose as I get. What are you up to, Shepherd? I know that tone of voice."

"Nothing, Peter. Jesus, take it easy."

"Tell me. You know how I hate surprises."

"I've invited a couple of people to join us tonight."

"People?"

"Girls, actually. In fact, they've just arrived."

Pope followed Jordan's gaze toward the front of the bar. There were two women, both young, both very attractive. The women spotted Shepherd Ramsey and Jordan and joined them at the bar.

"Peter, this is Barbara. But most people call her Baby."

"That's understandable. Pleasure to meet you, Barbara."

Barbara looked at Shepherd. "God, you were right! He's a doll." She spoke with a working-class London accent. "Are we eating in the Grill?"

"Yes. In fact, our table should be ready."

The maître d'hôtel showed them to their table. There was no way Pope could listen to their conversation from the bar. He needed to be seated at the next table. Gazing through the entrance of the dining room, Pope could see the table beside them was empty but had a small RESERVED sign on it. No problem, he thought. He quickly crossed the bar and went out into the street. Dicky was waiting in the front of the van. Pope waved for him to come inside. Dicky climbed out and crossed the street.

"What is it, Robert?"

"We're having dinner. I need you to make the reservation."

Pope sent Dicky to speak to the maître d'hôtel. The first time Dicky asked for the table, the man shook his head, frowned, and waved his hands to show there were no tables to be had. Then Dicky leaned down and whispered something into his ear that made him turn white and start to tremble. A moment later they were being seated at the table next to Peter Jordan and Shepherd Ramsey.

"What did you say to him, Dicky?"

"I told him if he didn't give us this table I'd rip out his Adam's apple and drop it into that flaming pan over there."

"Well, the customer is always right. That's what I say."

They opened their menus. Pope said, "Are you going to start with the smoked salmon or the pâté de foie gras?"

"Both, I think. I'm starving. You don't suppose they serve bangers and mash here, do you, Robert?"

"Not bloody likely. Try the coq au vin. Now keep quiet so I can hear what these Yanks are saying."

It was Dicky who followed them outside after dinner. He watched as they placed the two women into a taxi and set out along the Strand.

"You might at least have been civil."

"I'm sorry, Shepherd. We didn't have much to talk about."

"What's there to talk about? You have a few drinks, a few laughs, you take her home and have a wonderful evening in bed. No questions asked."

"I had trouble getting past the fact that she kept using her knife to check her lipstick."

"Do you know what she could have done to you with those lips? And did you get a look at what she had beneath that dress? My God, Peter, that girl has one of the worst reputations in London."

"I'm sorry to disappoint you, Shepherd. I just wasn't interested."

"Well, when are you going to get interested?"

"What are you talking about?"

"Six months ago you promised me you were going to start dating."

Jordan lit a cigarette and angrily waved out the match. "I would like to meet an intelligent, interesting grown-up. I don't need you to go out and find me a girl. Listen, Shep, I'm sorry——"

"No, you're right. It's none of my business. It's just that my mother died when my father was forty. He never remarried. As a result he died a lonely, bitter old man. I don't want the same thing to happen to you."

"Thanks, Shepherd, it won't."

"You'll never find another woman like Margaret."

"Tell me something I don't know." Jordan flagged down a taxi and climbed in. "Can I give you a lift?"

"Actually, I have a previous engagement."

"Shepherd."

"She's meeting me back at my room in half an hour. I couldn't resist. Forgive me, but the flesh is weak."

"More than the flesh. Have a good time, Shep."

The taxi drove off. Dicky peeled away and looked for the van. Pope pulled over to the curb a few seconds later and Dicky climbed inside. They followed the taxi back into Kensington, saw Peter Jordan to his door, and stayed there a half hour, waiting for the night shift to arrive.

CHAPTER TWENTY

LONDON

It had been Alfred Vicary's inability to repair a motorbike that led to his shattered knee. It happened on a glorious autumn day in the north of France, and without a doubt it was the worst day of his life.

Vicary had just finished a meeting with a spy who had gone behind enemy lines in a sector where the British planned to attack at dawn the next morning. The spy had discovered a large bivouac of German soldiers. The attack, if it went forward as planned, would be met with heavy resistance. The spy gave Vicary a handwritten note on the strength of the German troops and the number of artillery pieces he had spotted. He also gave Vicary a map showing exactly where they were camped. Vicary placed them in his leather saddlebag and set out back to headquarters.

Vicary knew he was carrying intelligence of vital importance; lives were at stake. He opened the throttle full and drove perilously fast along the narrow track. Large trees lined both sides of the path, a canopy of limbs overhead, the sunlight on the autumn leaves creating a flickering tunnel of fire. The path rose and fell rhythmically beneath him. Several times he felt the exhilarating thrill of his Rudge motorbike soaring airborne for a second or two.

The engine rattle began ten miles from headquarters. Vicary eased off the throttle. Over the next mile the rattle progressed to a loud clatter. A mile later he heard the sound of snapping metal, followed by a loud bang. The engine suddenly lost power and died.

With the roar of the bike gone, the silence was oppressive. He bent down and looked at the motor. The hot greasy metal and twisting cables meant nothing to him. He remembered actually kicking the thing and debating whether he should leave it by the roadside or drag it back to headquarters. He took hold of it by the handlebars and began pushing at a brisk pace.

The afternoon light diminished to a frail pink dusk. He was still miles from headquarters. If he were lucky, Vicary might run into someone from his own side who could give him a lift. If he were unlucky he might find himself face-to-face with a patrol of German scouts.

When the last of the twilight had died away, the shelling began. The first shells fell short, landing harmlessly in a field. The next shells soared overhead and thudded against a hillside. The third volley landed on the track directly in front of him.

Vicary never heard the shell that wounded him.

He regained consciousness sometime in the early evening as he lay freezing in a ditch. He looked down and nearly fainted at the sight of his knee, a mess of splintered bone and blood. He forced himself to crawl out of the ditch back up to the path. He found his bike and blacked out beside it.

Vicary came to in a field hospital the next morning. He knew the attack had gone forward because the hospital was overflowing. He lay in his bed all day, head swimming in a drowsy morphine haze, listening to the moaning of the wounded. At twilight the boy in the next bed died. Vicary closed his eyes, trying to shut out the sound of the death rattle, but it was no good.

Brendan Evans—his friend from Cambridge who had helped Vicary deceive his way into the Intelligence Corps—came to see him the next morning. The war had changed him. His boyish good looks were gone. He looked like a hardened, somewhat cruel man. Brendan pulled up a chair and sat down next to the bed.

"It's all my fault," Vicary told him. "I knew the Germans were waiting. But my motorbike broke down and I couldn't fix the damned thing. Then the shelling started."

"I know. They found the papers in your saddlebag. No one's blaming you. It was just bloody awful luck, that's all. You probably couldn't have done anything to repair the bike in any case."

Sometimes, Vicary still heard the screams of the dying in his sleep—even now, almost thirty years later. In recent days his dream had taken a new twist—he dreamed it was Basil Boothby who had sabotaged his motorbike.

Ever read Vogel's file?

No.

Liar. Perfect liar.

Vicary had tried to refrain from the inevitable comparisons between then and now, but it was unavoidable. He did not believe in fate, but someone or something had given him another chance—a chance to redeem himself for his failure on that autumn day in 1916.

Vicary thought the party in the pub across the street from MI5 headquarters would help him take his mind off the case. It had not. He had lingered at the fringes, thinking about France, gazing into his beer, watching while other officers flirted with the pretty typists. Nicholas Jago was giving a rather good account of himself at the piano.

He was jolted out of his trance when one of the Registry Queens began singing "I'll Be Seeing You." She was an attractive crimson-lipped blonde named Grace Clarendon. Vicary knew she and Harry had carried on a rather public affair early in the war. Vicary understood the attraction. Grace was bright, witty, and cleverer than the rest of the girls in Registry. But she was also married, and Vicary did not approve. He didn't tell Harry how he felt; it was none of his business. He thought, Besides, who am I to lecture on matters of the heart? He suspected it was Grace who had told Harry about Boothby and the Vogel file.

Harry walked in, bundled in his overcoat. He winked at Grace, then walked over to Vicary and said, "Let's head back to the office. We need to talk."

"Her name was Beatrice Pymm. She lived alone in a cottage outside Ipswich," Harry began, as they walked upstairs to Vicary's office. He had spent several hours in Ipswich that morning, delving into Beatrice Pymm's past. "No friends, no family. Her mother died in 1936. Left her the cottage and a fair amount of money. She didn't have a job. She had no boyfriends, no lovers, not even a cat. The only thing she did was paint."

"Paint?" Vicary asked.

"Yeah, paint. The people I spoke to said she painted almost every day. She left the cottage early in the morning, went into the surrounding countryside, and spent all day painting. A detective from the Ipswich police showed me a couple of her paintings: landscapes. Very nice, actually."

Vicary frowned. "I didn't know you had an eye for art, Harry."

"You think boys from Battersea can't appreciate the finer things? I'll have you know my sainted mother regularly dragged me to the National Gallery."

"I'm sorry, Harry. Please continue."

"Beatrice didn't own a car. She either rode her bicycle or walked or took the bus. She used to paint too long, especially in the summer when the light was good, and miss the last bus back. Her neighbors would spot her arriving home late at night on foot carrying her painting things. They say she spent the night in some godawful places, just to catch the sunrise."

"What do they think happened to her?"

"The official version of the story—accidental drowning. Her belongings were found on the banks of the Orwell, including an empty bottle of wine. The police think she may have had a little too much to drink, lost her footing, slipped into the water, and drowned. No body was found. They investigated for some time but couldn't find any evidence to support any other theory. They declared her death an accidental drowning and closed the case."

"Sounds like a very plausible story."

"Sure, it could have happened that way. But I doubt it. Beatrice Pymm was very familiar with the area. Why on that particular day did she have a little too much to drink and fall into the river?"

"Theory number two?"

"Theory number two goes as follows: she was picked up by our spy after dark, stabbed in the heart, and her body loaded into a van. Her things were left on the riverbank in order to make it appear like an accidental drowning. In reality, the corpse was driven across the country, mutilated, and buried outside Whitchurch."

They arrived in Vicary's office and sat down, Vicary behind the desk, Harry opposite. Harry leaned back in his chair and propped up his feet.

"Is this all supposition, or do you have facts to support your theory?"

"Half and half, but it all fits your guess that Beatrice Pymm was murdered in order to conceal the spy's entry into the country."

"Let's hear it."

"I'll start with the corpse. The body was discovered in August 1939. I spoke to the Home Office pathologist who examined it. Judging from the decomposition, he estimated it had been in the ground six to nine months. That's consistent with Beatrice Pymm's disappearance, by the way. The bones of the face had been almost completely shattered. There were no teeth to compare dental records. There were no fingerprints to be taken because the hands had badly decomposed. He was unable to fix a cause of death. He did find one interesting clue, though, a nick on the bottom rib of the left side. That nick is consistent with being stabbed in the chest."

"You say the killer may have used a van? What's your evidence?"

"I asked the local police forces for reports on any crimes or disturbances around Whitchurch the night of Beatrice Pymm's murder. Coincidentally, a van was deserted and set deliberately ablaze outside a village called Alderton. They ran a check on the van's identification number."

"And?"

"Stolen in London two days earlier."

Vicary rose and began pacing. "So our spy is in the middle of nowhere with a van blazing on the side of the road. Where does she go now? What does she do?"

"Let's assume she comes back to London. She flags down a passing car or lorry and asks for a lift. Or maybe she walks to the nearest station and takes the first train into London."

"Too risky," Vicary said. "A woman alone in the middle of the countryside late at night would be very unusual. It's November, so it's cold too. She might be spotted by the police. The murder of Beatrice Pymm was perfectly planned and executed. Her killer wouldn't leave her escape to chance."

"How about a motorbike in the back of the van?"

"Good idea. Run a check, see if any motorbikes were stolen about that time."

"She rides back to London and ditches the bike."

"That's right," Vicary said. "And when war breaks out we don't look for a Dutch woman named Christa Kunst because we assume incorrectly that she's dead."

"Clever as hell."

"More ruthless than clever. Imagine, killing an innocent British civilian to better conceal a spy. This is no ordinary agent, and Kurt Vogel is no ordinary control officer. I'm convinced of that." Vicary paused to light a cigarette. "Has the photograph yielded any leads?"

"Nothing."

"I think that leaves our investigation dead in the water."

"I'm afraid you're right. I'll make a few more calls tonight."

Vicary shook his head. "Take the rest of the night off. Go down to the party." Then he added, "Spend some time with Grace."

Harry looked up. "How did you know?"

"This place is filled with intelligence officers, if you haven't noticed. Things get around, people talk. Besides, you two weren't exactly circumspect. You used to leave the number of Grace's flat with the night operators in case I was looking for you."

Harry's face reddened.

"Go to her, Harry. She misses you, any fool can see that."

"I miss her too. But she's married. I broke it off because I felt like a complete cad."

"You make her happy and she makes you happy. When her husband comes home, *if* her husband comes home, things will go back to normal."

"And where does that leave me?"

"That's up to you."

"It leaves me with a broken heart, that's where it leaves me. I'm crazy about Grace."

"Then be with her and enjoy her company."

"There's something else." Harry told him about the other aspect of his guilt over his affair with Grace—that fact that he was in London chasing spies while Grace's husband and other men were risking their lives in the military. "I just don't know what I would do under fire, how I would react. Whether I would be brave or whether I would be a coward. I also don't know whether I'm doing any damned good here. I could name a hundred other detectives who can do what I do. Sometimes I think about giving Boothby my resignation and joining up."

"Don't be ridiculous, Harry. When you do your job right you save lives on the battlefield. The invasion of France is going to be won or lost before the first soldier ever sets foot on a French beach. Thousands of lives may depend on what you do. If you don't think you're doing your bit, think of it in those terms. Besides, I need you. You're the only one I can trust around here."

They sat in an awkward, embarrassed silence for a moment, the way Englishmen are apt to do after sharing private thoughts. Harry stood up, started for the door, then stopped and turned around. "What about you, Alfred? Why is there no one in your life? Why don't you come downstairs to the party and find a nice woman to spend some time with?"

Vicary beat his breast pockets for his half-moon reading glasses and thrust them onto his face. "Good night, Harry," he said, a little too firmly, as he leafed through a stack of papers on the desk in front of him. "Have fun at the party. I'll see you in the morning."

When Harry was gone Vicary picked up the telephone and dialed Boothby's number. He was surprised when Boothby answered his own telephone. When Vicary asked if he was free, Sir Basil wondered aloud whether it could wait until Monday morning. Vicary said it was important. Sir Basil granted him an audience of five minutes and told Vicary to come upstairs straightaway.

"I've drafted this memorandum to General Eisenhower, General Betts, and the prime minister," Vicary said, when he finished briefing Boothby on Harry's discoveries that day. He handed it to Boothby, who remained standing, feet slightly apart as if for balance. He was in a hurry to leave for the country. His secretary had packed a secure briefcase of weekend reading material and a small leather grip of personal items. An overcoat hung over his shoulders, sleeves dangling at his sides. "To keep quiet about this any longer would be a dereliction of duty in my opinion, Sir Basil."

Boothby was still reading; Vicary knew this because his lips were moving. He was squinting so hard his eyes had vanished into his lush brows. Sir Basil liked to pretend he still had perfect vision and refused to wear his reading glasses in front of the staff.

"I thought we'd discussed this once already, Alfred," Boothby said, waving the sheet of paper through the air. A problem, once dealt with, should never resurface—it was one of Sir Basil's many personal and professional maxims. He was apt to grow agitated when subordinates raised matters already dispensed with. Careful deliberation and second-guessing were the province of weaker minds. Sir Basil valued quick decision making over all else. Vicary glanced at Sir Basil's desk. It was clean, polished, and absolutely void of paper or files, a monument to Boothby's management style.

"We *have* discussed this once already, Sir Basil," Vicary said patiently, "but the situation has changed. It appears they've managed to insert an agent into the country and that agent has met with an agent in place. It appears that their operation—whatever it may be—is now under way. To sit on this information instead of passing it on is to court disaster."

"Nonsense," Boothby snapped.

"Why is it nonsense?"

"Because this department is not going to officially inform the Americans and the prime minister that it is incapable of performing its job. That it is incapable of controlling the threat posed to the invasion preparations by German spies."

"That's not a valid reason for concealing this information."

"It is a valid reason, Alfred, if I say it is a valid reason."

Conversations with Boothby often assumed the characteristics of a cat chasing its own tail: shallow contradiction, bluff and diversion, point-scoring contests. Vicary bunched his hands judicially beneath his chin and pretended to study the pattern of Boothby's costly rug. The room was silent except for the sound of the floorboards creaking beneath Sir Basil's muscular bulk.

"Are you prepared to forward my memorandum to the director-general?" Vicary asked. His tone of voice was as unthreatening as possible.

"Absolutely not."

"Then I'm prepared to go directly to the DG myself."

Boothby bent his body and put his face close to Vicary's. Vicary, seated in Boothby's deep couch, could smell gin and cigarettes on his breath.

"And I'm prepared to squash you, Alfred."

"Sir Basil—"

"Let me remind you how the system works. You report to me, and I report to the director-general. You have reported to me, and I have determined it would be inappropriate to forward this matter to the DG at this time."

"There is one other option."

Boothby's head snapped back as if he had been punched. He quickly regained his composure, setting his jaw in an angry scowl. "I don't report to the prime minister, nor do I serve at his pleasure. But if you go around the department and speak directly to Churchill, I'll have you brought up before an internal review committee. By the time the committee is finished with you, they'll need dental records to identify the body."

"That's completely unfair."

"Is it? Since you've taken charge of this case it's been one disaster after another. My God, Alfred—a few more German spies running loose in this country and they could form a rugby club."

Vicary refused to be baited. "If you're not going to present my report to the director-general, I want the official record of this affair to reflect the fact that I made the suggestion at this time and you turned it down."

The corners of Boothby's mouth lifted into a terse smile. Protecting one's flank was something he understood and appreciated. "Already thinking of your place in history, are you, Alfred?"

"You're a complete bastard, Sir Basil. And an incompetent one as well."

"You're addressing a senior officer, Major Vicary!"

"Believe me, I haven't missed the irony."

Boothby snatched up the briefcase and his leather grip, then looked at Vicary and said, "You have a great deal to learn."

"I suppose I could learn it from you."

"And what in God's name is that supposed to mean?"

Vicary got to his feet. "It means you should start thinking more about the security of this country and less about your personal advancement through Whitehall."

Boothby smiled easily, as if he were trying to seduce a younger woman. "But my dear Alfred," he said, "I've always considered the two to be completely intertwined."

CHAPTER TWENTY-ONE

EAST LONDON

Catherine Blake had a stiletto hidden in her handbag the following evening as she hurried along the pavement toward the Popes' warehouse. She had demanded a meeting alone with Vernon Pope, and, as she approached the warehouse, she saw no sign of Pope's men. She stopped at the gate and turned the latch. It was unlocked, just as Pope said it would be. She pulled it open and stepped inside.

The warehouse was a place of shadows, the only illumination from a light hanging at one end of the room. Catherine walked toward the light and found the freight lift. She stepped inside, pulled the gate closed, and pressed the button. The lift groaned and shuddered upward toward Pope's office.

The lift emptied onto a small landing with a set of black double doors. Catherine knocked and heard Pope's voice on the other side tell her to enter. He was standing at a drinks trolley, a bottle of champagne in one hand, a pair of glasses in the other. He held one out toward Catherine as she walked across the floor.

"No, thank you," she said. "I'm just staying for a minute."

"I insist," he said. "Things got a little tense the last time we were together. I want to make it up to you."

"Is that why you had me followed?" she said, accepting the wine.

"I have everyone followed, darling. That's how I stay in business. My boys are good at it, as you'll see when you read this." He held out an envelope toward Catherine, then pulled it away as her hand reached for it. "That's why I was so surprised when you managed to give Dicky the slip. That was smooth—ducking into the underground and then jumping on a bus."

"I changed my mind." She drank some of the champagne. It was ice cold and excellent. Pope held out the envelope again and this time allowed Catherine to take it. She set down her glass and opened it.

It was exactly what she needed, a minute-by-minute accounting of Peter Jordan's movements around London: where he worked, the hours he kept, the places he did his eating and drinking, even the name of a friend.

While she finished reading, Pope took the champagne from the ice bucket and poured another glass for himself. Catherine reached inside her handbag, took out the money, and dropped it on the table. "Here's the rest," she said. "I think that concludes our business. Thank you very much."

She was slipping the report on Peter Jordan into her purse when Pope stepped forward and loosened her grip on the bag. "Actually, Catherine darling, our business together has just begun."

"If it's more money you want—"

"Oh, I want more money. And if you don't want me to make a call to the police, you're going to give it to me." He took another step closer to her, pressed his body against hers, and ran his hand over her breasts. "But there's something else I want from you."

The bedroom doors opened and Vivie stood there, wearing nothing but one of Vernon's shirts unbuttoned to her waist. "Vivie, meet Catherine," Pope said. "Lovely Catherine has agreed to stay for the evening."

They didn't prepare her for situations like this at the Abwehr spy school in Berlin. They taught her how to count troops, how to assess an army, how to use her radio, how to recognize the insignia of units and the faces of senior officers. But they never taught her how to deal with a London gangster and his kinky girlfriend who planned to spend the evening taking turns with her body. She had the sensation of being trapped in some silly pubescent fantasy. She thought, This can't really be happening. But it *was* happening, and Catherine could think of nothing from her training to get her through it.

Vernon Pope led her through the doors into the bedroom. He pushed her down at the end of the bed, then sat down in a chair in the corner of the room. Vivie stood in front of her and undid the last two buttons of the shirt. She had small upturned breasts and pale skin that shone in the dim light of the room. She took hold of Catherine's head and pulled it to her breasts. Catherine played along with the depraved game, taking Vivie's nipple into her mouth, while she thought about how best to kill them both.

Catherine knew once she submitted to blackmail it would never end. Her financial resources were not unlimited. Vernon Pope could bleed her dry very quickly. With no money, she would be rendered useless. She decided there was little risk involved; she had covered her tracks carefully. The Popes and their men did not know where to find her. They only knew she worked as a volunteer nurse at St. Thomas Hospital, and Catherine had given the hospital a false address. They would also be reluctant to go to the police. The police would ask questions—answering them truthfully would mean admitting to following an American naval officer for money.

All of it hinged on killing Vernon Pope as quickly and quietly as possible.

Catherine took Vivie's other breast into her mouth and sucked the nipple until it became firm. Vivie's head rolled back and she moaned. She took Catherine's hand and guided it between her legs. Already she was warm and wet. Catherine had turned off all her emotions. She was just mechanically going through the movements of giving physical pleasure to this woman. She felt neither fear nor revulsion; she simply tried to remain calm and to think clearly. Vivie's pelvis began to work against Catherine's fingers, and a moment later her body trembled with an orgasm.

Vivie pushed Catherine down onto the bed, sat astride her hips, and began undoing the buttons of her sweater. She unhooked Catherine's brassiere and massaged her breasts. Catherine saw Vernon rise from his seat and begin to undress. For the first time she became nervous. She didn't want him on top of her or inside her. He might be a cruel and sadistic lover. He might hurt her. On her back, with her legs spread, she would be vulnerable. She would also be subject to his superior weight and strength. All the fighting techniques she had learned hinged on speed and maneuverability. If she were pinned beneath Vernon Pope's heavy body she would be defenseless.

Catherine had to play their game. Better still, she had to control it.

She reached up and took Vivie's breasts in her hands and stroked the nipples. She could see Vernon watching them. He was feeding on them with his eyes, drinking in the sight of the two women caressing each other. She drew Vivie toward her and guided her mouth to her breasts. Catherine thought how easy it would be to take Vivie's head in her hands and twist it until her neck snapped, but it would be a mistake. She needed to kill Pope first. Vivie would be easy after that.

Pope walked toward the bed and nudged Vivie aside.

Before Vernon could lie down on top of her, Catherine sat up and kissed him. She got to her feet as his tongue thrashed wildly about inside her mouth. She fought off an impulse to gag. For a moment she considered allowing him to make love to her, then killing him afterward when he was drowsy and satisfied. But she didn't want it to go on longer than was absolutely necessary.

She stroked his penis. He groaned and kissed her harder.

He was helpless now. She turned him so that his back faced the bed.

Then she slammed her knee viciously into his groin.

Pope doubled over, gasping for breath, hands between his thighs. Vivie screamed.

Catherine spun and drove her elbow into the bridge of his nose. She could hear the sound of the bone and cartilage snapping. Pope collapsed onto the floor at the foot of the bed, blood pouring from his nostrils. Vivie was kneeling on the bed, screaming. She was no threat to Catherine now.

She turned and moved quickly for the door. Pope, still on the floor, swung his leg.

It smashed into Catherine's right ankle and caused her own legs to become entangled. She crashed to the floor, the heavy fall taking her breath away. She saw stars for a moment and tears spilled into her eyes. She feared she was about to lose consciousness.

She struggled to her hands and knees and was about to climb to her feet when Pope grabbed her ankle in a vice grip and began dragging her toward him. She rolled quickly onto her side and drove the heel of her shoe into his broken nose.

Pope screamed in agony, but his grip on her ankle seemed only to tighten.

She kicked him a second time, then a third.

Finally, he let her go.

Catherine scrambled to her feet and ran to the couch, where Pope had made her leave her handbag. She opened it and unzipped the inner compartment. The stiletto was there. She took hold of the handle and pressed the release. The blade snapped into place.

Pope was on his feet, plunging through the darkness, hands reaching out for her. Catherine spun around and lashed out wildly with the weapon. The tip of the blade tore a gash across his right shoulder.

Pope grabbed the wound with his left hand, screaming in pain as blood began to pump between his fingers. His arm was across his chest—no way to plunge the stiletto into his heart. The Abwehr had taught her another method that made her cringe just to think about. But she would have to use it now. No other choice.

Catherine took a step closer, drew back the stiletto, and rammed it through Vernon Pope's eye.

Vivie was in the corner of the bedroom, lying on the floor in a fetal position, weeping hysterically. Catherine took her by the arm, pulled her to her feet, and pushed her back against the wall.

"Please—don't hurt me."

"I'm not going to hurt you."

"Don't hurt me."

"I'm not going to hurt you."

"I promise I won't tell anyone, not even Robert. I swear."

"Nor the police?"

"I won't tell the police."

"Good. I knew I could trust you."

Catherine stroked her hair, touched her face. Vivie seemed to relax. Her body went limp and Catherine had to hold her up to keep her from collapsing onto the floor.

"What are you?" Vivie asked. "How could you do that to him?"

Catherine said nothing, just stroked Vivie's hair while her other hand gently searched for the soft spot at the bottom of the rib cage. Vivie's eyes opened wide as the stiletto slid into her heart. A cry of pain caught in her throat and came out as a low gurgle. She died quickly and quietly, blank eyes staring into Catherine's.

Catherine released her. The motion of the body sliding down the wall pulled the stiletto from her heart. Catherine looked at the human wreckage all around her, the blood. *My God, what have they made of me?* Then she fell to her knees next to Vivie's dead body and was violently sick.

She conducted the rituals of escape with surprising calmness. In the bathroom, she washed their blood from her hands, from her face, and from the blade of the stiletto. There was nothing she could do about the blood on her sweater except conceal it beneath her leather coat. She walked through the bedroom, past the body of the woman, and into the next room. She went to the window and looked down into the street. Pope, it appeared, had kept his word. There was no one outside the warehouse. They would surely find his body in the morning, though, and when they did, they would come after her. For now, at least, she was safe. She collected her handbag and, from the table, the one hundred pounds in cash she had given Pope. She took the lift down, crossed the warehouse floor, and slipped out into the night.

CHAPTER TWENTY-TWO

EAST LONDON

Detective-Superintendent Andrew Kidlington, unlike most members of his profession, avoided murder scenes when he could. A lay preacher in his local church, he had lost his taste for the more ghoulish side of his profession long ago. He had assembled a thoroughly professional team of officers and believed it best to give them free rein. He had a legendary ability to deduce more about a murder from a good file than from a visit to the crime scene, and he made certain every shred of paper generated by his department crossed his desk. But it wasn't every day that someone stuck a knife in a man like Vernon Pope. This one he had to see for himself.

The uniformed officer standing watch outside the warehouse door moved aside as Kidlington approached. "The lift is at the far end of the warehouse, sir. Take it up one level. There's another man on the landing. He'll show you the way."

Kidlington slowly crossed the warehouse floor. He was tall and angular with a head of woolly gray hair and the look of someone perpetually preparing to break bad news. As a result his men tended to tread lightly around him.

A young detective-sergeant named Meadows was waiting for him on the landing. Meadows was too flashy for Kidlington's taste and put himself about with too many women. But he was an excellent detective and had promotion written all over him.

"Pretty messy in there, sir," Meadows said.

Kidlington could taste blood in the air as Meadows led him inside. Vernon Pope's body lay on an oriental rug next to the couch. The dark circle of blood extended beyond the gray covering sheet. Kidlington, despite thirty years on the Metropolitan Police, still felt bile rising in his throat when Meadows knelt beside the body and drew back the sheet.

"Good Lord," Kidlington said, beneath his breath. He made a face and turned away for a moment to regain his composure.

"I've never seen one like this," Meadows said.

The dead body of Vernon Pope was lying naked, face up, in a pool of dried black blood. It was obvious to Kidlington that the fatal wound was struck only after a brutal struggle. There was a large ragged slash across his shoulder. The nose had been badly broken. Blood had drained from both nostrils into the mouth, which had fallen open in death, as if to issue one last scream. Then there was the eye. Kidlington had trouble looking at it. Blood and ocular fluid had drained down the side of his face. The eyeball was destroyed, the pupil no longer visible. It would take an autopsy to determine the true depth of the wound, but it appeared to be the fatal blow. Someone had shoved something through Vernon Pope's eye and into his brain.

Kidlington broke the silence. "Approximate time of death?"

"Sometime last night, perhaps early evening."

"Weapon?"

"Hard to say. Certainly not an ordinary knife. Look at the shoulder. The edges of the wound are ragged."

"Conclusion?"

"Something sharp. A screwdriver, an ice pick perhaps."

Kidlington glanced across the room. "Pope's is still on the drinks trolley. Unless your killer is walking around with his own ice pick, I doubt it was the murder weapon." Kidlington looked down at the body again. "I'd say it was a stiletto. It's a stabbing weapon, not a slashing weapon. That would account for the ragged wound on the shoulder and the clean puncture wound in the eye."

"Right, sir."

Kidlington had seen enough. He rose to his feet and gestured for Meadows to cover the body.

"The woman?"

"In the bedroom. This way, sir."

Robert Pope sat in the passenger seat of the van, pale and shaking visibly, as Dicky Dobbs drove at speed toward St. Thomas Hospital. It was Robert who had discovered the bodies of his brother and Vivie earlier that morning.

He had waited for Vernon at the East End café where they ate breakfast each morning and became alarmed when he didn't appear. He fetched Dicky from his flat and went to the warehouse. When he saw the bodies he screamed and put his foot through the glass table.

Robert and Vernon Pope were realistic men. They realized they were in a risky line of work and that one or both of them might die young. Like all siblings they fought sometimes, but Robert Pope loved his older brother more than anything else in the world. Vernon had been like a father to him when their own father, an abusive unemployed alcoholic, walked out and never came back. It was the *way* he died that had horrified Robert the most: stabbed through the eye, left on the floor naked. And Vivie, an innocent, stabbed through the heart.

It was possible the killings were the work of one of their enemies. Their operation had thrived during the war and they had branched out into new territory. But it didn't look like any gang murder he had ever seen. Robert suspected it had something to do with the woman: Catherine, or whatever her name really was. He had made an anonymous call to the police—they would have to get involved at some point—but he wouldn't rely on them to find his brother's killer. He would do it himself.

Dicky parked along the river and entered the hospital through a service door. He came out again five minutes later and walked back to the van.

Pope asked, "Was he there?"

"Yeah. He thinks he can get it for us."

"How long?"

"Twenty minutes."

Half an hour later a thin man with a pinched face dressed in an orderly's uniform emerged from the back of the hospital and trotted over to the van.

Dicky wound down the window.

"I got it, Mr. Pope," he said. "A girl in the front office gave it to me. She said it was against the rules but I sweet-talked her. Promised her a fiver. Hope you don't mind."

Dicky held out his hand and the orderly gave him a slip of paper. Dicky passed it across to Pope.

"Good work, Sammy," Pope said, looking at it. "Give him his money, Dicky."

The orderly took the money, a disappointed look on his face.

Dicky said, "What's wrong, Sammy? Ten bob, just like I promised."

"What about the fiver for the girl?"

"Consider that your overhead," Pope said.

"But Mr. Pope—"

"Sammy, you don't want to fuck with me just now."

Dicky dropped the van into gear and sped away, tires squealing.

"Where's the address?" Dicky asked.

"Islington. Move it!"

Mrs. Eunice Wright of Number 23 Norton Lane, Islington, was very much like her house: tall, narrow, mid-fifties, all Victorian sturdiness and Victorian manners. She did not know—nor would she ever know, even when the entire disagreeable episode was over—that the house had been used as a false address by an agent of German military intelligence called Catherine Blake.

For two weeks Eunice Wright had been waiting for a repairman to come look at her cracked boiler. Before the war the tenants in her well-kept boardinghouse were mostly young men, who were always willing to help when something went wrong with the pipes or the stove. Now all the young men were away in the army. Her own son, never far from her thoughts, was somewhere in North Africa. She took no pleasure in her present tenants— two old men who talked a great deal about the last war, two rather daft country girls who had fled their dreary East Midlands village for factory jobs in London. When Leonard was alive he saw to all the repairs, but Leonard had been dead for ten years.

She stood in the window of the drawing room, sipping tea. The house was quiet. The men were upstairs playing draughts. She had insisted they play without slapping the pieces so as not to wake the girls, who had just come off a night shift. Bored, she switched on the wireless and listened to the news bulletin on the BBC.

The van, when it drew to a halt in front of her house, struck her as odd. It bore no markings—no company name painted on the side—and the two men in front didn't look like any repairmen she had ever seen. The one behind the wheel was tall and thick, with close-cropped hair and a neck so enormous it looked as though his head were simply attached to his shoulders. The other one was smaller, dark-haired, and looked mad at the world. Their clothing was odd too. Instead of workman's overalls they wore suits, quite expensive suits by the look of them.

They opened the doors and got out. Eunice took note of the fact they carried no tools. Perhaps they wanted to survey the damage to her boiler before dragging all the tools inside. Just being thorough, making sure they bring only those tools that are necessary for the job. She studied them more carefully as they moved toward her front door. They looked reasonably healthy. Why weren't they in the army? She noticed the way they glanced over their shoulders into the street as they came closer, as though they were trying to make their approach unobserved. Suddenly, she wished Leonard were here.

There was nothing polite about the knock. She imagined policemen knocked that way when they thought a criminal was on the other side. Another knock, so forceful it rattled the glass of the drawing room window.

Upstairs, the game of draughts went quiet.

She went to the door. She told herself there was no reason to be afraid; they just lacked the good manners common to most English handymen. It was the war. The experienced repairmen were in the service, working on bombers or frigates. The bad ones—like the pair outside—were holding down jobs at home.

Slowly she opened the door. She wanted to ask them to be as quiet as possible so they would not wake the girls. She never got the words out. The large one—the one with no neck—shoved back the door with his forearm, then clamped his hand over her mouth. Eunice tried to scream but it seemed to die quietly in the back of her throat, making almost no audible sound.

The smaller one put his face to her ear and spoke with a serenity that only frightened her more.

"Just give us what we want, luv, and no one gets hurt," he said.

Then he pushed past her and started up the stairs.

Detective-Sergeant Meadows considered himself a minor authority on the Pope gang. He knew how they made their money—legally and illegally— and he could recognize most of the gang members by name and face. So when he heard the description of the two men who just ransacked a boardinghouse in Islington he wrapped up his business at the murder scene and headed there to see things for himself. The first description matched Richard "Dicky" Dobbs, the Popes' main muscle boy and enforcer. The other matched Robert Pope himself.

Meadows, as was his habit, paced the drawing room while Eunice Wright, sitting bolt upright in a chair, patiently recounted the story again, even though she had told it twice already. Her cup of tea had given way to a small glass of sherry. Her face bore the handprint of her assailant, and she had received a bump on the head when shoved to the floor. Otherwise, she was not seriously injured.

"And they didn't tell you who or what they were looking for?" Meadows asked, ceasing his pacing only long enough to ask the question.

"No."

"Did they call each other by name?"

"No, I don't believe so."

"Did you happen to see the plate number on the van?"

"No, but I did give a description to one of the other officers."

"It's a very common model, Mrs. Wright. I'm afraid the description alone won't be of much value to us. I'll have one of the men check with the neighbors."

"I'm sorry," she said, rubbing the back of her head.

"Are you all right?"

"He gave me a nasty bump on the head, the ruffian!"

"Perhaps you should see a doctor. I'll have one of the officers give you a lift when we're finished here."

"Thank you. That's very kind of you."

Meadows picked up his raincoat and put it on. "Did they say anything else that you can remember?"

"Well, they did say one other thing." Eunice Wright hesitated a moment, and her face colored. "The language is a little on the rough side, I'm afraid."

"I assure you I won't be offended."

"The smaller one said, 'When I find that' "—she paused, lowering her voice, embarrassed to say the words—" 'when I find that *fucking bitch* I'm going to kill her myself.' "

Meadows frowned. "You're certain of that?"

"Oh, yes. When you don't often hear language like that, it's hard to forget."

"I'll say." He handed her his card. "If you think of anything else, please don't hesitate to call. Good morning, Mrs. Wright."

"Good morning, Detective-Sergeant."

Meadows put on his hat and saw himself to the door. So they were looking for a woman. Maybe it wasn't the Popes after all. Maybe it was just two blokes looking for a girl. Maybe the similar descriptions were just coincidence. Meadows didn't believe in coincidence. He would drive back to the Popes' warehouse and see if anyone had spotted a woman hanging around there lately.

CHAPTER TWENTY-THREE

LONDON

Catherine Blake assumed that Allied officers who knew the most important secret of the war had been made aware of the threat posed by spies. Why else would Commander Peter Jordan handcuff his briefcase to his wrist for a short walk across Grosvenor Square? She also assumed that officers had been warned about approaches by women. Earlier in the war she had seen a poster outside a club frequented by British officers. It showed a luscious, big-breasted blonde in a low-cut evening gown, waiting for an officer to light her cigarette for her. Across the bottom of the poster were the words KEEP IT MUM, SHE'S NOT SO DUMB. Catherine thought it was the most ridiculous thing she had ever seen. If there were women like that—tarts who hung around clubs or parties listening for gossip and secrets—she did not know about them. She *did* suspect that such indoctrination would make Peter Jordan distrustful of a beautiful woman suddenly vying for his attention. He was also a successful, intelligent, and attractive man. He would be very discriminating in the women he chose to spend time with. The scene at the Savoy the other night was evidence of that. He had become angry with his friend Shepherd Ramsey for setting him up with a young, stupid girl. Catherine would have to make her approach very carefully.

Which explained why she was standing on a corner near the Vandyke Club with a bag of groceries in her arms.

It was shortly before six o'clock. London was shrouded in the blackout. The evening traffic gave off just enough light for her to see the doorway of the club. A few minutes later a man of medium height and build emerged. It was Peter Jordan. He paused for a moment to button his overcoat. If he kept to his evening routine he would walk the short distance to his house. If he broke his routine by flagging down a taxi, Catherine would be out of luck. She would be forced to come back again tomorrow night with her bag of groceries.

Jordan turned up the collar of his overcoat and started walking her way. Catherine Blake waited for a moment and then stepped directly in front of him.

When they collided there was the sound of paper splitting and tins of food tumbling to the pavement.

"I'm sorry, I didn't see you there. Please, let me help you up."

"No, it's my fault. I'm afraid I've misplaced my blackout torch and I've been wandering around out here lost. I feel like such a fool."

"No, it's my fault. I was trying to prove to myself that I could find my way home in the dark. Here, I have a torch. Let me turn it on."

"Do you mind turning the beam toward the pavement? I believe my rations are rolling toward Hyde Park."

"Here, take my hand."

"Thank you. By the way, you can stop shining the light in my face any time now."

"I'm sorry, you're just—"

"Just what?"

"Never mind. I don't think that sack of flour survived."

"That's all right."

"Here, let me help you pick these things up."

"I can manage. Thank you."

"No, I insist. And let me replace the flour for you. I have plenty of food at my house. My problem is I don't know what to do with it."

"Doesn't the navy feed you?"

"How did—"

"I'm afraid the uniform and the accent gave you away. Besides, only an American officer would be silly enough to intentionally walk the streets of London without using a torch. I've lived here all my life, and I still can't find my way round in the blackout."

"Please, let me replace the things you've lost."

"That's a very kind offer but it's not necessary. It was a pleasure bumping into you."

"Yes—yes, it was."

"Can you kindly point me in the direction of Brompton Road?"

"It's that way."

"Thank you very much."

She turned and started to walk away.

"Hold on a minute. I have another suggestion."

She stopped walking and turned around.

"And what might that be?"

"I wonder if you might have a drink with me sometime."

She hesitated, then said, "I'm not sure I want to drink with a frightful American who insists on walking the streets of London without a torch. But I suppose you look harmless enough. So the answer is yes."

She walked away again.

"Wait, come back. I don't even know your name."

"It's Catherine," she called. "Catherine Blake."

"I need your telephone number," Jordan said helplessly.

But she had melted into the darkness and was gone.

When Peter Jordan arrived home he went into his study, picked up the telephone, and dialed. He identified himself, and a pleasant female voice instructed him to remain on the line. A moment later he heard the English-accented voice of the man he knew only as Broome.

CHAPTER TWENTY-FOUR

KENT, ENGLAND

Alfred Vicary was being stretched to the breaking point. Despite the intense pressure to capture the spies, Vicary had kept his old caseload—the Becker network. He had considered asking to be relieved of it until after the spies had been arrested, but he quickly rejected the idea. He was the genius behind the Becker network; it was his masterpiece. It had taken countless hours to build and countless more to sustain. He would keep control of it and try to capture the spies at the same time. It was a brutal assignment. His right eye was beginning to twitch the way it did during final examinations at Cambridge, and he recognized the early symptoms of nervous exhaustion.

Partridge was the code name of a degenerate lorry driver whose routes happened to take him into restricted military zones in Suffolk, Kent, and East Sussex. He subscribed to the beliefs of Sir Oswald Mosley, the British Fascist, and he used the money he made from spying to buy whores. Sometimes he brought the girls along on his trips so they could give him sex while he drove. He liked Karl Becker because Becker always had a young girl stashed away and he was always willing to share—even with the likes of Partridge.

But Partridge existed only in Vicary's imagination, on the airwaves, and in the minds of his German control officers in Hamburg. Luftwaffe surveillance photos had detected new activity in southeast England, and Berlin had asked Becker to assess the enemy activity and report back within one week. Becker had given the assignment to Partridge—or, rather, Vicary had done it for him. It was the opportunity Vicary had been waiting for, an invitation from the Abwehr to transmit false intelligence about the ersatz First United States Army Group being assembled in southeast England.

Partridge—according to Vicary's concocted scenario—had driven through the Kent countryside at midday. In fact, Vicary had journeyed the same route that morning in the back of a department Rover. From his perch on the leather seat, wrapped in a traveling rug, Vicary imagined the signs of a military buildup an agent like Partridge might see. He might see more military lorries on the road. He might spot a group of American officers at the pub where he ate lunch. At the garage where he stopped for petrol, he might hear rumors that nearby roads were being widened. The information was trivial, the clues small, but totally consistent with Partridge's cover. Vicary couldn't allow him to discover something extraordinary like General Patton's field headquarters; his Abwehr controllers would never believe an agent like Partridge was capable of that. But Partridge's small clues, when incorporated into the rest of the deception scheme, would help paint the picture British Intelligence wanted the Germans to see—a massive Allied force waiting to strike across the Channel at Calais.

Vicary composed Partridge's message as he rode back into London. The report would be encoded into an Abwehr cipher and Karl Becker would transmit it to Hamburg late that evening from his cell. Vicary envisioned another night with little or no rest. When he finished the message, he closed his eyes and leaned his head against the window, wadding his mackintosh into a ball for a pillow. The swaying of the Rover and the low rumble of its engine lulled him into a light fitful sleep. He dreamed of France again, except this time it was Boothby—not Brendan Evans—who came to him in the field hospital. *A thousand men are dead, Alfred, and it's all your fault! If you had captured the spies they'd be alive today!* Vicary forced open his eyes and caught a glimpse of the passing countryside before drifting off again.

This time he is lying in bed on a fine spring morning twenty-five years ago, the morning he made love to Helen for the first time. He is spending the weekend at the sprawling estate owned by Helen's father. Through his bedroom window, Vicary can see the morning sun gradually casting a pink light over the hillsides. It is the day they plan to inform Helen's father of their plans to marry. He hears the gentle knock at the door—in his dream it sounds exactly the same—and turns his head just in time to spot Helen, beautiful and fresh from sleep, slipping into his room wearing nothing but a white nightgown. She climbs into bed next to him and kisses him on the mouth. *I've been thinking about you all morning, Alfred darling.* She reaches beneath the blanket, unties his pajamas, and touches him lightly with her long, beautiful fingers. *Helen, I thought you wanted to wait until we were—* She quiets him by kissing his lips. *I don't want to discuss it anymore. We have to hurry, though. If Daddy finds out he'll kill us both.* She straddles his hips, carefully, so she doesn't hurt his knee. She lifts her nightgown and guides him with her hands. There is a moment of resistance. Helen presses down harder, utters a short gasp of pain, and he is inside her. She draws his hands to her breasts. He has touched them before but only through her clothing and stiff underwear. Now they are free within her gown and they feel soft and wonderful. He tries to unbutton her gown but she won't let him. *Quickly, darling, quickly.* When it is over he wants her to stay—to hold her and do it all over again—but she quickly straightens her nightgown, kisses him, and hurries back to her room.

Vicary awakened in the eastern suburbs of London, a slight smile on his face. He had not found the first time with Helen disappointing, it was just *different* from what he expected. The sex of his youthful fantasies always involved women with enormous breasts who screamed and cried with ecstasy. But with Helen it had been slow and gentle, and instead of screaming she smiled and kissed him tenderly. It was not passionate but it was perfect. And it was perfect because he loved her desperately.

It was that way with Alice Simpson too, but for other reasons. Vicary was fond of her; he even supposed he might be in love with her, whatever that meant. More than anything else he enjoyed her company. She was intelligent and witty and, like Helen, a touch irreverent. She taught literature at a minor school for girls and wrote mediocre plays about rich people who always seemed to have cathartic, life-altering discourse while sipping pale sherry and Earl Grey tea in a handsomely furnished drawing room. She also wrote romantic novels under a pseudonym, which Vicary, while not a fan of the genre, thought were rather good. Once Lillian Walford, his secretary at University College, caught him reading one of Alice Simpson's books. The next day she brought him a stack of Barbara Cartland novels. Vicary was mortified. The characters in Alice's novels, when they made love, all heard waves crashing and felt the heavens raining down on them. In real life she was shy and tender and somewhat ticklish, and she always insisted on making love in the dark. More than once Vicary closed his eyes and saw the image of Helen in her white nightgown bathed in morning sunlight.

His relationship with Alice Simpson had lapsed with the war. They still spoke at least once a week. She had lost her flat early in the blitz and stayed in Vicary's house in Chelsea for a time. They saw each other occasionally for dinner, but it had been months since they had made love. He realized suddenly that this was the first time Alice Simpson had entered his thoughts since Edward Kenton, walking across the drive of Matilda's cottage, had spoken Helen's name.

HAM COMMON, SURREY

The large, rather ugly three-story Victorian mansion was surrounded by a pair of perimeter fences and a picket to shield it from view from the outside world. Nissen huts had been erected around the ten-acre grounds to house most of the staff. Once it had been known as Latchmere House, an asylum and recuperation center for victims of shellshock during the First War. But in 1939 it was converted into MI5's main interrogation and incarceration center and assigned the military designation Camp 020.

The room into which Vicary was shown smelled of mildew, disinfectant, and vaguely of boiled cabbage. There was no place to hang his coat—the Intelligence Corps guards went to great lengths to guard against suicide—so he kept it on. Besides, the place was like a medieval dungeon: cold, damp, a breeding ground for bronchial infection. The room had one feature that made it highly functional—a tiny arrow slit of a window through which an aerial had been strung. Vicary opened the lid on the Abwehr-issue suitcase radio he had brought with him, the very one he had seized from Becker in 1940. He attached the aerial and switched on the power. The lights glowed yellow as Vicary selected the proper frequency.

He yawned and stretched. It was 11:45 P.M. Becker was scheduled to send his message at midnight. He thought, Damn, why does the Abwehr always choose such godawful hours for their agents to send messages?

Karl Becker was a liar, a thief, and a sexual deviant—a man without morals or loyalty. Yet he could be charming and intelligent, and over the years Becker and Vicary had developed something approaching a professional friendship. He came into the room, sandwiched between a pair of hulking guards, hands cuffed. The guards removed the cuffs and wordlessly went out. Becker smiled and stuck out his hand. Vicary shook it; it was cool as cellar limestone.

There was a small table of rough-hewn wood and a pair of battered old chairs. Vicary and Becker sat down on opposite sides of the table, as if facing off for a game of chess. The edges of the table had been burned black by unattended cigarettes. Vicary handed Becker a small package and, like a child, he opened it right away. In it were a half dozen packets of cigarettes and a box of Swiss chocolates.

Becker looked at the things, then at Vicary. "Cigarettes and chocolate—you're not here to seduce me, are you, Alfred?" Becker managed a small chuckle but prison life had changed him. His lustrous French suits had been replaced with a dour gray overall, neatly pressed and surprisingly well fitted through the shoulders. Officially he was on a suicide watch—which Vicary thought was absurd—and he wore flimsy canvas slippers with no laces. His skin, once deeply tanned, had faded to a dungeon white. His taut little body had assumed a sudden discipline imposed by small places; gone were the flailing arms and abandoned laughter that Vicary had seen in the old surveillance photographs. He sat ramrod straight, as though someone were holding a gun to his back, and arranged the chocolate, cigarettes, and matches as if he were laying down a boundary across which Vicary was not to venture.

Becker opened a packet of cigarettes and tapped out two of them, giving one to Vicary and keeping one for himself. He struck a match and held it out to Vicary before lighting his own cigarette. They sat in silence for a while, each studying his own spot on the cell wall—old chums who have told every story they know and now are content just to be in each other's presence. Becker savored his cigarette, rolling the smoke on his tongue like an excellent bordeaux before blowing it in a slender stream at the low stone ceiling. In the tiny chamber, smoke gathered overhead like storm clouds.

"Please send my love to Harry," Becker finally said.

"I will."

"He's a good man—a bit on the dogged side, like all policemen. But he's not a bad sort."

"I'd be lost without him."

"And how's brother Boothby?"

Vicary let out a long breath. "As ever."

"We all have our Nazis, Alfred."

"We're thinking of sending him over to the other side."

Becker, laughing, used the stub of his cigarette to light another. "I see you've brought my radio," he said. "What heroic deed have I done for the Third Reich now?"

"You've broken into Number Ten and stolen all the prime minister's private papers."

Becker threw his head back and emitted a short, brutal burst of laughter. "I hope I'm demanding more money from those cheap bastards! And not the counterfeit that got me into trouble last time."

"Of course."

Becker looked at the radio, then at Vicary. "In the good old days you would have left a revolver on the table and let me do the deed myself. Now you bring a radio made by some fine, upstanding German company and let me kill myself a dot and a dash at a time."

"It is a terrible world in which we live, Karl. But no one forced you to become a spy."

"Better than the Wehrmacht," Becker said. "I'm an old man, like you, Alfred. I would be conscripted and sent off to the East to fight the fucking Ivans. No, thank you. I'll wait out the war right here in my pleasant little English sanitarium."

Vicary glanced at his watch—ten minutes until Becker was scheduled to go on the air. He reached inside his pocket and withdrew the coded message Becker was to send. Then he took out the photograph taken from the passport of the Dutch woman named Christa Kunst. A look of distant recollection flashed across Becker's face, then dissipated.

"You know who she is, don't you, Karl."

"You've found Anna," he said, smiling. "Well done, Alfred. Well done indeed. Bravo!"

Vicary sat like a man straining to hear distant music, hands folded on the table, making no notes. He knew it was best to ask as few questions as possible, best to allow Becker to lead him where he wanted. Like a deer stalker, Vicary made no movements, stayed downwind. His cigarette, untouched, burned to gray dust in the metal ashtray at his elbow. Through the arrow-slit window he could hear an evening rainstorm smacking on the exercise yard. As always Becker started the story somewhere in the middle and with himself. He held his body with a regimental stillness for a time, but as the story built he began waving his arms and using his precise little fingers to weave a tapestry before Vicary's eyes. Like all Becker monologues there were blind alleys and detours for accounts of bravery, moneymaking, and sexual conquest. At times he would lapse into a long speculative silence; at other times he would tell it so quickly he would be overcome with a fit of coughing. "It's the goddamned damp in my cell," he said by way of explanation. "That's one thing you English do very well.

"People like me, they get almost no training," he said. "Oh, sure, a few lectures by some idiots in Berlin who've never seen England except on a map. This is how you estimate the size of an army, they tell you. This is how you use your radio. This is how you bite into your suicide capsule in the highly unlikely event that MI-Five kicks down your door. Then they send you off to England in a boat or a plane to win the war for the Führer."

He paused to light another cigarette and open the box of chocolates. "I was lucky. I was posing as a legal. I came by plane with a Swiss passport. You know what they did to another fellow? Put him ashore in Sussex in a rubber raft. But the U-boat left France without special unmarked Abwehr rafts. They had to use one of the U-boat's life rafts with a Kriegsmarine insignia on it. Can you believe such a thing?"

Vicary could believe it; the Abwehr was horrendously slipshod with the way it prepared and inserted its agents into England. He remembered the boy he pulled off the Cornish beach in September 1940. The Special Branch men who searched him found in his pocket a packet of matches from a popular Berlin nightclub. Then there was the case of Gösta Caroli, a Swedish citizen who parachuted into Northamptonshire near the village of Denton. He was discovered by an Irish farmhand named Paddy Daly, sleeping beneath a hedge. He wore a decent suit of gray flannel and a tie knotted continental style. Caroli admitted he had parachuted into England and handed over his automatic pistol and three hundred pounds in cash. The local authorities passed him on to MI5 and he was promptly taken to Camp 020.

Becker popped one of the chocolates into his mouth and held the box out to Vicary. "You British took the espionage business more seriously than we Germans. You had to because you were weak. You had to use deception and trickery to mask your frailty. But now you've got the Abwehr by the balls."

"But there were others they took more care with," Vicary said.

"Yes, there were others."

"Different kinds of agents."

"Absolutely," Becker said as he dug out another chocolate. "These are delicious, Alfred. Are you sure you won't have one?"

Becker was a surprisingly precise keyer—precise and very fast. Vicary attributed this to the fact that he was a classically trained violinist before his life took whatever unfortunate turn it was that landed him where he was now. Vicary listened on a spare pair of headphones as Becker identified himself and waited for the confirmation signal from the operator in Hamburg. As always it gave Vicary a brief chill. He took enormous pleasure from the fact that he was deceiving the enemy—lying to him so skillfully. He enjoyed the intimate contact: being able to hear the enemy's voice, even if it was just an electronic bleep amid a vapor of atmospheric hiss. Vicary imagined how appalled he would feel if *he* were the one being deceived. For some reason he found himself thinking of Helen.

The Hamburg operator ordered Becker to proceed. Becker looked down at Vicary's message and quickly tapped it out. When he was finished he waited for Hamburg to confirm, then signed off. Vicary slipped off his headphones and shut off the radio. Becker would sulk for a while—he always did after sending one of Vicary's Double Cross messages—like a man who feels the hot flash of guilt after copulating with his mistress and wishes to be alone with his troubled thoughts. Vicary always suspected Becker was ashamed of betraying his own service—that his rantings about Abwehr bumbling and incompetence were just an attempt to conceal his own guilt over being a failure and a coward. Not that he had much of a choice; the first time Becker refused to send one of Vicary's messages he would be marched off to Wandsworth Prison for an appointment with the hangman.

Vicary feared he had lost him. Becker smoked, and he ate a few more chocolates without offering any to Vicary. Vicary slowly packed away the radio.

"I saw her once in Berlin," Becker said suddenly. "She was immediately separated from the rest of us mere mortals. I don't want you to quote me on this, Alfred—I'm just going to tell you what I heard. The rumors, the talk. If it doesn't turn out to be totally accurate I don't want Stephens to come in here and start throwing me off the fucking walls."

Vicary nodded sympathetically. Stephens was Colonel R.W.G. Stephens, the commandant of Camp 020, better known as Tin-Eye. A former Indian Army officer, Stephens was monocled, maniacal, and always dressed immaculately in a forage cap and uniform of the Peshawar Rifles. He was half German and spoke the language fluently. He was also detested by the prisoners and MI5 staff alike. Once he had given Vicary a thorough public dressing down because he arrived five minutes late for an interrogation. Even senior staff like Boothby were not immune to his tirades and fits of vile temper.

"You have my word, Karl," Vicary said, taking his place at the table again.

"They said her name was Anna Steiner—that her father was some sort of aristocrat. Prussian, rich bastard, dueling scar on the cheek, dabbled in diplomacy. You know the type, don't you?" Becker didn't wait for an answer. "Christ, she was beautiful. Tall as hell. Spoke perfectly accented British English. The rumors said she had an English mother. That she was living in Spain the summer of thirty-six, fucking some Spanish Fascist bastard named Romero. Turns out Señor Romero was a talent spotter for the Abwehr. He calls Berlin, collects a finder's fee, and hands her over. The Abwehr puts the screws to her. They tell lovely Anna that her Fatherland needs her; if she doesn't cooperate, Papa von Steiner gets shipped off to a concentration camp."

"Who was her control officer?"

"I don't know his name. Sour-looking bastard. Smart, like you, only ruthless."

"Was his name Vogel?"

"I don't know—could be."

"You never saw her again?"

"No, just that once."

"So what happened to her?"

Becker was overcome by another fit of coughing that a fresh cigarette seemed to cure.

"I'm telling you what I *heard,* not what I *know.* You understand the difference?"

"I understand the difference."

"We heard there was a camp, somewhere in the mountains south of Munich. Very isolated, all surrounding roads closed. Hell for the locals. According to the rumors it was a place where they sent a few special agents—the ones they planned to bury deep."

"She was one of those agents?"

"Yes, Alfred. We've covered that ground already. Stay with me, please." Becker was digging through the chocolates again. "It was as if an English village had dropped from the sky and landed in the middle of Bavaria. There was a pub, a small hotel, cottages, even an Anglican church. Each agent was assigned to a cottage for a minimum stay of six months. In the morning they read London newspapers at the café over tea and buns. They did their shopping in English and listened to popular radio programs of the day on the BBC. Me, I never heard *It's That Man Again* until I came to London."

"Go on."

"They had special codes and special rendezvous procedures. They were given more weapons training. Silent killing. At night they even sent the boys English-speaking whores so they could fuck in English."

"And what about the woman?"

"They say she was fucking her control officer—what did you say his name was, Vogel? Again, it was only a rumor."

"Did you ever meet her in Britain?"

"No."

"I want the truth, Karl!" Vicary snapped, so loudly that one of the guards stuck his head inside the door to make sure there was no problem.

"I'm telling you the truth! Jesus Christ, you're Alfred Vicary one minute and Heinrich Himmler the next. I never saw her again."

Vicary switched to German. He didn't want the guards eavesdropping on the conversation.

"Do you know her cover name?"

"No." Becker responded in the same language.

"Do you know her address?"

"No."

"Do you know if she's operating in London?"

"She could be operating on the moon for all I know."

Vicary exhaled loudly in frustration. It was all interesting information but, like the discovery of Beatrice Pymm's murder, it put him no closer to his quarry. "Have you told me everything you know about her, Karl?"

Becker smiled. "She's supposed to be an incredible fuck." Becker noticed the color in Vicary's cheeks. "I'm sorry, Alfred. Jesus Christ, I forget what a prude you are sometimes."

Still speaking in German, Vicary said, "Why haven't you told us this before—the business about the special agents?"

"But I have, Alfred old man."

"Who have you told? You've never told me."

"I told Boothby."

Vicary felt blood streaming to his face, and his heart began to beat furiously. Boothby? Why in the world would Boothby be interrogating Karl Becker? And why would he do it without Vicary being present? Becker was *his* agent. Vicary arrested him, Vicary turned him, Vicary ran him.

His face calm, Vicary said, "When did you tell Boothby?"

"I don't know. It's hard to keep track of time in here. A couple of months ago. September maybe. No, maybe it was October. Yes, I believe October."

"What did you tell him, exactly?"

"I told him about the agents, I told him about the camp."

"Did you tell him about the woman?"

"Yes, Alfred, I told him everything. He's a vicious bastard. I don't like him. I'd watch out for him if I were you."

"Was there anyone with him?"

"Yes, tall fellow. Handsome, like a film star. Blond, blue eyes. A real German superman. Thin, though, skinny as a stick."

"Did the stick have a name?"

Becker threw his head back and made a show of searching his memory.

"Christ, it was a funny name. A tool or something." Becker pinched the bridge of his nose. "No, something you use in the house. Mop? Bucket? No, Broome! That's it, Broome! Imagine that—the guy looks like a fucking stick and calls himself Broome. You English have a marvelous sense of humor sometimes."

Vicary had collected the suitcase radio and was rapping his knuckle against the thick door.

"Why don't you leave the radio, Alfred. It gets lonely here sometimes."

"Sorry, Karl."

The door opened and Vicary stepped through.

"Listen, Alfred, the cigarettes and chocolate were wonderful, but next time bring a girl, will you?"

Vicary went to the chief guard's office and asked for the logbooks for October and November. It took him a few moments, but he found the entry he was looking for.

DATE: 5-10-43
PRISONER: *Becker, K.*
NUMBER OF VISITORS: *2*
NAMES/DEPT: *No thank you.*

CHAPTER TWENTY-FIVE

BERLIN

"My God, but it's cold this morning," said Brigadeführer Walter Schellenberg.

"At least you still have a roof over your head," replied Admiral Wilhelm Canaris. "The Halifaxes and Lancasters had quite a time last night. Hundreds dead, thousands homeless. So much for the invulnerability of our illustrious thousand-year Reich."

Canaris looked to Schellenberg for reaction. As always, he was struck by how young the man was. At just thirty-three he was head of Section VI of the *Sicherheitsdienst*—better known as the SD—the intelligence and security service of the SS. Section VI was responsible for gathering intelligence on the Reich's enemies in foreign countries, an assignment very similar to that of the Abwehr. As a result, the two men were locked in a desperate competition.

They were a mismatched pair: the short, laconic, white-haired old admiral who spoke with a slight lisp; the handsome, energetic, and thoroughly ruthless young brigadeführer. The son of a Saarland piano maker, Schellenberg was personally recruited to the Nazi security apparatus by Reinhard Heydrich, the chief of the SD who was assassinated by Czechoslovakian resistance fighters in May 1942. One of the Nazi Party's bright lights, Schellenberg thrived in its dangerous, paranoid atmosphere. His cathedral-like office was thoroughly bugged and he had machine guns built into his desk, giving him the ability to kill a threatening visitor with the press of a button. On those rare occasions when he permitted himself to relax, Schellenberg liked to spend time with his elaborate collection of pornography. Once, he displayed the photographs to Canaris the way a man might show snapshots of his family, boasting about the pictures he choreographed himself to satisfy his own bizarre sexual appetites. On his hand Schellenberg wore a ring with a blue stone, beneath which lay a capsule of cyanide. He had also been fitted with a false tooth containing a lethal measure of the poison.

Now, Schellenberg had just two goals: destroy Canaris and the Abwehr and bring Adolf Hitler the most important secret of the war, the time and place of the Anglo-American invasion of France. Schellenberg had nothing but disdain for the Abwehr and the cluster of old officers surrounding Canaris, whom he derisively referred to as Santa Clauses. Canaris knew perfectly well Schellenberg was gunning for him, yet between the two there existed an uneasy truce. Schellenberg treated the old admiral with deference and respect; Canaris genuinely admired the brash, brilliant young officer and enjoyed his company.

Which was why they began most mornings the same way, riding side by side on horseback through the Tiergarten. It gave each man a chance to check up on what the other was doing—to spar, to probe for weakness. Canaris liked their rides for one other reason. He knew that for at least one hour each morning the young general was not actively plotting his demise.

"There you go again, Herr Admiral," Schellenberg said. "Always looking at the dark side of things. I suppose that makes you a cynic, doesn't it."

"I'm not a cynic, Herr Brigadeführer. I'm a skeptic. There's an important difference."

Schellenberg laughed. "That's the difference between us in the *Sicherheitsdienst* and you old-school types in the Abwehr. We see nothing but endless possibility. You see nothing but danger. We are bold, not afraid to take risks. You prefer to have your head in the sand—no offense, Herr Admiral."

"None taken, my young friend. You are entitled to your opinion, however misinformed it might be."

Canaris's horse threw back its head and snorted. The breath froze into a cloud, then drifted away on the gentle morning wind. Canaris looked around him at the devastation of the Tiergarten. Most of the lime and chestnut trees were gone, burned by Allied incendiary bombs. Ahead of them, on the pathway, was a bomb crater the size of a *Kübelwagen*. Thousands more were scattered throughout the park. Canaris, tugging on the reins, led his horse around it. A pair of Schellenberg's security men trailed softly after them on foot. Another walked a few feet in front of them, head slowly wheeling from side to side. Canaris knew there were more he could not see, even with his well-trained eye.

"Something very interesting landed on my desk yesterday evening," Schellenberg said.

"Oh, really? What was her name?"

Schellenberg, laughing, spurred the horse into a light trot.

"I have a source in London. He did some work for the NKVD a long time ago, including recruiting an Oxford student who is now an officer inside MI-Five. He still talks to the man from time to time, and he hears things. He passes those things on to me. The MI-Five officer is a Russian agent, but I share in the harvest, so to speak."

"Remarkable," Canaris said dryly.

"Churchill and Roosevelt don't trust Stalin. They keep him in the dark. They have refused to tell him anything about the time and place of the invasion. They think Stalin might leak the secret to us so the Allies will be destroyed in France. With the British and Americans out of the fight, Stalin would try to finish us off alone and grab all of Europe for himself."

"I've heard that theory. I'm not sure I put much stock in it."

"In any case, my agent says MI-Five is in crisis. He says your man Vogel has mounted an operation that has scared the pants off them. The investigation is being led by a case officer named Vicary. Ever heard of him?"

"Alfred Vicary," Canaris said. "A former professor at University College in London."

"Very impressive," Schellenberg said genuinely.

"Part of being an effective intelligence officer is knowing your opponent, Herr Brigadeführer." Canaris hesitated, allowing time for Schellenberg to absorb the jab. "I'm glad Kurt is giving them a run for their money."

"The situation is so tense Vicary has met with Churchill personally to update him on the progress of his investigation."

"That's not so surprising, Herr Brigadeführer. Vicary and Churchill are old friends." Canaris cast a sideways glance at Schellenberg to see if his face registered any trace of surprise. Their conversations often turned into point-scoring contests, each man trying to surprise the other with tidbits of intelligence. "Vicary is a well-known historian. I've read his work. I'm surprised you haven't. He has a keen mind. He thinks like Churchill. He was warning the world about you and your friends long before anyone took notice."

"So what is Vogel up to? Perhaps the SD can be of some assistance."

Canaris permitted himself a rare but short burst of laughter.

"Please, Brigadeführer Schellenberg. If you're going to be so transparent, these morning rides will lose their appeal very quickly. Besides, if you want to know what Vogel is doing, just ask the chicken farmer. I know he's bugged our telephones and planted his spies inside Tirpitz Ufer."

"Interesting you should say that. I raised that very question with Reichs-führer Himmler over dinner last night. It seems Vogel is very careful. Very secretive. I hear he doesn't even keep his files in the Abwehr central registry."

"Vogel is a true paranoid and extremely cautious. He keeps everything in his office. And I wouldn't think about trying to get rough with him. He has an assistant named Werner Ulbricht who's seen the worst of this war. The man's always cleaning his Lugers. Even *I* don't go near Vogel's office."

Schellenberg pulled back on the reins until his horse came to a stop. The morning was still and quiet. In the distance came the growl of the morning's first traffic along the Wilhelmstrasse.

"Vogel is the kind of man we like in the SD—intelligent, driven."

"There's only one problem," Canaris said. "Vogel's a human being. He has a heart and a conscience. Something tells me he wouldn't fit in with your crowd."

"Why don't you let the two of us meet? Perhaps we can think of some way to pool our resources for the good of the Reich. There's no reason for the SD and the Abwehr to be always at each other's throats, like this."

Canaris smiled. "We're at each other's throats, Brigadeführer Schellenberg, because you are convinced I am a traitor to the Reich and because you tried to have me arrested."

Which was true. Schellenberg had assembled a file containing dozens of allegations of treason committed by Canaris. In 1942 he gave the file to Heinrich Himmler, but Himmler took no action. Canaris kept dossiers too, and Schellenberg suspected the Abwehr file on Himmler contained material the Reichsführer would rather not be made public.

"That was a long time ago, Herr Admiral. It's in the past."

Canaris jabbed the heel of his riding boot into his horse and they started moving again. The stables appeared in the distance.

"May I be so bold as to offer an interpretation of your offer to be of assistance, Brigadeführer Schellenberg?"

"Of course."

"You would like to be a part of this operation for one of two reasons. Reason one, you could sabotage the operation in order to further lower the reputation of the Abwehr. Or, reason two, you could steal Vogel's intelligence and claim all the credit and glory for yourself."

Schellenberg slowly shook his head. "This mistrust between us, such a pity. So distressing."

"Yes, isn't it."

They rode together into the stables and dismounted. A pair of stableboys scampered out and led the horses away.

"A pleasure as always," Canaris said. "Shall we take breakfast together?"

"I'd love to, but I'm afraid duty calls."

"Oh?"

"A meeting with Himmler and Hitler, eight o'clock sharp."

"Lucky you. What's the topic?"

Walter Schellenberg smiled and laid his gloved hand on the older man's shoulder.

"Wouldn't you like to know."

"How was the Old Fox this morning?" Adolf Hitler said as Walter Schellenberg walked through the door at precisely eight o'clock. Himmler was there, sitting on the overstuffed sofa sipping coffee. It was the image Schellenberg liked to present to his superiors—too busy to arrive for a meeting early and engage in small talk, disciplined enough to be prompt.

"As cagey as ever," Schellenberg said, pouring himself a cup of the steaming coffee. There was a jug with real milk. Even the staff at the SD had trouble securing a steady supply these days. "He refused to tell me anything about Vogel's operation. He claims he knows nothing about it. He has permitted Vogel to work under extremely secretive circumstances, allowing himself to be kept in the dark about the details."

"Perhaps it's better that way," Himmler said, his face impassive, his voice betraying no emotion whatsoever. "The less the good admiral knows, the less he can betray to the enemy."

"I've done some investigating of my own," Schellenberg said. "I know that Vogel has sent at least one new agent into England. He had to use the Luftwaffe for the drop, and the pilot who flew the mission was very cooperative." Schellenberg opened his briefcase and withdrew two copies of the same file, handing one to Hitler and the other to Himmler. "The agent's name is Horst Neumann. The Reichsführer may remember that business in Paris sometime back. An SS man was killed in a bar in Paris. Neumann was the man involved in that."

Himmler let the file fall from his hands onto the coffee table around which they were seated. "For the Abwehr to use such a man is a direct slap in the face to the SS and the memory of the man he murdered! It shows Vogel's contempt for the party and the Führer."

Hitler was still reading the file and seemed genuinely interested in it.

"Perhaps Neumann is simply the right man for the job, Herr Reichsführer. Look at his dossier: born in England, decorated member of the *Fallschirm-jäger*, Knight's Cross, Oak Leaves. On paper a very remarkable man."

The Führer was more lucid and reasonable than Schellenberg had seen him in some time.

"I agree," Schellenberg said. "Except for the one blight on his record, Neumann appears to be an extraordinary soldier."

Himmler cast a cadaverous glance at Schellenberg. He didn't appreciate being contradicted in front of the Führer, no matter how brilliant Schellenberg might be.

"Perhaps we should make our move against Canaris now," Himmler said. "Remove him, place Brigadeführer Schellenberg in charge, and combine the Abwehr and the SD into one powerful intelligence agency. That way Brigadeführer Schellenberg can oversee Vogel's operation personally. Things seem to have a way of going awry where Admiral Canaris is involved."

Again, Hitler disagreed with his most trusted aide. "If Schellenberg's Russian friend is correct, this man Vogel seems to have the British on the run. To step in now would be a mistake. No, Herr Reichsführer, Canaris remains in place for the time being. Perhaps he's doing something right for a change."

Hitler stood up.

"Now, if you gentlemen will excuse me, I have other matters that demand my attention."

Two Mercedes staff cars were waiting at the curbside, engines running. There was an awkward moment while deciding whose car to take, but Schellenberg quietly relented and climbed in the back of Himmler's. He felt vulnerable when he wasn't surrounded by his security men, even when he was with Himmler. During the short drive, Schellenberg's armored Mercedes never strayed more than a few feet from the rear bumper of Himmler's limousine.

"An impressive performance as always, Herr Brigadeführer," Himmler said. Schellenberg knew his superior well enough to realize the remark was not meant as a compliment. Himmler, the second most powerful man in Germany, was peeved at being contradicted in front of the Führer.

"Thank you, Herr Reichsführer."

"The Führer wants the secret of the invasion so badly it is clouding his judgment," Himmler said matter-of-factly. "It is our job to protect him. Do you understand what I'm saying to you, Herr Brigadeführer?"

"Absolutely."

"I want to know what Vogel is playing at. If the Führer won't let us do it from the inside, we'll have to do it from the outside. Put Vogel and his assistant Ulbricht under twenty-four-hour surveillance. Use every means at your disposal to penetrate Tirpitz Ufer. Also, find some way of getting a man into the radio center at Hamburg. Vogel has to communicate with his agents. I want someone listening to what's being said."

"Yes, Herr Reichsführer."

"And Walter, don't look so glum. We'll get our hands around the Abwehr soon enough. Don't worry. It will be all yours."

"Thank you, Herr Reichsführer."

"Unless, of course, you ever contradict me in front of the Führer again."

Himmler rapped on the glass partition so softly it was almost inaudible. The car pulled to the side of the curb, as did Schellenberg's, directly behind them. The young general sat motionless until one of his security men appeared at the door to accompany him on the ten-foot walk back to his own car.

CHAPTER TWENTY-SIX

LONDON

Catherine Blake was by now thoroughly regretting her decision to go to the Popes for help. Yes, they had given her a meticulous account of Peter Jordan's life in London. But it had come at a very steep price. She had been threatened with extortion, drawn into a bizarre sexual game, and been forced to murder two people. Now the police were involved. The murder of a prominent black marketeer and underworld figure like Vernon Pope was big news in all the London newspapers. The police had misled the newspapermen, though—they said the victims had been found with their throats slit, not stabbed through the eye and through the heart. They were obviously trying to filter out crank leads from real ones. Or was MI5 already involved? According to the newspapers, the police wanted to question Robert Pope but had been unable to find him. Catherine could be of assistance. Pope was sitting twenty feet from her in the Savoy bar, angrily nursing a whisky.

Why was Pope there? Catherine thought she knew the answer. Pope was there because he suspected Catherine was involved in his brother's murder. Finding her would not be difficult for him. Pope knew Catherine was looking for Peter Jordan. All he had to do was go to the places frequented by Peter Jordan, and there was a good chance Catherine would appear.

She turned her back to him. She was not afraid of Robert Pope; he was more a nuisance than a threat. As long as she remained in full view he would be reluctant to take action against her. Catherine had expected this. As a precaution she had started carrying her pistol at all times. It was necessary but annoying. She had to carry a larger handbag to conceal the weapon. It was heavy and banged against her hip when she walked. The gun, ironically, was also a threat to her security. Try explaining to a London police officer why you're carrying a German-made Mauser pistol equipped with a silencer.

Deciding whether to kill Robert Pope was not Catherine Blake's biggest worry, for at that moment Peter Jordan walked into the bar of the Savoy along with Shepherd Ramsey.

She wondered which man would make the first move. Things were about to get interesting.

"I'll say one good thing about this war," Shepherd Ramsey said, as he and Peter Jordan sat down at a corner table. "It's done wonders for my net worth. While I've been over here playing hero, my stocks have been soaring. I've made more money during the past six months than I did for ten years working at Dad's insurance company."

"Why don't you tell old Dad to shove off?"

"He'd be lost without me."

Shepherd signaled the waiter and ordered a martini. Jordan ordered a double scotch.

"Tough day at the office, honey?"

"Brutal."

"The rumor mill says you're working on a diabolical new secret weapon."

"I'm an engineer, Shep. I build bridges and roads."

"Any idiot could do that. You're not over here building a goddamned highway."

"No, I'm not."

"So when are you going to tell me what you're working on?"

"I can't. You know I can't."

"It's just me, old Shep. You can tell me anything."

"I'd love to, Shepherd, but if I told you I'd have to kill you, and then Sally would be a widow and Kippy would have no father."

"Kippy's in trouble at Buckley again. Goddamned kid gets in more trouble than I did."

"Now that's saying something."

"The headmaster's threatening to throw him out. Sally had to go over the other day and listen to a lecture about how Kippy needs a strong male influence in his life."

"I never knew he had one."

"Very funny, asshole. Sally's having trouble with the car. Says the thing needs tires but she can't buy new ones because of rationing. Says they couldn't open up the Oyster Bay house for Christmas this year because there was no fuel oil to heat the damned thing."

Shepherd noticed Jordan was studying his drink.

"I'm sorry, Peter, am I boring you?"

"No more than usual."

"I just thought some news from home might cheer you up."

"Who says I need cheering up?"

"Peter Jordan, I haven't seen that look on your face in a very long time. Who is she?"

"I have no idea."

"Would you like to explain that?"

"I bumped into her in the blackout, literally. Knocked her groceries out of her arms. It was very embarrassing. But there was something about her."

"Did you get her telephone number?"

"No."

"How about a name?"

"Yes, I got a name."

"Well, that's something. Jesus Christ! I'd say you're a little out of practice. Tell me how she looked."

Peter Jordan told him: tall, brown hair falling across her shoulders, a wide mouth, beautiful cheekbones, and the most spectacular eyes he had ever seen.

"That's interesting," Shepherd said.

"Why?"

"Because *that* woman is standing right over there."

Men in uniform generally made Catherine Blake nervous. But as Peter Jordan crossed the bar toward her she thought she had never seen a man look quite so handsome as he did in his dark blue American naval uniform. He was a strikingly attractive man—she had not noticed how attractive the previous evening. His uniform jacket fitted him perfectly through his square shoulders and chest, as though it had been cut for him by a tailor in Manhattan. He was trim at the waist, and his walk had a smooth confidence about it that only self-possessed, successful men have. His hair was dark, nearly black, and in striking contrast to his pale complexion. His eyes were a distracting shade of green—pale green, like a cat's—his mouth soft and sensuous. It broke into an easy smile when he noticed she was looking at him.

"I believe I bumped into you in the blackout last night," he said, and stuck out his hand. "My name is Peter Jordan."

She took his hand, then absently allowed her fingernails to trail across the palm of his hand when she released her grip.

"My name is Catherine Blake," she said.

"Yes, I remember. You look as though you're waiting for someone."

"I am, but it appears he's stood me up."

"Well, I'd say he's a damned fool then."

"He's just an old friend, actually."

"Can I buy you that drink now?" Jordan asked.

Catherine looked at Jordan and smiled; then she glanced across the bar at Robert Pope, who was watching them intently.

"Actually, I would love to go somewhere a little more quiet to talk. Do you still have all that food at your house?"

"A couple of eggs, some cheese, maybe a can of tomatoes. And lots of wine."

"Sounds like the makings of a wonderful omelet to me."

"Let me get my coat."

Robert Pope, standing at the bar, watched them as they slipped through the crowd and into the salon. He calmly finished his drink, waited a few seconds, then left the bar and trailed quietly after them. Outside the hotel, they were shown into a cab by the doorman. Pope, walking quickly across the street, watched the cab drive away. Dicky Dobbs was sitting behind the wheel of the van. He started the motor as Pope climbed inside. The van slipped away from the curb, into the evening traffic. No need to rush, Pope told Dicky. He knew where they were headed. He leaned back and closed his eyes for a few minutes as Dicky drove westward toward Jordan's town house in Kensington.

During the taxi ride to Peter Jordan's house, Catherine Blake realized quite suddenly that she was nervous. It was not because a man who possessed the most important secret of the war was sitting next to her. She was just not very good at this—the rituals of courtship and dating. For the first time in a very long time she thought about her appearance. She knew she was an attractive woman—a beautiful woman. She knew most men desired her. But during her time in Britain she had gone to great lengths to conceal her appearance, to blend in. She had adopted the look of an aggrieved war widow: heavy dark stockings that hid the shape of her long legs, poor-fitting skirts that masked the curve of her hips, chunky mannish sweaters that concealed her rounded breasts. Tonight, she was dressed in a striking gown she had bought before the war, appropriate for drinks at the Savoy. Even so, for the first time in her life, Catherine worried about whether she was pretty enough.

Something else was bothering Catherine. Why did it take circumstances like these for her finally to be with a man like Peter Jordan? He was intelligent and attractive and successful and—well, apparently *normal*. Most of the other men Catherine had known would be behaving very differently by now. She remembered the first time with Maria Romero's father, Emilio. He had not bothered with flowers or romance; he barely even kissed her. He just pushed her down onto the bed and fucked her. And Catherine had not minded. In fact, she rather liked it that way. Sex was not something to be done out of love and respect. She didn't even enjoy the conquest. For Catherine it was an act of pure physical gratification. Emilio Romero understood; unfortunately, Emilio understood many things about her.

She had given up long ago on the idea of falling in love, getting married, and having children. Her obsessive independence and deeply ingrained mistrust of people would never allow her to make the emotional commitment to a marriage; her selfishness and self-indulgence would never permit her to care for a child. She never felt safe with a man unless she was in total control, emotionally and physically. These feelings manifested themselves in the act of sex itself. Catherine had discovered long ago that she was incapable of having an orgasm unless she was on top.

She had formed an image of the kind of life she wanted for herself. When the war was over she would go somewhere warm—the Costa del Sol, the south of France, Italy perhaps—and buy herself a small villa overlooking the sea. She would live alone and cut off her hair and lie on the beach until her skin was deep brown, and if she needed a man she would bring him to her villa and use his body until she was satisfied and then she would throw him out and sit by her fire and be alone again with the sound of the sea. Perhaps she would let Maria stay with her sometimes. Maria was the only one who understood her. That's why it hurt Catherine so much that Maria had betrayed her.

Catherine didn't hate herself for the way she was, nor did she love herself. On the few occasions when she had reflected on her own psychology, she had thought of herself as a rather interesting character. She had also come to the realization that she was perfectly suited to being a spy—emotionally, physically, and intellectually. Vogel had recognized this, and so had Emilio. She loathed them both but she could not find fault with their conclusions. When she gazed at her reflection in the mirror now, one word came to mind: *spy*.

The taxi drew to a halt in front of Jordan's house. He took her hand to help her out of the car, then paid off the driver. He unlocked the front door to the house and showed her inside. He closed the door before turning on the lights—blackout rules. For an instant Catherine felt disoriented and exposed. She didn't like being in a strange place with a strange man in the dark. Jordan quickly switched on the lights and illuminated the room.

"My goodness," she said. "How did you get a billet like this? I thought all American officers were packed into hotels and boardinghouses."

Catherine knew the answer, of course. But she needed to ask the question. It was rare for an American officer to be living alone in such a place.

"My father-in-law bought the house years ago. He spent a great deal of time in London on both business and pleasure and decided he wanted a pied à terre here. I have to admit I'm glad he bought it. The thought of spending the war packed like a sardine in Grosvenor House really doesn't appeal to me. Here, let me take your coat."

He helped her off with her overcoat and went to hang it in the closet. Catherine surveyed the drawing room. It was handsomely furnished with the sort of deep leather couches and chairs one finds in a private London club. The walls were paneled; the wood floors were stained a deep brown and polished to a lustrous shine. The rugs scattered about were of excellent quality. There was one unique feature about the room—the walls were covered with photographs of bridges.

"You're married, then," Catherine said, making sure there was a slight note of disappointment in her voice.

"I beg your pardon?" he said, returning to the room.

"You said your father-in-law owns this house."

"I suppose I should say my former father-in-law. My wife was killed in an automobile accident before the war."

"I'm sorry, Peter. I didn't mean to—"

"Please, it's fine. It was a long time ago."

She nodded toward the wall and said, "You like bridges."

"You might say that, yes. I build them."

Catherine walked across the room and looked at one of the photographs close up. It was the Hudson River bridge for which Jordan had been named Engineer of the Year in 1938.

"You designed these?"

"Actually, architects design them. I'm an engineer. They put a design on paper and I tell them whether the thing will stand up or not. Sometimes I make them change the design. Sometimes, if it's terrific like that one, I find a way to make it work."

"Sounds challenging."

"It can be," he said. "But sometimes it can be tedious and dull, and it makes for boring conversation at cocktail parties."

"I didn't know the navy needed bridges."

"They don't." Jordan hesitated. "I'm sorry. I can't discuss my—"

"Please. Believe me, I understand the rules."

"I could do the cooking, but I couldn't guarantee that the food would be edible."

"Just show me where the kitchen is."

"Through that door. If you don't mind, I'd like to change. I still can't get used to wearing this damned uniform."

"Certainly."

She watched his next movements very carefully. He removed his keys from his trouser pocket and unlocked a door. That would be his study. He switched on the light and was inside for less than a minute. When he emerged Jordan was no longer carrying his briefcase. He probably locked it inside his safe. He climbed the stairs. His bedroom was on the second floor. It was perfect. While he was sleeping upstairs she could break into his safe and photograph the contents of his briefcase. Neumann would make sure the photographs reached Berlin, and the Abwehr analysts would examine them to discover the nature of Peter Jordan's work.

She went through the doorway into the kitchen and was struck by a flash of panic. Why was he suddenly changing out of his uniform? Had she done something wrong? Made some mistake? Was he on the phone right now to MI5? Was MI5 calling Special Branch? Would he come downstairs and sweet-talk her until they broke down the door and arrested her?

Catherine forced herself to relax. It was ludicrous.

When she opened the door to the refrigerator she realized something. She didn't have the vaguest idea how to make an omelet. Maria made excellent omelets—she would just imitate everything she did. From the refrigerator she took three eggs, a small pat of butter, and a chunk of cheddar.

She opened the door to the small pantry and found a tin of tomatoes and a bottle of wine. She opened it, found the wineglasses, and poured for them both. She didn't wait until Jordan returned to try the wine; it was delicious. She could taste wildflowers and lavender and apricot, and it made her think of her imaginary villa. Warm the tomatoes first—that's what Maria did, except before, in Paris, the tomatoes were fresh tomatoes, not these beastly tinned ones.

She opened the tomatoes, drained off the water, chopped them, and dropped them into a hot pan. The kitchen immediately took on the smell of the tomatoes, and she drank some more wine before cracking and beating the eggs and grating the cheese into a bowl. She had to smile—the domestic routine of making dinner for a man felt so odd to her. Then she thought, Perhaps Kurt Vogel should add a cooking course to his little Abwehr spy school.

Jordan set the table in the dining room while Catherine finished with the omelet. He had changed into cotton khaki trousers and a sweater, and Catherine was again struck by his looks. She wanted to let down her hair—to do something to make herself more attractive to him—but she stayed within the character she had created for herself. The omelet was surprisingly good and they both ate it very quickly before it could go cold, washing it down with the wine, a prewar bordeaux Jordan had brought to London from New York. By the end of the meal Catherine felt pleasant and relaxed. Jordan seemed that way too. He appeared to suspect nothing—appeared to accept that their meeting was wholly coincidental.

"Have you ever been to the States?" he asked, as they cleared away the dishes and carried them into the kitchen.

"Actually, I lived in Washington for two years when I was a little girl."

"Really?"

"Yes, my father worked at the Foreign Office. He was a diplomat. He was posted in Washington in the early twenties, after the Great War. I liked it very much. Except for the heat, of course. My goodness, but Washington is oppressive in the summer! My father rented a cottage for us on the Chesapeake Bay for the summers. I have very fond memories of that time."

All true, except Catherine's father had worked for the German Foreign Ministry, not the British Foreign Office. Catherine had decided it was best to draw on as many aspects of her own life as possible.

"Is your father still a diplomat?"

"No, he died before the war."

"And your mother?"

"My mother died when I was a very little girl." Catherine stacked the dirty dishes in the sink. "I'll wash if you dry."

"Forget it. I have a woman who comes a couple of times a week. She'll be here in the morning. How about a glass of brandy?"

"That would be nice."

There were photographs in silver frames over the fireplace, and she looked at them while Jordan poured the brandy. He joined her in front of the fire and handed her one of the glasses.

"Your wife was very beautiful."

"Yes, she was. Her death was very hard on me."

"And your son? Who's caring for him now?"

"Margaret's sister, Jane."

She sipped her brandy and smiled at him. "You don't sound terribly thrilled about that."

"My God, is it that obvious?"

"Yes, it is."

"Jane and I never really got along very well. And frankly, I wish Billy wasn't in her care. She's selfish and petty and spoiled rotten, and I'm afraid she's going to make Billy the same way. But I really had no choice. The day after I joined the navy I was sent to Washington, and two weeks after that I was flown to London."

"Billy is the image of his father," Catherine said. "I'm certain you have nothing to worry about."

Jordan smiled and said, "I hope you're right. Please, sit down."

"Are you sure? I don't want to keep you—"

"I haven't had an evening as pleasant as this in a very long time. Please stay a little longer."

They sat down next to each other on the large leather couch.

Jordan said, "So tell me how it is that an incredibly beautiful woman like you isn't married."

Catherine felt her face flush.

"My goodness, you're actually blushing. Don't tell me no one has ever told you before that you're beautiful."

She smiled and said, "No, it's just been a very long time."

"Well, that makes two of us. It's been a very long time since I've told a woman that she was beautiful. In fact, I can remember the last time. It was when I woke up and saw Margaret's face on the day she died. I never thought

I could find another woman beautiful after that. Until I made a fool of myself by crashing into you in the blackout last night. You took my breath away, Catherine."

"Thank you. I can assure you the attraction was mutual."

"Is that why you didn't give me your telephone number?"

"I didn't want you to believe I was a wanton woman."

"Darn, I was hoping you were a wanton woman."

"Peter," she said, and jabbed him in the leg with her finger.

"Are you ever going to answer my question? Why aren't you married?"

Catherine stared into the fire for a moment. "I *was* married. My husband, Michael, was shot down over the Channel the first week of the Battle of Britain. They never were able to recover his body. I was pregnant at the time, and I lost the baby. The doctors said it was the shock of Michael's death that did it." Catherine's gaze shifted from the fire to Jordan's face. "He was handsome and brave and he was my entire world. For the longest time after his death, I never looked twice at another man. I started dating a short time ago, but nothing at all serious. And then some foolish American who wasn't using his blackout torch smashed into me on a pavement in Kensington. . . ."

There was a long and slightly uncomfortable moment of silence. The fire was dying. Catherine could hear the sound of a rainstorm getting up and pattering against the pavement outside the window. She realized she could stay like this for quite a while, sitting next to the fire with her brandy and this kind and gentle man. *My God, Catherine, what's got into you?* She tried for a moment to make herself hate him but she could not. She hoped he never did anything to threaten her, anything that would force her to kill him.

She made a show of looking at her wristwatch. "My goodness, look at the time," she said. "It's eleven o'clock. I've imposed on you too long. I should really be going—"

"What were you thinking just now?" Jordan asked, as if he had not heard a word she had just said.

What was she thinking? A very good question.

"I realize you can't talk about your work, but I'm going to ask you one question and I want you to tell me the truth."

"Cross my heart."

"You're not going to run off and get yourself killed, are you?"

"No, I'm not going to get myself killed. I promise."

She leaned over and kissed him on the mouth. His lips did not respond.

She pulled away, thinking, Did I make a mistake? Perhaps he wasn't ready for this?

He said, "I'm sorry. It's just been a very long time."

"It's been a very long time for me too."

"Maybe we need to try again."

She smiled and kissed him again. This time his mouth responded to hers. He pulled her close to him. She enjoyed the sensation of her breasts pressing against him.

After a moment she drew away.

"If I don't leave now I don't think I ever will."

"I'm not sure I want you to leave."

She gave him a final kiss and said, "When am I going to see you again?"

"Will you let me take you to dinner tomorrow night—a proper dinner, that is? Somewhere we can dance."

"I'd love that."

"How about the Savoy again, around eight o'clock."

"That sounds perfect."

Catherine Blake was brought back to reality by the cold blast of rain and the sight of Pope and Dicky sitting in a parked van. At least they had not interfered. Perhaps they were content to watch from a distance for the time being.

The late-night traffic was light. She quickly flagged down a taxi on Brompton Road. She climbed in and asked the cabbie to take her to Victoria Station. Turning around, she saw Pope and Dicky following.

At Victoria she paid off the driver and went inside, melting into a crowd of passengers stepping from a late-arriving train. She glanced over her shoulder as Dicky Dobbs came running into the terminus, head wheeling from side to side.

Quickly, she walked out through another door, vanishing into the blackout.

CHAPTER TWENTY-SEVEN

BAVARIA, GERMANY: MARCH 1938

Her cottage in Vogel's secret village is flimsy and drafty, the coldest place she has ever known. There is a fireplace, though, and in the afternoon while she studies codes and radio procedures an Abwehr man comes and lays kindling and dry fir logs for the night.

The fire has burned low, the cold is creeping into the cottage, so she rises and tosses a pair of large logs onto the embers. Vogel is lying on the floor silently behind her. He is a terrible lover: boring, selfish, all elbows and knees. Even when he tries to please her he is clumsy and rough and preoccupied. It is a wonder she has been able to seduce him at all. She has her reasons. If he falls in love with her or becomes obsessed with her, Vogel will be reluctant to send her to England. It seems to be working. When he was inside her a moment ago he professed love for her. Now, as he lies on the rug, staring at the ceiling, he seems to be regretting his words.

"Sometimes I don't want you to go," he says.

"Go where?"

"To England."

She comes back, lies down next to him on the rug, and kisses him. His breath is horrible: cigarettes, coffee, bad teeth.

"Poor Vogel. I've made a shambles of your heart, haven't I?"

"Yes, I think so. Sometimes I think about taking you back to Berlin with me. I can get you a flat there."

"That would be lovely," she says, but she is thinking it might be better to be arrested by MI5 than spend the war as Kurt Vogel's mistress in some hovel of a flat in Berlin.

"But you are far too valuable to Germany to spend the war in Berlin. You must go behind enemy lines to England." He pauses and lights a cigarette. "And then there's something else I think. I think, Why would a beautiful woman fall in love with a man

such as myself? And then I have my answer. She thinks he won't send her to England if he loves her."

"I'm not clever or cunning enough to do something like that."

"Of course you are. That's why I chose you."

She feels anger rising within her.

"But I've enjoyed our time together. Emilio said you were very good in bed. 'The best fuck of my entire fucking life'—that's the way Emilio described it. But then, Emilio tends to be a bit of a vulgarian. He said you were better than even the most expensive whores. He said he wanted to keep you in Spain as his mistress. I had to pay twice his usual fee. But believe me, you were well worth the money."

She gets to her feet. "Get out of here, now! I'm leaving in the morning. I've had enough of this hellhole!"

"Oh, yes, you're leaving in the morning. But it's not where you think. There's just one problem. Your trainers tell me that you are still reluctant to kill with your knife. They say you shoot very well, better than the boys, even. But they say you are slow with your stiletto."

She says nothing, just glares at him, lying on the rug in the firelight.

"I have a suggestion for you. Whenever you must use your stiletto, think of the man who hurt you when you were a little girl."

Her mouth drops open in horror. She has told only one person about it in her entire life: Maria. But Maria must have told Emilio—and Emilio, the bastard, told Vogel.

"I don't know what you're talking about," she says, but there is no conviction to her words.

"Of course you do. It's what made you what you are, a heartless fucking bitch."

She reacts instinctively. She takes a step forward and kicks him viciously beneath his chin. His head snaps back and crashes violently against the floor. He is very still, perhaps unconscious. Her stiletto is on the floor next to the fire; they have trained her to keep it near at all times. She picks it up and presses the release, and the shiny blade snaps into place. In the firelight it is bloodred. She takes a step toward Vogel. She wants to kill him, to plunge the stiletto into one of the kill zones they have taught her: the heart, the kidneys, through the ear or the eye. But Vogel is leaning on one elbow now, and there is a gun in his hand aimed at her head.

"Very good," he says. Blood is pouring from his mouth. "I think you're ready now. Put away the knife and sit down. We need to talk. And please, put on some clothes. You look ridiculous standing there like that."

She puts on a robe and stirs the embers while he dresses and tends to his mouth.

"You're a complete bastard. I'd be a fool to work for you, Vogel."

"Don't even think of trying to back out now. I'd provide the Gestapo very con-

vincing evidence of your father's treachery against the Führer. You wouldn't want to see the things they do to people like that. And if you ever cross me once you're in England, I'll deliver you to the British on a silver platter. If you think that fellow hurt you when you were a little girl, just think about being raped repeatedly by a bunch of stinking British guards. You'll be their favorite prisoner, believe me. I doubt they would ever bother to hang you."

She has gone very still in the dark. She thinks how she can smash his skull with the cast-iron poker but Vogel is still holding his gun. She realizes she has been manipulated by him. She thought she was deceiving him—she thought she was in control—but all the while it was Vogel. He was trying to instill in her the ability to kill. She realizes he has done a very good job indeed.

Vogel is talking again. "By the way, I killed you tonight while you were letting me fuck you. Anna Katerina von Steiner, age twenty-seven, died in an unfortunate road accident outside Berlin about an hour ago. A terrible pity. Such a waste of talent."

Vogel is dressed now, holding a wet cloth against his mouth. It is stained with his blood.

"You're going to Holland in the morning, just as we planned. You stay there for six months, firmly establish your identity; then you go to England. Here are your papers for Holland, your money, and your train ticket. I have people in Amsterdam who will contact you and guide you from there."

He comes forward and stands very close to her.

"Anna wasted her life. But Catherine Blake can do great things."

She hears the door close behind him, hears the sound of his boots crunching through the snow outside her cottage. It is very quiet now, only the popping of the fire and the hiss of the bitter wind stirring the fir trees outside her window. She is still for a moment; then she feels her body begin to convulse. Standing is no longer possible. She falls to her knees in front of the fire and begins to weep uncontrollably.

BERLIN: JANUARY 1944

Kurt Vogel was sleeping on the camp bed in his office when he heard a dull scraping sound that made him sit up with a start. "Who's there?"

"It's only me, sir."

"Werner, for God's sake! You scared me to death, dragging your damned wooden leg like that. I thought it was Frankenstein coming to murder me."

"I'm sorry, sir. I thought you would want to see this right away." Ulbricht handed him a signal flimsy. "It just came in from Hamburg—a message from Catherine Blake in London."

Vogel read it quickly, heart pounding.

"She's made contact with Jordan. She wants Neumann to begin making regular pickups as soon as possible. My God, Werner, she's actually done it!"

"Obviously, a remarkable agent. And a remarkable woman."

"Yes," Vogel said distantly. "Signal Neumann at Hampton Sands at the first opportunity. Tell him to begin pickups on the prearranged schedule."

"Yes, sir."

"And leave word with Admiral Canaris's office. I want to brief him on the developments first thing in the morning."

"Yes, sir."

Ulbricht went out, leaving Vogel alone in the dark. He wondered how she had done it. He hoped one day she would come out so he could debrief her. *Stop fooling yourself, old man.* He wanted her to come out so he could see her just one more time, explain why he had treated her so horribly on the last night. It was for her own good. She couldn't see it then but maybe, with the passing of time, she could see it now. He imagined her now. *Is she frightened? Is she in danger?* Of course she was in danger. She was trying to steal Allied secrets in the heart of London. One false move and she would end up in the arms of MI5. But if there was one woman who could pull it off, it was her. Vogel had the broken heart and the broken jaw to prove it.

Heinrich Himmler was working his way through a stack of paperwork at his office on Prinz Albrechtstrasse when the call from Brigadeführer Walter Schellenberg was routed through to his desk. "Good evening, Herr Brigadeführer. Or should I say good morning."

"It's two A.M. I didn't think you would still be at the office."

"No rest for the weary. What can I do for you?"

"It's about the Vogel affair. I was able to convince an officer in the Abwehr communication room that it was in his interest to cooperate with us."

"Very good."

Schellenberg told Himmler about the message from Vogel's agent in London.

Himmler said, "So, your friend Horst Neumann is about to be brought into the game."

"It appears that way, Herr Reichsführer."

"I'll brief the Führer on the developments in the morning. I'm sure he'll be very pleased. This man Vogel seems to be a very capable officer. If he steals the most important secret of the war I wouldn't be surprised if the Führer were to name him Canaris's successor."

"I can think of more worthy candidates for the job, Herr Reichsführer," Schellenberg said.

"You'd better find some way of getting control of the situation. Otherwise you might find yourself out of contention."

"Yes, Herr Reichsführer."

"You're riding with Admiral Canaris in the Tiergarten in the morning?"

"As usual."

"Perhaps you can find out something useful for a change. And do give the Old Fox my warmest regards. Good night, Herr Brigadeführer."

Himmler gently replaced the receiver in the cradle and returned to his eternal paperwork.

CHAPTER TWENTY-EIGHT

HAMPTON SANDS, NORFOLK

A gray dawn was leaking through thick clouds as Horst Neumann crossed the pine grove and climbed to the top of the dunes. The sea opened before him, gray and still in the windless morning, small breakers collapsing onto the seemingly endless expanse of beach. Neumann wore a gray track suit, a rollneck sweater beneath for warmth, and a pair of soft black leather running shoes. He breathed deeply of the cold crisp air and then scrambled down the dunes and walked across the soft sand. The tide was going out and there was a wide swath of hard flat sand, perfect for running. He stretched his legs, blew on his hands, and set out at an easy pace. Terns and gulls squawked in protest and moved away.

He had received a message from Hamburg earlier that morning instructing him to begin regular pickups of material from Catherine Blake in London. It was to be done on the schedule Kurt Vogel had given him at the farm outside Berlin. The material was to be placed through a doorway in Cavendish Square, where it would be collected by a man from the Portuguese embassy and sent to Lisbon inside the diplomatic pouch. It sounded simple. But Neumann understood that courier work on the streets of London would take him straight into the teeth of the British security forces. He would be carrying information that would guarantee him a trip to the gallows if he was arrested. In combat he always knew where the enemy was. In espionage work the enemy could be anywhere. He could be in the next seat in a café or on a bus, and Neumann might never know.

It took several minutes for Neumann to feel warm and for the first beads of sweat to appear on his forehead. The running worked its magic, the same magic it had worked on him since he was a boy. He was taken with a pleasant floating sensation, almost flight. His breathing was regular and relaxed, and he could feel the tension melting out of his body. He picked out an imaginary finish line about a half mile down the beach and increased his pace.

The first quarter mile was good. He glided along the beach, his long stride eating up the ground, shoulders and arms loose and relaxed. The last quarter mile was tougher. Neumann's breath grew harsh and ragged. The cold air tore at his throat. His arms felt as though he were carrying lead weights. His imaginary finish line loomed two hundred yards ahead. The backs of his thighs tightened suddenly, and his stride shortened. He pretended it was the homestretch of the 1,500-meter final of the Olympic Games—*the games I missed because I was sent off to kill Poles and Russians and Greeks and French!* He imagined there was just one man in front of him, and he was gaining ground excruciatingly slowly. The finish line was fifty yards away. It was a clump of sea grass stranded by the high tide, but in Neumann's imagination it was a real finish line with a tape and men in white jackets with stopwatches and the Olympic banner flapping over the stadium in a gentle breeze. He pounded his feet savagely against the hard sand and leaned across the sea grass, stumbled to a halt, and struggled to catch his breath.

It was a silly game—a game he had played with himself since he was a child—but it served a purpose. He had proved to himself that he was finally fit again. It had taken him months to recover from the beating he suffered at the hands of the SS men, but he had finally done it. He felt he was physically ready for anything he might be confronted with. Neumann walked for a moment before breaking into a light jog. It was then that he noticed Jenny Colville, watching him from atop the dunes.

Neumann smiled at her as she approached. She was more attractive than he remembered—a wide, mobile mouth, eyes large and blue, her pale complexion flushed from the morning cold. She wore a heavy wool sweater, a woolen cap, an oilskin coat, trousers haphazardly tucked inside Wellington boots. Behind her, beyond the dunes, Neumann could see white smoke from a doused fire drifting through the pine trees. Jenny drew nearer. She looked tired and her clothes appeared slept in. Yet she smiled with considerable charm as she stood, arms akimbo, and examined him.

"Very impressive, Mr. Porter," she said. Neumann always found her broad, singsong Norfolk accent difficult to comprehend. "If I didn't know better I'd say you were in training for something."

"Old habits are hard to break. Besides, it's good for the body and the soul. You should try it sometime. It would take those extra pounds off you."

"Ah!" She pushed him playfully. "I'm too skinny as it is now. All the boys in the village say so. They like Eleanor Carrick because she has big—well, you know. She goes down to the beach with them and they give her money to unbutton her blouse."

"I saw her in the village yesterday," Neumann said. "She's a fat cow. You're twice as pretty as Eleanor Carrick."

"You think so?"

"I do indeed." Neumann rubbed his arms briskly and stamped his feet. "I need to walk. Otherwise I'm going to be stiff as a board."

"Would you like some company?"

Neumann nodded. It was not the truth but Neumann saw no harm in it. Jenny Colville had a terrible schoolgirl crush on him; it was obvious. She made up some excuse to drop by the Dogherty cottage every day and never turned down an invitation from Mary to stay for tea or supper. Neumann had tried to pay an appropriate amount of attention to Jenny and carefully avoided putting himself in any situation where he might be alone with her. Until now. He would try to turn the conversation to his advantage—to take stock of how well his cover story was holding up in the village. They walked in silence, Jenny staring out at the sea. Neumann grabbed up a handful of stones and skipped them across the waves.

Jenny said, "Do you mind talking about the war?"

"Of course not."

"Your wounds—were they bad?"

"Bad enough to cut short my fighting days and give me a one-way ticket home."

"Where were you wounded?"

"In the head. Someday, when I know you better, I'll lift up my hair and show the scars."

She looked at him and smiled. "Your head looks fine to me."

"And what do you mean by that, Jenny Colville?"

"It means you're a handsome man. And you're smart too. I can tell."

The wind blew a strand of hair across Jenny's face. She tucked it back under her woolen cap with a brush of her hand.

"I just don't understand what you're doing in a place like Hampton Sands."

So his cover story had aroused suspicion in the village!

"I needed a place to rest and get well. The Doghertys offered to let me come here and stay with them, and I took them up on it."

"Why don't I believe that story?"

"You should, Jenny. It's the truth."

"My father thinks you're a criminal or a terrorist. He says Sean used to be a member of the IRA."

"Jenny, can you really picture Sean Dogherty as a member of the Irish Republican Army? Besides, your father has serious problems of his own."

Jenny's face darkened. She stopped walking and turned to face him. "And what's that supposed to mean?"

Neumann feared he had taken it too far. Perhaps it was better to disengage, make an excuse, and change the subject. But something made him want to finish what he started. He thought, Why can't I keep my mouth shut and walk away from this? He knew the answer, of course. His own stepfather had been a vicious bastard, quick with a backhand across the face or a cruel remark that brought tears to his eyes. He felt certain Jenny Colville had endured worse physical abuse than he ever had. He wanted to say something to her that would let her know that things did not always have to be this way. He wanted to tell her she was not alone. He wanted to *help* her.

"It means he drinks far too much." Neumann reached out and touched her face gently. "And it means he mistreats a beautiful, intelligent young girl who's done absolutely nothing in the world to deserve it."

"Do you mean that?" she asked.

"Mean what?"

"That I'm beautiful and intelligent. No one's ever said that to me before."

"Of course I mean it."

She took his hand and they walked some more.

"Do you have a girl?" she asked him.

"No."

"Why not?"

Why not indeed? The war. It was the easy answer. He had never had time for a girl really. His life had been one long series of obsessions: an obsession to lose his Englishness and become a good German, an obsession to become an Olympic champion, an obsession to become the most decorated member of the *Fallschirmjäger*. His last lover had been a French farm girl from the village near his listening post. She had been tender when Neumann was in desperate need of tenderness, and each night for a month she let him in the back door of her cottage and took him secretly to her bed. When he closed his eyes Neumann could still see her body, rising to his in the flickering candlelight of her bedroom. She had taken a vow to kiss his head every night until it healed. In the end, Neumann was overcome with the guilt of an occupier and broke it off. He feared now what would happen to her when the war was over.

"Your face became sad for a moment," Jenny said.

"I was thinking about something."

"I'd say you were thinking about *someone*. And by the look on your face that someone was a woman."

"You're a very perceptive girl."

"Was she pretty?"

"She was French and she was very beautiful."

"Did she break your heart?"

"You might say that."

"But you left *her*."

"Yes, I suppose I did."

"Why?"

"Because I loved her too much."

"I don't understand."

"You will someday."

"And what do you mean by that?"

"It means you're far too young to be hanging around with the likes of me. I'm going to finish my run. I suggest you go home and change into some clean clothes. You look like you've been sleeping on the beach all night."

They looked at each other in a way that said they both knew it was the truth. She turned to leave, then stopped.

"You'd never do anything to hurt me, would you, James?"

"Of course not."

"You promise?"

"I promise."

She stepped forward and kissed him on the mouth very briefly before turning and running across the sand. Neumann shook his head; then he turned in the opposite direction and ran back down the beach.

CHAPTER TWENTY-NINE

LONDON

Alfred Vicary felt he was sinking in quicksand. The more he struggled, the deeper he descended. Each time he unearthed a new clue or lead he seemed to fall farther behind. He was beginning to doubt his chances of ever catching the spies.

The source of his despair was a pair of decoded German messages that had arrived from Bletchley Park that morning. The first message was from a German agent in Britain asking Berlin to begin making regular pickups. The second was from Hamburg to a German agent in Britain asking the agent to do just that. It was a disaster. The German operation—whatever it might be—appeared to be succeeding. If the agent had requested a courier, it was logical the agent had stolen something. Vicary was struck by the fear that if he ever *did* catch up with the spies he might be too late.

The red light shone over Boothby's door. Vicary pressed the buzzer and waited. A minute passed and the light still was red. So like Boothby to demand an urgent meeting, then keep his victim waiting.

Why haven't you told us this before?

But I have, Alfred, old man. . . . I told Boothby.

Vicary pressed the buzzer again. Was it really possible Boothby had known of the existence of the Vogel network and kept it from him? It made absolutely no sense. Vicary could think of only one possible explanation. Boothby had vehemently opposed Vicary's being assigned to the case and had made that clear from the outset. But would Boothby's opposition include actively trying to sabotage Vicary's efforts? Quite possible. If Vicary could display no momentum in solving the case, Boothby might have grounds to sack him and give the case to someone else, someone he trusted—a career officer, perhaps, not one of the new recruits that Boothby so detested.

The light finally shone green. Vicary, slipping through the grand double doors, vowed not to leave again without first clearing the air.

Boothby was seated behind his desk. "Let's have it, Alfred."

Vicary briefed Boothby on the content of the two messages and his theory about what they meant. Boothby listened, fidgeting and squirming in his chair.

"For God's sake!" he snapped. "The news gets worse every day with this case."

Vicary thought, Another sparkling contribution, Sir Basil.

"We've made some progress on piecing together background on the female agent. Karl Becker identified her as Anna von Steiner. She was born in Guy's Hospital in London on Christmas Day 1910. Her father was Peter von Steiner, a diplomat and a wealthy West Prussian aristocrat. Her mother was an Englishwoman named Daphne Harrison. The family remained in London until war broke out, then moved to Germany. Because of Steiner's position, Daphne Harrison was not interned during the war, as many British citizens were. She died of tuberculosis in 1918 at the Steiner estate in West Prussia. After the war Steiner and his daughter drifted from posting to posting, including another brief stint in London in the early twenties. Steiner also worked in Rome and in Washington."

"Sounds like he was a spy to me," Boothby said. "But go on, Alfred."

"In 1937, Anna Steiner vanished. We can only speculate after that. She undergoes Abwehr training, is sent to the Netherlands to establish a false identity as Christa Kunst, then enters England. By the way, Anna Steiner was allegedly killed in an auto accident outside Berlin in March 1938. Obviously, Vogel fabricated that."

Boothby rose and paced his office. "It's all very interesting, Alfred, but there's one fatal flaw. It's based on information given to you by Karl Becker. Becker would say anything to ingratiate himself."

"Becker has no reason to lie to us about this, Sir Basil. And his story is perfectly consistent with the few things we know for certain."

"All I'm saying, Alfred, is that I very much doubt the veracity of anything the man says."

"So why did you spend so much time with him last October?" Vicary said.

Sir Basil was standing in the window, looking down at the last light slipping out of the square. His head snapped around before he regained his composure and turned slowly to face Vicary.

"The reason I spoke to Becker is none of your affair."

"Becker is my agent," Vicary said, anger creeping into his voice. "I arrested him, I turned him, I run him. He gave you information that might have proved useful to this case, yet you kept that information from me. I'd like to know why."

Boothby was very calm now. "Becker told me the same story he told you: special agents, a secret camp in Bavaria, special codes and rendezvous procedures. And to be honest with you, Alfred, I didn't believe him at the time. We had no other evidence to support his story. Now we do."

It was a perfectly logical explanation—on the surface, at least.

"Why didn't you tell me about it?"

"It was a long time ago."

"Who's Broome?"

"Sorry, Alfred."

"I want to know who Broome is."

"And I'm trying to tell you as politely as I can that you're not entitled to know who Broome is." Boothby shook his head. "My God! This isn't some college club where we sit around and swap insights. This department is in the business of counterintelligence. And it operates on a very simple concept: need to know. You have no need to know who Broome is because it does not affect any case to which you have been assigned. Therefore it is none of your business."

"Is the concept of need to know a license to deceive other officers?"

"I wouldn't use the word *deceive*," Boothby said, as though it were an obscenity. "It simply means that, for reasons of security, an officer is entitled to know only what is necessary for him to carry out his assignment."

"How about the word *lie*? Would you use that word?"

The discussion seemed to be causing Boothby physical pain.

"I suppose at times it might be necessary to be less than truthful with one officer to safeguard an operation being carried out by another. Surely this doesn't come as a surprise to you."

"Of course not, Sir Basil." Vicary hesitated, deciding whether to continue with his line of questioning or disengage. "I was just wondering why you lied to me about reading Kurt Vogel's file."

The blood seemed to drain from Boothby's face, and Vicary could see him bunching and unbunching his big fist inside his trouser pocket. It was a risky strategy, and Grace Clarendon's neck was on the block. When Vicary was gone, Boothby would call Nicholas Jago in Registry and demand answers. Jago would surely realize Grace Clarendon was the source of the leak. It was no small matter; she could be sacked immediately. But Vicary was betting they wouldn't touch Grace because it would only prove her information had been correct. He hoped to God he was right.

"Looking for a scapegoat, Alfred? Someone or something to blame for your inability to solve this case? You should know the danger in that more than any of us. History is replete with examples of weak men who have found it expedient to acquire a convenient scapegoat."

Vicary thought, And you're not answering my question.

He rose to his feet. "Good night, Sir Basil."

Boothby remained silent as Vicary walked toward the door.

"There's one more thing," Boothby finally said. "I shouldn't think I need to tell you this, but I shall in any case. We don't have an unlimited amount of time. If there isn't progress soon we may have to make—well, changes. You understand, don't you, Alfred?"

CHAPTER THIRTY

LONDON

As they walked into the Savoy Grill, the band began playing "And a Nightingale Sang in Berkeley Square." It was a rather poor rendition—choppy and a bit rushed—but it was pretty, regardless. Jordan took her hand without speaking and they walked onto the dance floor. He was an excellent dancer, smooth and confident, and he held her very closely. He had come directly from his office and was wearing his uniform. He had brought his briefcase with him. Obviously it contained nothing important because he had left it behind at the table. Still, he never seemed to take his eyes off it for very long.

After a moment Catherine noticed something: everyone in the room seemed to be staring at them. It was terribly unnerving. For six years she had done everything in her power *not* to be noticed. Now she was dancing with a dazzling American naval officer at the most glamorous hotel in London. She felt exposed and vulnerable, yet at the same time she derived a strange satisfaction from doing something completely normal for a change.

Her own appearance certainly had something to do with the attention they were drawing. She had seen it in Jordan's eyes a few minutes earlier when she walked into the bar. She looked stunning tonight. She wore a dress of black crepe material with a deep plunge in the back and a neckline that showed off the shape of her breasts. She wore her hair down, held back by a smart jeweled clasp, and a double strand of pearls at her throat. She had taken care with her makeup. The wartime cosmetics were of extremely poor quality but she didn't require much—a little lipstick to accentuate the shape of her generous mouth, a little rouge to bring out her prominent cheekbones, a bit of liner around her eyes. She derived no special satisfaction from her appearance. She had always thought of her own beauty in dispassionate terms, the way a woman might evaluate her favorite china or a cherished antique rug. Still, it had been a very long time since she had walked through a room and watched heads turn her way. She was the kind of woman that both sexes noticed. The men could hardly keep their mouths closed, the women frowned with envy.

Jordan said, "Have you noticed that everyone in this room is staring at us?"

"I've noticed that, yes. Do you mind?"

"Of course not." He drew away a few inches so he could look at her face. "It's been a very long time since I've felt this way, Catherine. And to think I had to come all the way to London to find you."

"I'm glad you did."

"Can I make a confession?"

"Of course you can."

"I didn't get much sleep after you left last night."

She smiled and drew him near, so her mouth was next to his ear. "I'll make a confession too. I didn't sleep at all."

"What were you thinking about?"

"You tell me first."

"I was thinking how much I wished you hadn't left."

"I was having very similar thoughts."

"I was thinking about kissing you."

"I think I *was* kissing you."

"I don't want you to leave tonight."

"I think you would have to throw me out bodily if you wanted me to leave."

"I don't think you need to worry about that."

"I think I'd like you to kiss me again right now, Peter."

"What about all these people staring at us? What do you think they'll do if I kiss you?"

"I'm not sure. But it's 1944 in London. Anything can happen."

"Compliments of the gentleman at the bar," the waiter said, opening a bottle of champagne as they came back to the table.

"Does the gentleman have a name?" Jordan asked.

"None that he gave, sir."

"What did he look like?"

"Rather like a sunburned rugby player, sir."

"American naval officer?"

"Yes, sir."

"Shepherd Ramsey."

"The gentleman wishes to join you for a glass."

"Tell the gentleman thank you for the champagne, but forget it."

"Of course, sir."

"Who's Shepherd Ramsey?" Catherine asked when the waiter left.

"Shepherd Ramsey is my oldest and dearest friend in the world. I love him like a brother."

"So why don't you let him come over for a drink?"

"Because for once in my adult life I'd like to do something without him. Besides, I don't want to share you."

"Good, because I don't want to share you either." Catherine raised her champagne glass. "To the absence of Shepherd."

Jordan laughed. "To the absence of Shepherd."

They touched glasses.

Catherine added, "And to the blackout, without which I would never have bumped into you."

"To the blackout." Jordan hesitated. "I know this probably sounds like a terrible cliché, but I can't take my eyes off of you."

Catherine smiled and leaned across the table.

"I don't want you to take your eyes off me, Peter. Why do you think I wore this dress?"

"I'm a little nervous."

"I am too, Peter."

"You look so beautiful, lying there in the moonlight."

"You look beautiful too."

"Don't. My wife—"

"I'm sorry. It's just that I've never seen a man who looked quite like you. Try not to think about your wife for just a few minutes."

"It's very hard, but you're making it a little easier."

"You look like a statue, kneeling there like that."

"A very old, crumbling statue."

"A beautiful statue."

"I can't stop touching you—touching them. They're so beautiful. I've been dreaming of touching them like this since the first moment I saw you."

"You can touch them harder. It won't hurt."

"Like this?"

"Oh, God! Yes, Peter, just like that. But I want to touch you too."

"That feels so nice when you do that."

"It does?"

"Ahh, yes, it does."

"It's so hard. It feels wonderful. There's something else I want to do to it."

"What?"

"I can't say it out loud. Just come closer."

"Catherine——"

"Just do it, darling. I promise you won't regret it."

"Oh, my God, that feels so incredible."

"Then I shouldn't stop?"

"You look so beautiful doing that."

"I want to make you feel good."

"I want to make *you* feel good."

"I can show you how."

"I think I know how."

"Ahh, Peter, your tongue feels so wonderful. Oh, please, touch my breasts while you do that."

"I want to be inside you."

"Hurry, Peter."

"Ohh, you're so soft, so wonderful. Oh, God, Catherine, I'm going to——"

"Wait! Not yet, darling. Do me a favor and lie down on your back. Let me do the rest."

He did as she asked. She took him in her hand and guided him inside her body. She could have just lain there and let him finish but she wanted it this way. She always knew Vogel would do this to her. Why else would he want a female agent except to seduce Allied officers and steal their secrets? She always thought the man would be fat and hairy and old and ugly, not like Peter. If she was going to be Kurt Vogel's whore, she might as well enjoy it. *Oh, God, Catherine, you shouldn't be doing this. You shouldn't be losing control like this.* But she couldn't help it. She *was* enjoying it. And she *was* losing control. Her head rolled back and her hands went to her breasts and she stroked her nipples with her fingers and after a moment she felt his warm release within her and it washed over her in wave after wonderful wave.

It was late, at least four o'clock, though Catherine couldn't be sure because it was too dark to see the clock on the bedstand. It didn't matter. All that mattered was that Peter Jordan was sleeping soundly next to her. His breathing was deep and regular. They had eaten a large meal, had a lot to drink, and made love twice. Unless he was a very light sleeper, he would probably sleep through a Luftwaffe night raid right now. She slipped out of bed, put on the silk dressing robe he had given her, and padded quietly across the room. The bedroom door was closed halfway. Catherine opened it a few inches, slipped through the doorway, and closed it behind her.

The silence rang in her ears. She could feel her heart pounding in her chest. She forced herself to be calm. She had worked too hard—risked too much—just to get to this point. One silly mistake and it would destroy all she had done. She moved quickly down the narrow staircase. The stair creaked. She froze, waiting to hear if Jordan woke up. Outside a car whooshed through standing water. Somewhere a dog was barking. In the distance a lorry horn blared. She realized these were just the average sounds of the night that people slept through all the time. She walked quickly down the stairs and along the hall. She found his keys on a small table, next to her handbag. She picked them both up and went to work.

Catherine had limited objectives tonight. She wanted to guarantee herself regular access to Jordan's study and his private papers. For that she needed her own copy of the keys to the front door, to the study door, and to his briefcase. Jordan's key ring held several keys. The key to the front door was obvious; it was larger than the rest. She reached in her purse and removed a block of soft brown clay. She singled out the skeleton key and pressed it into the clay, making a neat imprint. The key to the briefcase was also obvious; it was the smallest. She repeated the same process, making another neat imprint. The study would be more difficult; there were a number of keys that looked as though they might be the one. There was only one way to find out which it was. She picked up her handbag and Jordan's briefcase, carried everything down the hall to the study door, and began trying the different keys. The fourth key she tried fit the lock. She removed it and pressed it into her block of clay.

Catherine could stop now, and it would be a very successful evening. She could make duplicate keys and she could come back when Jordan wasn't home and photograph everything in his study. She *would* do that; but she wanted more tonight. She wanted to prove to Vogel that she had done it, that she was a talented agent. By her estimate she had been out of bed less than two minutes. She could afford two more.

She unlocked the study door, went inside, and switched on the light. It was a handsome room, furnished like the drawing room in a masculine way.

There was a large desk and a leather chair and a drafting table with a tall wooden stool in front of it. Catherine reached inside her handbag and withdrew two items, her camera and her silenced Mauser pistol. She laid the Mauser on the desk. She raised the camera to her eye and clicked off two photographs of the room. Next she unlocked Jordan's briefcase. It was virtually empty—just a billfold, a case for eyeglasses, and a small leatherbound appointment book. She thought, It's a start at least. Perhaps there were names of important men with whom Jordan had met. If the Abwehr knew whom he was meeting, perhaps they could discover the nature of his work.

How many times had she done this at the training camp? God, but she had lost count: a hundred at least, always with Vogel standing over her with his bloody stopwatch. *Too long! Too loud! Too much light! Not enough! They're coming for you! You're caught! What do you do now?* She laid the appointment book on the desk and switched on the desk lamp. It had a pliable arm and a dome over the bulb to focus the light downward, perfect for photographing documents.

Three minutes. Work quickly now, Catherine. She opened the notebook and adjusted the lamp so the light shone directly onto the page. If she did it at the wrong angle, or if the light was too close, the negatives would be ruined. She did it just as Vogel had instructed and started snapping off the photographs. Names, dates, short notes written in his scrawling hand. She photographed a few more pages and then found something very interesting. One page contained crude sketches of a boxlike figure. There were numbers on the page that appeared to represent dimensions. Catherine photographed that page twice to make certain she captured the image.

Four minutes. One more item tonight: the safe. It was bolted to the floor, next to the desk. Vogel had given her a combination that was supposed to unlock it. Catherine knelt and turned the dial. Six digits. When she turned to the last number she felt the tumbler settle into place. She took hold of the latch and applied pressure. The latch snapped into the open position; the combination worked. She pulled open the door and looked inside: two binders filled with papers, several looseleaf notebooks. It would take hours to photograph everything. She would wait. She aimed the camera at the inside of the safe and took a photograph.

Five minutes. Time to put everything back in its original place. She closed the safe door, returned the latch to the locked position, and spun the dial. She placed the block of clay in her handbag carefully, so as not to damage the imprints. The camera and the Mauser were next. She returned Jordan's appointment book to its place inside his briefcase and locked it. Then she shut off the lights and went out. She closed the door and locked it.

Six minutes. Too long. She carried everything back into the hall and placed the keys, his briefcase, and her handbag back on the table. Done! She needed an excuse: she was thirsty. It was true—her mouth was parched from nerves. She went into the kitchen, took a glass down from the cabinet, and filled it with cold water from the tap. She drank it down immediately, refilled it, and carried the glass upstairs to the bedroom.

Catherine felt relief washing over her and at the same time an amazing sense of power and triumph. Finally, after months of training and years of waiting, she had done something. She realized suddenly that she liked spying—the satisfaction of meticulously planning and executing an operation, the childlike pleasure of knowing a secret, learning something that someone doesn't want you to know. Vogel had been right all along, of course. She was perfect for it—in every way.

She opened the door and went back into the bedroom.

Peter Jordan was sitting up in bed in the moonlight.

"Where have you been? I was worried about you."

"I was dying of thirst." She couldn't believe the calm, collected voice was really hers.

"I hope you brought me some too," he said.

Oh, thank God. She could breathe again.

"Of course I did."

She handed him the glass of water, and he drank it.

Catherine asked, "What time is it?"

"Five o'clock. I have to be up in an hour for an eight o'clock meeting."

She kissed him. "So we have one hour left."

"Catherine, I couldn't possibly—"

"Oh, I bet you could."

She let the silk gown fall from her shoulders and drew his face to her breasts.

Catherine Blake, later that morning, strode along the Chelsea Embankment as a light, bitterly cold rain drifted across the river. During her preparation Vogel had provided her with a sequence of twenty different rendezvous, each in a different location in central London, each at a slightly different time. He had forced her to commit them to memory, and she assumed he had done the same thing with Horst Neumann before sending him into England. Under the rules it was Catherine who would decide whether the meeting would take place. If she saw anything she didn't like—a suspicious face, men in a parked car—she could call it off and they would try again at the next location on the list at the specified time.

Catherine saw nothing out of the ordinary. She glanced at her wristwatch: two minutes early. She continued walking and, inevitably, thought about what had happened last night. She worried she had taken things with Jordan too far, too fast. She hoped he hadn't been shocked by the things she had done to his body or by the things she had asked him to do to hers. Perhaps a middle-class Englishwoman wouldn't have behaved like that. *Too late for second thoughts now, Catherine.*

The morning had been like being in a dream. It felt as if she had been magically turned into someone else and dropped into their world. She dressed and made coffee while Jordan shaved and showered; the placid domestic scene felt bizarre to her. She felt a stab of fear when he unlocked the study door and went inside. *Did I leave anything out of place? Does he realize I was in there last night?* They had shared a taxi. During the short ride to Grosvenor Square she was struck by another thought: What if he doesn't want to see me again? It had never occurred to her before that moment. All of it would have been for nothing unless he truly cared for her. Her concerns had been groundless. As the taxi arrived at Grosvenor Square he asked her to have dinner with him that evening at an Italian restaurant in Charlotte Street.

Catherine turned around and retraced her steps along the Embankment. Neumann was there now, walking toward her, hands plunged into the pockets of his reefer coat, collar up against the rain, slouch hat pulled down close to his eyes. He had a good look for a field agent: small, anonymous, yet vaguely menacing. Put a suit on him and he could attend a Belgravia cocktail party. Dressed as he was now, he could walk the toughest docks in London and no one would dare look at him twice. She wondered if he had ever studied acting, like she had.

"You look like you could use a cup of coffee," he said. "There's a nice warm café not too far from here."

Neumann held out an arm to her. She took it and they strolled along the Embankment. It was very cold. She gave him the film and he carelessly dropped it into his pocket, as though it were spare change. Vogel had trained him well.

Catherine said, "You know where to deliver this, I assume?"

"Cavendish Square. A man from the Portuguese embassy named Hernandez will pick it up at three o'clock this afternoon and place it in the diplomatic pouch. It will go to Lisbon tonight and be in Berlin in the morning."

"Very good."

"What is it, by the way?"

"His appointment book, some photographs of his study. Not much, but it's a start."

"Very impressive," Neumann said. "How did you get it?"

"I let him take me to dinner; then I let him take me to bed. I got up in the middle of the night and slipped into his study. The combination worked, by the way. I also saw the inside of his safe."

Neumann shook his head. "That's risky as hell. If he comes downstairs you're in trouble."

"I know. That's why I need these." She reached into her handbag and gave him the block of clay with the imprints of the keys. "Find someone to make copies of these and deliver them to my flat today. Tomorrow, when he goes to work, I'm going to go back inside his house and photograph everything in that study."

Neumann pocketed the block of clay.

"Right. Anything else?"

"Yes, from now on, no more conversations like this. We bump into each other, I give you the film, you walk away and deliver it to the Portuguese. If you have a message for me, write it down and give it to me. Understood?"

"Understood."

They stopped walking. "Well, you have a very busy day ahead of you, Mr. Porter." She kissed his cheek and said into his ear, "I risked my life for those things. Don't fuck it up now."

Then she turned and walked away down the Embankment.

The first problem confronting Horst Neumann that morning was finding someone to make copies of Peter Jordan's keys. No reputable shop in the West End would make a duplicate key based on an imprint. In fact they would probably call the Metropolitan Police and have him arrested. He needed to go to a neighborhood where he might find a shopkeeper willing to do the job for the right price. He walked along the Thames, crossed Battersea Bridge, and headed into South London.

It didn't take Neumann long to find what he was looking for. The shop's windows had been blown out by a bomb. Now they were boarded up with plywood. Neumann stepped inside. There were no customers, just an older man behind the counter wearing a heavy blue shirt and a grimy apron.

Neumann said, "You make keys, mate?"

The clerk inclined his head toward the grinder.

Neumann took the clay from his pocket. "You know how to make keys from something like this?"

"Yep, but it will cost you."

"How's ten shillings sound?"

The clerk smiled; he had about half his teeth. "Sounds like sweet music." He took the clay. "Be ready by tomorrow noon."

"I need them right now."

The clerk was smiling his horrid smile again. "Well, now, that's going to cost you another ten bob."

Neumann laid the money on the counter. "I'll wait here while you cut them, if you don't mind."

"Suit yourself."

In the afternoon the rain stopped. Neumann walked a great deal. When he wasn't walking he was jumping on and off buses and rushing in and out of the underground. He had only the vaguest memories of London from when he was a boy, and he actually enjoyed spending the day in the city. It was a relief from the boredom of Hampton Sands. Nothing to do there except run on the beach and read and help Sean in the meadows with the sheep. Leaving the hardware shop, he pocketed the duplicate keys and recrossed Battersea Bridge. He took Catherine's block of clay, crushed it so as to erase the imprints, and tossed it into the Thames. It broke the surface with a deep *bloop* and vanished into the swirling water.

He meandered through Chelsea and Kensington and finally into Earl's Court. He placed the keys in an envelope and the envelope through Catherine's letter box. Then he took his lunch at a window table of a crowded café. A woman two tables away made eyes at him throughout the meal, but he had brought a newspaper for protection and looked up only occasionally to smile at her. It was tempting; she was attractive enough and it might be an enjoyable way to kill the rest of the afternoon and get off the streets for a while. It was insecure, however. He paid his bill, winked at her, and walked out.

Fifteen minutes later he stopped at a phone box, picked up the receiver,

and dialed a local number. It was answered by a man who spoke heavily accented English. Neumann politely asked for a Mr. Smythe; the fellow at the
other end of the line protested a little too vehemently that there was no one
named Smythe at this number. Then he violently rang off. Neumann smiled
and returned the receiver to its cradle. The exchange was a crude code. The
man was the Portuguese courier, Carlos Hernandez. When Neumann called
and asked for someone with a name beginning with an *S,* the courier was to
go to Cavendish Square and collect the material.

He still had an hour to kill. He walked in Kensington, skirting Hyde Park,
and arrived at Marble Arch. The clouds thickened and it started to rain—
just a few cold, fat drops to begin with, then a steady downpour. He ducked
into a bookshop in a small street off Portman Square. He browsed for a bit,
dismissing an offer of assistance from the dark-haired girl standing atop a
ladder stocking books on the top shelves. He selected a volume of T. S. Eliot
and a new novel by Graham Greene called *The Ministry of Fear.* While he was
paying, the girl professed love for Eliot and invited Neumann for coffee
when she took her break at four o'clock. He declined but said he was frequently in the area and would come back. The girl smiled, placed the books
in a brown paper bag, and said she would like that. Neumann walked out,
accompanied by the tinkle of the little bell attached to the top of the door.

He arrived in Cavendish Square. The rain diminished to a chilly drizzle.
It was too cold for him to wait on a bench in the square, so he walked around
it several times, never taking his eye from the doorway on the southwest
corner.

After twenty minutes of this, the fat man arrived.

He wore a gray suit, gray overcoat, and bowler hat and carried himself as
though he were about to rob a bank. He shoved his key in the door as though
he were entering enemy territory and went inside. When the door closed
Neumann crossed the square, removed the film from his jacket pocket, and
dropped it through the mail slot. On the other side of the door he heard the
fat man grunting as he stooped to pick it up. Neumann walked away and
continued his tour of the square, again never taking his eyes from the house.
The Portuguese diplomat emerged five minutes later, found a taxi after a
moment, and was gone.

Neumann looked at his wristwatch. More than an hour before his train.
He thought about going back to the bookshop for the girl. The idea of coffee and intelligent conversation appealed to him. But even innocent discourse was a potential minefield. Speaking the language and understanding

the culture were two different things. He might make a stupid remark and she might become suspicious. It was not worth the risk.

He left Cavendish Square, books beneath his arm, and took the underground east to Liverpool Street, where he boarded the late-afternoon train for Hunstanton.

PART
THREE

CHAPTER THIRTY-ONE

BERLIN: FEBRUARY 1944

"It's called Operation Mulberry," Admiral Canaris began, "and as of now we don't have the slightest idea what it's all about."

A smile flickered across Brigadeführer Walter Schellenberg's lips and evaporated as quickly as summer rain. When the two men had ridden together earlier that morning in the Tiergarten, Canaris had not told Schellenberg the news. Catching a glimpse of Schellenberg's reaction now, Canaris felt no guilt about keeping it from the young general. Their horseback meetings had one unspoken ground rule: each man was expected to use them for his own advantage. Canaris decided to share or withhold information based on a simple formula: did it help his cause? Outright lying was frowned upon. Lying led to reprisals, and reprisals spoiled the affable atmosphere of the rides.

"A few days ago, the Luftwaffe shot these surveillance photographs." Canaris laid two enlargements on the low, ornate coffee table around which they were seated. "This is Selsey Bill in the south of England. We are almost certain these work sites are connected to the project." Canaris used a silver pen as a pointer. "Obviously, something very large is being hastily constructed at these sites. There are huge stockpiles of cement and steel girding. In this photograph a scaffolding is visible."

"Impressive, Admiral Canaris," Hitler said. "What else do you know?"

"We know that several topflight British and American engineers are working on the project. We also know that General Eisenhower is intimately involved. Unfortunately, we are missing one very important piece of the puzzle—the purpose of the giant concrete structures." Canaris paused for a moment. "Find that missing piece, and we may very well solve the puzzle of the Allied invasion."

Hitler was visibly impressed with Canaris's briefing. "I have just one more question, Herr Admiral," Hitler said. "The source of your information—what is it?"

Canaris hesitated. Himmler's face twitched, then he said, "Surely, Admiral Canaris, you don't think anything said here this morning would go beyond this room?"

"Of course not, Herr Reichsführer. One of our agents in London is getting the information directly from a senior member of the Mulberry team. The source of the leak does not know he has been compromised. According to Brigadeführer Schellenberg's sources, British Intelligence knows about our operation but has been unable to stop it."

"This is true," Schellenberg said. "I have it from an excellent source that MI-Five is operating in crisis mode."

"Well, well. Isn't this refreshing, the SD and the Abwehr working together for a change instead of clawing at each other's throats. Perhaps this is a sign of good things to come." Hitler turned to Canaris. "Perhaps Brigadeführer Schellenberg can help you unlock the riddle of those concrete boxes."

Schellenberg smiled and said, "My thoughts precisely."

CHAPTER THIRTY-TWO

LONDON

Catherine Blake tossed stale bread to the pigeons on Trafalgar Square. A stupid place for a rendezvous, she thought. But Vogel liked the image of his agents meeting so near the seat of British power. She had entered from the south, having crossed St. James's Park and walked along Pall Mall. Neumann was supposed to come from the north, from St. Martin's Place and Soho. Catherine, as usual, was a minute or two early. She wanted to see if he was being followed before deciding whether to proceed. The square shone with the morning's rain. A chill wind rose from the river and whistled through a pile of sandbags. A sign pointing to the nearest shelter swayed with the gusts, as though confused about the direction.

Catherine looked north, toward St. Martin's Place, as Neumann entered the square. She watched his approach. A thick crowd of pedestrians jostled along the pavement behind him. Some continued on St. Martin's Place; some broke away and, like Neumann, walked across the square. There was no way to know for certain whether he was being followed. She scattered the rest of the bread and got up. The birds startled, broke into flight, and turned like a squadron of Spitfires toward the river.

Catherine walked toward Neumann. She was especially anxious to deliver this film. Jordan had brought home a different notebook last night—one she had never seen before—and locked it in his safe. That morning, after he left for his office in Grosvenor Square, she returned to the house. When Jordan's cleaning lady left, Catherine slipped inside, using her keys, and photographed the entire book.

Neumann was a few feet away. Catherine had placed the rolls in a small envelope. She withdrew the envelope and prepared to slip it into Neumann's hand and keep walking. But Neumann stopped in front of her, took the envelope, and handed her a slip of paper.

"Message from our friend," he said, and melted into the crowd.

She read the message from Vogel while drinking weak coffee in a café in Leicester Square. She read it again to make certain she understood it. When she finished she folded the note and placed it in her handbag. She would burn it back at her flat. She left change on the table and went out.

Vogel began the message with a commendation for the work Catherine had done so far. But he said more specific information was required. He also wanted a written report on every step she had taken thus far: how she made her approach, how she gained entry to Jordan's private papers, everything he had said to her. Catherine thought she knew what that meant. She was delivering high-grade intelligence, and Vogel wanted to make certain the source was not compromised.

She walked north up Charing Cross Road. She paused now and again to gaze into shop windows and check to see if she was being followed. She turned into Oxford Street and joined a bus queue. The bus came right away and she climbed on board and took a seat upstairs near the rear.

She had suspected the material Jordan brought home would not paint a complete picture of his work. It made sense. Based on the watch report given to her by the Popes, Jordan moved between a pair of offices during the day, one at the SHAEF headquarters on Grosvenor Square and another smaller office nearby. Whenever he carried material between the two offices it was handcuffed to his wrist.

Catherine needed to see that material.

But how?

She considered a second bump, a chance meeting on Grosvenor Square. She could entice him back to his house for an afternoon in bed together. It was fraught with risk. Jordan might become suspicious about another coincidental encounter. There was no guarantee he would go home with her. And even if he did it would be almost impossible to sneak out of bed in the middle of the afternoon and photograph the contents of the briefcase. Catherine remembered something Vogel said to her during her training: *When desk officers grow careless, field agents die.* She decided she would be patient and wait. If she continued to enjoy Peter Jordan's trust, eventually the secret of his work would appear in his briefcase. She would give Vogel his written report, but she would not change her tactics for now.

Catherine looked out the window. She realized she did not know where she was—still in Oxford Street, but where in Oxford Street? She was concentrating so hard on Vogel and Jordan that she had momentarily lost her bearings. The bus crossed Oxford Circus and she relaxed. It was then she noticed the woman watching her. She was seated across the aisle, facing Catherine, and she was staring directly at her. Catherine turned away and pretended to look out the window, but the woman still was staring at her. *What's wrong with that damned woman? Why is she looking at me like that?* She glanced at the woman's face. Something about it was distantly familiar.

The bus was nearing the next stop. Catherine gathered up her things. She would take no chances. She would get off right away. The bus slowed and pulled to the curbside. Catherine prepared to get to her feet. Then the woman reached across the aisle, touched her arm, and said, "Anna, darling. Is it really you?"

The recurring dream began after she killed Beatrice Pymm. It starts the same way each time. She is playing on the floor of her mother's dressing room. Her mother, seated before her vanity, powders a flawless face. Papa comes into the room. He is wearing a white dinner jacket with medals pinned to his breast. He leans over, kisses her mother's neck, and tells her they must hurry or they will be late. Kurt Vogel arrives next. He is wearing a dark suit, like an undertaker, and he has the face of a wolf. He is holding her things: a beautiful silver stiletto with diamonds and rubies in the shape of a swastika on the grip, a Mauser with a silencer screwed into the barrel, a suitcase with a radio inside. "Hurry," he whispers to her. "We mustn't be late. The Führer is extremely anxious to meet you."

She rides through Berlin in a horse-drawn carriage. Vogel the wolf is loping easily in their wake. The party is like a candlelit cloud. Beautiful women are dancing with beautiful men. Hitler is holding forth at the center of the room. Vogel encourages her to go talk to the Führer. She slips through the shimmering crowd and notices everyone is looking at her. She thinks it is because she is beautiful but after a moment everyone has stopped talking, the band has stopped playing, and everyone is staring at her.

"You're not a little girl! You're a spy for the Abwehr!"

"No, I'm not!"

"Of course you are! That's why you have a stiletto and that radio!"

"No! It's not true!"

Then Hitler says, "You're the one who killed that poor woman in Suffolk—Beatrice Pymm."

"It's not true! It's not true!"

"Arrest her! Hang her!"

Everyone is laughing at her. Suddenly she is naked and they laugh even more. She turns to Vogel for help but he has run away and left her. And then she screams and sits up in bed, bathed in sweat, and tells herself it was only a dream. Just a silly, bloody dream.

Catherine Blake took a taxi to Marble Arch. The episode on the bus had left her badly shaken. She chastised herself for not handling it better. She had rushed off the bus, alarmed, after the woman called her by her real name. She should have stayed in her seat and calmly explained to the woman that she was mistaken. It was a dreadful miscalculation. Several people on the bus had seen her face. It was her worst nightmare.

She used the taxi ride to calm down and think it through. She knew it was always a remote possibility—the possibility that she might run into someone who recognized her. She had lived in London for two years after her mother's death, when her father was assigned to the German embassy here. She had attended an English school for girls but made no close friends. She came to the country one other time after that—with Maria Romero on a brief holiday in 1935. They had stayed with friends of Maria and met many other young, rich people at parties and restaurants and theaters. She'd had a brief affair with a young Englishman whose name she could not remember. Vogel had decided it was an acceptable risk. The chances of actually bumping into someone she knew were remote. If she did she was to have a standard response: *I'm sorry, but you must have me confused with someone else.* For six years it did not happen. She had grown careless. When it did happen she panicked.

She finally remembered who the woman was. Her name was Rose Morely, and she had been the cook at her father's house in London. Catherine barely remembered her—only that she cooked rather poorly and always served the meat overdone. Catherine had had very little contact with the woman. It was amazing she recognized her.

She had two choices: ignore it and pretend it never happened or investigate and try to determine the extent of the damage.

Catherine chose the second option.

She paid off the driver at Marble Arch and got out. Dusk was fading quickly into the blackout. A number of bus routes converged on Marble Arch, including the bus she had just fled. With luck, Rose Morely would get off here and change for another bus. The bus she was on would turn down Park Lane to Hyde Park Corner. If Rose stayed on the bus, Catherine would try to slip on without her noticing.

The bus approached. Rose Morely was still in the same seat. As the bus slowed she got to her feet. Catherine had guessed right. The bus stopped. Rose disembarked from the rear doorway.

Catherine stepped forward and said, "You're Rose Morely, aren't you."

The woman's mouth dropped open in surprise. "Yes—and you *are* Anna. I knew it was you. It had to be. You haven't changed a bit since you were a little girl. But how did you get here so—"

"When I realized it was you, I followed in a taxi," Catherine said, cutting her off. The sound of her real name, spoken in a crowd of people, made her shudder. She took Rose Morely by the arm and headed into the gloom of Hyde Park.

"Let's walk for a while," Catherine said. "It's been *so* long, Rose."

That evening Catherine typed her report to Vogel. She photographed it, burned it in the bathroom sink, then burned the ribbon, just as Vogel had taught her. She looked up and caught sight of her own reflection in the mirror. She turned away. The sink was black with the ink and the ash. Her fingers were black too, her hands.

Catherine Blake—*spy.*

She picked up the soap and began working it through her fingers.

It was not a difficult decision. It was worse than she could have imagined. *I emigrated to England before the war,* she had explained, as they walked along the pathway in the gathering darkness. *I couldn't bear the thought of living under Hitler any longer. It was truly horrifying, the things he was doing to the Jews especially.*

Catherine Blake—*liar.*

They must have given you a rough time.

What do you mean?

The authorities, the police. A whisper: *Military Intelligence.*

No, no, it wasn't difficult at all.

I work for a man named Commander Higgins now. I care for his children. His wife was killed in the blitz, poor dearie. Commander Higgins works for the Admiralty. He says anyone who entered the country before the war was assumed to be a German spy.

Oh, really?

I'm sure Commander Higgins will be interested to know you were not harassed.

There's no need to mention any of this to Commander Higgins, is there, Rose?

But there was no escaping it. The British public was very aware of the threat posed by spies. It was everywhere: the newspapers, on the radio, in the movies. Rose was not a foolish woman. She would mention the encounter to Commander Higgins, and Commander Higgins would telephone MI5, and MI5 would be crawling all over central London looking for her. All the meticulous preparation that went into creating her cover would be blown away because of one chance encounter with a domestic who had read too many spy thrillers.

Hyde Park in the blackout. It might have been Sherwood Forest if not for the distant drone of traffic on Bayswater Road. They had switched on their blackout torches, two pencils of fragile yellow light. Rose carried her shopping in her other hand. *Goodness, try feeding children on four ounces of meat a week. I'm afraid they're going to be stunted.* A grove of trees loomed ahead of them, a shapeless black blob against the last light in the western sky. *I have to be going now, Anna. So nice to see you.* They walk a little farther. Do it here, in the trees. No one will see. The police will blame it on some ruffian or refugee. Everyone knows street crime has reached alarming levels in the West End with the war. Take her food and her money. Make it look like a robbery that went wrong. *It was lovely seeing you after all these years, Rose.*

They parted in the trees, Rose walked north, Catherine south. Then Catherine turned around and walked after her. She reached into her handbag and withdrew the Mauser. She needed a very quick kill. *Rose, I forgot something.* Rose stopped and turned around. Catherine raised the Mauser and before Rose could utter a sound shot her through the eye.

The damned ink wouldn't come off. She lathered her hands once more and scrubbed them with a brush until they were raw. She wondered why she hadn't become sick this time. Vogel said it would be easier after a while. The brush took the ink away. She looked up in the mirror again, but this time she held her own gaze. Catherine Blake—*assassin.*

Catherine Blake—*murderer.*

CHAPTER THIRTY-THREE

LONDON

Alfred Vicary felt an evening at home might do him some good. He wanted to walk so he left the office an hour before sunset, enough time for him to make it into Chelsea before becoming stranded in the blackout. It was a fine afternoon, cold but no rain and scarcely a wind. Puffy gray clouds, their bellies pink from the setting sun, drifted over the West End. London was alive. He watched the crowds in Parliament Square, marveled at the antiaircraft guns on Birdcage Walk, drifted through the silent Georgian canyons of Belgravia. The wintry air felt wonderful in his lungs, and he forced himself not to smoke. He had developed a dry hacking cough—like the one he had during final exams at Cambridge—and he vowed to give the damn things up when the war was over.

He crossed Belgrave Square and walked toward Sloane Square. The spell was broken; the case was in his thoughts again. It never really left him. Sometimes he was able to push it slightly farther away than others. January had turned to February. Soon spring would come, then the invasion. And whether it would succeed or fail might be resting squarely on Vicary's shoulders.

He thought about the latest decoded message sent to him by the codebreakers at Bletchley Park. The message was sent the previous night to an agent operating inside Britain. The message contained no code name but Vicary assumed it was one of the spies he was pursuing. It said the information received thus far had been good but more was needed. It also asked for a report on how the agent had contacted the source. Vicary looked for a silver lining. If Berlin needed more intelligence, it did not have a complete picture. If it did not have a complete picture, there still was time for Vicary to plug the leak. Such was the bleak nature of the case that he took heart from logic like that.

He crossed Sloane Square and drifted into Chelsea. He thought of evenings like this a long time ago—before the war, before the bloody blackout—when he would walk home from University College with a briefcase bulging with books and papers. His worries had been much simpler then. Did I put my students to sleep with my lecture today? Will I finish my next book before deadline?

Something else occurred to him as he walked. He was a damned good intelligence officer, no matter what Boothby might say. He was also well suited to it by nature. He was without vanity. He didn't require public praise or accolades. He was perfectly content to toil in secret and keep his victories to himself. He liked the fact that no one knew what he really did. He was secretive and private by nature, and being an intelligence officer only reinforced that.

He thought of Boothby. Why did he pull Vogel's file and lie about it? Why did he refuse to forward Vicary's warning to Eisenhower and Churchill? Why did he interrogate Karl Becker but not pass on the evidence of a separate German network? Vicary could think of no logical explanation for his actions. They were like notes that Vicary could not arrange into a pleasing melody.

He arrived at his home in Draycott Place. He pushed back the door and waded through several days of unanswered post into his darkened drawing room. He considered inviting Alice Simpson to dinner but decided he didn't have the strength for polite conversation. He filled the bath with hot water and soaked his body while listening to sentimental music on the wireless. He drank a glass of whisky and read the newspapers. Since his induction into the secret world he no longer believed a word in them. Then the telephone started ringing. It had to be the office; no one else ever bothered to call him any longer. He struggled out of the bath and covered himself in a robe. The telephone was in the study. He picked up the receiver and said, "Yes, Harry?"

"Your conversation with Karl Becker gave me an idea," Harry said without preamble.

Vicary was dripping bathwater on the papers scattered over his desk. The cleaning lady knew it was verboten even to consider entering his study. As a result it was an island of academic clutter in his otherwise sterile and immaculate home.

"Anna Steiner lived in London with her diplomat father for two years in the early twenties. Rich foreign diplomats have servants: cooks, butlers, maids."

"All true, Harry. I hope this is leading somewhere."

"For three days I've been checking with every agency in town, trying to find the names of the people who worked in that household."

"Good idea."

"I've got a few. Most are dead; the others are old as the hills. There was one promising name, though: Rose Morely. As a young woman she worked as a cook in the Steiner house. Today I discovered she works for a Commander Higgins of the Admiralty at his house in Marylebone."

"Good work, Harry. Set up an appointment first thing in the morning."

"I planned to, but someone just shot her through the eye and left her body in the middle of Hyde Park."

"I'll be dressed in five minutes."

"There's a car waiting outside your house."

Five minutes later Vicary let himself out and locked the door behind him. He realized at that moment that he had completely forgotten about his lunch date with Helen.

The driver was an attractive young Wren who didn't make a sound during the short journey. She took him as close to the scene as she could—about two hundred yards away, at the bottom of a gentle rise. The rain had started up again, and he borrowed her umbrella. He climbed out and softly closed the door, as though arriving at a cemetery for a burial. Ahead of him he saw several long beams of white light bouncing back and forth, like miniature searchlights trying to pick a Heinkel bomber out of the night sky. One of the beams caught his approach, and he had to shade his eyes from the glare. The walk was longer than he estimated; the gentle rise was more like a small hill. The grass was long and very damp. His trousers were soaked from the knee down, as though he had just forded a stream. The torch beams were lowered like swords at his approach. A Detective Chief Superintendent Something-or-Other took him gently by the elbow and walked him the rest of the way. He had the good sense not to speak Vicary's name.

A tarpaulin had been hastily erected over the body. The rain pooled in the center and spilled over one edge like a tiny waterfall. Harry was squatting next to the ruined skull. Harry in his element, Vicary thought. He looked so casual and relaxed hovering over the corpse, he might as well have been resting in the shade on a warm summer's day. Vicary surveyed the scene.

The body had fallen backward and landed with its arms and legs spread wide, like a child making angels in snow. The earth around the head was black with blood. One hand still clung to a cloth shopping bag, and inside the bag Vicary saw tins of vegetables and some kind of meat wrapped in butcher's paper. The paper was leaking blood. The contents of a handbag were strewn about the feet. Vicary saw no money among the things.

Harry noticed Vicary standing there silently and came over to him. They stood side by side for a long moment, neither speaking, like mourners at a graveside, Vicary softly beating his pockets for his half-moon reading glasses.

"It could be a coincidence," Harry said, "but I really don't believe in them. Especially when it involves a dead woman with a bullet through the eye." Harry paused, finally showing emotion. "Christ, I've never seen anyone do it like that. Street thugs don't shoot people in the face. Only professionals do."

"Who found the body?"

"A passerby. They've questioned him. His story seems to check out."

"How long has she been dead?"

"Just a few hours. Which means she would have been killed in the late afternoon or early evening."

"And no one heard the shot?"

"No."

"Perhaps the weapon was silenced?"

"Could have been."

The superintendent came over.

"Well, if it isn't Harry Dalton, the man who cracked the Spencer Thomas case." The superintendent glanced at Vicary; then his gaze returned to Harry. "I'd heard you were working for the irregulars now."

Harry managed a weak smile. "Hello, guv."

Vicary said, "I'm declaring this a security matter as of now. You'll have the necessary paperwork on your desk in the morning. I want Harry to coordinate the investigation. Everything should go through him. Harry will draft a statement in your name. I want this described as a robbery that went wrong. Describe the wound accurately. Don't play around with the details of the crime scene. I want the statement to say the police are searching for a pair of refugees of undetermined origin seen in the park around the time of the murder. And I want your men to proceed with discretion. Thank you, Superintendent. Harry, I'll see you first thing in the morning."

Harry and the superintendent watched Vicary limp down the hill and vanish into the soggy blackness. The superintendent turned to Harry. "Jesus Christ, what's his bloody problem?"

Harry stayed in Hyde Park until the body was taken away. It was after midnight. He hitched a lift from one of the police officers. He could have called for a department car but he didn't want the department to know where he was going. He got out of the car a short distance from Grace Clarendon's flat and walked the rest of the way. She had given him his old key back, and he let himself inside without knocking. Grace always slept like a child—on her stomach, arms and legs sprawled, a pale foot poking from beneath the covers. Harry undressed quietly in the dark and tried to slip into bed without waking her. The bedsprings groaned beneath his weight. She stirred, rolled over, and kissed him.

"I thought you'd left me again, Harry."

"No, just a very long, very dirty night."

She leaned on one elbow. "What happened?"

Harry told her. Harry told her everything.

"It's possible she was killed by the agent we're looking for."

"You look like you've seen a ghost."

"It was bad. She was shot in the face. It's hard to forget something like that, Grace."

"Can I make you forget?"

He had just wanted to sleep. He was exhausted, and being around a body always made him feel dirty. But she began to kiss him, very slowly at first, and softly. Then she was begging him to help her out of her flowered flannel nightshirt, and the madness began. She always made love to him as if she were possessed, clawing and scratching at his body, pulling at him as if trying to draw venom from a wound. And when he entered her she wept and pleaded with him never to leave her again. And afterward, as she lay next to him sleeping, Harry was struck by the most awful thought of his life. He found himself hoping her husband would never come back from the war.

CHAPTER THIRTY-FOUR

LONDON

They gathered around a large model of a Mulberry harbor the following afternoon in a secret room at 47 Grosvenor Square: senior American and British officers assigned to the project; Churchill's personal chief of staff, General Sir Hastings Ismay; and a pair of generals from Eisenhower's staff who sat so still they might have been statues.

The meeting began cordially enough, but after a few minutes tempers flared. There were charges and countercharges, accusations of foot-dragging and distortion, even a few quickly regretted personal insults. *The British construction estimates were too rosy! You Americans are being too impatient, too—well, too bloody American!* It was the pressure, they all agreed, and they started over at the beginning.

With little more than three months remaining until D-Day, the Mulberry project was falling hopelessly behind schedule. *It's the bloody Phoenixes,* drawled an English officer who happened to be assigned to one of Mulberry's more successful components.

But it was the truth: the giant concrete caissons, backbone of the entire project, were perilously behind schedule. There were so many problems it might have been funny if the stakes weren't so high. There were critical shortages of concrete and critical shortages of steel for reinforcement rods. There were too few construction sites and no room in Britain's south coast harbors to moor finished units. There were shortages of skilled workers, and the workers they had on the job were weak and malnourished because there were critical shortages of food.

It was a disaster. Without the caissons acting as a breakwater, the entire Mulberry project was unworkable. They needed someone to go to the construction sites first thing in the morning to make a realistic assessment of whether the Phoenixes could be completed on time, someone who had overseen large projects and knew how to make design modifications in the field once construction was under way.

They chose the former chief engineer of the Northeast Bridge Company, Commander Peter Jordan.

CHAPTER THIRTY-FIVE

LONDON

The Hyde Park shooting made the first editions of the London evening papers. All the papers printed quotes from the bogus police statement. Investigators were treating the murder as a robbery that went wrong; police were searching for two men thought to be Eastern European in origin—very probably Polish—seen near the site of the murder shortly before it occurred. Harry even had invented two rather vague descriptions of the suspects. The newspapers all bemoaned the shocking rise in violent street crime in the West End that had come with the war. The stories contained accounts of men and women who had been beaten and robbed in recent months by bands of roving refugees, drunken soldiers, and deserters.

Vicary felt a tinge of guilt as he leafed through the newspapers at his desk early that afternoon. He believed in the sanctity of the written word and felt bad about misleading the press and the public. His guilt was easily assuaged. It was impossible to the tell the truth—that Rose Morely might very well have been murdered by a German spy.

By midafternoon Harry Dalton and a team of officers from the Metropolitan Police had pieced together the final hours of Rose Morely's life. Harry was in Vicary's office, his long legs propped up on the desk, so that Vicary was treated to a view of his worn soles.

"We interviewed the maid at the home of Commander Higgins," Harry said. "She said Rose had gone out to do her shopping. She went most afternoons before the children arrived home from school. The receipt we found in her bag was from a shop in Oxford Street near Tottenham Court Road. We interviewed the shopkeeper. He remembered her. In fact he remembered almost every item she purchased. He said she bumped into another woman that she knew, a domestic like herself. They took tea together at a café across the street. We spoke to the waitress there. She confirmed it."

Vicary was listening intently, studying his hands.

"The waitress says Rose crossed Oxford Street and queued for a westbound bus. I put a man on as many buses as I could. About a half hour ago we found the ticket collector who was on Rose's bus. He remembered her very well. Said she had a brief conversation with a very tall, very attractive woman who jumped off the bus in quite a hurry. Said that when the bus arrived at Marble Arch, the same very tall, very attractive woman was waiting there. He said he would have called us on his own, but the papers said the police already had their suspects and neither one was a very tall, very attractive woman."

A typist poked her head in the door and said, "Sorry to interrupt but you have a call, Harry. A Detective-Sergeant Colin Meadows. Says it's urgent."

Harry took the call at his desk.

"You the same Harry Dalton that cracked the Spencer Thomas case?"

"I'm the man," Harry said. "What can I do for you?"

"It's concerning the Hyde Park shooting. I think I have something for you."

"Spill it, Detective-Sergeant. We're under a bit of time pressure over here."

"I hear the real suspect is a woman," Meadows said. "Tall, attractive, thirty to thirty-five years old."

"Could be. What do you know?"

"I've been working the Pope murder."

"I read about it," Harry said. "I can't believe someone had the balls to slit the throats of Vernon Pope and his girl."

"Actually, Pope was stabbed in the eye."

"Really!"

"Yeah," Meadows said. "And his girlfriend got it in the heart. One stab wound—surgical, almost."

Harry remembered what the Home Office pathologist had said about the body of Beatrice Pymm. The last rib on her left side had been nicked. Possible stab wound to the chest.

Harry said, "But the papers—"

"You can't trust what you read in the papers, can you, Harry? We changed the descriptions of the wounds to weed out the crazies. You'd be surprised how many people want to take credit for killing Vernon Pope."

"Not really. He was a right bastard. Keep going."

"A woman matching your girl's description was seen entering the Popes' warehouse the night Pope was killed. I have two witnesses."

"Jesus Christ!"

"It gets better. Immediately after the murder, Robert Pope and one of his muscle boys broke into a boardinghouse in Islington looking for a woman. It seems they had the wrong address. Took off like a pair of jackrabbits. But not before they roughed up the landlady."

"Why am I hearing this only now?" Harry snapped. "Pope was killed nearly two weeks ago!"

"Because my super thinks I'm on a wild-goose chase. He's convinced Pope was killed by a rival. He doesn't want us to waste time pursuing *alternative theories,* as he puts it."

"Who's the super?"

"Kidlington."

"Oh, Christ! Saint Andrew?"

"One and the same. There's one other thing. I questioned Robert Pope once last week. I want to question him again but he's gone to ground. We haven't been able to locate him."

"Is Kidlington there now?"

"I can see him sitting in his office doing his bloody paperwork."

"Keep watching. I think you'll enjoy this."

Harry nearly killed himself sprinting from his desk into Vicary's office. He told it very quickly, running over the details so fast that Vicary twice had to ask him to stop and go back to the beginning. When he was finished, Harry dialed the number for him and handed Vicary the receiver.

"Hello, Detective Chief Superintendent Kidlington? This is Alfred Vicary calling from the War Office. . . . I'm fine, thank you. But I'm afraid I need your rather serious help. It's about the Pope murder. I'm declaring it a security matter as of now. A man from my staff will come to your office right away. His name is Harry Dalton. You may remember him. . . . You do? Good. I'd like a complete copy of the entire case file. . . . Why? I'm afraid I can't say any more, Superintendent. Thank you for your cooperation. Good afternoon."

Vicary rang off. He slammed the palm of his hand onto the desk and looked up at Harry, smiling for the first time in weeks.

❖

Catherine Blake packed her handbag for the evening: her stiletto, her Mauser pistol, her camera. She was meeting Jordan for dinner. She assumed they would go back to his house together afterward to make love; they always did. She made tea and read the afternoon newspapers. The murder of Rose Morely in Hyde Park was the big news of the day. The police believed the murder was a robbery that spun out of control and ended in murder. They even had a pair of suspects. Just as she thought. It was perfect. She undressed and took a long bath. She was toweling her wet hair when the telephone rang. Only one person in all of Britain knew her number—Peter Jordan. Catherine pretended to be surprised when she heard his voice at the other end of the line.

"I'm afraid I'm going to have to cancel dinner. I apologize, Catherine. It's just that something very important has come up."

"I understand."

"I'm still at the office. I need to stay here very late tonight."

"Peter, you're not obliged to give me an explanation."

"I know, but I want to. I have to leave London very early tomorrow morning, and I have a lot of work to do before then."

"I'm not going to pretend I'm not disappointed. I was looking forward to being with you tonight. I haven't seen you for two days."

"It seems like a month. I wanted to see you too."

"Is it completely out of the question?"

"I'm not going to be home until at least eleven o'clock."

"That's fine."

"And I have a car picking me up at my house at five in the morning."

"That's fine too."

"But Catherine—"

"Here's my suggestion. I'll meet you in front of your house at eleven. I'll make us something to eat. You can relax and get ready for your trip."

"I need to get some sleep."

"I'll let you sleep, I promise."

"We haven't been sleeping much lately."

"I'll do my best to restrain myself."

"I'll see you at eleven."

"Wonderful."

❖

The red light shone over Boothby's double door for a very long time. Vicary reached out to press the buzzer a second time—a flagrant violation of one of Boothby's edicts—but stopped himself. From the other side of the heavy doors he heard two voices elevated in argument, one distinctly female, the other Boothby's. *You can't do this to me!* It was the woman's voice, suddenly loud and slightly hysterical. Boothby's voice grew calmer in response, a parent quietly lecturing an errant child. Vicary, feeling like an idiot, leaned his ear against the seam in the doors. *Bastard! Bloody bastard!* It was the woman again. Then the sound of a door slamming. The light suddenly shone green. Vicary ignored it. Sir Basil's office had a private entrance, used only by the lord and master himself and by the director-general. It was not all that private; if Vicary waited long enough, the woman would turn the corner and he could get a look at her. He heard the sound of her high-heeled shoes, smacking angrily against the corridor floor. She turned the corner. It was Grace Clarendon. She stopped walking and narrowed her vivid green eyes at Vicary in disgust. A tear tumbled down her cheek. She punched it away, then disappeared down the hallway.

The office was dark except for the single lamp burning on Boothby's desk. The room reeked of the cigarette smoldering untouched at Boothby's elbow. Boothby was working through a file in his braces and his shirtsleeves. Without looking up, he commanded Vicary to sit by jabbing his gold pen at one of the chairs in front of the desk. "I'm listening," he said.

Vicary brought him quickly up to date. He told Boothby about the results of the daylong investigation into the murder of Rose Morely. He told him about the possible link between the German agent and the murder of Vernon Pope. He explained that finding Robert Pope and questioning him was imperative. He requested every available man to assist in the search for Pope. Boothby maintained a stoic silence throughout Vicary's briefing. His habitual fidgeting and pacing had been suspended, and he seemed to be listening more intently than usual.

"Well," Boothby said. "This is the first piece of good news we've had when it comes to this case. I do hope for your sake that you're right about the connection between these killings."

He began making noises about the importance of patience and legwork. Vicary was thinking of Grace Clarendon. He was tempted to ask Boothby why she had just been in his office but couldn't bear the thought of another lecture about need to know. Vicary felt terrible about it. He had miscalculated. He had put Grace's head on the block for the sake of scoring a useless point in a lost argument, and Boothby had chopped it off. He wondered if she had been sacked or had escaped with only a stern warning. She was a valuable member of the staff, intelligent and dedicated. He hoped Boothby had spared her.

Boothby said, "I'll telephone the head of the watchers straightaway, order him to give you as many men as he can possibly spare."

"Thank you, Sir Basil," Vicary said, standing up to leave.

"I know we've had our differences over this case, Alfred, and I *do* hope you're right about all this." Boothby hesitated. "I spoke with the director-general a few minutes ago."

"Oh?" Vicary said.

"He's given you the proverbial twenty-four hours. If all this doesn't produce a break I'm afraid you're going to be removed from the case."

When Vicary was gone, Boothby reached across his desk and picked up the receiver of his secure telephone. He dialed the number and waited for the answer.

As usual the man at the other end of the line did not identify himself, just said, "Yes?"

Boothby did not identify himself either. "It seems our friend is closing in on his prey," Boothby said. "The second act is about to begin."

The man at the other end of the line murmured a few words, then broke the connection.

Her taxi stopped outside Peter Jordan's house at five minutes after eleven. Catherine could see him standing on the pavement outside his front door, blackout torch in hand. She climbed out and paid the driver. An engine started somewhere down the street. The taxi drove off. She took a step toward Jordan and heard the roar of an engine, the sound of tires spinning on the wet street. She turned her head in the direction of the sound and saw a van bearing down on her. It was just a few feet off, too close to get out of the way. She closed her eyes and waited to die.

Dicky Dobbs had never actually killed anyone before. Sure, he had broken his share of bones, ruined his share of faces. He'd even crippled one bloke who refused to cough up protection money. But he had never actually taken a human life. *I should enjoy killing the bitch.* She had murdered Vernon and Vivie. She had given him the slip so many times he had lost count. And God knows what she was doing with the American officer. The taxi turned onto the darkened street. Dicky gently turned the key, igniting the van's engine. He opened the throttle a bit, feeding fuel to the motor. Then he placed his hand on the gearshift and waited. The taxi drove off. The woman started across the street. Dicky dropped the van into gear and opened the throttle full.

A soft, warm darkness surrounded her. She was aware of nothing, only a distant ringing in her ears. She tried to open her eyes but could not. She tried to breathe but could not. She thought of her father and mother. She thought of Maria and she dreamed she was in Spain again, lying on a warm rock beside the stream. There had never been a war; Kurt Vogel had never entered her life. Then, slowly, she became aware of a sharp pain at the back of her head and a great weight pressing down on her body. Her lungs cried out for oxygen. Her body retched but she still could not breathe. She saw bright lights, like comets, shooting across a vast black emptiness. Something was shaking her. Someone was calling her name. And quite suddenly she realized she was not dead after all. The retching stopped and she was finally able to draw a breath. Then she opened her eyes and saw Peter Jordan's face. *Catherine, can you hear me, darling? Are you all right? Jesus Christ, I think he was trying to kill you! Catherine, can you hear me?*

Neither of them felt much like eating. Both of them wanted something to drink. Jordan had a briefcase chained to his wrist—it was the first time he had brought one home with him like that. He went to the study and unlocked it. Catherine heard him working the combination of the safe, pulling open the heavy door, then closing it again. He came out and went into the drawing room. He poured two very large glasses of brandy and carried them upstairs to the bedroom.

They undressed slowly while they drank the brandy. Catherine was having trouble holding on to her glass. Her hands shook, her heart was pounding inside her chest, she felt as if she were about to be sick. She forced herself to drink some of the brandy. The warmth of it took hold of her, and she felt herself begin to relax.

She had made a terrible miscalculation. She should never have gone to the Popes. She should have thought of some other way. But she had made one *other* mistake. She should have killed Robert Pope and Dicky Dobbs too, when she had the chance.

Jordan sat down on the bed next to her. "I don't know how you can be so calm about this," he said. "After all, you were almost killed just now. You're allowed to show some emotion."

Another mistake. She should be acting more frightened. She should be asking him to hold her and tell her everything was all right. She should be thanking him for saving her life. She was no longer thinking clearly. It was spinning out of control, she could feel it. Rose Morely . . . the Popes. . . . She thought of the briefcase Jordan just locked away in his safe. She thought about the contents. She thought about the fact that he had brought it home chained to his wrist. The most important secret of the war—the secret of the invasion—might very well be within her grasp. And if it was really there? If she could really steal it? She wanted to come out. She no longer felt safe. No longer capable of living the double life she had lived for six years. No longer capable of carrying on this affair with Peter Jordan. No longer capable of giving him her body each night and then sneaking into his study. *One assignment, then out.* Vogel had promised. She would hold him to it.

Catherine finished undressing and lay down on the bed. Jordan was still sitting on the edge, drinking his brandy, staring into the darkness.

"It's called English reserve," she said. "We're not allowed to show our emotions, even when we're nearly run over in the blackout."

"When *are* you allowed to show your emotions?" he said, still staring away.

"You could have been killed tonight too, Peter," she said. "Why did you do it?"

"Because I realized something when I saw that damned idiot bearing down on you. I realized that I was desperately, madly, completely in love with you. I have been since the moment you walked into my life. I never thought anyone would ever make me happy again. But you have, Catherine. And I'm terrified of its all going away again."

"Peter," she said softly. His back was to her. She reached up and took hold of his shoulder to pull him down, but his body had gone rigid.

"I always wondered where I was the exact moment she died, what I was doing. I know it sounds morbid, but I was obsessed with it for the longest time. It was because I wasn't there for her. It was because my wife died alone in a rainstorm on a Long Island highway. I always wondered if there wasn't something I could have done. And standing there tonight I saw the whole thing happening all over again. But this time I could do something— something to stop it. So I did."

"Thank you very much for saving my life, Peter Jordan."

"Believe me, the reasons were purely selfish. I waited a very long time to find you, Catherine Blake, and I don't ever want to be without you again."

"Do you mean that?"

"I mean it with all my heart."

She reached for him again, and this time he came to her. She kissed him again and again and said, "God, I love you so much, Peter." She was surprised by how easily the lie came to her lips. He suddenly wanted her very badly. She lay down on her back and opened her legs to him, and when he entered her Catherine felt her body rising toward his. She arched her back to him and felt him deep inside her. It happened so suddenly it made her gasp. When it was over she found she was laughing helplessly.

He laid his head on her breasts. "What's so damned funny?"

"You just make me very happy, Peter—so very happy."

Alfred Vicary maintained a restless vigil at St. James's Street. At nine o'clock he took the stairs to the canteen for something to eat. The fare was atrocious as usual, potato soup and some steamed white fish that tasted as though it came from the river. But he discovered he was ravenously hungry and actually had a second helping. Another officer—a former barrister who looked chronically hung over—asked Vicary for a game of chess. Vicary played poorly and without enthusiasm but managed to pull out the game with a series of rather brilliant moves at the end. He hoped it was an allegory for the way the case would turn out.

Grace Clarendon passed him in the stairwell. She was clutching a batch of files in her arms like a schoolgirl carrying books. She shot Vicary a malevolent glance and clattered downward toward the dungeon of Registry.

Back in his office he tried to work—the Becker network was demanding attention—but it was no good.

Why haven't you told us this before?

I told Boothby.

Harry checked in for the first time—nothing.

He needed an hour of sleep. The clatter of the teleprinters next door, once so pacifying, sounded like jackhammers. His tiny camp bed, once his deliverance from insomnia, became a symbol of all that was wrong with his life. For thirty minutes he moved it around his office, placing it first against one wall, then another, then in the center of the room. Mrs. Blanchard, the supervisor of the night typists, poked her head in Vicary's door, alarmed by the racket. She poured Vicary an enormous glass of whisky, ordered him to drink it, and returned the cot to its usual place.

Harry called again—nothing.

He picked up the telephone and dialed Helen's number. An annoyed man answered. *Hello. . . . Hello. . . . Dammit, who's there?* Vicary quietly replaced the receiver.

Harry checked in for the third time—still nothing.

Vicary, dejected, drafted a letter of resignation.

Ever read Vogel's file?

No.

He tore the letter to shreds and placed the shreds in his burn bag. He lay on his bed, the desk lamp shining on his face, and stared at the ceiling.

He wondered why she had become involved with the Popes. Were they operating in complicity with her, involved in espionage as well as black marketeering and protection rackets? Unlikely, he thought. Perhaps she went to them because of services they could provide: black market petrol, weapons, men to mount a surveillance operation. Vicary could never be certain until he apprehended and questioned Robert Pope. Even then he planned to put the Pope operation under a microscope. If he saw anything he didn't like he would charge the lot of them with spying for Germany and throw them in prison for a very long time. And what about Rose Morely? Was it possible the whole thing was a dreadful coincidence? That Rose had recognized Anna Steiner and had paid for that with her life? Very possible, Vicary thought. But he would assume the worst-case scenario—that Rose Morely actually was an agent too. He would conduct a thorough investigation of her background before closing the book on her murder.

He looked at his wristwatch: one o'clock in the morning. He picked up the telephone and dialed the number once more. This time it was Helen's voice on the other end of the line. It was the first time he had heard it in twenty-five years. *Hello. . . . Hello. . . . Who is this, please?* Vicary wanted to speak but could not. *Oh, bloody hell!* And the connection was broken.

Catherine unlocked the study door, went inside, and closed it softly behind her. She switched on the desk lamp. From her handbag she removed her camera and her Mauser pistol. She laid the pistol on the desk carefully, the butt facing her, so she could swing it up rapidly into the firing position if necessary. She knelt in front of the safe and rotated the dial back and forth. She turned the latch and the door was open. Inside was the briefcase—locked. She unlocked it with her own key, opened it, and looked inside.

A black bound book with the words TOP SECRET—BIGOT ONLY on the cover.

She felt her heart begin to beat faster.

Catherine took the book to the desk, laid it down, and photographed the cover.

She opened it and read the first page:

PHOENIX PROJECT
1) **design specifications**
2) **construction schedule**
3) **deployment**

Catherine thought, My God, I've actually done it!

She photographed that page and turned another.

Page after page of designs—she photographed all of them.

A page labeled CREW REQUIREMENTS—she photographed it.

Another page labeled TOWING REQUIREMENTS—she photographed it.

She ran out of film. She removed the spent film and reloaded the camera. She photographed two more pages.

Then she heard the noise upstairs—Jordan, getting out of bed.

She turned another page and photographed it.

Catherine heard him walking across the floor.

She turned another page and photographed it.

She heard water running in the bathroom.

She photographed two more pages. She would never have access to this document again, that she knew. If it truly contained the secret of the invasion, she had to keep working. While she photographed, she thought what she would do if he walked in on her. Kill him with the Mauser. No one would hear it because of the silencer. She could finish photographing the documents, leave, go to Hampton Sands, find Neumann, and signal the submarine. *Keep working.* . . . And what would happen when SHAEF counterintelligence found the body of an officer who knew the secret of the invasion? They would launch an immediate investigation. They would discover he had been seen with a woman. They would look for the woman and, unable to locate her, conclude she was an agent. They would conclude the documents in his safe had been photographed, that the secret of the invasion had been compromised. She thought, *Don't come in here, Peter Jordan. For your sake and mine.*

She heard the sound of the toilet flushing.

Just a few more pages. She photographed them quickly. Done! She closed the binder, returned it to the briefcase, and placed the briefcase back in the safe. She closed the door quietly and spun the lock. She picked up the Mauser, pulled the slide into the firing position, and turned out the light. She opened the door and crept out into the hall. Jordan was still upstairs.

Think quickly, Catherine!

She walked down the hallway and pushed back the door of the drawing room. She put the Mauser in the handbag and the handbag on the floor. She turned on the light and walked to the drinks trolley. *Calm down. Take a deep breath.* She picked up a glass and was pouring herself a brandy when Peter Jordan walked in.

Harry Dalton was waiting outside the Popes' warehouse in a department surveillance van. He had two men with him, Detective-Sergeant Meadows from the Metropolitan Police and a watcher named Clive Roach. Harry was in the front passenger seat, Roach behind the wheel. Meadows was getting a few minutes of sleep in the back.

It was dawn. It had been a long and dreadfully boring night. Harry was exhausted, but each time he tried to sleep he saw one of two disparate visions: Rose Morely lying dead in Hyde Park or Grace Clarendon's face as they made love. He wanted to climb into her bed and sleep around the clock. He wanted to hold her in his arms and never let go. He was under her spell again.

The visions of Grace were broken by the sound of a van drawing up in front of the warehouse. A tall, thick man climbed out of the driver's-side door. Harry could make him out in the weak morning light.

"Know him?" Clive Roach asked.

Harry said, "Yeah. His name is Dicky Dobbs."

"Looks like trouble."

"He's Pope's main muscle boy and enforcer."

"If I was on the run I think I'd want that one around for protection."

"You're right," Harry said. "Wake up Sleeping Beauty back there."

Dobbs unlocked the judas gate and went inside the warehouse. A moment later the main door was pulled upward. Dobbs emerged and climbed back inside the van.

Roach started the engine as Meadows sat up.

Dobbs pulled the van inside the warehouse.

Roach opened the throttle and gunned the motor, nosing the van inside the warehouse before Dobbs could close the door again.

Harry jumped out of the van.

Dobbs yelled, "What the fuck do you think you're doing?"

Meadows said, "Turn around, put your fucking hands in the air, and shut the fuck up!"

Harry stepped forward and threw open the rear door of the van. Robert Pope was sitting on the floor. He looked up, smiled, and said, "Well, if it isn't my old friend Harry Dalton."

Catherine Blake took a taxi to her flat. It was early, just after dawn, the sky a flat mother-of-pearl gray. She had six hours until she was to meet Horst Neumann on Hampstead Heath. She washed her face and neck and changed out of her clothes into a nightgown and a bathrobe. She desperately needed a few hours of sleep, but she had something to do first.

It had been too close tonight. If Jordan had come downstairs a few seconds earlier she would have been forced to kill him. She told him she had been unable to sleep—she was upset about nearly being killed and thought a glass of brandy would help to calm her nerves. He seemed to accept her excuse for leaving his bed in the middle of the night, but she doubted he would buy it twice.

She went into the sitting room and sat down at the writing table. She opened the drawer and removed a single sheet of paper and a pen. On the paper she wrote four words: *Get me out now!* She placed the piece of paper on the desk and adjusted the lamp so the light was at the proper angle. She removed her camera from her handbag and held it to her eye. She placed her left hand next to the paper. Vogel would recognize it; there was a scar across the thumb where she had been cut during one of his damned silent killing classes. She photographed her hand and the note twice, then burned the note in the bathroom sink.

CHAPTER THIRTY-SIX

LONDON

Harry Dalton thought, One more minute of this bullshit and I'm going to handcuff Pope to a chair and beat his face bloody. They were in a small glass-enclosed office on the warehouse floor, Pope seated on an uncomfortable wooden chair, Harry pacing like a caged jungle cat. Vicary had settled himself quietly in the shadows and seemed to be listening to different music. Harry and Vicary had not revealed their true affiliation; to Pope they were just a pair of Metropolitan Police officers. For one hour Pope had denied any knowledge of the woman whose photograph Harry kept waving in front of him. Pope's face remained bored, placid, and insolent, the look of a man who had broken the law his entire life and never seen the inside of a prison cell. Harry thought, I'm not getting to him. He's beating me.

Harry said, "All right, let's try this one more time."

Pope looked at his watch. "Not again, Harry. I've business to attend to."

Harry felt himself losing control. "You've never seen this woman before?"

"I've told you a hundred times. No!"

"I've got a witness who says this woman entered your warehouse the day your brother was murdered."

"Then your witness is wrong. Let me talk to him. I'm sure I could make him see the error of his ways."

"I'm sure you could! Where were you when your brother was killed?"

"At one of my clubs. I've got a hundred witnesses that will tell you that."

"Why have you been avoiding the police?"

"I haven't been avoiding the police. You blokes managed to find me." Pope looked over at Vicary, who was looking down at his hands. "That one ever speak?"

"Shut up and look at me, Pope. You *have* been avoiding the police, because you know who killed Vernon and you want to pay them back your own way."

"You're talking nonsense, Harry."

"There's a very nice lady in Islington who says you broke into her boardinghouse two hours after Vernon's murder, looking for a woman."

"Your very nice lady in Islington is obviously mistaken."

"Don't bullshit me, Pope!"

"Temper, temper, Harry."

"You've been looking for her for days and you haven't been able to find her. Do you ever wonder why she was able to elude you and your thugs?"

"No, I never wondered that because I don't know what the *fuck* you're talking about."

"Do you ever wonder why you were never able to find out where she lives?"

"I never tried because I never met the woman!"

Harry noticed a sheen of perspiration on Pope's face. He thought, I'm finally getting to him.

Vicary must have noticed it too, because he chose that moment to speak for the first time. "You're not being honest with us, Mr. Pope," he said politely, still studying his hands. Then he looked up and said, "But then, we haven't been exactly honest with you, have we, Harry."

Harry thought, Perfect timing, Alfred. Well done. He said, "No, Alfred, we haven't been completely honest with Mr. Pope here."

Pope looked thoroughly confused. "What the fuck are you two talking about?"

"We're connected with the War Office. We deal in security."

A shadow passed over Pope's face. "What does my brother's murder have to do with the war?" His voice had lost conviction.

"I'm going to be honest with you. We know this woman is a German spy. And we know she came to you for help. And if you don't start talking we're going to be forced to take some rather drastic action."

Pope turned to Harry, as if Harry had been appointed his lawyer. "I can't tell him what he wants to know because I don't know anything. I've never seen that woman in my life."

Vicary seemed disappointed. "Well, then, you're under arrest, Mr. Pope."

"On what bloody charges?"

"Espionage."

"Espionage! You can't do that! You have no evidence!"

"I have enough evidence and enough power to lock you away and throw away the fucking key." Vicary's voice had taken on a menacing edge. "Unless you want to spend the rest of your life in a filthy, stinking jail, I suggest you start talking *now!*"

Pope blinked rapidly, looking first at Vicary, then at Harry. He was defeated.

"I begged Vernon not to take the job but he wouldn't listen," Pope said. "He just wanted to get under her skirt. I always knew there was something wrong with her."

Vicary said, "What did she want from you?"

"She wanted us to follow an American officer. She wanted a complete report on his movements around London. Paid us two hundred quid for it. She's been seeing a lot of him ever since."

"Where?"

"In restaurants. At his house."

"How do you know?"

"We've been following them."

"What does she call herself?"

"Catherine. No last name."

"And what was the officer's name?"

"Commander Peter Jordan, U.S. Navy."

Vicary immediately detained Robert Pope and Dicky Dobbs. He saw no reason to keep his word to a professional thief and liar. Besides, he couldn't have them running around loose on the street. Vicary made arrangements to have them stored on ice at an MI5 lockup outside London.

Harry Dalton telephoned the Americans at Grosvenor Square and asked whether there was a naval officer named Peter Jordan assigned to SHAEF headquarters. Fifteen minutes later someone else called back and said, "Yeah, who wants to know?" When Harry asked about Jordan's assignment, the American said, "Above your pay grade, fella—yours *and* mine."

Harry told Vicary about the conversation. Vicary felt the blood drain from his face.

For ninety minutes no one could find Basil Boothby. It was still early, and he had not arrived at his office. Vicary rang his home at Cadogan Square, and a testy butler said Sir Basil was no longer there. His secretary professed a guarded ignorance about Sir Basil's whereabouts; she expected him quite soon. Boothby, according to the gossip mill, believed he was stalked by his enemies and was notoriously vague about his personal movements. Finally, shortly after nine o'clock, he arrived at his office looking inordinately pleased with himself. Vicary—who hadn't bathed, slept, or changed his clothes in nearly two days—followed him inside and broke the news.

Boothby walked to his desk and picked up the receiver of his secure telephone. He dialed a number and waited. "Hello, General Betts? This is Boothby calling from Five. I need to run a check on an American naval officer named Peter Jordan."

A pause. Boothby drummed his fingers on the desk, Vicary softly kicked at the pattern in Boothby's Persian rug with the scuffed toe of his shoe.

Boothby said, "Yes, I'm still here. . . . He is? Oh, bloody hell! You'd better find General Eisenhower. I need to see him straightaway. I'll contact the prime minister's office myself. I'm afraid we have a rather serious problem."

Boothby slowly replaced the receiver and looked up at Vicary, his face the color of ash.

Frozen fog hung like gunsmoke over Hampstead Heath. Catherine Blake, sitting on a bench surrounded by beech trees, lit a cigarette. She could see for several hundred yards in every direction. She was confident she was alone. Neumann appeared out of the fog, hands pushed deeply into his coat pockets, walking like a man with somewhere to go. When he was a few feet away Catherine said, "I want to talk to you. It's all right, we're alone." He sat down on the bench next to her and she gave him a cigarette, which he lit with hers.

She handed him an envelope containing the film. "I'm fairly certain this is what they're looking for," she said. "He brought it home with him last night—a book detailing the project he's working on. I photographed the entire thing."

Neumann pocketed the envelope. "Congratulations, Catherine. I'll make sure it gets safely into the hands of our friend from the Portuguese embassy."

"There's something else on that film," she said. "I've asked Vogel to pull us out. Some things have gone wrong. I don't think my cover is going to hold up much longer."

"Would you like to tell me about it?"

"The less you know the better, believe me."

"You're the professional. I'm just the errand boy."

"Just be ready to pull out at a moment's notice."

She stood up and walked away.

"Come in and sit down, Alfred," Boothby said. "I'm afraid we have a Force Twelve disaster on our hands." Boothby gestured toward one of the chairs in front of his desk. He had just walked in the door, and his cashmere overcoat still hung like a cape from his shoulders. He shed the coat and handed it to his secretary, who was eyeing him with the intensity of a retriever, waiting for his next command. "Coffee, please. And no interruptions. Thank you."

Vicary lowered himself into the chair. He was feeling peeved. Sir Basil had been gone three hours. The last time Vicary had seen Boothby he was rushing out the door muttering something about mulberries. The code word meant nothing to Vicary. For all he knew it was a tree that produced sweet fruit. Vicary had spent the entire time pacing his office, wondering how bad the damage really was. But there was something else that bothered him. The case had been his from the beginning, and yet it was Boothby who was briefing Eisenhower and Churchill.

The secretary came in, bearing a tray with a silver pot of coffee and dainty china cups. She placed it carefully on Boothby's desk and went out again. Boothby poured. "Milk, Alfred? It's real."

"Yes, thank you."

"What I am about to tell you is highly classified," Boothby began. "Very few people even know of its existence—a handful of top invasion planners and the men on the project itself. Even I knew only the barest details. Until today, that is."

Boothby reached inside his briefcase, withdrew a chart, and spread it over the surface of the desk. He put on his reading glasses, which he had never worn in Vicary's presence, and used his gold pen as a pointer.

"Here are the beaches of Normandy," he began, tapping the map with his pen. "Here is the Baie de la Seine. The invasion planners have concluded that the only way to bring men and supplies ashore quickly enough to sustain the operation is through a large, fully functioning harbor. Without one, the invasion would be a complete fiasco."

Vicary, listening intently, nodded.

"There is just one problem with a harbor—we aren't planning on capturing one," Boothby said. "The result is this." Boothby reached inside his briefcase again and withdrew another chart of the same section of the French coast, except this one had a series of markings depicting a structure along the shoreline. "It's called Operation Mulberry. We're constructing two complete *artificial* harbors here in Britain and towing them across the Channel on D-Day."

"Good Lord," Vicary muttered.

"You're about to be inducted into a very small fraternity, Alfred. Pay close attention." Boothby was using his pen as a pointer again. "These are giant steel floats that will be moored a couple of miles from the coastline. They're designed to dampen the waves as they roll toward shore. Here, they're going to sink several old merchantmen in a line to create a breakwater. That part of the operation is code-named Gooseberry. These are floating roadways with pier heads at the end. The Liberty ships will dock at the pier heads. The supplies will be loaded directly onto trucks and brought to shore."

"Remarkable," Vicary said.

"The backbone of the entire project is these things, here, here, and here," Boothby said, tapping three points on the chart with his pen. "Their code name is Phoenix. They do not rise, however. They sink. They're giant concrete and steel caissons that will be towed across the Channel and sunk in a row to create an inner breakwater. They are *the* most critical component of Operation Mulberry." Boothby hesitated a moment. "Commander Peter Jordan is assigned to that operation."

"My God," Vicary muttered.

"It gets worse, I'm afraid. The Phoenix project is in trouble. They're planning to build one hundred and forty-five of them. The structures are huge—sixty feet high. Some have their own crew quarters and antiaircraft batteries. They require immense amounts of concrete, steel reinforcement, and highly skilled labor. The project has been hampered with shortages of raw materials and construction delays from the beginning."

Boothby folded up the charts and locked them in his desk drawer.

"Last night Commander Peter Jordan was ordered to tour the construction sites in the south and make a realistic assessment of whether the Phoenix units can be completed on time. He walked out of Forty-seven Grosvenor Square with a briefcase chained to his wrist. Inside that briefcase were the plans for the Phoenixes."

"Good God almighty!" Vicary said. "Why the hell did he do that?"

"His family owns the home he's living in here in London. There's a secure safe inside. SHAEF Intelligence inspected it and gave it their stamp of approval."

Vicary thought, None of this would have happened if Boothby had passed on my damned security alert! He said, "So if Commander Jordan has been compromised it's possible a major portion of the plans for Operation Mulberry have fallen into German hands."

"I'm afraid so," Boothby said. "And there's more bad news. Mulberry, by its nature, could betray the secret of the invasion. The Germans know we need ports to successfully carry out an invasion of the Continent. They expect us to stage a frontal assault on a port and reopen it as quickly as possible. If they discover we're building an artificial harbor—some means of circumventing the heavily fortified ports of Calais—they may very well conclude we're coming at Normandy."

"My God! Who in the bloody hell is Commander Peter Jordan?"

Boothby dug in his briefcase again. He brought out a thin file and tossed it across the desk. "He used to be the chief engineer at the Northeast Bridge Company. It's one of the largest bridge construction companies in America. He's considered something of a wunderkind. He was brought onto Operation Mulberry because of his experience overseeing large construction projects."

"Where is he now?"

"Still in the south inspecting the sites. He's due back at Grosvenor Square at seven o'clock. He was supposed to meet with Eisenhower and Ismay at eight o'clock to brief them on his findings. I want you and Harry to pick him up at Grosvenor Square—very quietly—and take him to the house at Richmond. We'll question him there. I want you to handle the interrogation."

"Thank you, Sir Basil." Vicary rose.

"At the very least you're going to need Jordan's help to roll up your network."

"True," Vicary said. "But we may need more help, depending on the extent of the damage."

"You have an idea, Alfred?"

"The beginnings of one." Vicary rose. "I'd like to see the inside of Jordan's house before I question him. Any objections?"

"No," Boothby said. "But softly, Alfred, very softly."

"Don't worry. I'll be discreet."

"Some of the watchers specialize in that sort of thing—breaking and entering, you know."

"Actually, I have someone in mind for the job."

Harry Dalton worked the thin metal tool inside the lock on Peter Jordan's front door. Vicary stood facing the street, shielding Harry from view. After a moment Vicary heard the faint click of the lock giving way. Harry, like a consummate professional thief, opened the door as if he owned the place and led them inside.

"You're damned good at that," Vicary said.

"I saw someone do it in a movie once."

"Somehow, I don't believe that story."

"I always knew you were an intelligent bloke." Harry closed the door. "Wipe your feet."

Vicary opened the door to the drawing room and went inside. His eyes ran over the leather-covered furniture, the rugs, the photographs of bridges on the walls. He walked to the fireplace and examined the silver-framed photos on the mantel.

"Must be his wife," Harry said. "She was beautiful."

"Yes," Vicary said. He had quickly read the copy of Jordan's service file and background check given to him by Boothby. "Her name was Margaret Lauterbach-Jordan. She was killed in an automobile accident on New York's Long Island shortly before the war broke out."

They crossed the hall and looked inside the dining room and the kitchen. Harry tried the next door and found it was locked. Vicary said, "Open it."

Harry knelt down and worked the tool inside the lock. A moment later he turned the latch and they went inside. It was furnished as a working office, certainly for a man: a desk of dark stained wood, a chair of fine leather, and, a unique feature that said much about the occupant, a drafting table and stool that an engineer or an architect might use. Vicary switched on the desk lamp and said, "What a perfect place to photograph documents." The safe was next to the desk. It was old and looked as though it weighed at least five hundred pounds. Vicary looked closely at the legs and noticed they were bolted to the floor. He said, "Let's take a look upstairs."

There were three bedrooms, two overlooking the street, a third larger room at the back of the house. The two in front were obviously guest rooms. The wardrobes were empty and there were no personal touches of any kind. Vicary led them into Jordan's room. The double bed was unmade, the shades raised on windows overlooking a small, unkempt walled garden. Vicary opened the Edwardian wardrobe and looked inside: two U.S. Navy uniforms, several pairs of wool civilian trousers, a stack of sweaters, and several neatly folded shirts bearing the name of a men's shop in Manhattan. He closed the wardrobe and looked around the room. If she had been here she had left no trace, only a faint breath of perfume that hung in the air and reminded Vicary of the fragrance that Helen had worn.

Who is this, please? Oh, bloody hell!

Vicary looked at Harry and said, "Go downstairs, quietly open the door to the study, go inside, and close it again."

Harry came back two minutes later. "Did you hear anything?"

"Not a sound."

"So it's possible she may be slipping into his study at night and photographing everything he brings home."

"We have to assume that, yes. Check out the bathroom. See if she's left any personal items here at all."

Vicary could hear Harry rattling around inside the medicine chest. He came back into the bedroom and said, "Nothing belonging to a woman in there."

"All right. I've seen enough for now."

They went downstairs again, made certain the door to the study was locked, and let themselves out the front door. They had parked around the corner. As they turned onto the pavement Vicary looked up at the terrace of houses across the street. He looked down again very quickly. He could have sworn he saw a face in a darkened window looking back at him. A man's face—dark eyes, black hair, thin lips. He glanced upward again but this time the face was gone.

Horst Neumann played a game with himself to help ease the tedium of waiting: he memorized faces. He had become good at it. He could glance at several faces—on the train or in a crowded square—commit each to memory, then mentally flip through them, the way one looks at photographs in an album. He was spending so much time on the Hunstanton-to-Liverpool-Street run that he was beginning to see familiar faces all the time. The chubby salesman who always fondled his girlfriend's leg before kissing her good-bye at Cambridge and going home to his wife. The spinster who seemed forever on the verge of tears. The war widow who always gazed out the window and, Neumann imagined, saw her husband's face in the passing gray-green countryside. In Cavendish Square he knew all the regulars: the residents of the houses surrounding the square, the people who liked to come sit on the benches among the dormant plants. It was monotonous work, but it kept his mind sharp and helped pass the time.

The fat man came at three o'clock—the same gray overcoat, the same bowler hat, the same jittery air of a decent man embarking on a life of crime. The diplomat unlocked the door to the house and went inside. Neumann crossed the square and slipped the envelope through the slot. He heard the familiar grunt as the chubby diplomat stooped to retrieve it.

Neumann returned to his spot on the square and waited. The diplomat came out a few minutes later, found a taxi, and was gone. Neumann waited for a few minutes to make certain the taxi was not being followed.

Neumann had two hours before his train. He stood up and started walking toward Portman Square. He passed by the bookshop and saw the girl through the window. The shop was empty. She was sitting behind the counter reading the same volume of Eliot she had sold him last week. She seemed to sense someone was watching her, because she looked up suddenly as if startled. Then she recognized him, smiled, and gestured for him to come inside. Neumann opened the door and walked in. "It's time for my break now," she said. "There's a café across the street. Will you join me? My name's Sarah, by the way."

Neumann thought, Oh, what the hell. He said, "I'd love to, Sarah."

Rain beat softly on the roof of the Humber. Cold infiltrated the interior, so they saw their breath when they spoke. Grosvenor Square was unusually quiet, indistinguishable in the blackout. They might have been parked outside the Reichstag for all Vicary could tell. An American staff car slipped into the square, headlamps shrouded. The street shone with the rain in the puddle of light thrown off by the vehicle. Two men climbed out; neither was Jordan. A moment later a motorcycle courier plunged through the darkness. Vicary reflexively thought of France.

He closed his eyes to squeeze away the images and instead saw the face of the man in the Kensington window. Probably nothing more than a nosy neighbor, he told himself. Something troubled him, though—the way the man stood a few feet back from the glass, the way the room was in darkness. He pictured the face: dark hair, dark eyes, a narrow mouth, pale skin, the features arranged in a way to obscure national origin. Maybe German, maybe Italian; maybe Greek or Russian. *Or English.*

Harry lit a cigarette, then Vicary lit a cigarette, and after a moment the back of the Humber was thick with smoke. Vicary wound down his window an inch to release the cloud. The cold poured in and sliced at his face.

Vicary said, "I never knew you were such a star, Harry. Every policeman in London knows your name."

"The Spencer Thomas case," Harry said.

"How did you catch him?"

"The dumb bastard wrote everything down."

"What do you mean?"

"He wanted to remember the details of the murders but he didn't trust his memory. So he kept this bizarre diary. I found it when I searched his room. You'd be surprised at the things some people put in writing."

No, I wouldn't, thought Vicary, remembering the letter from Helen. *I have proven my love for you in a way that I can do for no other man. But I am unwilling to sacrifice my relationship with my father for the sake of a marriage.*

"How's Grace Clarendon?" Vicary asked. He had never asked about her before and the question sounded unnatural, as though he had just asked Harry about rugby or cricket.

Harry said, "She's fine. Why do you ask?"

"I saw her outside Boothby's office last night."

"Boothby always asks for Grace to deliver files to his office personally. Grace thinks it's because he likes to look at her legs. Half the people in the department think she's having it off with him."

Vicary had heard those rumors once upon a time himself: Boothby had slept with everything in the department that wasn't nailed down, and Grace Clarendon had been one of his favorite conquests.

You can't do this to me! Bastard! Bloody bastard!

Vicary had assumed Boothby disciplined Grace over the Vogel file. But it was possible he had just overheard a lover's quarrel. He decided he would not tell Harry any more about it.

The car entered the square a moment later.

Vicary's first image of Jordan would linger with him for a long time, faintly irritating, like the odor of foul cooking trapped in clothes. He heard the low rumble of the approaching staff car and spun his head in time to see Jordan slip past his window. He saw him for less than a split second, but his mind had frozen Jordan's likeness as surely as film traps light. He saw the eyes, looking across the square, as if for hidden enemies. He saw the jawline, taut and crisp, as if steeled for a contest. He noted the cap, pulled tightly to the brow, and the overcoat, buttoned tightly to the throat.

Jordan's staff car stopped in front of Number 47. The engine started and they pulled forward very quickly. Harry got out of the car and pursued Jordan across the pavement.

The rest Vicary watched like a pantomime: Harry asking Jordan to come away and get in the second Humber, which seemed to have materialized from thin air; Jordan looking at Harry as though he were from outer space.

Harry identifying himself in the overpolite manner of a London police of-ficer; Jordan telling him very clearly to fuck off. Harry seizing Jordan's arm, a little too firmly, and leaning over to murmur something into his ear.

All color bleeding from Jordan's face.

CHAPTER THIRTY-SEVEN

RICHMOND UPON THAMES, ENGLAND

The redbrick Victorian mansion was not visible from the road. It stood atop the highest point of the grounds at the end of a ragged ribbon of gravel. Vicary, alone in the back of the freezing Humber, doused the light as he approached the house. During the drive he had read the contents of Jordan's briefcase. His eyes burned and his head was throbbing. If this document was in German hands, it was possible the Abwehr could use it to unlock the secret of the invasion. They could use it to peer through the smoke and the fog of Double Cross and Fortitude. They could use it to win the war! Vicary imagined the scene in Berlin. Hitler would be dancing on the tabletops, clicking the heels of his jackboots. *And it's all because I couldn't find a way to catch that damned spy!*

Vicary rubbed a clear patch in his fogged window. The mansion was dark except for a single yellow light burning over the entrance. MI5 had purchased it before the war from bankrupt relatives of the original owner. The plan had been to use it for clandestine meetings and interrogations and as lodgings for sensitive guests. Used infrequently, it had grown seedy and derelict and looked as though it had been abandoned by a retreating army. The only signs of habitation were the dozen staff cars parked haphazardly in the weedy drive.

A Royal Marine guard appeared out of the darkness and opened Vicary's door. He led him into the cold timeworn hall and through a series of rooms—a drawing room of covered furniture, a library of empty bookshelves—and finally through a pair of double doors that led into a large room overlooking the darkened grounds. It smelled of woodsmoke and brandy and faintly of wet dog. A billiards table had been pushed aside and a heavy oaken banquet table laid in its place. A bonfire burned in the huge fireplace. A pair of dark-eyed Americans from SHAEF Intelligence sat quietly as altar boys in the chairs nearest the flames. Basil Boothby paced slowly in the shadows.

Vicary found his spot at the table. He placed Jordan's briefcase on the floor next to his chair and began slowly unpacking his own. He looked up, caught Boothby's eye, and nodded. Then he looked down again and continued preparing his place. He heard doors opening and two pairs of footsteps crossing the wooden floor. He recognized one set as Harry's and knew the other to be Peter Jordan's.

A moment later Vicary heard Jordan's weight settling into the chair directly across the table from him. Still, he did not look at him. He removed his notebook and a single yellow pencil and laid them on the table carefully, as if arranging a place setting for royalty. Next he removed Jordan's file and laid it on the table. He sat down, opened the first page of his notebook, and licked the tip of his pencil.

Then, finally, Vicary lifted his head and looked Peter Jordan directly in the eye for the first time.

"How did you meet her?"

"I bumped into her in the blackout."

"What do you mean by that?"

"I was walking down the sidewalk without a blackout torch and we collided. She was carrying a bag of groceries. They spilled everywhere."

"Where did this happen?"

"Kensington, outside the Vandyke Club."

"When?"

"About two weeks ago."

"When exactly?"

"Jesus, I don't remember! It might have been a Monday."

"What time in the evening?"

"Around six o'clock."

"What did she call herself?"

"Catherine Blake."

"Had you ever met her before that night?"

"No."

"Had you ever *seen* her before that night?"

"No."

"You didn't recognize her?"

"No."

"And how long were you with her that first night?"

"Less than a minute."

"Did you make arrangements to see her again?"

"Not exactly. I asked her to have a drink sometime. She said she'd like that, and then she walked away."

"She gave you her address?"

"No."

"A telephone number?"

"No."

"So how were you supposed to contact her?"

"Good question. I assumed she didn't want to see me again."

"When *did* you see her again?"

"The next night."

"Where?"

"The bar of the Savoy Hotel."

"What were the circumstances?"

"I was having a drink with a friend."

"The friend's name?"

"Shepherd Ramsey."

"And you saw her in the bar?"

"Yes."

"And she came to your table?"

"No, I went to her."

"What happened next?"

"She said she was supposed to meet a fellow there but she'd been stood up. I asked if I could buy her a drink. She said she would rather leave. So I left with her."

"Where did you go?"

"To my house."

"What did you do?"

"She cooked dinner and we ate. We talked for a while and she went home."

"Did you make love to her that night?"

"Listen, I'm not going to—"

"Yes, you bloody well are, Commander Jordan! Now answer the question! Did you make love to her that night?"

"No!"

"Are you telling me the truth?"

"What?"

"I said are you telling me the truth?"

"Of course I am."

"You don't intend to lie to me tonight, do you, Commander Jordan?"

"No, I don't."

"Good, because I wouldn't advise it. You're in enough trouble as it is. Now, let's continue."

Vicary abruptly changed course, guiding Jordan into calmer waters. For one hour he walked Jordan through his personal history: his childhood on the West Side of Manhattan, his education at Rensselaer Polytechnic Institute, his work with the Northeast Bridge Company, his marriage to the wealthy and beautiful debutante Margaret Lauterbach, her death in an automobile accident on Long Island in August 1939. Vicary asked the questions without notes and as if he did not know the answers, even though he had memorized Jordan's file during the drive. He made certain he controlled the pace and the cadence of the conversation. When Jordan seemed to be too comfortable, Vicary would derail him. All the while Vicary was writing religiously in his notebook. The interrogation was being recorded with hidden microphones, yet Vicary was scribbling as if his little notebook would be the permanent chronicle of the evening's proceedings. Whenever Jordan spoke, there was the maddening sound of Vicary's pencil scratching across the page. Every few minutes Vicary's pencil would dull. He would apologize, force Jordan to stop, then make a vast show of fishing out a new one. Each time he would retrieve just one new pencil—never an extra, just one. Each search seemed to take longer than the last. Harry, watching from the shadows, marveled at Vicary's performance. He wanted Jordan to underestimate him, to think him something of a dolt. Harry thought, Go ahead, you dumb bastard, and he'll cut your balls off. Vicary turned to a fresh page in his notebook and withdrew a new pencil.

"Her name isn't really Catherine Blake. And she isn't really English. Her real name is Anna Katarina von Steiner. But I will never refer to her by that name again. I would like you to forget you ever heard it. My reasons will be made clear to you later. She was born in London before the First War to an English mother and a German father. She returned to England in November 1938 using this false Dutch passport. Do you recognize the photograph?"

"It's her. She looks different now, but that's her."

"We assume she came to the attention of German intelligence because of her background and her language ability. We believe she was recruited in 1936 and sent to a camp in Bavaria, where she was given training in codes and radios, taught how to assess an army, and taught how to kill. In order to conceal her own entry into the country she brutally murdered a woman in Suffolk. We think she's murdered three other people as well."

"That's very difficult to believe."

"Well, believe it. She's different from the rest. Most of Canaris's spies were useless idiots, poorly trained and ill-suited to espionage. We rolled up their networks at the beginning of the war. But we think Catherine Blake is one of their stars, a different kind of agent. We call them sleepers. She never used her radio, and it appears she never engaged in any other operation. She simply melted into British society and waited to be activated."

"Why did she choose me?"

"Allow me to phrase the question differently, Commander Jordan. Did she choose you or did you choose her?"

"What are you talking about?"

"It's simple, really. I want to know why you've been flogging our secrets to the Germans."

"I haven't!"

"I want to know why you've been betraying us."

"I haven't betrayed anybody!"

"I want to know why you're acting as an agent of German intelligence."

"That's ridiculous!"

"Is it? What are we supposed to think? You've been carrying on an affair with Germany's top agent in Britain. You bring home a briefcase full of classified material. Why did you do that? Why couldn't you just *tell* her the secret of Operation Mulberry? Did she ask you to bring home the documents so she could photograph them?"

"No! I mean—"

"Did you volunteer to bring them home?"

"No!"

"Well, why were you walking around with this in your briefcase?"

"Because I was leaving early in the morning to inspect the construction sites in the south. Twenty people will verify that. Personnel security inspected my home and the vault in my study. Under certain circumstances I was allowed to take classified documents there if they were locked in the vault."

"Well, that was obviously an enormous mistake. Because I think you've been bringing those documents home and handing them over to Catherine Blake."

"That's not true."

"I'm just not sure whether you're a German agent or whether you've been seduced into spying."

"Go fuck yourself! I've had enough of this."

"I want to know if you've betrayed us for sex."

"No!"

"I want to know if you've betrayed us for money."

"I don't need money."

"Are you working in collusion with the woman known to you as Catherine Blake?"

"No."

"Have you knowingly or willingly supplied Allied secrets to the woman known to you as Catherine Blake?"

"No!"

"Are you working directly for German military intelligence?"

"That's a ridiculous question."

"Answer it!"

"No! Goddammit, no!"

"Are you involved in a sexual relationship with the woman known to you as Catherine Blake?"

"That's my business."

"Not anymore, Commander. I ask you again. Are you involved in a sexual relationship with Catherine Blake?"

"Yes."

"Are you in love with Catherine Blake? Commander, did you hear the question? Commander? Commander Jordan, are you in love with Catherine Blake?"

"Until a couple hours ago I was in love with the woman I *thought* was Catherine Blake. I didn't know she was a German agent and I didn't willingly give her Allied secrets. You must believe me."

"I'm not sure I do, Commander Jordan. But let's move on."

❖

"You enlisted in the navy last October."

"That's correct."

"Why not sooner?"

"My wife is dead. I didn't want to leave my son alone."

"Why did you change your mind?"

"Because I was *asked* to join the navy."

"Tell me how it was done."

"Two men came to my office in Manhattan. It was clear they had already checked out my background, both personal and professional. They said my services were required for a project connected with the invasion. They didn't tell me what that project was. They asked me to go to Washington, and I never saw them again."

"What were their names?"

"One was called Leamann. I don't recall the other man's name."

"Were they both American?"

"Leamann was an American. The other one was British."

"But you don't remember his name?"

"No."

"How did he look?"

"He was tall and thin."

"Well, that narrows it to about half the country. What happened when you went to Washington?"

"After my security clearance came through, I was briefed on Mulberry and shown the actual plans."

"Why did they need you?"

"They wanted someone who'd had experience on large construction projects. My company had built some of the biggest bridges in the East."

"And what were your initial impressions?"

"I thought Mulberry was feasible technically, but I thought the construction schedule was a farce—far too optimistic. I could see right away that there would be delays."

"And what were your conclusions after the inspection you carried out today?"

"That the project is dangerously behind schedule. That the chance of actually completing the Phoenixes on time is about one in three."

"Did you share these conclusions with Catherine Blake?"

"Please. Let's not go through this again."

"You're not answering my question."

"No, I did not share those conclusions with Catherine Blake."

"Did you see her before we picked you up at Grosvenor Square?"

"No. I went to SHAEF directly from the construction sites."

Vicary reached in his briefcase and laid two photographs on the table, one of Robert Pope and the other of Dicky Dobbs.

"Have you ever seen these men?"

"They look vaguely familiar, but I can't tell you where I've seen them."

Vicary opened Jordan's file and flipped a page. "Tell me about the house you're living in."

"My father-in-law purchased it before the war. He spent a fair amount of time in London on business and pleasure and wanted a comfortable place to stay when he was in town."

"Anyone else use the house?"

"Margaret and I used it when we came to Europe on vacation."

"Did your father-in-law's bank have German investments?"

"Yes, many. But he liquidated most of them before the war."

"Did he oversee that liquidation personally?"

"Most of the work was done by a man named Walker Hardegen. He's the number-two man at the bank. He also speaks fluent German and knows the country inside and out."

"Did he travel to Germany before the war?"

"Yes, several times."

"Did you ever accompany him?"

"No. I have nothing to do with my father-in-law's business."

"Did Walker Hardegen use the house in London?"

"He may have, I'm not certain."

"How well do you know Walker Hardegen?"

"I know him very well."

"Then I suppose you're good friends?"

"No, not really."

"You know him well but you're not friends?"

"That's right."

"Are you enemies?"

"Enemies is a strong word. We just don't get along well."

"Why not?"

"He dated my wife before I met her. I think he was always in love with her. He drank quite a bit at my going-away party. He accused me of killing her to make a business deal."

"I think someone who made a remark like that to me would be my enemy."

"I thought about knocking the hell out of him at the time."

"Do you blame yourself for your wife's death?"

"Yes, I always have. If I hadn't asked her to come into the city for that goddamned business dinner she'd still be alive."

"How much does Walker Hardegen know about your work?"

"Nothing."

"He knows you're a gifted engineer?"

"Yes."

"He knows you were sent to London to work on a secret project?"

"He could probably deduce that, yes."

"Have you ever mentioned Operation Mulberry in your letters home?"

"Never. They were all cleared by the censor."

"Did you ever tell any other member of your family about Operation Mulberry?"

"No."

"Ever tell any of your friends?"

"No."

"This fellow Shepherd Ramsey. Ever tell him?"

"No."

"Does he ever ask about it?"

"All the time—in a joking manner, of course."

"Did you have plans to see Catherine Blake again?"

"I don't have plans to see her. I never want to see her again."

"Well, that may not be possible, Commander Jordan."

"What are you talking about?"

"In due time. It's late. I think we all could use some sleep. We'll continue in the morning."

Vicary rose and walked to where Boothby was sitting. He leaned down and said, "I think we should talk."

"Yes," Boothby said. "Let's go in the next room, shall we?" He uncoiled himself from his chair and took Vicary by the elbow. "You did a marvelous job with him," he said. "My God, Alfred, when did you become such a bastard?"

Boothby pulled open a door and held out his hand for Vicary to enter first. Vicary brushed past Boothby and stepped inside the room.

He couldn't believe his eyes.

Winston Churchill said, "Hello, Alfred. So good to see you again. I wish it could be under different circumstances. I'd like to introduce you to a friend of mine. Professor Alfred Vicary, meet General Eisenhower."

Dwight Eisenhower rose from his seat and stuck out his hand.

The room had been a study once. There were bookshelves built into the walls, a writing desk, and a pair of wing chairs where Churchill and Eisenhower sat now. A wood fire burned brightly in the hearth, but it had failed to take the chill off the room. A woolen blanket lay across Churchill's knees. He was gnawing on the damp end of a dead cigar and drinking brandy. Eisenhower lit a cigarette and sipped black coffee. On the table between them was a small speaker, which they had used to monitor the interrogation of Jordan. Vicary knew this because the microphones were still turned on and he could hear a scrape of chairs and a murmur of voices coming from the next room. Boothby glided forward and turned down the volume. The door opened and a fifth man entered the room. Vicary recognized the tall, bearlike build: Brigadier General Thomas Betts, the deputy chief of intelligence at SHAEF and the man charged with safeguarding the secret of the invasion.

"Is he telling the truth, Alfred?" Churchill asked.

"I'm not sure," Vicary said, pouring himself a cup of coffee at the sideboard. "I want to believe him but something is bothering me, and I'm damned if I know what it is."

Boothby said, "Nothing in his background would suggest he's a German agent or that he's willingly betrayed us. After all, we came to him. He was *recruited* to work on Mulberry, he didn't volunteer. If he was an agent the entire time, he would have been banging on the door early in the war, trying to work himself into a position of importance."

"I agree," Eisenhower said.

"His background is sterling," Boothby continued. "You saw his file. His FBI background check didn't turn up a thing. He has all the money in the world. He's not a Communist. He doesn't bugger little boys. We have no reason to think he's sympathetic to the German cause. In short, we have no reason to suspect this man is a spy or has been coerced into spying."

"All true," Vicary said, thinking, When the hell did Boothby become chairman of the Peter Jordan fan club? "But what about this man Walker Hardegen? Was he checked out before Jordan came to the Mulberry team?"

"Thoroughly," General Betts said. "The FBI was concerned about his German contacts long before the War Department ever approached Jordan about working on Mulberry. They looked into Hardegen's background with a microscope. They didn't turn up a blessed thing. Hardegen is clean as a whistle."

"Well, I'd feel better if they took another look," Vicary said. "How in the bloody hell did she know to go after him? And how's she getting the material? I've been inside his house. It's possible she's getting into his papers without his knowledge, but it would be very dangerous. And what about his friend Shepherd Ramsey? I'd like to put him under surveillance and have the FBI look deeper into his background."

Churchill said, "I'm sure General Eisenhower won't have a problem with that, would you, General?"

"No," Eisenhower said. "I want you gentlemen to take whatever steps you feel are necessary."

Churchill cleared his throat. "This debate is very interesting, but it doesn't address our most pressing problem," he said. "It appears this fellow—intentionally or not—has delivered a very significant portion of the plans for Operation Mulberry directly into the hands of a German spy. Now, what are we going to do about it? Basil?"

Boothby turned to General Betts. "How much can the Germans discern about Operation Mulberry from that one document?"

"It's difficult to say," Betts said. "The document Jordan had in his briefcase doesn't give them a complete picture, just a damned important slice of it. There are many more components of Mulberry, as I'm sure you're well aware. This just tells them about the Phoenixes. If that document is truly on its way to Berlin, their analysts and engineers are going to be poring all over it. If they're able to determine the purpose of the Phoenixes, it won't be difficult for them to unlock the secret of the artificial harbor project." Betts hesitated, his face grave. "And gentlemen, if they're convinced we're building an artificial harbor, it's very possible they could make the leap and conclude we're coming at Normandy, not Calais."

Vicary said, "I think we should *assume* that is the case and proceed accordingly."

"My suggestion is that we use Jordan to lure Catherine Blake into the open," Boothby said. "We arrest her, put her under the bright lights, and turn her. We use her to funnel smoke back to the Germans—confuse them, try to convince them that Mulberry is anything but an artificial harbor meant for Normandy."

Vicary cleared his throat gently and said, "I fully agree with the second half of that proposal, Sir Basil. But I suspect the first half wouldn't be quite as easy as it sounds."

"Your point, Alfred?"

"Everything we know about this woman suggests she is highly trained and thoroughly ruthless. I doubt we'd succeed in convincing her to cooperate with us. She's not like the others."

"It's been my experience that everyone cooperates when they're faced with the prospect of a hanging, Alfred. But what are you suggesting?"

"I suggest that Peter Jordan continue to see her. But from now on, we control what's inside that briefcase and what goes home into that safe. We let her run and we watch her. We discover how she's getting the material back to Berlin. We discover the other agents in the network. Then we arrest her. If we roll up the network cleanly, we'll be able to feed Double Cross material directly to the highest levels of the Abwehr—right up to the invasion."

Churchill said, "Basil, what do you think of Alfred's plan?"

"It's brilliant," Boothby said. "But what if Alfred's fears about Commander Jordan are correct? What if he truly is a German agent? Jordan would be in a position to do irreparable damage."

"That would be true under your scenario as well, Sir Basil. I'm afraid it's a risk we're going to have to take. But Jordan will never be alone with her or anyone else for a second. As of now he is under round-the-clock surveillance. Wherever he goes, we go. If we see or hear anything we don't like, we move in, arrest Catherine Blake, and do it your way."

Boothby nodded. "Do you think Jordan can pull it off? After all, he just told us he was in love with this woman. She betrayed him. I don't think he's going to be in any condition to continue carrying on a romantic relationship with her."

"Well, he simply has to," Vicary said. "He's the one who got us into this damned mess, and he's the only one who can get us out. It's not as though we could move the chairs around and slip a professional in there. They *chose* him. No one else will do. They'll believe what they see in *Jordan's* briefcase."

Churchill looked at Eisenhower. "General?"

Eisenhower crushed out his cigarette, thinking for a moment, and then said, "If there's truly no other way to do it, I support the professor's plan. General Betts and I will make certain you have the necessary support from SHAEF to make it work."

"Then it's done," Churchill said. "And God help us if it doesn't work."

❖

"My name is Vicary, by the way, Alfred Vicary. This is Harry Dalton—he works with me. And this gentleman is Sir Basil Boothby. He's in charge."

It was early the next morning, an hour after dawn. They were walking a narrow footpath through the trees—Harry a few paces ahead, like a scout, Vicary and Jordan side by side, Boothby looming over them from behind. The rain had stopped during the night, but the sky was still thick with cloud. The nickeled winter light bleached all color from the trees and the hills. A gauze of fog covered the ground in the low spots, and the air smelled of woodsmoke from the fires burning inside the house. Jordan's gaze settled briefly on each of them as they were introduced, but he did not offer his hand. Both remained jammed in the pockets of the jacket that had been left in his room, along with a pair of woolen trousers and a heavy country sweater.

They moved along the path in silence for a time, like old schoolmates walking off a heavy breakfast. The cold felt like a nail in Vicary's knee. He walked slowly, hands clasped behind his back, head down as if looking for a lost object. The trees broke and the Thames appeared before them. A pair of wooden benches stood on the bank. Harry sat on one, Vicary and Jordan on the other. Boothby remained standing.

Vicary explained to Jordan what they wanted him to do. Jordan listened without looking at anyone. He sat motionless, hands still in his pockets, legs stretched out before him, gaze fixed on some obscure point on the surface of the river. When Vicary finished, Jordan said, "Find some other way to do it. I'm not up to it. You'd be a fool to use me."

"Believe me, Commander Jordan. If there were some other way to reverse the damage that's been done, I'd do it. But there isn't. You *must* do this. You owe it to us. You owe it to all the men who will risk their lives trying to storm the beaches of Normandy." He paused a moment and followed Jordan's gaze onto the water. "And you owe it to yourself, Commander Jordan. You made a terrible mistake. Now you have to help repair the damage."

"Is that supposed to be a pep talk?"

"No, I don't believe in pep talks. It's the truth."

"How long will it last?"

"As long as necessary."

"You're not answering my question."

"That's right. It could be six days or six months. We just don't know.

This isn't an exact science. But I will end it as soon as I can. On that you have my word."

"I didn't think the truth counted for much in your line of work, Mr. Vicary."

"Not usually. But it will in this case."

"What about my work on Operation Mulberry?"

"You'll go through the motions of being an active member of the team, but the truth is you're finished." Vicary stood up. "We should get back to the house, Commander Jordan. We have a few papers for you to sign before we leave."

"What sort of papers?"

"Oh, just something that binds you to never breathe a word of this for the rest of your life."

Jordan turned away from the river and finally looked at Vicary.

"Believe me, you don't need to worry about that."

CHAPTER THIRTY-EIGHT

RASTENBURG, GERMANY

Kurt Vogel was fussing with his collar. He was wearing his Kriegsmarine uniform for the first time in longer than he could remember. It fit before the war but Vogel, like almost everyone else, had lost weight. Now his tunic hung on him like prison pajamas.

He was nervous as hell. He had never met the Führer; in fact he had never been in the same room with the man. Personally, he thought Hitler was a lunatic and a monster who had led Germany to the brink of catastrophe. But he found he was eager to meet him and, for some inexplicable reason, he wanted to make a good impression. He wished he had a better speaking voice. He chain-smoked to ease his nerves. He had smoked the entire flight from Berlin and now he was smoking again in the car. Canaris finally pleaded with him to put the damned thing out for the sake of the dachshunds. They were lying at Vogel's feet like fat sausages, glaring up at him malevolently. Vogel cracked the window and tossed his cigarette into the swirling snow.

The staff Mercedes stopped at the outer checkpoint of Hitler's *Wolf-schanze*. Four SS guards descended on the car, threw open the hood and the trunk, and used mirrors to search the undercarriage. The SS men waved them forward and they drove a half mile toward the compound. It was late afternoon, but the forest floor burned with brilliant white arc light. Guards with Alsatians patrolled the footpaths.

The car stopped again in the compound, and again they were set upon by SS men. This time the inspection was personal. They were ordered out of the car and body-searched. Vogel was shocked at the sight of Wilhelm Canaris, the chief of Germany's intelligence service, standing with his arms in the air, an SS man patting him down as if he were a beerhall drunk.

A guard demanded Vogel's briefcase, and he reluctantly handed it over.

It contained the photographs of the Allied documents and the hastily produced analysis from the Abwehr technical staff in Berlin. The SS man dug inside the briefcase with a gloved hand and then returned it to Vogel, satisfied it contained no weapons or explosives.

Vogel joined Canaris, and they walked wordlessly toward the stairs that descended into the bunker. Two of the photographs Vogel had left behind in Berlin, locked in his file cabinets—the photographs of the note. The hand was hers; Vogel recognized the jagged scar at the base of her thumb. He was torn. Accede to her wishes and extract her from Britain or leave her in place? He suspected the decision would be made for him.

Another SS man waited at the top of the stairs, just in case the Führer's visitors were somehow able to arm themselves during the walk across the compound. Canaris and Vogel stopped and submitted to yet another search.

Canaris looked at Vogel and said, "Welcome to Camp Paranoia."

Vogel and Canaris were the first to arrive. "Smoke now before the chicken farmer gets here," Canaris said. Vogel cringed at the remark; surely the room was thoroughly bugged. Leafing through his files, he fought off the craving for tobacco.

Vogel watched as the most powerful men of the Third Reich filed into the room one by one: Reichsführer SS Heinrich Himmler, Brigadeführer Walter Schellenberg, Field Marshal Gerd von Rundstedt, Field Marshal Erwin Rommel, and Hermann Göring.

They all rose when Hitler entered the room, twenty minutes behind schedule. He wore slate-gray trousers and a black tunic. He remained standing after everyone else sat. Vogel watched him, fascinated. The hair was graying, the skin sallow, the eyes red-rimmed. The dark circles beneath them were so pronounced they looked like bruises. Yet there was a daunting energy about him. For two hours he dominated the other men in the room as he led the conference on preparations for the invasion—probing, challenging, dismissing information or insight deemed irrelevant. It was clear to Vogel that Adolf Hitler knew as much, if not more, about the disposition of his forces in the West than his senior military officers. His attention to detail was astonishing. He demanded to know why there were three fewer antiaircraft guns in the Pas de Calais than in the previous week. He wanted to know the exact kind of concrete used for the Atlantic Wall fortifications and the precise thickness at which it was laid.

Finally, at the end of the conference, he turned to Canaris and said, "So.

I'm told the Abwehr has uncovered another piece of information that might shed some light on the enemy's intentions."

"Actually, my Führer, the operation was conceived and executed by Captain Vogel. I'll allow him to brief you on his findings."

"Fine," Hitler said. "Captain Vogel?"

Vogel remained seated. "My Führer, two days ago in London one of our agents took possession of a document. As you know, we have discovered the enemy is engaged in something called Operation Mulberry. Based on these new documents we are now closer to learning exactly what Mulberry is."

"Closer?" Hitler said, his head tilting back. "So you are still engaging in guesswork, Captain?"

"If I may continue, my Führer."

"Please, but I have limited patience this evening."

"We now know much more about the giant concrete and steel structures being built at several points around England. We now know they are code-named Phoenix. We also know that when the invasion comes they will be towed across the English Channel and sunk off the coast of France."

"Sunk? For what possible purpose, Captain Vogel?"

"For the past twenty-four hours, our technical analysts have been poring over the documents stolen in London. Each of the submersible units contains quarters for a crew and a large antiaircraft gun. It is possible the enemy is planning to create a huge coastal antiaircraft complex to provide additional cover for their troops during the invasion."

"Possible," Hitler said. "By why go to so much trouble to construct an antiaircraft facility? All your estimates indicate the British are desperately short of raw materials—steel, concrete, aluminum. You've been telling me that for months. Churchill has bankrupted Britain with this foolish war. Why waste precious supplies on such a project?"

Hitler turned and glared at Göring. "Besides, I'm afraid we must assume that the enemy will enjoy supremacy in the air during the invasion."

Hitler turned back toward Vogel. "Do you have a second theory, Captain Vogel?"

"We do, my Führer. It is a minority opinion, very preliminary, and still open to a great deal of interpretation."

"Let's hear it," he snapped.

"One of our analysts believes the submersible units might actually be components of some sort of artificial harbor, a device that could be constructed in Britain, towed across the Channel, and installed along the French coast during the first hours of the invasion."

Hitler, intrigued, was pacing again. "An artificial harbor? Is such a thing possible?"

Himmler cleared his throat gently. "Perhaps your analysts are misreading the information provided by the agent, Captain Vogel. An artificial harbor sounds a little far-fetched to me."

"No, Herr Reichsführer," Hitler said, "I think Captain Vogel may be on to something here." Hitler paced the room violently. "An artificial harbor! Imagine the arrogance, the audacity of such a project! I see the fingerprints of that madman Churchill all over this."

"My Führer," Vogel said hesitantly, "an artificial harbor is only one possible explanation for these concrete units. I would caution against putting too much emphasis on these early findings."

"No, Captain Vogel, I am intrigued by this theory of yours. Let's take it to the next level, just for argument's sake. If the enemy is actually engaged in an attempt to build something as elaborate as an artificial harbor, where would he put it? Von Rundstedt, you first."

The old field marshal rose, walked to the map, and tapped at it with his baton. "If one studies the failed enemy assault on Dieppe in 1942, one can learn valuable lessons. The enemy's primary objective was to seize and open a major port as quickly as possible. The enemy failed, of course. The problem is this: the enemy knows we will deny him the use of ports for as long as possible and that we will cripple those ports before surrendering them. I suppose it is possible the enemy might be constructing facilities in Britain that would allow him to reopen the ports more quickly. That makes sense to me. *If* that is the case—and I stress that Captain Vogel and his colleagues have no conclusive proof it is so—I still believe it is Calais. An invasion at Calais still makes the most sense militarily and strategically. This cannot be ignored."

Hitler listened carefully, then turned to Vogel. "What do you think of the field marshal's analysis, Captain Vogel?"

Vogel looked up. Von Rundstedt's icy gaze had settled on him. He knew he had to proceed very carefully.

"Field Marshal von Rundstedt's argument is extremely sound." Vogel paused as von Rundstedt nodded in acknowledgment. "But for the sake of discussion, may I offer a second interpretation?"

"Do so," Hitler said.

"As the field marshal has pointed out, the enemy desperately needs port facilities if he is to build up supplies quickly enough to sustain an invasion force. We estimate that would require at least ten thousand tons of supplies each day during the first phase of the operation. Any of the ports on the Pas de Calais could sustain such a massive buildup—Calais, Boulogne, Dunkirk for example. But as Field Marshal von Rundstedt pointed out, the enemy knows we will demolish those ports before surrendering them. The enemy also knows those ports will be heavily defended. A frontal assault on any one of them would be very costly."

Vogel could see that Hitler was fidgeting, growing impatient. He hurried things along.

"Along the Normandy coast there are a number of small fishing ports, none of them large enough to handle the necessary buildup of matériel and heavy equipment. Even Cherbourg might not be large enough. Remember, it was designed as a passenger terminal for transatlantic liners, not for discharging cargo."

"Your point, Captain Vogel," Hitler said, an edge to his voice.

"My Führer, what if it were possible for the enemy to build up his supplies and equipment on open beaches rather than through a port? If that were indeed possible, the enemy could avoid our strongest defenses, land on the less heavily defended beaches of Normandy, and attempt to supply an invasion force through the use of an artificial harbor."

Hitler's eyes flickered. He was clearly intrigued by Vogel's analysis.

Field Marshal Erwin Rommel was shaking his head. "A scenario such as yours would be a recipe for disaster, Captain Vogel. Even in spring the weather along the Channel coast can be extremely hazardous—rain, high winds, heavy seas. My staff has studied the patterns. If history is a guide, the enemy can expect periods of good weather for no more than three or four days at a time. If he attempts to build up his forces on an open beach, with no harbor and no sheltered water, the enemy will be totally at the mercy of nature. And no portable device, no matter how ingenious, will survive a springtime gale on the English Channel."

Hitler stepped in. "A fascinating discussion, gentlemen—but enough. Obviously, Captain Vogel, your agent needs to discover more about the project. I assume the agent is still in place?"

Vogel proceeded carefully.

"There *is* a problem, my Führer," Vogel said. "The agent feels the British security forces may be closing in—that it may not be safe to remain in England much longer."

Walter Schellenberg spoke for the first time. "Captain Vogel, our own source in London says quite the opposite—that the British know there is a leak but have been unable to plug it. Your agent is imagining the danger at this time."

Vogel thought, Arrogant ass! Who's this great source the SD has in London? He said, "The agent in question is highly trained and exceptionally intelligent. I think—"

Himmler cut Vogel off. "Surely you don't assume Brigadeführer Schellenberg's source is less credible than your own, Captain Vogel."

"With respect, I have no way to judge the credibility of the brigadeführer's source, Herr Reichsführer."

"A very diplomatic answer, Herr Captain," Himmler said. "But clearly your agent should remain in place until we know the truth about these concrete objects, wouldn't you agree?"

Vogel was trapped. To disagree with Himmler would be like signing his own death warrant. They could manufacture evidence of treason against him and hang him with piano wire like they did the others. He thought of Gertrude and the children. The barbarians would go after them too. He trusted Anna's instincts, but to pull her out now would be suicide. He had no choice. She would remain in place.

"Yes. I agree, Herr Reichsführer."

Himmler invited Vogel for a walk around the grounds. Night had fallen. Beyond the sphere of arc light the forest was very dark. A sign warned not to stray from the footpath because of mines. Wind stirred the tops of the conifers. Vogel could hear a dog barking; it was difficult to tell how far away because the new snow reduced all sound to a dull muffle. It was bitter cold. During the tense meeting he had perspired heavily beneath his tunic. Now, in the cold, it felt as if his clothes had frozen to his body. He craved a cigarette but decided not to risk offending Himmler further for one day. Himmler's voice, when he finally spoke, was nearly inaudible. Vogel wondered if it was possible to bug a forest.

"A remarkable achievement, Captain Vogel. You are to be commended."

"I'm honored, Herr Reichsführer."

"Your agent in London is a woman."

Vogel said nothing.

"It was always my impression that Admiral Canaris distrusted female agents. That he believed they are too susceptible to emotion for clandestine work and lack the necessary objectivity."

"I can assure you, Herr Reichsführer, that the agent involved has none of those shortcomings."

"I must admit I find the practice of inserting female agents behind enemy lines a bit distasteful myself. The SOE persists in sending women into France. When they are arrested, I'm afraid the women suffer the same fate as the men. To inflict such suffering on a woman is regrettable, to say the least." He paused, cheek muscle twitching, and breathed deeply of the cold night air. "Your achievement is even more remarkable because you succeeded in spite of Admiral Canaris."

"I'm not sure what you mean, Herr Reichsführer."

"What I mean is that the admiral's days at the Abwehr are numbered. We have been unhappy with his performance for some time. He is at least an incompetent. And if my suspicions are correct, he's a traitor to the Führer as well."

"Herr Reichsführer, I've never——"

Himmler cut him off with a wave of his hand.

"I know you feel a certain loyalty to Admiral Canaris. After all, he is personally responsible for your rapid rise through the ranks of the Abwehr. But nothing you can say now can possibly change my opinion of Canaris. And a word to the wise. Be careful when coming to the aid of a drowning man. You may be dragged under as well."

Vogel was stunned. He said nothing. The barking of the dog faded slowly away, then was gone. The wind rose and blew snow across the path, erasing the border with the forest. Vogel wondered how close they laid the mines. He turned his head and glimpsed a pair of SS men trailing softly after them.

"It is now February," Himmler resumed. "I can predict with some certainty that Admiral Canaris will be dismissed soon, perhaps even by the end of the month. I intend to bring all the security and intelligence agencies of Germany under my control, including the Abwehr."

Vogel thought, The Abwehr under Himmler's control? It would be laughable if he wasn't serious.

"You are obviously a man of considerable talent," Himmler continued. "I want you to remain at the Abwehr. With a considerable promotion, of course."

"Thank you, Herr Reichsführer." It was as if someone else said the words for him.

Himmler stopped. "It's cold. We should start back."

They walked past the security men, who waited until Himmler and Vogel were out of earshot before falling in quietly behind them.

Himmler said, "I'm glad we were able to reach agreement on the matter of leaving the agent in place. I think it is the prudent course of action at this time. And besides, Herr Vogel, it is never wise for one's personal feelings to cloud one's judgment."

Vogel stopped walking and looked into Himmler's desolate eyes. "What do you mean by that?"

"Please, don't treat me like a fool," Himmler said. "Brigadeführer Schellenberg spent some time in Madrid on another matter this past week. He met a friend of yours there—a man named Emilio Romero. Señor Romero told Brigadeführer Schellenberg all about your most prized possession."

Vogel thought, Damn Emilio for talking to Schellenberg! Damn Himmler for sticking his nose into places it doesn't belong! The SS men seemed to sense tension, and they drifted silently forward.

"I understand she's very beautiful," Himmler said. "It must have been difficult to give up a woman like that. It must be tempting to bring her home and lock her away. But she is to remain in place in England. Is that clear, Captain Vogel?"

"Yes, Herr Reichsführer."

"Schellenberg has his faults: arrogant, too flashy, and this obsession with pornography—" Himmler shrugged. "But he's a clever and resourceful intelligence officer. I know you're going to enjoy working more closely with him."

Himmler turned abruptly and walked away. Vogel stood alone, shivering in the intense cold.

"You don't look well," Canaris said when Vogel returned to the car. "I usually feel that way after conversations with the chicken farmer. But I must admit I do a better job of hiding it than you."

There was a scratching at the side of the car. Canaris opened his door, and the dogs scampered inside and settled at Vogel's feet. Canaris rapped his knuckle on the glass divider. The engine turned over and the car crunched over the snow toward the gate. Vogel felt relief wash over him as the glare of the compound receded behind them and they returned once more to the gloom of the forest.

"The little corporal was very proud of you tonight," Canaris said, contempt in his voice. "And what about Himmler? Did you stick the dagger in me during your little moonlight stroll?"

"Herr Admiral—"

Canaris leaned over and put his hand on Vogel's arm. There was a look in his ice-blue eyes Vogel had never seen.

"Be careful, Kurt," he said. "It is a dangerous game you are playing. A very dangerous game."

And with that Canaris leaned back, closed his eyes, and was immediately asleep.

CHAPTER THIRTY-NINE

LONDON

The operation was hastily code-named Kettledrum—who chose the name and why Vicary did not know. It was too complex and too sensitive to be run from his cramped quarters in St. James's Street, so for his command post Vicary procured a stately Georgian house in a terrace in West Halkin Street. The drawing room was converted into a situation room, with extra telephones, a wireless set, and a large-scale map of metropolitan London tacked to the wall. The upstairs library was turned into an office for Vicary and Harry. There was a rear entrance for the watchers and a pantry stocked with food. The typists volunteered to do the cooking, and Vicary, arriving at the house early that evening, was struck by the aroma of toast and bacon and the lamb stew bubbling on the stove.

A watcher led him upstairs to the library. A coal fire burned in the fireplace; the air was dry and warm. He struggled out of his sodden mackintosh, hung it on a hanger, and hung the hanger on the back of the door. One of the girls had left him a pot of tea, and he poured himself a cup. Vicary was exhausted. He had slept poorly after interrogating Jordan, and his hope of catching a little sleep in the car had been dashed by Boothby, who suggested they ride back to the office together so they could use the time to talk.

Overall control of Kettledrum was Boothby's. Vicary would run Jordan and be responsible for keeping Catherine Blake under surveillance. At the same time he would try to discover the rest of the agents in the network and their means of communication with Berlin. Boothby would be the liaison to the Twenty Committee, the interdepartmental group that supervised the entire Double Cross apparatus, so named because the symbol of Double Cross and the Roman numeral for twenty are the same: XX. Boothby and the Twenty Committee would produce the misleading documents for Jordan's briefcase and integrate Kettledrum into the rest of Double Cross and Bodyguard. Vicary did not ask about the nature of the misinformation, and Boothby did not tell him. Vicary knew what it meant. He had discovered the existence of the new German network and traced the leak back to Jordan. But now he was being shoved into a supporting role. Basil Boothby was fully in command.

"Nice digs," Harry said, as he entered the room. He poured himself a cup of tea and warmed his backside against the fire. "Where's Jordan?"

"Upstairs sleeping."

"Dumb bastard," Harry said, his voice lowered.

"He's *our* dumb bastard now, Harry, don't forget that. What have you got?"

"Fingerprints."

"What?"

"Fingerprints, latent fingerprints from someone other than Peter Jordan, all over the inside of that study. On the desk, on the exterior of the safe. He says the cleaning lady was never allowed to go in. We should assume those latent fingerprints were left by Catherine Blake."

Vicary shook his head slowly.

"Jordan's house is ready to go," Harry continued. "We put so many microphones in that place you can hear a mouse fart. We evicted the family across the street and established a static post. The view is perfect. Anyone goes near that house gets their picture taken."

"What about Catherine Blake?"

"We traced her telephone number to a flat in Earl's Court. We took over a flat in the building opposite."

"Good work, Harry."

Harry looked at Vicary a long moment, then said, "Don't take this the wrong way, Alfred, but you look like hell."

"I can't remember the last time I slept. What's keeping you going?"

"A couple of Benzedrine and ten quarts of tea."

"I'm going to have a bite to eat, then try to get some sleep. What about you?"

"Actually, I had plans for the evening."

"Grace Clarendon?"

"She asked me to dinner. I thought I'd take the opportunity. I don't think we're going to have much free time the next few weeks."

Vicary rose and poured himself another cup of tea. "Harry, I don't want to take advantage of your relationship with Grace, but I'm wondering if she could do me a favor. I'd like her to run a couple of names quietly through Registry and see what comes up."

"I'll ask her. What are the names?"

Vicary carried his tea across the room and stood in front of the fire next to Harry.

"Peter Jordan, Walker Hardegen, and anyone or anything called Broome."

Grace never liked to eat before making love. Afterward Harry lay in her bed, smoking a cigarette, listening to Glenn Miller on the gramophone and the clatter of Grace cooking in her tiny kitchen. She came back into the bedroom ten minutes later. She wore a robe, loosely tied at her slender waist, and carried a tray with their supper on it: soup and bread. Harry sat up against the headboard and Grace leaned against the footboard. The tray was between them. She handed him a bowl of the soup. It was nearly midnight and they both were starved. Harry loved to watch her—the way she seemed to take such pleasure from the simple meal. The way her robe parted to reveal her taut, perfect body.

She noticed him looking at her and said, "What are you thinking, Harry Dalton?"

"I was thinking how much I never want this to end. I was thinking how much I wish every night of my life could be just like this."

Her face became very grave; she was absolutely incapable of hiding her emotions. When she was happy her face seemed to light up. When she was angry her green eyes smoldered. And when she was sad, like now, her body became very still.

"You mustn't say things like that, Harry. It's against the rules."

"I know it's against the rules, but it's the truth."

"Sometimes it's better to keep the truth to yourself. If you don't say it out loud, it doesn't hurt so much."

"Grace, I think I'm in love—"

She slammed down her spoon on the tray. "Jesus, Harry! Don't say things like that! You make it so damned hard sometimes. First you say you can't see me because you're feeling guilty, and now you're telling me you're in love with me."

"I'm sorry, Grace, it's just the truth. I thought we could always tell each other the truth."

"All right, here's the truth. I'm married to a wonderful man I care for very much and don't want to hurt. But I've fallen desperately in love with a detective-turned-spycatcher named Harry Dalton. And when this damned war is over I have to give him up. And it hurts like bloody hell every time I let myself think about it." Her eyes welled with tears. "Now shut up and eat your soup. Please. Let's talk about something else. I'm stuck in dreary Registry all day with Jago and his wretched pipe. I want to know what's going on in the rest of the world."

"All right. I have a favor to ask of you."

"What kind of favor?"

"A professional favor."

She smiled at him wickedly. "Damn, I was hoping it was a sexual favor."

"I need you to quietly run a couple of names through the Registry index. See if anything comes up."

"Sure, what are they?"

Harry told her.

"Okay, I'll see what I can find."

She finished the soup, leaned back, and watched Harry while he ate the rest of his soup. When he was done she stacked the dishes on the tray and set the tray on the floor next to the bed. She turned out the lights and lit a candle on the bedstand. She took off her robe, and she made love to him in a way she never had before: slowly, patiently, as if his body were made of crystal. Her eyes never strayed from his face. When it was over she fell forward onto his chest, her body limp and damp, her warm breath against his neck.

"You wanted the truth, Harry. That's the truth."

"I have to be honest with you, Grace. It didn't hurt."

It began a few minutes past ten o'clock the following morning when Peter Jordan, standing in the upstairs library of Vicary's house in West Halkin Street, dialed the number for Catherine Blake's flat. For a long time the recording of this one-minute conversation held the distinction of the most listened-to wiretap in the history of the Imperial Security Service. Vicary himself would listen to the damned thing a hundred times, searching for imperfections like a master jeweler examining a diamond for flaws. Boothby did the same. A copy of the recording was rushed back to St. James's Street by motorcycle courier, and for one hour the red light burned over Sir Basil's door as he listened over and over again.

The first time Vicary heard only Jordan. He was standing a few feet away, his back politely turned, his eyes fixed on the fire.

"Listen, I'm sorry I haven't had a chance to call sooner. I've just been busy as hell. I was out of town a day longer than I expected, and there was no way for me to call."

Silence, while she tells him there's no need to apologize.

"I missed you very much. I thought about you the entire time I was away."

Silence, while she tells him she missed him terribly and can't wait to see him again.

"I want to see you too. In fact, that's why I'm calling. I booked us a table at the Mirabelle. I hope you're free for lunch."

Silence, while she tells him that sounds wonderful.

"Good. I'll meet you there at one o'clock."

Silence, while she says she loves him very much.

"I love you too, darling."

Jordan was quiet when it was over. Vicary, watching him, was reminded of Karl Becker and the dark mood he slipped into whenever Vicary forced him to send a Double Cross message. They killed the rest of the morning with chess. Jordan played a precise mathematical match; Vicary engaged in deception and subterfuge. While they played they could hear the banter of the watchers and the clatter of the typists downstairs in the situation room. Jordan was beating Vicary badly so Vicary resigned.

At noon Jordan went to his room and dressed in his uniform. At twelve-fifteen he walked out the rear door of the house and clambered into the back of a department van. Vicary and Harry settled into their places downstairs in the situation room while Jordan was driven at speed up Park Lane like a high-security prisoner. He was taken to a secluded rear door of SHAEF headquarters in Blackburn Street and went inside. For the next six minutes, no one from Vicary's team saw him.

Jordan emerged from the front entrance of SHAEF at 12:35. He walked across the square, a briefcase chained to his wrist, and vanished into another doorway. This time his absence was ten minutes. When he reappeared, the briefcase was gone. From Grosvenor Square he walked to South Audley Street and from South Audley Street to Curzon Street. During his journey he was quietly shadowed by three of the department's best watchers, Clive Roach, Tony Blair, and Leonard Reeves. None of them saw any signs that Jordan was under surveillance by the opposition.

At 12:55 Jordan arrived at the Mirabelle. He waited outside, just as Vicary had instructed him to do. At precisely one o'clock a taxi braked to a halt in front of the restaurant and a tall, attractive woman stepped into view.

Ginger Bradshaw, the department's best surveillance photographer, was crouched in the back of a department van parked across the street; as Catherine Blake took Peter Jordan's hand and kissed his cheek, he quickly shot six photographs. The film was rushed back to West Halkin Street, and the prints were sitting in front of Vicary in the situation room by the time they had finished lunch.

When it was over Blair would say it was his fault; Reeves said no, it was his. Roach, being the senior man, took responsibility himself. All three agreed she was a cut above every other German agent they had ever followed: the best, bar none. And if they ever made a mistake, got too close, fingers would surely be burned.

After leaving the Mirabelle, Catherine and Peter walked together back to Grosvenor Square. They stopped on the southwest corner of the square and talked for two minutes. Ginger Bradshaw took several more photographs, including one of their very brief kiss good-bye. When Jordan walked away, Catherine flagged down a taxi and climbed inside. Blair, Roach, and Reeves jumped into the surveillance van and followed the taxi east to Regent Street. The taxi then headed north to Oxford Street, where Catherine paid off the cabbie and climbed out.

Later, Roach would call her stroll along Oxford Street the best demonstration of streetcraft he had ever seen. She paused in at least a half dozen storefronts. She doubled back twice, once so quickly that Blair had to dive into a café to get out of the way. At Tottenham Court Road she descended into the underground and purchased a ticket for Waterloo. Roach and Reeves both managed to get on the train with her—Roach, twenty feet away in the same car, Reeves in the next one. When the doors opened at Leicester Square she remained still, as if she were going to continue on; then suddenly she stood up and stepped onto the platform. Roach had to squeeze through the closing doors to stay with her. Reeves was stuck on the train; he was out of the game.

She melted into the crowd on the staircase and Roach lost her momentarily. When she reached street level she quickly crossed Charing Cross Road and took the stairs back into the Leicester Square station.

Roach could have sworn he saw her climb onto a waiting bus, and for the rest of the afternoon he berated himself for making such a stupid mistake. He rushed across the street and jumped onto the bus as it pulled away from the curb. Ten seconds later he realized he had the wrong woman. He got off the bus at the next stop and telephoned Vicary at West Halkin Street to tell him she had given them the slip.

"Clive Roach has never lost a German agent before," Boothby said, glaring at the watch report that evening in his office. He looked up at Vicary. "The man could follow a gnat through Hampstead Heath."

"He's the best. She's just damned good."

"Look at this: a taxi, a long walk to check her tail, and then into the underground, where she buys a ticket for one station and gets out at another."

"She's extremely careful. That's why we've never caught on to her."

"There's another explanation, Alfred. It's possible she spotted the tail."

"I know. I've thought about that possibility."

"And if that's the case, the entire operation is blown even before it's started." Boothby tapped the thin metal attaché case containing the first batch of Kettledrum material. "If she knows she's under surveillance and we give her this, we might as well publish the secret of the invasion in the *Daily Mail* under a bloody banner headline. They'll know they're being deceived. And if they know they're being deceived, they'll know the opposite is true."

"Roach is convinced she didn't spot him."

"Where is she now?"

"She's in her flat."

"What time is she supposed to meet Jordan?"

"Ten o'clock, at Jordan's house. He told her he was working late tonight."

"What were Jordan's impressions?"

"He said he detected no change in her demeanor, no sign of nerves or tension." Vicary paused. "He's good, our Commander Jordan, damned good. If he weren't such an excellent engineer he'd make a marvelous spy."

Boothby tapped the metal attaché case with his thick forefinger. "If she spotted the tail, why is she sitting in her flat? Why isn't she making a run for it?"

Vicary said, "Perhaps she wants to see what's inside that briefcase."

"It's not too late, Alfred. We don't have to go through with this. We can arrest her right now and think of some other way to repair the damage."

"I think that would be a mistake. We don't know the other agents in the network, and we don't know how they're communicating with Berlin."

Boothby rapped his knuckle against the attaché case. "You haven't asked what's inside this briefcase, Alfred."

"I didn't want another lecture about need to know."

Boothby chuckled and said, "Very good. You're learning. You don't *need* to know this, but since it's your brilliant idea I'm going to tell you. The Twenty Committee wants to convince them that Mulberry is actually an offshore antiaircraft complex bound for Calais. The Phoenix units already have crew quarters and antiaircraft guns, so it's a rather neat fit. They've just altered the drawings a bit."

"Perfect," Vicary said.

"They have some other schemes in mind to help sell the deception through other channels. You'll be briefed on those as necessary."

"I understand, Sir Basil."

They sat in silence for a time, each studying his own private spot on the paneled walls.

"It's your call, Alfred," Boothby said. "You control this part of the operation. Whatever you recommend, I'll back you up on it."

Vicary thought, Why do I feel as though I'm being measured for the drop? He did not take comfort from Boothby's offer of support. The first sign of trouble and Boothby would be diving for the nearest foxhole. The easiest thing to do would be to arrest Catherine Blake and do it Boothby's way— try to turn her and force her to cooperate with them. Vicary remained convinced it would not work, that the only way to funnel the Double Cross material directly through her was to do it without her knowledge.

"I remember a time when men didn't have to make decisions like this," Boothby said wistfully. "If we make the wrong one, we could very well lose the war."

"Thank you for reminding me," Vicary said. "You don't have a crystal ball behind that desk, do you, Sir Basil?"

"I'm afraid not."

"How about a coin?"

"Alfred!"

"A poor attempt at levity, Sir Basil."

Boothby was tapping on the attaché again. "What's your decision, Alfred?"

"I say we let her run."

Boothby said, "I hope to God you're right. Give me your right arm."

Vicary stuck out his arm. Boothby shackled the attaché case to his wrist.

❖

Half an hour later Grace Clarendon was standing in Northumberland Avenue, stomping her feet against the pavement for warmth as she watched the evening traffic rushing past. Finally, she spotted Boothby's large black Humber when the driver winked the shaded headlamps. The car pulled over. Boothby threw open the back door and Grace climbed inside.

Grace shivered. "Bloody cold outside! You were supposed to meet me fifteen minutes ago. I don't know why we can't just do this in your office."

"Too many watchful eyes, Grace. Too much at stake."

She stuck a cigarette into her mouth and lit it. Boothby closed the glass partition.

"Now, what do you have for me?"

"Vicary wants me to run a couple of names through Registry for him."

"Why doesn't he come to me for a chit?"

"I suppose he thinks you won't give it to him."

"What are the names?"

"Peter Jordan and Walker Hardegen."

"Clever bastard," Boothby murmured. "Anything else?"

"Yes. He wanted me to run a trace on the word Broome."

"How broad?"

"Names of our own personnel. Code names of agents, German and British. Operational code names, existing or closed."

"For Christ's sake," Boothby said. He turned and watched the traffic. "Did Vicary come to you directly, or did he make the request through Dalton?"

"Harry did it."

"When?"

"Last night."

Boothby turned and smiled at her. "Grace, have you been a naughty girl again?"

She didn't respond, just said, "What do you want me to tell him?"

"Tell him you searched for the names of Jordan and Hardegen in every index you could think of and found nothing. The same for Broome. Understood, Grace?"

She nodded.

Boothby said, "Don't look so glum. You're making an invaluable contribution to your nation's defense."

She turned at him, narrowing her green eyes in anger. "I'm deceiving someone I care about very much. And I don't like it."

"It will all be over soon. When it is I'll treat you to a nice dinner out, just like the old days."

She pulled the door latch, a little too forcefully, and put a foot out the door. "I'll let you take me to an expensive dinner, Basil. But that's all. The old days are definitely over."

She got out, slammed the door, and watched Boothby's car vanish into the dark.

Vicary waited upstairs in the library. The girls brought him the updates, one by one.

2115 hrs: The static post at Earl's Court spots Catherine Blake leaving her flat. Photographs to follow.

2117 hrs: Catherine Blake walks north toward Cromwell Road. One watcher trailing on foot. Surveillance van following.

2120 hrs: Catherine Blake catches a taxi and heads east. Surveillance van collects watcher on foot and tails the taxi.

2135 hrs: Catherine Blake arrives Marble Arch and leaves taxi. New watcher leaves the surveillance van and follows on foot.

2140 hrs: Catherine Blake catches another taxi in Oxford Street. Surveillance van nearly loses her. Unable to pick up watcher on foot.

2150 hrs: Catherine Blake leaves taxi at Piccadilly Circus. Walking west on Piccadilly. New watcher trailing on foot. Surveillance van following.

2153 hrs: Catherine Blake catches bus. Surveillance van following.

2157 hrs: Catherine Blake leaves bus. Enters Green Park on footpath. One watcher following.

Five minutes later, Harry came into the room. "We lost her in Green Park," he said. "She doubled back. The watcher had to keep going."

"That's all right, Harry, we know where she's going."

But for the next twenty minutes no one saw her. Vicary came downstairs and nervously paced the situation room. Through the microphones, Vicary could hear Jordan prowling the inside of his house, waiting for her. Had she seen the watchers? Did she spot the surveillance van? Had she been attacked in Green Park? Was she meeting with another agent? Was she trying to escape? Outside, Vicary heard the rattle of the surveillance van returning, then the soft footfalls of the dejected watchers slipping back into the house. She had beaten them again. Then Boothby telephoned. He was monitoring the operation from his office and wanted to know what the hell was going on. When Vicary told him, Boothby muttered something unintelligible and rang off.

Finally the static post outside Jordan's house came on the air.

2225 hrs: Catherine Blake approaching Jordan's door. Catherine Blake pressing the buzzer.

This piece of information Vicary did not need to know, for Jordan's house had been bugged and wired so thoroughly that the door buzzer, over the speakers in the situation room, sounded like an air-raid alert.

Vicary closed his eyes and listened. Their voices rose and fell as they moved from room to room, out of the range of one microphone and into the next. Vicary, listening to them trade banalities, was reminded of the dialogue in one of Alice Simpson's romance novels: *Can I top up your drink? No, it's fine. How about something to eat? You must be famished. No, I had a little something earlier. But there is something I want desperately right now.*

He listened to the sound of their kissing. He searched her voice for false notes. He had a team of officers waiting in the house across the street, just in case it all went wrong and he decided to arrest her. He listened to her telling him how much she loved him, and for some horrid reason he found himself thinking of Helen. They had stopped talking. Clinking glass. Running water. Footsteps ascending the stairs. Silence, as they moved through a dead zone on the microphone coverage. The sound of Jordan's bed, creaking beneath the weight of their bodies. The sound of clothing being removed. Whispers. Vicary had heard enough. He turned to Harry and said, "I'm going upstairs. Come get me when she makes her move."

Clive Roach heard it first, then Ginger Bradshaw. Harry had fallen asleep on the couch, his long legs dangling over the armrest. Roach reached out and smacked him on the sole of his shoe. Harry, startled, sat up, listening intently. He bounded up the stairs and nearly broke down the door to the library. Vicary had brought his camp bed from his office. He slept, as was his habit, with the light shining on his face. Harry reached down and shook his shoulder. Vicary came awake suddenly and looked at his wristwatch: 2:45 A.M. He followed Harry wordlessly down the stairs and into the situation room. Vicary had experimented with captured German cameras and recognized the sound immediately. Catherine Blake was locked inside Jordan's study, rapidly photographing the first batch of Kettledrum material. After a minute it stopped. Vicary heard the sound of papers being straightened and the door to the safe being closed. Then a *click,* as she turned out the lights and walked back upstairs.

CHAPTER FORTY

LONDON

"Well, if it isn't the man of the hour!" Boothby sang, flinging open the rear door of his Humber. "Come inside, Alfred, before you freeze to death out there. I just finished briefing the Twenty Committee. Needless to say, they're thrilled. They've asked me to pass on their congratulations to you. So, congratulations, Alfred."

"Thank you, I suppose," Vicary said, thinking, When did he have time to brief the Twenty Committee? It was barely seven in the morning: raining, colder than hell, London veiled in the dull half-light of wintry dawn. The car pulled away from the curb into the silent, shimmering street. Vicary slumped down on the seat, leaned his head back, and closed his eyes, just for a moment. He was beyond exhaustion. Fatigue pulled at his limbs. It pressed on his chest like the winner of a schoolyard wrestling match, squeezed his head like a vise. He had not slept again, not after listening to Catherine Blake photographing the Kettledrum material. What was it that kept him awake, the excitement of so skillfully deceiving the enemy or disgust at the manner in which it was done?

Vicary opened his eyes. They were heading east, across the Georgian bleakness of Belgravia, then Hyde Park Corner, then Park Lane to Bayswater Road. The streets were deserted—a few taxis here and there, a lorry or two, solitary pedestrians rushing along the pavement like scared survivors of a plague.

Vicary, closing his eyes again, said, "What's this all about anyway?"

"Remember I told you the Twenty Committee was considering using some of our other Double Cross assets to help bolster the credibility of Kettledrum in Berlin?"

"I remember," Vicary said. He also remembered he had been stunned by the speed at which the decision had been reached. The Twenty Committee was notorious for bureaucratic warfare. Each and every Double Cross message had to be approved by the Twenty Committee before it could be sent to the Germans through turned agents. Vicary sometimes waited days for the Committee to approve Double Cross messages for his Becker network. Why were they able to move so quickly now?

He was too tired to search his brain for possible answers. He closed his eyes again. "Where are we going?"

"East London. Hoxton, to be precise."

Vicary opened his eyes to a slit, then let them close again. "If we're going to East London, why are we traveling west along Bayswater Road?"

"To make certain we're not being followed by members of any other service, friendly or hostile."

"Who's going to be following us, Sir Basil, the Americans?"

"Actually, Alfred, *I'm* more worried about the Russians."

Vicary lifted his head and twisted it around at Boothby before letting it fall back onto the leather seat. "I'd ask for an explanation of that remark, but I'm too tired."

"In a few minutes everything will be made clear to you."

"Will there be coffee there?"

Boothby chuckled. "Yes, I can guarantee that."

"Good. You won't mind if I use this opportunity to get a few minutes of sleep?"

But Vicary had drifted off and didn't hear Boothby's answer.

The car jerked to a halt. Vicary, floating in a light sleep, felt his head roll forward, then snap back. He heard the metallic crunch of a door latch giving way, felt a blast of cold air clawing at his face. He came awake suddenly. He looked to his left and seemed surprised to see Boothby sitting there. He glanced at his wristwatch. Good heavens, nearly eight o'clock!—they had been driving the London streets for an hour. His neck ached from the awkward position in which he had slept, slumped down in his seat with his chin pressing against the top of his rib cage. His head throbbed with a craving for caffeine and nicotine. He took hold of the armrest and pushed himself into a sitting position. He looked out the window: East London, Hoxton, an ugly Victorian terrace that looked like a factory fallen on hard times. The terrace on the other side had been bombed—a house here, a pile of rubble there, then a house, then rubble—like a mouth of rotting teeth.

He heard Boothby say, "Wake up, Alfred, we're here. What on earth were you dreaming about anyway?"

He felt suddenly self-conscious. What *had* he dreamt? Had he talked in his sleep? He hadn't dreamt of France since—since when?—since they cornered Catherine Blake. He wondered if he had dreamt of Helen. Climbing out of the car, he was overcome by a wave of fatigue and had to steady himself by putting a hand on the rear fender of the car. Boothby seemed not to notice, for he was standing on the pavement, glaring back at Vicary impatiently, rattling loose change in his pocket. Rain fell harder now. The bleak landscape somehow made it seem colder. Vicary, joining Boothby on the pavement, breathed deeply of the raw, damp air and immediately felt better.

Boothby led the way through the front door into the hall. The house must have been turned into flats, because there were metal letter boxes on one wall. At the back of the hall—directly opposite the door—was a staircase. Vicary let the door close and they were enveloped in darkness. He reached out and groped for a light switch—he had seen one there, somewhere. He found it, flipped it. Nothing.

"They take the blackout a little more seriously here than we do up West," Boothby said. Vicary dug a blackout torch from the pocket of his mackintosh. He handed it to Boothby, and Boothby led the way up the wooden stairs.

Vicary could see almost nothing, just the outline of Boothby's broad back and a puddle of listless light leaking from the weak torch. Like a blind man the rest of his senses were suddenly alive. He was treated to a tour of foul odors—urine, stale beer, disinfectant, dried egg frying in old fat. Then the sounds—a parent striking a child, a couple quarreling, another couple noisily copulating. Somewhere he heard notes on an organ and a chorus of male voices. He wondered if there was a church nearby, then realized it was the BBC. Only then did he comprehend that it was Sunday. Kettledrum and the search for Catherine Blake had robbed him of the days of the week.

They reached the landing on the top floor. Boothby shone the torch down the hall. The light reflected in the yellow eyes of a skinny cat. It hissed at them in anger before scurrying away. Boothby followed the sound of the church services. The singing had stopped, and the congregation was reciting the Lord's Prayer. Boothby had a key. He stuck it in the lock and switched off the torch before going inside.

❖

It was a squalid little room: an unmade bed no larger than Vicary's at MI5 headquarters, a tiny galley kitchen where coffee burned on a gas ring, a small café table where two men sat still as statues, listening to the radio. Both had vile Gauloise cigarettes in their mouths, and the air was blue with smoke. The lights were doused; the only illumination came from narrow windows that looked over the back of a terrace on the next street. Vicary walked to the window and looked out at an alley strewn with rubbish. Two little boys were tossing tin cans into the air and hitting them with sticks. A wind rose, lifting old newspaper into the air like circling gulls. Boothby was dumping the burnt coffee into two suspect enamel mugs. He gave one to Vicary and kept one for himself. The coffee was vile—bitter, stale, and too strong— but it was hot and it had caffeine.

Boothby used his chipped cup to make the introductions, tipping it first toward the older and larger of the two men. "Alfred Vicary, this is Pelican. That's not his real name, mind you, that's his code name. You don't get to know his real name, I'm afraid. I'm not sure even *I* know his real name." He tipped his mug at the second man sitting at the table. "And this fellow is Hawke. That's not a code name, that's his real name. Hawke works for us, don't you, Hawke?"

But Hawke gave no indication he had heard Boothby speak. He was not a Hawke—more like a Stick or a Rod or a Cane, cadaverous and painfully thin. His cheap wartime suit hung from his bony shoulders as if it had been thrown over a valet. He had the pallor of someone who worked at night and beneath ground. His blond hair was thinning and going rapidly gray, even though he was no older than the boys Vicary had tutored his last term at the university. He held his Gauloise like a Frenchman, between the tip of his long thumb and forefinger. Vicary had the uncomfortable feeling he had seen him somewhere before—in the canteen, maybe, or leaving Registry with a batch of files beneath his arm. Or was it leaving Boothby's office by the secret passageway, the way he had seen Grace Clarendon leaving that night? Hawke didn't look at Vicary. The only time he moved was when Boothby took a couple of steps toward him. Then he only inclined his head away a fraction of an inch and tightened his face, as if he feared Boothby might strike him.

Vicary looked next at Pelican. He might have been a writer or he might have been a dockworker, he might be German or he might be French. Polish, perhaps—they were everywhere. Unlike Hawke, Pelican stared straight back at Vicary, holding him in a steady, slightly bemused gaze. Vicary couldn't quite see Pelican's eyes because he wore the thickest glasses

Vicary had ever seen, tinted slightly, as if he was sensitive to bright light. Beneath his black leather coat he wore two sweaters, a gray rollneck and a frayed beige cardigan that looked as though it had been made for him by a well-meaning relative with eyes as good as his. He smoked his Gauloise to a stub, then crushed it out, using the cracked nail of his thick thumb.

Boothby removed his coat and turned down the radio. Then he looked at Vicary and said, "Well, now. Where should I begin?"

Hawke didn't work for *us,* Hawke worked for Boothby.

Boothby knew Hawke's father. Worked with him in India. Security. He met young Hawke in Britain in 1935 at a luncheon at the family's Kent estate. Young Hawke was drinking and talking too much, berating his father and Boothby for the kind of work they did, reciting Marx and Lenin like Shakespeare, waving his arms at the splendid gardens as though they were proof of the corruption of the English ruling classes. After lunch Hawke Senior smiled weakly at Boothby to apologize for his son's abominable behavior: children these days . . . you know . . . rot they're learning at school . . . expensive education gone to waste.

Boothby smiled too. He had been looking for a Hawke for a very long time.

Boothby had a new job: keep an eye on the Communists. Especially at the universities, Oxford and Cambridge. The Communist Party of Great Britain, with love and encouragement from its Russian masters, was trolling the universities for new members of the flock. The NKVD was looking for spies. Hawke went to work for Boothby at Oxford. Boothby seduced Hawke. Boothby gave direction to his directionless heart. Boothby was good at that. Hawke ran with the Communists: drank with them, quarreled with them, played tennis with them, fornicated with them. When the Party came for him, Hawke told them to fuck off.

Then the Pelican came for him.

Hawke called Boothby. Hawke was a good boy.

The Pelican was German, Jewish, and a Communist; Boothby saw the possibilities immediately. He had been a Communist street brawler in Berlin in the 1920s, but with Hitler in power he thought it best to find safer shores.

He emigrated to England in 1933. The NKVD knew about the Pelican from his days in Berlin. When they found out he had settled in England they recruited him as an agent. He was supposed to be a talent spotter only, no heavy lifting. The first talent he spotted was Boothby's agent, Hawke. At the next meeting between Hawke and the Pelican, Boothby appeared out of nowhere and put the fear of God into him. Pelican agreed to go to work for Boothby.

Are you still with me, Alfred?

Vicary, listening at the window, thought, Oh, yes. In fact, I'm four moves ahead of you.

In August 1939, Boothby brought Hawke to MI5. On Boothby's orders, the Pelican told his Moscow controllers that his star recruit was now working in British Intelligence. Moscow was ecstatic. Pelican's star rose. Boothby used Pelican to funnel true but harmless material back to the Russians, all of it allegedly from his source inside MI5—Hawke—all information the Russians could verify from other sources. Pelican's star soared.

In November 1939, Boothby sent the Pelican to the Netherlands. A young, arrogant SS intelligence officer named Walter Schellenberg was making regular trips into Dutch territory under an assumed name to meet with a pair of MI6 agents.

Schellenberg was posing as a member of the *Schwarze Kapelle* and was asking the British for assistance. In truth, he wanted the British to give him the names of *real* German traitors so he could arrest them. The Pelican met Schellenberg in a café in a Dutch town just across the border and offered to work for him as a spy in Britain. He admitted he had done a job or two for the NKVD, including recruiting an Oxford boy named Hawke, who had just joined MI5 and with whom Pelican was still in regular contact. As a sign of goodwill the Pelican presented Schellenberg with a gift, a collection of Asian erotica. Schellenberg gave Pelican a thousand pounds, a camera, and a radio transmitter and sent him back to Britain.

In 1940, MI5 reorganized. Vernon Kell, the old director-general who founded the department in 1909, was abruptly fired by Churchill. Sir David Petrie took charge. Boothby knew him from India. Boothby was kicked upstairs. He turned over the Pelican to a case officer—*an amateur like you, Alfred: a solicitor, though, not a professor*—but he kept a firm hand on him.

Pelican was too important to be left to someone who barely knew his way to the canteen. Besides, the Pelican's dealings with Schellenberg were getting damned interesting.

Schellenberg was impressed with the Pelican's first reports. The material was all good but harmless stuff—munitions production, troop movements, bomb damage assessment. Schellenberg drank greedily of it, even though he knew it was coming from a Jewish Communist who had worked as a talent spotter for the NKVD. He and the rest of the SS despised Canaris and the professional intelligence officers at the Abwehr. They mistrusted the information Canaris was giving the Führer. Schellenberg saw his opportunity. He could create a separate network in Britain that reported directly to him and Heinrich Himmler, bypassing the Abwehr altogether.

Boothby saw an opportunity too. He could use the Pelican network for two purposes: to verify misinformation being sent to Canaris through the Double Cross system and at the same time to sow mistrust between the two rival intelligence organizations. It was a delicate balancing act. MI5 wanted Canaris to remain on the job—after all, his agency had been totally compromised and manipulated—but a little palace intrigue was good too. British Intelligence could blow gently on the flames of dissension and treachery. Boothby started feeding Schellenberg information through the Pelican that raised questions about Canaris's loyalty—not enough for Schellenberg to plunge the dagger into the Old Fox's back, mind you, just enough to put the bloody thing in his hand.

In 1942, Boothby thought the game had spun out of control. Schellenberg compiled a lengthy list of Canaris's sins and presented it to Himmler. The Double Cross committee decided to throw Canaris a bone or two to untie the noose around his neck—high-grade intelligence he could show to the Führer to prove the Abwehr's effectiveness. It worked. Himmler stuck Schellenberg's file in the drawer, and the Old Fox stayed on the job.

Boothby was pouring another cup of the obscene coffee. Vicary had been unable to finish his first cup. It sat half empty in the window, next to a dead moth that was slowly turning to powder. The little boys had been chased from the alley by the wind. It gusted, hurling rain against the glass. The room was in darkness. The house had gone quiet after the morning's activities. The only sound was the floor creaking beneath Boothby's restless pacing. Vicary turned from the window and watched him. He looked out of place in the grimy flat—like a priest in a cathouse—but he seemed to be enjoying himself thoroughly. Even spies like telling secrets sometimes.

Boothby reached inside the breast pocket of his suit, pulled out a single sheet of paper, and handed it to Vicary. It was the memorandum he had written to Boothby weeks ago, asking him to issue a security alert. Vicary looked at the top left corner; it had been stamped ACTION. Next to the stamp were two nearly illegible initials: *BB*. Boothby reached out his hand and took the note back from Vicary. Then he gave it to Pelican.

Pelican moved for the first time. He laid Vicary's memo on the table and switched on the light. Vicary, standing over him, could see Pelican's eyes crinkle in discomfort behind the dark glasses. From his pocket he removed a German-issue camera, the same one Schellenberg had given him in 1940. He carefully took ten photographs of the document, like a professional, adjusting the light and the camera angle each time to make certain he had at least one clear negative. Then he raised the camera and pointed it at Hawke. The camera clicked twice and he put it back in his pocket.

"The Pelican is going to Lisbon tonight," Boothby said. "Schellenberg and friends have requested a meeting with him. We think they're going to give him a very thorough going over. Before they begin their interrogation, Pelican is going to give them this film. The next time Schellenberg and Canaris ride together in the Tiergarten, Schellenberg will tell him about it. Canaris and Vogel will take it as proof that Kettledrum is good as gold. Their agent has not been compromised. British Intelligence is in a panic. Therefore, the information she's sending about Operation Mulberry must be accurate. Get the picture, Alfred?"

Vicary and Boothby left first, Boothby leading, Vicary behind him again. Descending the stairs in the dark was harder than climbing them. Twice Vicary had to reach out in the gloom and steady himself on the soft shoulder of Boothby's cashmere coat. The cat reappeared and spat at them from a corner. The foul smells were the same; only the order was reversed. They reached the bottom of the stairs. Vicary felt the soles of his shoes scraping over the soiled linoleum of the hall. Boothby pushed open the door. Vicary, stepping back outside, felt the rain on his face.

He was never happier to be out of a place in his life. Walking to the car, he watched Boothby, who was watching him. Vicary felt as though he had just peered through the looking glass. He had been given a guided tour of a secret world of deception he never imagined existed. Vicary climbed into the car. Boothby got in next to him and closed the door. They were driven to Kingsland Road, then south toward the river. Vicary glanced at Boothby once, then averted his eyes. Boothby looked pleased with himself.

Vicary said, "You didn't have to show me all that. Why did you?"

"Because I wanted to."

"What happened to need to know? I had no need to know all that. You could have funneled my memo to Schellenberg and never told me about any of it."

"That's true."

"So why did you do it, to impress me?"

"In a way, yes," Boothby said. "You've impressed a great many people with your idea to leave Catherine Blake in place, including me. I realized I've underestimated you, Alfred—your intelligence and your ruthlessness. It takes a coldhearted bastard to send Peter Jordan back into that bedroom with a briefcase full of Double Cross. I wanted to show you the next level of the game."

"Is that how you think of this, Sir Basil, a game?"

"Not just *a* game, Alfred, *the* game."

Boothby smiled. It could be his greatest weapon. Vicary, gazing at his face, imagined it was the same smile he used on his wife, Penelope, when assuring her he had given up his latest little love.

The illusion of Kettledrum required Vicary to spend much of his day in his cramped office in St. James's Street—after all, they were trying to convince the Abwehr, and the rest of the department, that Vicary was still pursuing a German agent with access to top-secret material. He closed the door and sat down at his desk. He desperately needed sleep. He laid his head on the desk like a drowsy student and closed his eyes. When he did, he was immediately back in the grimy Hoxton flat. He saw the Pelican and he saw the Hawke. He saw the little boys in the filthy alleyway, pale malnourished legs poking from their shorts. He saw the moth turning to dust. He heard the organ music echoing through the grand cathedral. He thought of Matilda; guilt over missing her funeral flashed over him like hot water poured down his neck.

Damn. Why can't I turn it off just for a few minutes and sleep?

Then he saw Boothby, striding around the flat, telling the story of the Hawke and the Pelican and the elaborate deception he had foisted on Walter Schellenberg. He realized he had never seen Boothby happier: Boothby in the field, surrounded by his agents, Boothby drinking vile coffee from a chipped enamel mug. He realized he had misjudged Boothby or, more accurately, he had been misled by Boothby. The entire department had been. Boothby was a lie. The comic bureaucrat, preening around his grand office, the silly personal maxims, the red light and the green light, the ridiculous fetish about moisture rings on his precious furniture—it was all a lie. That was not Basil Boothby. Basil Boothby was not a pusher of paper, Basil Boothby was a runner of agents. A liar. A manipulator. A deceiver. Vicary, drifting off to sleep, found he loathed Boothby just a little less. But one thing troubled him. Why had Boothby lowered the veil? And why now?

Vicary felt himself descending into a dreamless sleep. In the distance Big Ben tolled ten o'clock. The chimes faded, only to be replaced by the muffled clatter of the teleprinters outside his closed door. He wanted to sleep for a long time. He wanted to forget about it all, just for a few minutes. But after a short while, the shaking began—gentle at first, then violent. Then the sound of a girl's voice—at first downy and pleasant, then slightly alarmed. "Professor Vicary . . . Professor Vicary. . . . Please wake up. . . . Professor Vicary. . . . Can you hear me?"

Vicary, his head still resting on his folded hands, opened his eyes. For an instant he thought it was Helen. But it was only Prudence, a flaxen angel from the typing pool. "I'm so sorry to wake you, Professor. But Harry Dalton's on the line, and he says it's urgent. Let me bring you a cup of hot tea, you poor lamb."

CHAPTER FORTY-ONE

LONDON

Catherine Blake left her flat shortly before 11 A.M., a light, cold rain falling. The darkening skies promised worse weather to come. She had three hours before her rendezvous with Neumann. On dreary days like these she was tempted to skip her painstaking ritual sojourns across London and proceed straight to the rendezvous site. It was monotonous, exhausting work, constantly stopping and checking her tail, jumping on and off underground trains and in and out of taxicabs. But it was necessary, especially now.

She paused in the door, knotting a scarf beneath her chin, looking into the street. A quiet Sunday morning, traffic light, shops still closed. Only the café across the street was open. A bald man sat in a window table reading a newspaper. He looked up for an instant, turned a page, and looked down again.

Outside the café a half dozen people waited for a bus. Catherine looked at the faces and thought she had seen one of them before, maybe at the bus stop, maybe somewhere else. She looked up at the flats across the street. *If they're watching you, they'll do it from a fixed position, a flat or a room over a shop.* She scanned the windows, looking for any changes, any faces looking back at her. She saw nothing. She finished tying her scarf, put up her umbrella, and started walking through the rain.

She caught her first bus in Cromwell Road. It was nearly empty: a pair of old ladies; an old man who mumbled to himself; a slight man who had shaved poorly, wore a soggy mackintosh, and read a newspaper. Catherine got off at Hyde Park Corner. The man with the newspaper did too. Catherine headed into the park. The man with the newspaper headed in the opposite direction, toward Piccadilly. What was it Vogel had said about the watchers of MI5? *Men you would walk past on the street and never give a second look*. If Catherine were selecting men to be MI5 watchers, she would have chosen the man with the newspaper.

She walked north on a footpath bordering Park Lane. At the northern edge of the park, at Bayswater Road, she turned around and walked back to Hyde Park Corner. Then she turned around and walked north again. She was confident no one was following her on foot. She walked a short distance along Bayswater Road. She stopped at a letter box and dropped an empty unmarked envelope into the slot, using the opportunity to check her tail once more. Nothing. The clouds thickened, the rain fell harder. She found a taxi and gave the driver an address in Stockwell.

Catherine sat back in her seat, watching the rain running in patterns down the window. Crossing Battersea Bridge, the wind gusted, causing the taxi to shudder. The traffic was still very light. Catherine turned around and looked through the small porthole of a rear window. Behind them, perhaps two hundred yards away, was a black van. She could see two people in the front seat.

Catherine turned around and noticed the cabbie was watching her in his rearview mirror. Their eyes met briefly; then he returned his gaze to the road. Catherine instinctively reached inside her handbag and touched the grip of her stiletto. The cab turned into a street lined with bleak, identical Victorian houses. There was not another human being in sight: no traffic, no pedestrians on the pavement. Catherine turned around again. The black van was gone.

She relaxed. She was especially anxious to make today's rendezvous. She wanted to know Vogel's response to her demand to be taken out of England. Part of her wished she had never sent it. She felt certain MI5 was closing in on her; she had made terrible mistakes. But at the same time she was gathering remarkable intelligence from Peter Jordan's safe. Last night she photographed a document emblazoned with the sword and shield of SHAEF and stamped MOST SECRET. It was quite possible she was stealing *the* secret of the invasion. She could not be sure from her vantage point—Peter Jordan's project was just one piece in a giant, complex puzzle. But in Berlin, where they were trying to fit that puzzle together, the information she was taking from Peter Jordan's safe might be invaluable, pure gold. She found she wanted to continue, but why? It was illogical, of course. She had never wanted to be a spy; she had been blackmailed into it by Vogel. She never felt any great allegiance to Germany. In fact, Catherine felt no allegiance to anything or anyone—she supposed that's what made her a good agent. There was something else. Vogel had always called it a game. Well, she was hooked on the game. She liked the challenge of the game. And she wanted to win the game. She didn't want to steal the secret of the invasion so Germany could win the war and the Nazis could rule Europe for a thousand years. She wanted to steal the secret of the invasion to prove she was the best, better than all the bumbling idiots the Abwehr sent to England. She wanted to show Vogel that she could play his game better than he could.

The taxi stopped. The cabbie turned around and said, "Are you sure this is the place?"

She looked out the window. They had stopped along a row of bombed and deserted warehouses. The streets were deserted. If anyone was following her they could not go undetected here. She paid off the driver and got out. The taxi drove away. A few seconds later a black van approached, two men in the front seat. It drove past her and continued down the road. Stockwell underground station was just a short distance away. She threw up her umbrella against the rain, walked quickly to the station, and bought a ticket for Leicester Square. The train was about to leave as she reached the platform. She stepped through the doors before they could close and found a seat.

Horst Neumann, standing in a doorway near Leicester Square, ate fish and chips from the newspaper wrapping. He finished the last bite of the fish and immediately felt sick. He spotted her entering the square amid a small knot of pedestrians. He crushed the oily newspaper, dropped it into a rubbish bin, and followed her. After a minute of walking he pulled alongside her. Catherine looked straight ahead, as if she did not know Neumann was walking next to her. She reached out her hand and placed the film into his. He wordlessly gave her a small slip of paper. They separated. Neumann sat down on a bench in the square and watched her go.

Alfred Vicary said, "Then what happened?"

"She went into Stockwell underground station," Harry said. "We sent a man into the station, but she had already boarded a train and left."

"Dammit," Vicary muttered.

"We put a man on the train at Waterloo and picked up her trail again."

"How long was she alone?"

"About five minutes."

"Plenty of time to meet another agent."

"Afraid so, Alfred."

"Then what?"

"Usual routine. Ran the watchers all over the West End for about an hour and a half. She finally went into a café and gave us a break for a half hour. Then to Leicester Square. She made one pass across the square and headed back to Earl's Court."

"No contact with anyone?"

"None that we observed."

"What about on Leicester Square?"

"The watchers didn't see anything."

"The letter box on Bayswater Road?"

"We confiscated the contents. We found an unmarked empty envelope on top of the pile. It was just a ploy to check her tail."

"Dammit, but she's good."

"She's a pro."

Vicary made a church steeple of his fingers. "I don't believe she's out there running around because she likes fresh air, Harry. She either made a dead drop somewhere or she met an agent."

"Must have been the train," Harry said.

"Could have been bloody anywhere," Vicary said. He thumped his arm on the side of the chair. "Dammit!"

"We just have to keep following her. Eventually, she'll make a mistake."

"I wouldn't count on that, Harry. And the longer we keep her under tight surveillance, the greater the chances are that she'll spot the tail. And if she spots the tail—"

"—we're dead," Harry said, finishing Vicary's thought for him.

"That's right, Harry. We're dead."

Vicary tore down his church steeple to free his hands to smother a long yawn. "Did you talk to Grace?"

"Yeah. She ran the names every way she could think of. She came up with nothing."

"What about Broome?"

"Same thing. It's not a code name for any operation or agent." Harry looked at Vicary for a long moment. "Would you like to explain to me now why you asked Grace to run those names?"

Vicary looked up and met Harry's gaze. "If I did, you'd have me committed. It's nothing, just my eyes playing tricks on me." Vicary looked at his wristwatch and yawned again. "I have to brief Boothby and collect the next batch of Kettledrum material."

"We're moving forward then?"

"Unless Boothby says otherwise, we're moving forward."

"What are you planning for tonight?"

Vicary struggled to his feet and pulled on his mackintosh. "I thought some dinner and dancing at the Four Hundred Club would be a nice change of pace. I'll need someone on the inside to keep an eye on them. Why don't you ask Grace to join you? Have a nice evening at the department's expense."

CHAPTER FORTY-TWO

BERCHTESGADEN

"I'd feel better if those bastards were in front of us instead of behind us," Wilhelm Canaris said morosely as the staff Mercedes sped along the white concrete autobahn toward the tiny sixteenth-century village of Berchtesgaden. Vogel turned and glanced through the rear window. Behind them, in a second staff car, were Reichsführer Heinrich Himmler and Brigadeführer Walter Schellenberg.

Vogel turned away and looked out his own window. Snow drifted gently over the picturesque village. In his foul mood he thought it made the place look like a cheap postcard: *Come to beautiful Berchtesgaden! Home of the Führer!* He was annoyed at being dragged so far from Tirpitz Ufer at such a critical time. He thought, Why can't he stay in Berlin like the rest of us? He's either buried in his *Wolfschanze* in Rastenburg or atop his *Adlersnest* in Bavaria.

Vogel had decided to make something good out of the trip; he planned to have dinner and spend the night with Gertrude and the girls. They were staying with Trude's mother in a village a two-hour drive from Berchtesgaden. God, how long had it been? One day at Christmas; two days in October before that. She had promised him a dinner of pork roast, potatoes, and cabbage and, in that playful voice of hers, promised to do wonderful things to his body in front of the fire when the children and her parents had gone off to bed. Trude always liked to make love that way, somewhere insecure where they might be caught. Something about it always made it more exciting for her, the way it had been twenty years ago when he was a student at Leipzig. For Vogel the excitement had gone out of it long ago. *She had done it—done it intentionally—as punishment for sending her to England.*

Watch me and remember this the next time you're with your wife.

Vogel thought, My God, why am I thinking of that now? He had managed to hide his feelings from Gertrude, the way he had managed to hide everything else from her. He was not a born liar, but he had become a good one. Gertrude still believed he was a personal in-house counsel to Canaris. She had no idea he was the control officer of the Abwehr's most secret spy network in Britain. As usual, he had lied to her about what he was doing today. Trude believed he was in Bavaria on a routine errand for Canaris, not ascending Kehlstein Mountain to brief the Führer on the enemy's plans to invade France. Vogel feared she would leave him if she knew the truth. He had lied to her too many times, deceived her for too long. She would never trust him again. He often thought it would be easier to tell her about Anna than confess he had been a spymaster for Hitler.

Canaris was feeding biscuits to the dogs. Vogel glanced at him, then looked away. Was it really possible? Was the man who had plucked him from the law and made him a top spy for the Abwehr a traitor? Canaris certainly made no attempt to conceal his disdain for the Nazis—his refusal to join the party, the constant stream of sarcastic remarks about Hitler. But had his disdain turned to treachery? If Canaris was a traitor, the consequences for the Abwehr networks in Britain were disastrous; Canaris was in a position to betray everything. Vogel thought, If Canaris is a traitor, why are most of the Abwehr networks in England still functioning? It didn't make sense. If Canaris had betrayed the networks, the British would have rolled them up overnight. The mere fact that the overwhelming majority of the German agents sent to England were still in place could be taken as proof that Canaris was not a traitor.

Vogel's own network was theoretically immune from treachery. Under their arrangement, Canaris knew only the vaguest details of the V-Chain. Vogel's agents did not cross paths with other agents. They had their own radio codes, rendezvous procedures, and separate lines of finance. And Vogel stayed clear of Hamburg, the control center for English networks. He remembered some of the idiots Canaris and the other control officers had sent to England, especially in the summer of 1940, when the invasion of Britain seemed at hand and Canaris threw all caution to the wind. His agents were poorly trained and poorly financed. Vogel knew some were given only two hundred pounds—a pittance—because the Abwehr and the General Staff believed Britain would fall as easily as had Poland and France. Most of the new agents were morons, like that idiot Karl Becker, a pervert, a glutton, in the espionage game only for the money and the adventure. Vogel wondered how a man like that managed to avoid capture. Vogel didn't like adventurers. He distrusted anyone who actually wanted to go behind enemy lines to work as a spy; only a fool would actually *want* to do that. And fools make bad agents. Vogel wanted only people who had the attributes and intelligence necessary to be a good spy. The rest of it—the motivation, the tradecraft, the willingness to use violence when necessary—he could provide.

Outside the temperature was dropping by degrees as they climbed higher along the winding Kehlsteinstrasse. The car's motor labored, tires skidding on the icy surface of the roadway. After a few moments the driver stopped in front of two huge bronze doors at the base of Kehlstein Mountain. A team of SS men carried out a rapid inspection, then opened the doors with the press of a single button. The car left the swirling snow of the Kehlsteinstrasse and entered a long tunnel. The marble walls shone in the light of the ornate bronze lanterns.

Hitler's famous elevator awaited them. It was more like a small hotel room, with plush carpet, deep leather chairs, and a bank of telephones. Vogel and Canaris stepped in first. Canaris sat down and immediately lit a cigarette, so that the elevator was filled with smoke when Himmler and Schellenberg arrived. The four men sat silently, each looking straight ahead, as the elevator whisked them toward the Obersalzberg, six thousand feet above Berchtesgaden. Himmler, annoyed by the smoke, raised his gloved hand to his mouth and coughed gently.

Vogel's ears popped with the rapid altitude change. He looked at the three men riding upward with him, the three most powerful intelligence officers in the Third Reich—a chicken farmer, a pervert, and a fussy little admiral who might very well be a traitor. In the hands of these men rested the future of Germany.

Vogel thought, God help us all.

The Nordic giant who served as the chief of Hitler's personal SS bodyguard showed them inside the salon. Vogel, normally indifferent to natural scenery, was stunned by the beauty of the panoramic view. Below, he could see the steeples and hills of Salzburg, the birthplace of Mozart. Near Salzburg was the Untersberg, the mountain where Emperor Frederick Barbarossa awaited his legendary call to rise and restore the glory of Germany. The room itself was fifty feet by sixty feet, and by the time Vogel reached the seating area next to the fire he was light-headed from the altitude. He settled down in the corner of a rustic couch while his eyes scanned the walls.

Huge oil paintings and tapestries covered them. Vogel admired the Führer's collection—a nude believed to have been painted by Titian, a landscape by Spitzweg, Roman ruins by Pannini. There was a bust of Wagner and a vast clock crowned by a bronze eagle. A steward silently poured coffee for the guests and tea for Hitler. The doors flew open a moment later and Adolf Hitler pounded into the room. Canaris, as usual, was the last one on his feet. The Führer gestured for them to return to their seats, then remained standing so he could pace.

"Captain Vogel," Hitler said, without preamble, "I understand your agent in London has scored another coup."

"We believe so, my Führer."

"Please, let's not keep it a secret any longer."

Vogel, under the watchful gaze of an SS man, opened his briefcase. "Our agent has stolen another remarkable document. This document provides us further clues about the nature of Operation Mulberry." Vogel hesitated. "We can now predict with much greater certainty just what role Mulberry will play in the invasion."

Hitler nodded. "Please continue, Captain Vogel."

"Based on the new documents, we believe Operation Mulberry is an antiaircraft complex. It will be deployed along the French coastline in an effort to provide protection from the Luftwaffe during the critical first hours of the enemy invasion." Vogel reached into his briefcase again. "Our analysts have used the designs in the enemy document to render a sketch of the complex." Vogel laid it on the table. Schellenberg and Himmler both looked at it with interest.

Hitler had walked away and stared out the windows toward his mountains. He believed he did his best thinking at the Berghof, where he was above it all. "And in your opinion, where will the enemy place this antiaircraft complex, Captain Vogel?"

"The plans stolen by our agent do not specify where Mulberry will be deployed," Vogel said. "But based on the rest of the intelligence collected by the Abwehr, it would be logical to conclude that Mulberry is destined for Calais."

"And your old theory about an artificial harbor at Normandy?"

"It was"—Vogel hesitated, searching for the right word—"premature, my Führer. I made a rush to judgment. I reached a verdict before all the evidence was in. I am a lawyer by training, my Führer—so you will forgive the metaphor."

"No, Captain Vogel, I believe you were right the first time. I believe Mulberry *is* an artificial harbor. And I believe it is destined for Normandy." Hitler turned and faced his audience. "This is just like Churchill, that madman! A grandiose, foolish contraption that betrays his intentions because it tells us where he and his American friends will strike! The man thinks of himself as a great thinker, a great strategist! But he is a fool when it comes to military matters! Just ask the ghosts of the boys he led to the slaughterhouse in the Dardanelles. No, Captain Vogel, you had it right the first time. It is an artificial harbor, and it is bound for Normandy. I know this"—Hitler thumped his chest—"here."

Walter Schellenberg cleared his throat. "My Führer, we do have other evidence to support Captain Vogel's intelligence."

"Let's hear it, Herr Brigadeführer."

"Two days ago in Lisbon, I debriefed one of *our* agents in England."

Vogel thought, Oh, Christ, here we go again.

Schellenberg dug a document out of his briefcase.

"This is a memorandum written by an MI-Five case officer named Alfred Vicary. It was approved by someone with the initials *BB* and forwarded to Churchill and Eisenhower. In it, Vicary warns that there is a new threat to security and that extra precautions should be taken until further notice. Vicary also warns that all Allied officers should be especially careful of approaches by women. Your agent in London—it's a woman, is it not, Captain Vogel?"

Vogel said, "May I see that?"

Schellenberg handed it to him.

Hitler said, "Alfred Vicary. Why does that name sound familiar to me?"

Canaris said, "Vicary is a personal friend of Churchill's. He was part of the group that had Churchill's ear during the 1930s. Churchill brought him to MI-Five when he became prime minister in May 1940."

"Yes, I remember now. Didn't he write a bunch of vile articles about National Socialism throughout the thirties?"

Canaris thought, All of which turned out to be true. He said, "Yes, he's the one."

"And who's *BB*?"

"Basil Boothby. He heads a division within MI-Five."

Hitler was pacing again, but slowly. The tranquillity of the silent Alps always had a soothing effect on him. "Vogel, Schellenberg, and Canaris all are convinced. Well, I'm not."

❖

"An interesting turn of events, wouldn't you say, Herr Reichsführer?" The storm had moved off. Hitler was watching the sun vanishing in the west, the mountain peaks purple and pink with the high Alpine dusk. Everyone had gone except Himmler. "First, Captain Vogel tells me Operation Mulberry is an artificial harbor; then it is an antiaircraft complex."

"Quite interesting, my Führer. I have my theories."

Hitler turned away from the window. "Tell me."

"Number one, he is telling the truth. He has received new information that he trusts, and he truly believes what he has told you."

"Possible. Go on."

"Number two, the intelligence he has just presented to you is totally fabricated and Kurt Vogel, like his superior Wilhelm Canaris, is a traitor bent on the destruction of the Führer and of Germany."

Hitler crossed his arms and tilted his head back. "Why would they deceive us about the invasion?"

"If the enemy succeeds in France and the German people see the war is lost, Canaris and the rest of the *Schwarze Kapelle* scum will turn on us and try to destroy us. If the conspirators succeed in grabbing power, they will sue for peace and Germany will end up the way she was after the First War— castrated, weak, the beggar of Europe, living off scraps from the tables of the British and the French and the Americans." Himmler paused. "And the Bolsheviks, my Führer."

Hitler's eyes seemed to catch fire, the very thought of Germans living under Russian domination too painful to imagine. "We must never let that happen to Germany!" he said, then looked at Himmler carefully. "I see by that look on your face that you have another theory, Herr Reichsführer."

"Yes, my Führer."

"Let's hear it."

"Vogel believes the information he is presenting to you is true. But he has been drinking from a poisoned well."

Hitler seemed intrigued. "Go on, Herr Reichsführer."

"My Führer, I have always been frank with you about my feelings for Admiral Canaris. I believe he is a traitor. I know he has had contact with British and American agents. If my fears about the admiral are correct, wouldn't it be logical to assume he has compromised the German networks in Britain? Wouldn't it also be logical to assume that the information from Canaris's spies in England is also compromised? What if Captain Vogel actually discovered the truth, and Admiral Canaris silenced him in order to protect himself?"

Hitler was pacing restlessly again. "Brilliant as usual, Herr Reichsführer. You are the only one I can trust."

"Remember, my Führer, a lie is the truth, only backward. Hold the lie up to a mirror, and the truth will be staring back at you in the glass."

"You have a plan. I can see it."

"Yes, my Führer. And Kurt Vogel is the key. Vogel can bring us the secret of the invasion and proof of Canaris's treachery once and for all."

"Vogel strikes me as an intelligent man."

"He was considered one of the brightest legal minds in Germany before the war. But remember, he was recruited by Canaris personally. Therefore, I have my doubts about his loyalty. He will have to be handled very carefully."

"That's your specialty, isn't it, Herr Reichsführer?"

Himmler smiled his cadaverous smile. "Yes, my Führer."

The house was dark when Vogel arrived. A heavy snowstorm had stretched the two-hour drive to four. He stepped from the back of the car and collected his small grip from the trunk. He sent the driver on his way; he had booked a room for him at the small hotel in the village. Trude was standing in the open door, arms folded tightly against her body for warmth. She looked absurdly healthy, her fair skin pink with the cold, her brown hair streaked by the mountain sun. She wore a heavy ski sweater, wool trousers, and mountain boots. Despite the chunky clothing Vogel could see she was fit from the outdoors. When Vogel took her into his arms she said, "My God, Kurt Vogel, you're nothing but a bag of bones. Are things so bad in Berlin?"

Everyone was in bed already. The girls shared a room upstairs. While Trude prepared his dinner, Vogel went up to look in on them. The room was cold. Nicole had climbed in bed with Lizbet. In the darkness it was hard to tell where one left off and the other began. He stood and he listened to their breathing and he smelled their scents—their breath, their hair, their soap, their warm bodies releasing the fragrance of the bedclothes. Trude always thought it was strange, but he loved the way they smelled more than anything else.

A plate of food and a glass of wine awaited him downstairs. Trude had eaten hours ago, so she just sat next to him and talked while he devoured the roast pork and potatoes. He was surprisingly hungry. He finished the first plate and she filled a second, which he forced himself to eat more slowly.

Trude talked about her parents and the girls and how the Wehrmacht had come to the village and taken the remaining men and the schoolboys. She thanked God they had been given two daughters and no sons. She asked no questions about his trip, and he volunteered no details.

He finished eating. Trude cleared away the dishes. She had made a pot of ersatz coffee and was standing at the stove, pouring him a cup, when there was a very faint tapping at the door. She crossed the room and opened the door, staring in disbelief at the figure, dressed all in black, standing before her.

"Oh, my God," she murmured as the cup and saucer fell from her grasp and shattered at her feet.

"I still can't believe Heinrich Himmler actually set foot in this house," Trude said, her voice flat, as though she were speaking to herself. She was standing before a weak fire in their bedroom, ramrod straight, arms folded. In the dim light Vogel could see her face was damp and her body was trembling. "When I first saw that face I thought I was dreaming. Then I thought we were all under arrest. And then it dawned on me—Heinrich Himmler was in my parents' house because he needed to confer with my husband."

She turned from the fire and looked at him. "Why is that, Kurt? Tell me you don't work for him. Tell me you're not one of Himmler's henchmen. Tell me, even if it's a lie."

"I don't work for Heinrich Himmler."

"Who was that other man?"

"His name is Walter Schellenberg."

"What does he do?"

Vogel told her.

"What do *you* do? And don't tell me you're just Canaris's lawyer."

"Before the war I looked for very special people. I trained them and sent them to England to be spies."

Trude absorbed this information as if part of her had suspected it for a long time.

"Why didn't you tell me this before?"

"I wasn't allowed to tell anyone, not even you. I deceived you in order to protect you. I had no other reason."

"Where were you today?"

It was no use lying to her any longer. "I was at Berchtesgaden for a meeting with the Führer."

"God almighty," she muttered, shaking her head. "What else have you lied to me about, Kurt Vogel?"

"I've lied to you about nothing else, only my work."

The look on her face said she didn't believe him.

"Heinrich Himmler, in this house. What happened to you, Kurt? You were going to be a great lawyer. You were going to be the next Herman Heller, maybe even sit on the Supreme Court. You loved the law."

"There is no law in Germany, Trude. There is only Hitler."

"What did Himmler want? Why did he come here so late at night?"

"He wants me to help him kill a friend."

"I hope you said you won't help him."

Vogel looked up at her.

"If I don't help him, he'll kill me. And then he'll kill you and he'll kill the girls. He'll kill us all, Trude."

PART
FOUR

CHAPTER FORTY-THREE

LONDON: FEBRUARY 1944

"Same thing as before, Alfred. She led the watchers on a merry chase for three hours and then headed back to her flat."

"Nonsense, Harry. She's meeting another agent, or she's making a dead drop somewhere."

"If she did, then we missed it. Again."

"Damn!" Vicary used the stub of his cigarette to light another. He was disgusted with himself. Smoking cigarettes was bad enough. Using one to light the next was intolerable. It was just the tension of the operation. It had entered its third week. He had allowed Catherine Blake to photograph four batches of Kettledrum documents. Four times she had led the watchers on long chases around London. And four times they had failed to detect how she was getting the material out. Vicary was getting edgy. The longer the operation continued in this manner, the greater the chances of a mistake. The watchers were exhausted, and Peter Jordan was ready to revolt.

Vicary said, "Perhaps we're just going about this the wrong way."

"What do you mean?"

"We're following her, hoping we can detect her drop. What if we changed our tactics and started looking for the agent who's making the pickup?"

"But how? We don't know who he is or what he looks like."

"Actually, we might. Every time Catherine goes out we go with her. And so does Ginger Bradshaw. He's taken dozens and dozens of photographs. Our man is bound to be in a couple of them."

"It's possible, certainly worth a try."

Harry returned ten minutes later with a stack of photographs a foot high. "One hundred and fifty photographs to be exact, Alfred."

Vicary sat down at his desk and put on his half-moon reading glasses. He picked up the photographs one at a time and scanned the images for faces, clothing, suspicious looks—anything. Cursed with a near photographic memory, Vicary stored each of the images in his mind and moved on to the next. Harry drank tea and paced quietly in the shadows.

Two hours later, Vicary thought he had a match.

"Look, Harry, here he is in Leicester Square. And here he is again outside Euston Station. Could be coincidence, could be two different people. But I doubt it."

"Well, I'll be damned!" Harry studied the figure in the photographs: small, dark-haired, with square shoulders and conventional clothing. Nothing about his appearance called attention to him—perfect for pavement work.

Vicary gathered up the remaining photographs and divided them in half.

"Start looking for him, Harry. Just him. No one else."

Half an hour later Harry picked him out of a photograph taken on Trafalgar Square, which proved to be the best one yet.

"He needs a code name," Vicary said.

"He looks like a Rudolf."

"All right," Vicary said. "Rudolf it is."

CHAPTER FORTY-FOUR

HAMPTON SANDS, NORFOLK

At that moment, Horst Neumann was pedaling his bicycle from Dogherty's cottage toward the village. He wore his heavy rollneck sweater, a reefer coat, and trousers tucked inside Wellington boots. It was a bright clear day. Plump white clouds, driven by the strong northerly winds, drifted across a sky of deep blue. Their shadows raced across the meadows and the hillsides and disappeared over the beach. It was the last decent day they would see for a while. Heavy weather was forecast for the entire east coast of the country, beginning midday tomorrow and lasting several days. Neumann wanted to get out of the cottage for a few hours while he had the chance. He needed to think. The wind gusted, making it nearly impossible to keep the bicycle upright on the pitted single-lane track. Neumann put his head down and pedaled harder. He turned and looked over his shoulder. Dogherty had given up. He had climbed off his bicycle and was pushing it morosely along the path.

Neumann pretended not to notice and continued toward the village. He leaned forward over the handlebars, elbows thrust out, and cycled furiously up a small hill. He reached the top and coasted down the other side. The track was hard with the previous night's freeze, and the bicycle rattled along the deep ruts so viciously Neumann feared the front tire might break loose. The wind eased and the village appeared. Neumann pedaled across the bridge over the sea creek and stopped on the other side. He laid the bicycle in the deep grass at the edge of the track and sat down next to it. He lifted his face toward the sun. It felt warm, despite the crisp air. A squadron of gulls circled silently overhead. He closed his eyes and listened to the beating of the sea. He was struck by an absurd notion—he would miss this little village when it was time to leave.

He opened his eyes and spotted Dogherty atop the hill. Dogherty removed his cap, wiped his brow, and waved. Neumann called, "Take your time, Sean." Then he gestured at the sun to explain why he was in no hurry to move. Dogherty climbed back onto the bicycle and coasted down.

Neumann watched Dogherty; then he turned and looked at the sea. The message he had received from Vogel early that morning troubled him. He had avoided thinking about it but he could avoid it no longer. The wireless operator in Hamburg had transmitted a code phrase that meant Neumann was to conduct countersurveillance on Catherine Blake in London. Countersurveillance, in the lexicon of the trade, meant he was supposed to follow Catherine to make certain she wasn't being followed by the opposition. The request could mean anything. It could mean that Vogel just wanted to make certain the information Catherine was receiving was good. Or it could mean he suspected she was being manipulated by the other side. If that was the case, Neumann might be walking straight into a very dangerous situation. If Catherine was under surveillance and he followed her too, he would be walking side by side with MI5 officers trained to recognize countersurveillance. He would be walking right into a trap. He thought, Damn you, Vogel, what are you playing at?

And what if she *was* being followed by the other side? Neumann had two choices. If possible, he was to contact Vogel by wireless and request authorization to extract Catherine Blake from England. If there was no time, he had Vogel's permission to act on his own.

Dogherty coasted across the bridge and stopped next to Neumann. A large cloud passed before the sun. Neumann shivered in the cold. He stood up and walked with Dogherty toward the village, each man pushing his bicycle. The wind gusted, whistling through the crooked headstones in the graveyard. Neumann turned up the collar of his coat.

"Listen, Sean, there's a chance I may need to be leaving soon, in a hurry."

Dogherty looked at Neumann, his face blank, then looked forward again.

Neumann said, "Tell me about the boat."

"Early in the war I was instructed by Berlin to create an escape route along the Lincolnshire coast, a way for an agent to get to a U-boat ten miles offshore. His name is Jack Kincaid. He has a small fishing boat in the town of Cleethorpes, at the mouth of the River Humber. I've seen the boat. It's a bit of a wreck—otherwise, it would have been seized by the Royal Navy—but it will do the trick."

"And Kincaid? What does he know?"

"He thinks I'm involved in the black market. Kincaid's into a lot of shady things, but I suspect he'd draw the line at working for the Abwehr. I paid him a hundred pounds and told him to be ready to do the job on short notice—anytime, day or night."

"Contact him today," Neumann said. "Tell him we might be coming soon."

Dogherty nodded.

Neumann said, "I'm not supposed to make you this offer, but I'm going to anyway. I want you and Mary to consider coming out with me when I leave."

Dogherty laughed to himself. "And what am I supposed to do in bloody Berlin?"

"You'll be alive, for one thing," Neumann said. "We've left too many footprints and the British aren't stupid, as much as you'd like to believe they are. They'll find you. And when they do they'll march you straight to the gallows."

"I've thought of that already. A lot of good men have given their life for the cause. My brother did. And I'm not afraid to give mine."

"That's a lovely speech, Sean. But don't be a fool. I'd say you bet on the wrong horse. You wouldn't be dying for the cause, you'd be dying because you engaged in espionage on behalf of the enemy—Nazi Germany. Hitler and his friends don't give a damn about Ireland. And helping them now isn't going to free Northern Ireland from English oppression—not now, not ever. Do you understand me?"

Dogherty said nothing.

"And there's something else you need to ask yourself. You may be willing to sacrifice your own life, but what about Mary's?"

Dogherty looked up at him sharply. "What do you mean?"

"Mary knows you were spying for the Abwehr and she knows I was an agent. If the British find out about that, they're not going to be happy, to say the least. She'll go to prison for a very long time—if she's lucky. If she's not lucky, they'll hang her too."

Dogherty waved his hand. "They won't touch Mary. She didn't have any part in it."

"It's what they call being an accessory, Sean. Mary was an accessory to your espionage."

Dogherty walked in silence for a while, thinking over Neumann's words.

Finally he said, "What the hell would I do in Germany? I don't want to go to Germany."

"Vogel can arrange passage for you to a third country—Portugal or Spain. He might even be able to get you back into Ireland."

"Mary will never go. She'll never leave Hampton Sands. If I go with you, I'd have to go on my own—leave her behind to face the bloody British."

They arrived at the Hampton Arms pub. Neumann leaned his bicycle against the wall and Dogherty did the same.

"Let me think about it tonight," Dogherty said. "I'll talk to Mary and give you an answer in the morning."

They went inside the Arms, empty except for the publican, who was behind the bar polishing glasses. A large fire burned on the hearth. Neumann and Dogherty removed their coats, hung them on a row of hooks next to the door, and sat down at the table nearest the fire. There was only one thing on the menu that day, pork pie. They ordered two pies and two glasses of beer. The fire was incredibly hot. Neumann removed his sweater. The publican brought the pies a few minutes later, and they ordered more beer. Neumann had helped Sean repair some fencing that morning, and he was starved. The only time Neumann looked up from his plate was when the door opened and a large man stepped inside. Neumann had seen him around the village and knew who he was. Jenny's father, Martin Colville.

Colville ordered whisky and stayed at the bar. Neumann, finishing the last of his pork pie, glanced up at him at regular intervals. He was a large powerful man, with black hair that fell into his eyes and a black beard flecked with gray. His coat was filthy and smelled of motor oil. His huge hands were cracked and permanently soiled. Colville drank the first whisky in one gulp and ordered a second. Neumann ate the last of his pie and lit a cigarette.

Colville finished the second whisky and glared in Neumann and Dogherty's direction. "I want you to stay away from my daughter," Colville said. "I hear you two have been seen together around the village, and I'm not happy about it."

Dogherty, through clenched teeth, said, "Stay out of it, mate."

"Jenny and I spend time together because we're friends," Neumann said. "Nothing more."

"You expect me to believe that! You want to get under her skirt. Well, Jenny's not that kind of girl."

"Frankly, I don't give a damn what you believe."

"I put up with her hanging around Paddy, here, and his wife, but I won't put up with the likes of you. You're no good for her. And if I ever hear about you two being together again"—Colville thrust out his forefinger at Neumann—"I'll be coming after you."

Dogherty said, "Just nod and smile and be done with it."

"She spends time with Sean and Mary because they care about her. They give her a pleasant, safe home. Which is more than I can say for you."

"Jenny's home is none of your affair. Just keep your nose out of it! And if you know what's good for you, you'll stay the fuck away from her!"

Neumann crushed out his cigarette. Dogherty was right. He should just sit there and keep his mouth shut. The last thing he needed now was to provoke a fight with a villager. He looked up at Colville. He knew the type. The bastard had terrorized everyone his entire life, including his own daughter. Neumann relished the opportunity to put him in his place. He thought, If I show him what it's like, maybe he'll never hurt Jenny again.

He said, "What are you going to do, hit me? That's your answer for everything, isn't it? Whenever something happens that you don't like, you just hit someone. That's why Jenny spends so much time with the Doghertys. That's why she can't stand to be around you."

Colville's face tightened. He said, "Who the fuck *are* you? I don't believe your story."

He crossed the pub in a few quick steps, took hold of the table, and threw it out of the way.

"You're mine—and I'm going to enjoy this."

Neumann got to his feet. "Lucky me."

A small knot of villagers, sensing trouble, gathered outside the pub around the two men. Colville threw a wild right hook that Neumann avoided easily. Colville threw two more punches. Neumann avoided them by moving his head just a few inches, keeping his hands protectively around his face and his eyes locked on Colville's, staying back on the defensive. If he tried to move close enough to land a punch, Colville might be able to grab him with his powerful arms and he might never get away again. He had to wait for Colville to make a mistake. Then he would go on the offensive and end this thing as quickly as possible.

Colville threw several more wild punches. He was already out of breath and laboring. Neumann could see frustration building in his face. Colville reached out his arms and charged like a bull. Neumann stepped quickly to the side and tripped Colville as he stormed past. He landed facedown with a heavy thud. Neumann moved in quickly, as Colville was rising to his hands and knees, and kicked him twice rapidly in the face. Colville raised a heavy forearm, absorbing a third blow, and scrambled back onto his feet.

Neumann had managed to break his nose. Blood streamed from both nostrils into his mouth.

Neumann said, "You've had enough, Martin. Let's stop this and go back inside."

Colville said nothing. He stepped forward, jabbed with his left hand, and unleashed a powerful roundhouse right. The blow landed high on Neumann's cheekbone, splitting the flesh. Neumann felt as if he had been hit by a sledgehammer. His head rang, tears flowed into his eyes, his vision blurred. He shook his head to clear the cobwebs and thought of Paris—lying in the filthy alley behind the café, his own blood running into the puddles of rainwater, the SS men above him, kicking him with their jackboots, beating him with their fists, their pistol butts, wine bottles, anything.

Colville unleashed another reckless punch. Neumann crouched, then pivoted and kicked sideways, landing a savage blow on Colville's right kneecap. The bigger man screamed in agony. Neumann rapidly kicked him three more times. Colville was crippled; Neumann wondered if he had dislodged the kneecap. Colville was also terrified. He had obviously never encountered anyone who fought like Neumann.

Neumann kept moving to his right, forcing Colville to put weight on his damaged leg. Colville could barely remain standing. Neumann thought his opponent was finished.

When Neumann's back was toward the pub, Colville shifted all his weight to his good leg and lunged. Neumann, surprised, couldn't get out of the way fast enough. Colville smashed into him and drove him back against the wall. It was like being hit by a speeding lorry. Neumann struggled to regain his breath. Colville raised his head viciously, catching Neumann beneath his chin. Neumann bit his own tongue and blood poured into his mouth.

Before Colville could strike again, Neumann raised a knee into his groin. Colville doubled over, groaning deep in his throat. Neumann raised his knee again, this time into Colville's face, shattering bone. Neumann stepped forward, raised his arm, and drove his elbow downward into the side of Colville's head.

Colville's knees buckled and he collapsed, barely conscious.

Neumann said, "Don't get up, Martin. If you know what's good for you, stay right where you are."

Then Neumann heard screaming. He looked up and saw Jenny running toward him.

❖

That night Neumann lay awake in his bed. He had slept for a while but the pain had awakened him. Now he lay very still, listening to the wind beating against the side of the cottage. In the distance he could hear the rush of the waves against the shoreline. He did not know the time. His wristwatch was lying on the little table next to the bed. He rose onto one elbow, reached out for it, groaning with pain, and looked at the luminous face. Nearly midnight.

He fell back onto his pillow and stared at the ceiling. Fighting with Martin Colville was a foolish mistake. He had endangered his cover and the security of the operation. And he had hurt Jenny. Outside the pub, she had screamed at him and beat her fists against his chest. She was furious with him for hurting her father. He had just wanted to teach the bastard a lesson, but it had all backfired. Now, lying in bed, listening to the confused rhythm of the ceaseless wind, he wondered whether the entire operation was doomed. He thought of Catherine's warning on Hampstead Heath: *Some things have gone wrong. I don't think my cover is going to hold up much longer.* He thought of Vogel's order to conduct countersurveillance. He wondered whether all of them—Vogel, Catherine, himself—had already made fatal mistakes.

Neumann took stock of his injuries. He seemed to hurt everywhere. His ribs were bruised and tender—every breath hurt—but it appeared he had suffered no broken bones. His tongue was swollen, and when he rubbed it along the roof of his mouth he felt the cut on the surface. He raised his hand and touched his cheek. Mary had done her best to close the wound without stitches—going to a doctor was out of the question. He checked to make certain the dressing was securely in place. Even the lightest touch made his face pound with pain.

Neumann closed his eyes and tried to sleep. He was beginning to drift off when he heard a footfall on the landing outside his door. Instinctively, he reached for his Mauser. He heard another footfall, then the floor creaking beneath the weight of a body. He raised the Mauser and leveled it at the door. He heard the rattle of someone turning the latch. He thought: If MI5 was coming for me, they certainly wouldn't be trying to sneak into my bedroom at night. But if it wasn't MI5 or the police, who the hell was it? The door pushed back and a small figure stood in the open space. Neumann, in the dim light of his open shade, could see it was Jenny Colville. He quietly laid the Mauser on the floor next to the bed and whispered, "What do you think you're doing?"

"I came to see if you were all right."

"Do Sean and Mary know you're here?"

"No. I let myself in." She sat down on the edge of the small bed. "How are you feeling?"

"I've been through worse. Your father packs quite a punch. But then, you know that better than anyone else."

She reached out in the darkness and touched his face. "You should have seen a doctor. That was quite a cut on your face."

"Mary did an excellent job."

Jenny smiled. "She's had a lot of practice with Sean. She said that when Sean was young, Saturday night wasn't Saturday night unless it ended with a good fight outside the pub."

"How's your father? I think I hit him one too many times."

"He'll be all right. Oh, his face is a mess. He was never very good-looking to begin with."

"I'm sorry, Jenny. The whole thing was ridiculous. I should have known better. I should have just ignored him."

"The publican said my father started it. He deserved what he got. He's had it coming for a long time."

"You're not angry with me anymore?"

"No. No one's ever stood up for me before. That was a very brave thing you did. My father is as strong as an ox. He could have killed you." She removed her hand from his face and ran it across his chest. "Where did you learn to fight like that?"

"In the army."

"It was terrifying. My God, but your body is covered with scars."

"I've lived a very rich and fulfilling life."

She came closer to him. "Who are you, James Porter? And what are you doing in Hampton Sands?"

"I came here to protect you."

"Are you my knight in shining armor?"

"Something like that."

Jenny stood up abruptly and pulled her sweater over her head.

"Jenny, what do you think you're—"

"Shhh, you'll wake Mary."

"You can't stay here."

"It's after midnight. You wouldn't send me out into a night like this, would you?"

Jenny had removed her Wellington boots and her trousers before he could answer the question. She climbed into bed and curled up next to him, beneath his arm.

Neumann said, "If Mary finds you here, she'll kill me."

"You're not afraid of Mary, are you?"

"Your father I can handle. But Mary's another story altogether."

She kissed him on the cheek and said, "Good night." After a few minutes, her breathing assumed the rhythm of sleep. Neumann leaned his head against hers, listening to the wind, and after a few moments he slept too.

CHAPTER FORTY-FIVE

BERLIN

The Lancasters came at two o'clock in the morning. Vogel, sleeping fitfully on the army cot in his office, rose and went to the window. Berlin shuddered beneath the impact of the bombs. He parted the blackout curtain and looked out. The car was still there—a large black sedan, parked across the street. It had been there all night and all afternoon before that. Vogel knew there were at least three men inside, because he could see the embers of their cigarettes glowing in the dark. He knew the engine was running, because he could see the exhaust drifting from the tailpipe into the freezing night air. The professional in him marveled at the shoddiness of their surveillance. Smoking, knowing full well the embers would be visible in the dark. Running the engine so they could have heat, even though the worst amateur could spot the exhaust. But then the Gestapo didn't need to worry much about technique and tradecraft. They relied on terror and brute force. Hammer blows.

Vogel thought about his conversation with Himmler at the house in Bavaria. He had to admit Himmler's theory made a certain amount of sense. The fact that most of the German intelligence networks in Britain were still operational was not proof of Canaris's loyalty to the Führer. It was proof of the opposite—his treachery. If the head of the Abwehr is a traitor, why bother to publicly arrest and hang his spies in Britain? Why not use those spies and, together with Canaris, try to fool the Führer with false and misleading intelligence?

Vogel thought it was a plausible scenario. But a deception of that magnitude was almost unimaginable. Every German agent would have to be in custody or turned by the other side. Hundreds of British case officers would have to be involved in the project, turning out reams of false intelligence reports to be transmitted by wireless back to Hamburg. Could there be such a deception? It would be a mammoth and risky undertaking, but Vogel concluded it was possible.

The concept was brilliant, but Vogel recognized one glaring weakness. It required total manipulation of the German networks in Britain. Every agent had to be accounted for—turned or locked away where they could do no harm. If there was a single agent outside MI5's web of control, that one agent could file a contradictory report and the Abwehr might smell a rat. It could use the reports from the one genuine agent to conclude that all the other intelligence it was receiving was bogus. And if all the other intelligence was pointing toward Calais as the invasion point, the Abwehr could conclude that in fact the opposite was true—the enemy was coming at Normandy.

He would have his answer soon. If Neumann discovered that Catherine Blake was under surveillance, Vogel could dismiss the information she was sending as smoke concocted by British Intelligence—part of a deception.

He turned from the window and lay on his army cot. A chill ran down him. He might very well uncover evidence that British Intelligence was engaged in a grand deception. And that in turn would strongly suggest that Admiral Wilhelm Canaris, the head of German military intelligence, was a traitor. Himmler would certainly take it as ironclad proof. There was only one punishment for such an offense: piano wire around the neck, a slow torturous death by strangulation, all captured on film so Hitler could watch it over and over again.

And what if he did uncover proof of a deception? The Wehrmacht would be waiting with their panzers at the invasion point. The enemy would be slaughtered. Germany would win the war, and the Nazis would rule Germany and Europe for decades.

There is no law in Germany, Trude. There is only Hitler.

Vogel closed his eyes and tried to sleep, but it was no good. The two incompatible aspects of his personality were in full conflict: Vogel the spymaster and manipulator and Vogel the believer in the rule of law. He was tantalized by the prospect of uncovering a massive British deception, of outwitting his British opponents, of destroying their little game. At the same time, he was terrified by what that victory would bring. Prove a British deception, destroy his old friend Canaris, win the war for Germany, secure the Nazis in power forever.

He lay on his cot awake, listening to the rumble of the bombers.

Tell me you don't work for him, Kurt.

Vogel thought, I do now, Trude. I do now.

CHAPTER FORTY-SIX

LONDON

"Hello, Alfred."

"Hello, Helen."

She smiled and kissed his cheek and said, "Oh, it's so good to see you again."

"It's good to see you too."

She threaded her arm through Vicary's and placed her hand inside his coat pocket, the way she used to do. They turned and walked silently along the footpath in St. James's Park. Vicary did not find the quiet awkward. In fact he found it rather pleasant. A hundred years ago it was one of the reasons why he knew he truly loved her—the way he felt when there was silence between them. He could enjoy her company when they talked and laughed, but he enjoyed her just as much when she said nothing at all. He loved sitting quietly with her on the veranda of her home or walking through the woods or lying by the lake. Just to have her body next to his—or her hand in his—was enough.

The afternoon air was thick and warm, a breath of August in February, the sky dark and unsettled. Wind moved in the trees, made waves on the surface of the pond. A fleet of ducks bobbed with the current as if lying at anchor.

He looked at her closely for the first time. She had aged well. In many ways she was more beautiful than before. She was tall and erect, and the little bit of weight she had put on over the years was hidden nicely behind her carefully tailored suit. Her hair, which she used to wear down the center of her back in a blond cape, was pulled back and pinned neatly in place. On her head she wore a gray pillbox hat.

Vicary allowed his gaze to settle on her face. Her nose, once a little too long for her face, now seemed perfectly appropriate. Her cheeks had hollowed a bit with age, making the bones of her face more prominent. She turned and noticed Vicary was staring at her. She smiled at him, but the smile did not extend to the eyes. There was a distant sadness there, as if someone close to her had died recently.

Vicary was the first to break the silence. He looked away from her and said, "I'm sorry about lunch, Helen. Something came up at work and I wasn't able to get away or even call you."

"Don't worry, Alfred, I just sat at a table alone at the Connaught and became miserably drunk." Vicary looked up sharply at her. "I'm only teasing you. But I won't pretend I wasn't disappointed. It took me a very long time to work up the courage to approach you. I acted so horribly before. . . ." Her voice trailed off and she left her thought unfinished.

Vicary thought, Yes, you did, Helen. He said, "It was a long time ago. How on earth did you find me?"

She had telephoned him at the office twenty minutes ago. He had picked up the receiver expecting to hear anything but her voice: Boothby, telling him to come upstairs for another display of his brilliance; Harry, telling him Catherine Blake had shot someone else in the face; Peter Jordan, telling him to fuck off, he wouldn't see her anymore. The sound of Helen's voice nearly made him choke. "Hello, darling, it's me," she had said, and, like a good agent, she had not used her name. "Will you still see me? I'm in a phone box opposite your office. Oh, please, Alfred."

"My father is friends with your director-general," she said, "and David is good friends with Basil Boothby. I've known for some time that you'd been pulled in."

"Your father, David, and Basil Boothby—all my favorite people."

"Don't worry, Alfred, they don't sit around discussing you."

"Well, thank heavens for that!"

She squeezed his hand. "How in the world did *you* end up doing *this*?"

Vicary told her the story. How he befriended Churchill before the war. How he was drawn into Churchill's circle of advisers at Chartwell. How Churchill put the hooks into him that afternoon in May 1940.

"He actually did it in the bath?" Helen exclaimed.

Vicary nodded, smiling at the memory of it.

"What does the prime minister look like naked?"

"He's very pink. It was awe-inspiring. I found myself humming 'Rule Britannia' for the rest of the day."

Helen laughed. "Your work must be terribly exciting."

"It can be. But it can also be dreadfully boring and tedious."

"Are you ever tempted to tell anyone all the secrets you know?"

"Helen!"

"Are you?" she insisted.

"No, of course not."

"I am," she said, and looked away. After a moment she looked back at him. "You look wonderful, Alfred. You're very handsome. This bloody war seems to be agreeing with you."

"Thank you."

"I must admit I miss the corduroy and tweed, though. Now you're all gray, just like the rest of them."

"It's the official uniform of Whitehall, I'm afraid. I've become accustomed to it. I've also enjoyed the change. But I'll be glad when it's over so I can get back to University College where I belong."

He couldn't believe the words had actually come out of his mouth. He had once thought of MI5 as his salvation. He knew now it definitely was not. He had enjoyed his time at MI5: the tension, the long hours, the inedible fare in the canteen, the battles with Boothby, the remarkable group of dedicated amateurs just like himself who toiled away in secret. He had once toyed with the idea of asking to stay on after the war. But it wouldn't be the same—not without the threat of national destruction hanging over them like Damocles' sword.

There was something else. While he was well suited intellectually to the actual business of intelligence, its very nature was abhorrent to him. He was a historian. By nature and training he was dedicated to searching out truth. Intelligence was about lying and deception. About betrayal. About means justifying ends. About stabbing one's enemy in the back—and maybe stabbing a friend in the back, if necessary. He was not at all certain he liked the person he had become.

Vicary said, "How's David, by the way?"

Helen exhaled heavily. "David is *David*," she said, as if no other explanation was necessary. "He's banished me to the countryside, and he stays here in London. He managed a commission and does something for the Admiralty. I come to see him once every few weeks. He likes it when I'm away. It gives him the freedom to pursue his other interests."

Vicary, uncomfortable with Helen's honesty, looked away. David Lindsay, along with being incredibly rich and handsome, was a notorious womanizer. Vicary thought, No wonder he and Boothby are such good friends.

Helen said, "You don't need to feign ignorance, Alfred. I am aware that everyone knows about David and his favorite pastime. I've grown used to it. David likes women, and they like him. It's a rather neat fit."

"Why don't you leave him?"

"Oh, Alfred," she said, and dismissed the suggestion with a wave of her gloved hand.

"Is there anyone else in your life?"

"Do you mean other men?"

Vicary nodded.

"I tried once, but he was the wrong man. He was David in different clothes. Besides, I made a promise in a country church twenty-five years ago, and I seem incapable of breaking it."

"I wish you had felt that way about the promise you made to me," Vicary said, and immediately regretted the note of bitterness that crept into his voice. But Helen just looked at him, blinked rapidly, and said, "Sometimes I wish that too. There, I've said it. My God, how thoroughly un-English of me. Please forgive me. I suppose it's all these bloody Americans in town."

Vicary felt his face flush.

Helen said, "Are you still seeing Alice Simpson?"

"How in the world do you know about Alice Simpson?"

"I know about all your women, Alfred. She's very pretty. I even like those wretched books she writes."

"She's slipped away. I told myself it was the war, my work. But the truth is, she wasn't you, Helen. So I let her slip away. Just like all the others."

"Oh, damn you, Alfred Vicary! Damn you for saying that."

"It's the truth. Besides, it's what you wanted to hear. That's why you sought me out in the first place."

"The truth is, I wanted to hear that you were happy," she said. Her eyes were damp. "I didn't want you to tell me I'd ruined your life."

"Don't flatter yourself, Helen. You haven't ruined my life. I'm not unhappy. I've just never found enough room in my heart for someone else. I don't trust people very much. I suppose I have you to thank for that."

"Truce," she said. "Please, let's call a truce. I didn't want this to turn into a continuation of our last conversation. I just wanted to spend some time with you. God, but I need a drink. Will you take me somewhere nice and pour a bottle of wine into me, darling?"

They walked to Duke's. It was quiet that time of the afternoon. They were shown to a corner table. Vicary kept expecting one of Helen and David's friends to come in and recognize them, but they were alone. Vicary excused himself to go to the telephone and tell Harry where he was. When he came back there was a ludicrously expensive bottle of champagne sitting in an ice bucket.

"Don't worry, darling," she said. "It's David's party."

He sat down and they drank half the wine very fast. They talked about Vicary's books, and they talked about Helen's children. They even talked about David some more. He never took his eyes from her face as she spoke. There was something about the remote sadness in her eyes—the vulnerability caused by her failed marriage—that made her even more attractive to him. She reached out her hand and laid it on Vicary's. He felt his heart beating inside his chest for the first time in twenty-five years.

"Do you ever think about it, Alfred?"

"Think about what?"

"That morning."

"Helen, what are you—"

"My God, Alfred, you can be so thick sometimes. The morning I came to your bed and ravaged your body for the first time."

Vicary swallowed the last of his wine and refilled their glasses. He said, "No—not really."

"My God, Alfred Vicary, but you *are* a terrible liar. How do you manage in your new line of work?"

"All right, yes. I *do* think about it." He thought: When was the last time? The morning in Kent, after composing a Double Cross message for his false agent code-named Partridge. "I catch myself thinking about it at the damnedest times."

"I lied to David, you know. I always told him he was the first. But I'm glad it was you." She fingered the base of her wineglass and looked out the window. "It was so fast—just a moment or two. But when I remember it now it lasts for hours."

"Yes. I know what you mean."

She looked back at him. "Do you still have your house in Chelsea?"

"I'm told it's still there. I haven't been there since 1940," Vicary added, jokingly.

She turned from the window and looked Vicary directly in the eyes. She leaned forward and whispered, "I wish you would take me there now and make love to me in your bed."

"I'd like that too, Helen. But you'd only break my heart again. And at my age, I don't think I could get over you a second time."

Helen's face lost all expression and her voice, when it finally came, was flat and toneless. "My God, Alfred, when did you become such a cold-hearted bastard?"

Her words sounded familiar to him. Then he remembered that Boothby, taking him by the arm after the interrogation of Peter Jordan, had asked him the same thing.

A shadow fell between them. It passed over her face, darkened it, then moved on. She sat very quiet and very still. Her eyes dampened. She blinked away the tears and regained her composure. Vicary felt like an idiot. The whole thing had gone too far—spun out of control. He was a fool to see her. Nothing good could come of it. The silence was like grinding metal now. He absently beat his breast pockets for his half-moon glasses and tried to think of some excuse to get away. Helen sensed his uneasiness. Still facing the window, she said, "I've kept you too long. I know you should be getting back."

"Yes. I really should. I'm sorry."

Helen was still talking to the window. "Don't be seduced by them. When the war is over, get rid of those awful gray suits and go home to your books. I liked you better then." Vicary said nothing, just looked at her. He leaned down to kiss her cheek but she lifted her face to him and, holding his neck with her fingers, kissed him lightly on the mouth. She smiled and said, "I hope you change your mind—and soon."

"I may, actually."

"Good."

"Good-bye, Helen."

"Good-bye, Alfred."

She took his hand. "I have one more thing to say to you. Whatever you do, don't trust Basil Boothby, darling. He's poison. Never, ever, turn your back on him."

And then he remembered what she had said about her one adulterous lover: *He was David in different clothes.*

No, Helen, he thought. He was Boothby.

He walked. If he could have run he would have. He walked without direction, without destination. He walked until the scar tissue in his knee burned like a brand. He walked until his smoker's cough sounded like consumption. The leafless trees of Green Park twisted with the wind. The rushing air sounded like white water. The wind lifted his unbuttoned mackintosh and nearly tore it from his body. He clutched it at the throat, and it flew from his shoulders like a cape. The blackout descended like a veil. In the darkness he bumped into a brassy American. *Hey, watch it, Mac!* Vicary muttered an apology—"So sorry, forgive me"—then regretted it. *Still our bloody country.*

He felt as though he were being conveyed—as though his movements were no longer his own. He suddenly remembered the hospital in Sussex where he recovered from his wounds. The boy who'd been shot in the spine and could no longer move his arms and legs. The way he described to Vicary the floating numbness he felt when the doctors moved his dead limbs for him. *God, Helen! How could you? Boothby! God, Helen!* Vile images of their lovemaking shot through his mind. He closed his eyes and tried to squeeze them away. *Bloody hell! Bloody hell! Anyone but Basil Boothby!* He marveled at the absurd way in which one part of his life had folded over and touched another. Helen and Boothby—absurd. Too absurd to contemplate. But it was true, he knew it.

Where was he now? He smelled the river and made for it. Victoria Embankment. Tugs hauling barges up the river, running lights doused, the far-off call of a foghorn. He heard a man moaning with pleasure and thought it was only his imagination again. He looked to his left and, in the darkness, could made out a tart with her hands inside a soldier's fly. *Oh, good Lord! Excuse me.*

He was walking again. He had an urge to walk up to Boothby's office and punch him in the face. He remembered Boothby's physical size and the rumors about his prowess with the martial arts and decided it would be tantamount to a suicide attempt. He had an urge to walk back to Duke's, find Helen, take her home with him, and to hell with the consequences. Then the images of the case began bursting through his mind, just like they always did. Vogel's empty file. Karl Becker in his soggy cell—*I told Boothby.* Rose Morely's exploded face. Grace Clarendon's tearful flight from Boothby's lair. The Pelican. The Hawke, Boothby's Oxford boy spy. He had the uncomfortable feeling he was being run. He thought, Am I a Hawke too?

Where was he now? Northumberland Avenue. He walked more slowly, listening to the pleasant growl of the late-afternoon traffic. He looked up and saw an attractive young woman staring impatiently at the passing cars. It was Grace Clarendon, there was no mistaking her shock of white-blond hair and her bloodred lips. A large black Humber pulled to the curb. Boothby's. The door opened and Grace climbed inside. The car slid into the traffic. Vicary turned his head and looked away as the car swept past him.

✦

Vicary rode to West Halkin Street. Night had fallen, and with it had come a drenching downpour like a springtime thunderstorm. Vicary rubbed a hole in the condensation on his window and looked out. Crowds of Londoners moved along the pavements like refugees fleeing an advancing army— huddled beneath raincoats and umbrellas, some turned inside out by the wind, blackout torches peering weakly into the wet gloom. Vicary thought of the strange twist of fate that had placed him in the back of a government car and not out there with the rest of them. He thought suddenly of Helen and wondered where she was—somewhere safe and dry, he hoped. He thought of Grace Clarendon, climbing into the back of Boothby's car, and wondered what the hell she was doing there. Was it a very simple answer? Was she sleeping with Boothby and Harry at the same time? Or was it something more sinister? He remembered the words shouted in anger at Boothby behind the closed doors of his office: *You can't do this to me! Bastard! Bloody bastard!* Vicary thought, Tell me what he made you do, Grace, because for the life of me I can't figure it out on my own.

The car stopped outside the house. Vicary climbed out and, holding his briefcase as a shield against the rain, hurried inside. It felt like a West End theater preparing for an uncertain opening night. He had come to enjoy the atmosphere of the place—the noisy chatter of the watchers as they dressed in their foul-weather gear for a night on the streets, the technician checking to make sure he was receiving a good signal from the microphones inside Jordan's house, the smell of cooking drifting from the kitchen.

Something about Vicary's appearance must have radiated tension, because no one spoke to him as he picked his way through the clutter of the situation room and climbed the stairs to the library. He removed his mackintosh and hung it on the hook behind the door. He placed his briefcase on the desk. Then he walked across the hall and found Peter Jordan standing in front of a mirror, dressing in his naval uniform.

He thought, If the watchers are my stagehands, Jordan is my star and the uniform his costume.

Vicary watched him carefully. He seemed uncomfortable putting on the uniform—the way Vicary felt when he dug out his black tie once a decade and tried to remember what went where and how. Vicary cleared his throat gently to announce his presence. Jordan turned his head, stared at Vicary for an instant, then returned his attention to his own image in the glass.

Jordan said, "When is it going to end?"

It had become part of their evening ritual. Each night, before Vicary sent Jordan off to meet Catherine Blake with a new load of Kettledrum material in his briefcase, Jordan asked the same question. Vicary always deflected it. But now he said, "Actually, it may be over very soon."

Jordan looked up sharply, then looked at an empty chair and said, "Sit down. You look like hell. When's the last time you slept?"

"I believe it was a night in May 1940," Vicary said, and lowered himself into the chair.

"I don't suppose you can tell me why this is all about to end soon, can you?"

Vicary shook his head slowly. "I'm afraid I can't."

"I didn't think so."

"Does it make a difference to you?"

"Not really, I suppose."

Jordan finished dressing. He lit a cigarette and sat down opposite Vicary. "Am I allowed to ask you any questions?"

"That depends entirely on the question."

Jordan smiled pleasantly. "It's obvious to me you're not a career intelligence officer. What did you do before the war?"

"I was a professor of European history at University College London." It sounded odd to Vicary just saying it, as though he were reading from someone else's résumé. It seemed like a lifetime ago—two lifetimes ago.

"How did you end up working for MI-Five?"

Vicary hesitated, decided he was violating no security edict by answering, and told him the story.

"Do you enjoy your work?"

"Sometimes. And then there are times when I detest it and can't wait to get back behind the walls of academia and bar the door."

"Like when?"

"Like now," Vicary said flatly.

Jordan had no reaction. It was as if he understood no intelligence officer, no matter how calloused, could actually enjoy an operation like this.

"Married?"

"No."

"Ever been?"

"Never."

"Why not?"

Vicary thought that sometimes God's coincidences were too vulgar to contemplate. Three hours earlier he had answered the same question in front of the woman who knew the answer. And now his agent was asking him the same bloody thing. He smiled weakly and said, "I suppose I never found the right woman."

Jordan was studying him. Vicary felt it and didn't quite like it. He was used to the relationship being the other way around—with Jordan and with the German spies he had handled. It was Vicary who did the prying, Vicary who broke open the locked vaults of emotion and picked at old wounds until they bled, Vicary who probed for the weak spots and thrust in the dagger. He supposed it was one of the reasons he was a good Double Cross officer. The job allowed him to gaze into the lives of strangers and exploit their personal defects without having to face his own. He thought of Karl Becker sitting in his cell in his drab prison pajamas. Vicary realized he liked being the one in total control, the one doing the manipulating and the deceiving, the one pulling the strings. He thought, Am I this way because Helen tossed me away twenty-five years ago? He dug a packet of Players from his jacket and absently lit one.

Jordan propped his elbow on the arm of his chair and rested his chin on his fist. He frowned and stared back at Vicary as if Vicary were an unstable bridge in danger of collapse.

"I think you probably found the right woman somewhere along the way and she didn't return the favor."

"I say—"

"Ah, so I'm right after all."

Vicary blew smoke at the ceiling. "You're an intelligent man. I always knew that."

"What was her name?"

"Her name was Helen."

"What happened?"

"Sorry, Peter."

"Ever see her now?"

Vicary, shaking his head, said, "No."

"Any regrets?"

Vicary thought of Helen's words. *I didn't want you to tell me I'd ruined your life.* Had she ruined his life? He liked to tell himself that she had not. Like most single men, he liked to tell himself how fortunate he was not to be burdened with a wife and a family. He had his privacy and his work and he liked not having to answer to anyone else in the world. He had enough money to do whatever he wanted. His house was decorated to his taste, and he didn't have to worry about anyone rummaging through his belongings or his papers. But in truth he was lonely—sometimes terribly lonely. In truth he wished he had someone to share his triumphs and his disappointments. He wished someone wanted to share theirs with him. When he stood back and looked at his life objectively, it was missing something: laughter, tenderness, a little noise and disorder sometimes. It was half a life, he realized. Half a life, half a home, ultimately half a man.

Do I have regrets? "Yes, I have a regret," Vicary said, surprised to hear himself actually saying the words. "I regret my failure to marry has deprived me of children. I always thought it must be wonderful to be a father. I think I would have been a good one, in spite of all my quirks and shortcomings."

A smile flickered across Jordan's face in the half darkness, then dissipated. "My son is my entire world. He's my link with the past and my glimpse into the future. He's all that I have left, the only thing that's real. Margaret's gone, Catherine was a lie." He paused, staring at the dying ember of his cigarette. "I can't wait for this to end so I can go home to him. I keep thinking what I'm going to say when he asks me, 'Daddy, what did you do in the war?' What in the hell am I supposed to tell him?"

"The truth. Tell him you were a gifted engineer, and you built a contraption that helped us win the war."

"But that's *not* the truth."

Something about the tone of Jordan's voice made Vicary look up sharply. He thought, Which part isn't the truth?

Vicary said, "Do you mind if I ask a couple of questions now?"

"I thought you were allowed to ask anything you liked, with or without my permission."

"Different setting, different reason for asking."

"Go ahead."

"Did you love her?"

"Have you ever seen her?"

Vicary realized he never *had* seen her in person, only in surveillance photographs.

"Yes, I loved her. She was beautiful, she was intelligent, she was charming, and obviously she was an incredibly talented actress. And believe it or not, I thought she would make a good mother for my son."

"Do you still love her?"

Jordan looked away. "I love the person I thought she was. I don't love the woman you tell me she is. Part of me almost believes this is all some kind of joke. So I suppose you and I have one thing in common."

"What's that?" Vicary asked.

"We both fell in love with the wrong woman."

Vicary laughed. He looked at his wristwatch and said, "It's getting late."

"Yes," Jordan said.

Vicary stood and led Jordan across the hall into the library. He unlocked his briefcase and removed a sheaf of papers from inside. He handed Jordan the papers and Jordan placed them inside his own briefcase. They stood in an awkward silence before Vicary said, "I'm sorry. If there was some other way to do this, I would. But there isn't. Not yet, at least."

Jordan said nothing.

"There's one thing that always bothered me about your interrogation: Why you couldn't remember the names of the men who first approached you about working on Operation Mulberry."

"I met dozens of people that week. I can't remember half of them."

"You said one of them was English."

"Yes."

"Was his name Broome, by any chance?"

"No, his name wasn't Broome," Jordan said without hesitation. "I think I'd remember that. I probably should be going."

Jordan moved toward the door.

"I just have one more question."

Jordan turned and said, "What's that?"

"You *are* Peter Jordan, aren't you?"

"What in the hell kind of question is that?"

"It's a rather simple one really. Are you Peter Jordan?"

"Of course I'm Peter Jordan. You know, you really should get some sleep, Professor."

CHAPTER FORTY-SEVEN

LONDON

Clive Roach was sitting at a window table in the café across the street from Catherine Blake's flat. The waitress brought his tea and his bun. He immediately placed a few coins on the table. It was a habit developed from his work. Roach usually had to leave cafés on short notice and in a hurry. The last thing he needed to do was attract attention. He sipped his tea and half-heartedly leafed through a morning paper. He was not really interested. He was more interested in the doorway across the street. The rain fell harder. He was not looking forward to going out in it again. It was the one aspect of his job he did not like—the constant exposure to foul weather. He'd had more colds and bronchial infections than he could remember.

Before the war he had been a teacher at a down-at-the-heel boys' school. He decided to enlist in the army in 1939. He was far from the ideal soldier—thin, pasty skin, sparse hair, an underpowered voice. Hardly officer material. At the induction center he noticed he was being watched by a pair of sharp-suited men in the corner. He also noticed they had requested a copy of his file and were poring over it with great interest. A few minutes later they pulled him from the queue, told him they were from Military Intelligence, and offered him a job.

Roach liked watching. He was a natural people watcher and he had a flair for names and faces. He knew there would be no medals for battlefield heroics, no stories he could tell down at the pub when the war was over. But it was an important job and Roach did it well. He ate his bun, thinking of Catherine Blake. He had followed many German spies since 1939, but she was the best. A real pro. She had embarrassed him once, but he had vowed he would never let it happen again.

He finished his bun and drank the last of his tea. He looked up from his table and saw her coming out of her block of flats. He marveled at her trade-craft. She always stood still for a moment, doing something prosaic, while scanning the street for any sign of surveillance. Today, she was fumbling with her umbrella as if it were broken. Roach thought, You're very good, Miss Blake. But I'm better.

He watched as she finally snapped up her umbrella and started walking. Roach got up, pulled on his coat, and walked out the door after her.

Horst Neumann came awake as the train clattered through London's north-eastern suburbs. He glanced at his wristwatch: 10:30. They were due in at Liverpool Street at 10:23. Miraculously, they would be only a few minutes late. He yawned, stretched, and sat up in his seat. He looked out the win-dow at the bleak Victorian tenement houses sweeping past. Dirty children waved at the passing train. Neumann, feeling ridiculously English, waved back. There were three other passengers in his compartment, a pair of sol-diers and a young woman who wore the overalls of a factory worker and pulled a frown of concern when she first saw Neumann's bandaged face. He glanced at each of them now. He always worried about talking in his sleep, though the last few nights he had dreamt in English. He leaned his head back and closed his eyes again. God, but he was tired. Up at five o'clock, out of the cottage by six so Sean could give him a lift to Hunstanton, the 7:12 from Hunstanton to Liverpool Street.

He had not slept well the previous night. It was the pain of his injuries and the presence of Jenny Colville in his bed. She had risen with him before dawn, slipped out of the Dogherty cottage, and pedaled home through the dark and the rain. Neumann hoped she made it safely. He hoped Martin wasn't waiting for her. It was a stupid thing to do, letting her spend the night with him. He thought about how she would feel when he was gone. When he never wrote and she never heard from him again. He worried about how she would feel if she ever discovered the truth—that he was not James Porter, a wounded British soldier looking for peace and quiet in a Norfolk village. That he was Horst Neumann, a decorated German paratrooper who came to England to spy and who had deceived her in the worst way. He had not deceived her about one thing. He cared for her. Not in the way she would like, but he did care about what happened to her.

The train slowed as it approached Liverpool Street. Neumann stood, pulled on his reefer coat, and stepped out of the compartment. The corri-dor was packed. He shuffled amid the other passengers toward the door.

Someone ahead of him threw it open, and Neumann stepped from the still-moving train. He gave his ticket to the ticket collector and walked along a dank passageway to the underground station. There, he purchased a ticket for Temple and caught the next train. A few minutes later, he was walking up the stairs and heading north toward the Strand.

Catherine Blake took a taxi to Charing Cross. The rendezvous point was a short distance away, in front of a shop on the Strand. She paid off the driver and threw up her umbrella against the rain. She started walking. At a phone box, she stopped, picked up the receiver, and pretended to place a call. She looked behind her. The heavy rain had reduced visibility, but she could see no sign of the opposition. She replaced the receiver, stepped from the phone box, and continued eastward along the Strand.

Clive Roach slipped from the back of a surveillance van and followed her along the Strand. During the brief ride he had shed his mackintosh and brimmed hat and changed into a dark green oilskin coat and woolen cap. The transformation was remarkable—from a clerk to a laborer. Roach watched as Catherine Blake stopped to place the ersatz telephone call. Roach paused at a newspaper vendor. Browsing through the headlines, he pictured the face of the agent Professor Vicary had code-named Rudolf. Roach's assignment was simple: tail Catherine Blake until she handed her material to Rudolf, then follow him. He looked up in time to see her replacing the receiver in the cradle and stepping from the phone box. Roach melted into the pedestrians and followed her.

Neumann spotted Catherine Blake walking toward him. He paused at a shop, eyes scanning the faces and the clothing of the pedestrians behind her on the pavement. As she drew closer, Neumann turned from the window and started walking toward her. The contact was brief, a second or two. But when it was over Neumann had the film in his hand and was shoving it into the pocket of his coat. She moved quickly on, disappearing into the crowd. Neumann continued in the opposite direction for a few feet, recording the faces. Then he abruptly stopped at another shop window, turned, and followed softly after her.

Clive Roach spotted Rudolf and saw the exchange. He thought, Smooth bastards, aren't you? He watched as Rudolf paused, then turned and walked in the same direction as Catherine Blake. Roach had witnessed many meetings by German agents since 1939, but never had he seen one agent turn and follow the other. Usually, they went their separate ways. Roach turned the collar of his oilskin up around his ears and floated carefully behind them.

❖

Catherine Blake walked eastward along the Strand, then down to Victoria Embankment. It was then she spotted Neumann behind her. Her first reaction was anger. Standard rendezvous procedure was to part company—and quickly—as soon as the handover was complete. Neumann knew the procedure and had executed it faultlessly every time. She thought, Why is he following me now?

Vogel must have ordered him to do it.

But why? She could think of two possible explanations: He had lost faith in her and wanted to see where she was going, or he wanted to determine whether she was under surveillance by the other side. She looked out at the Thames, then turned and glanced down the Embankment. Neumann made no attempt to conceal his presence. Catherine turned and continued walking.

She thought of the endless training lectures at Vogel's secret Bavarian camp. He had called it countersurveillance, one agent following another to make certain the agent was not being followed by the opposition. She wondered why Vogel would make such a move now. Perhaps Vogel wanted to verify that the information she was receiving was good by making certain she was not being followed by the other side. Just to contemplate the second explanation made her stomach burn with anxiety. Neumann was following her because Vogel *suspected* she was under MI5 surveillance.

She paused again and stared out at the river, forcing herself to remain calm. To think clearly. She turned and looked down the Embankment. Neumann still was there. He was intentionally avoiding her gaze, that was clear to her. He was looking out at the river or back up the Embankment, anywhere but in her direction.

She turned and started walking again. She could feel her heart pounding in her chest. She walked to Blackfriars underground station, went inside, and purchased a ticket for Victoria. Neumann followed her and did the same, except the ticket he purchased was for the next stop, South Kensington.

She walked quickly toward the platform. Neumann purchased a newspaper and followed her. She stood, waiting for the train. Neumann stood twenty feet away, reading the paper. When the train came, Catherine waited for the doors to open, then stepped into the carriage. Neumann stepped into the same carriage, but through the second set of doors.

She sat down. Neumann remained standing at the opposite end of the carriage. Catherine did not like the look on his face. She looked down, opened her handbag, and peered inside—a wallet filled with cash, a stiletto, and a loaded, silenced Mauser pistol with extra ammunition clips. She closed the bag and waited for Neumann to make the next move.

For two hours Neumann followed her as she moved through the West End, from Kensington to Chelsea, from Chelsea to Brompton, from Brompton to Belgravia, from Belgravia to Mayfair. By the time they reached Berkeley Square, he was convinced. They were good—damned good—but time and patience had finally depleted their resources and forced them to make a mistake. It was the man in the mackintosh walking fifty feet behind him. Five minutes earlier Neumann had been able to get a very good look at his face. It was the same face he had seen on the Strand nearly three hours earlier—when he had taken the film from Catherine—only then the man had been wearing a green oilskin coat and woolen cap.

Neumann felt desperately alone. He had survived the worst of the war—Poland, Russia, Crete—but none of the skills that helped him through those battles would come into play here. He thought of the man behind him—reedy, pasty, probably very weak. Neumann could kill him in an instant if he wanted. But the old rules didn't apply to this game. He could not radio for reinforcements, he could not count on the support of his comrades. He kept walking, surprised at how calm he was. He thought, They've been following us for hours; why haven't they arrested us both? He thought he knew the answer. They obviously wanted to know more. Where was the film to be dropped? Where was Neumann staying? Were there other agents in the network? As long as he didn't give them the answers to those questions, they were safe. It was a very weak hand but, if played skillfully, Neumann might be able to give them a chance to escape.

Neumann quickened his pace. Catherine, several feet in front of him, turned into Bond Street. She stopped to flag a taxi. Neumann walked faster, then broke into a light run. He called out, "Catherine! My God—it's been ages. How have you been?"

She glanced up, alarm on her face. Neumann took her by the arm.

"We need to talk," Neumann said. "Let's find a place to have some tea and do some catching up."

Neumann's sudden move landed on the command post in West Halkin Street with the impact of a thousand-pound bomb. Basil Boothby was pacing and talking tensely to the director-general by telephone. The director-general was in contact with the Twenty Committee and with the prime minister's staff in the Underground War Rooms. Vicary had made a patch of quiet around himself and was staring at the wall, hands bunched beneath his chin. Boothby slammed down the telephone and said, "The Twenty Committee says let them run."

"I don't like it," Vicary said, still staring at the wall. "They've obviously spotted the surveillance. They're sitting there now trying to figure out what to do."

"You don't know that for certain."

Vicary looked up. "We've never observed her meeting with another agent before. And now she's suddenly sitting in a Mayfair café having tea and toast with Rudolf?"

"We only had her under surveillance a short time. For all we know she and Rudolf have been meeting like this regularly."

"Something's not right. I think they've spotted the tail. What's more, I think Rudolf was looking for it. That's why he followed her after making the rendezvous in the Strand."

"The Twenty Committee has made its decision. They say let them run, so we let them run."

"If they've spotted the surveillance, it makes no sense to let them run. Rudolf is not going to make the drop, and he'll stay clear of any other agents in the network. Following them now does us no good whatsoever. It's over, Sir Basil."

"What do you suggest?"

"Move in now. Arrest them the moment they leave that café."

Boothby looked at Vicary as though he had uttered heresy. "Getting cold feet now, are you, Alfred?"

"What do you mean by that?"

"I mean this was your idea in the first place. You conceived it, you sold it to the prime minister. The director-general signed off on it, the Twenty Committee approved it. For weeks a group of officers has toiled night and day to provide the material for that briefcase. And now you want to shut it all down, just like that"—Sir Basil snapped his thick fingers so loudly it sounded like a gunshot—"because you have a hunch."

"It's more than a hunch, Sir Basil. Read the bloody watch reports. It's all there."

Boothby was pacing again, hands clasped behind his back, head raised slightly as if straining to hear something annoying in the distance. "They'll say he was good at the wireless game but he didn't have the nerve to play with live agents—that's what they'll say about you when this is all over: 'Not surprising, really. He was an amateur, after all. Just a university bright boy who did his bit during the war, then turned to dust when it was all over. He was good—very good—but he didn't have the balls to play in the high-stakes game.' Is that what you want them to say about you? Because if it is, pick up the telephone and tell the DG you think we should roll this all up now."

Vicary stared at Boothby. Boothby the agent runner; Boothby, patrician-cool under fire. He wondered why Boothby was trying to shame him into going forward when a blind man could see they were blown.

"It's over," Vicary said in a dull monotone. "They've spotted the surveillance. They're sitting there planning their next move. Catherine Blake knows she's been deceived, and she's going to tell Kurt Vogel about it. Vogel will conclude that Mulberry is exactly the opposite of what we told him. And then we're dead."

"They're everywhere," Neumann said. "The man in the mackintosh, the girl waiting for the bus, the man walking into the chemist's shop across the square. They've used different faces, different combinations, different clothing. But they've been following us from the moment we left the Strand."

A waitress brought tea. Catherine waited until she left before she spoke. "Did Vogel order you to follow me?"

"Yes."

"I don't suppose he said why?"

Neumann shook his head.

Catherine picked up her cup of tea, her hand trembling. She used her other hand to steady the cup and forced herself to drink.

"What happened to your face?"

"I had a little trouble in the village. Nothing serious."

Catherine looked at him doubtfully and said, "Why haven't they arrested us?"

"Any number of reasons. They've probably known about you for a very long time. They've probably been following you for a very long time. If that's true, then all the information you've been receiving from Commander Jordan is false—smoke put together by the British. And we've been funneling it back to Berlin for them."

She put down her cup. She glanced into the street, then looked back at Neumann, forcing herself not to look at the watchers. "If Jordan is working with British Intelligence, we can assume everything in his briefcase is false— information they wanted me to see, information designed to mislead the Abwehr about the Allied plans for the invasion. Vogel needs to know this." She managed a smile. "It's possible those bastards have just handed us the secret of the invasion."

"I suspect you're right. But there's just one problem. We need to tell Vogel in person. We have to assume the Portuguese embassy route is now compromised. We also have to assume that we cannot use our radios. Vogel thinks all the old Abwehr codes have been broken. That's why he uses the radio so sparingly. If we broadcast what we know to Vogel over the air, the British will know it too."

Catherine lit a cigarette, her hands still trembling. More than anything else, she was angry at herself. For years, she had gone to extraordinary lengths to make certain she was not being watched by the other side. Then, when it finally happened, she had missed it. She said, "How in the world are we going to get out of London?"

"We have a couple of things we can use to our advantage. Number one, this." Neumann tapped his pocket containing the film. "I could be wrong, but I don't think I've ever been followed. Vogel trained me well, and I'm very careful. I don't think they know how I deliver the film to the Portuguese: where it's done, whether there's a patter or any other recognition signal. Also, I'm certain I've not been followed to Hampton Sands. The village is so small I'd know if I was under surveillance. They don't know where I'm staying or whether I'm working with any other agents. Standard procedure is to find out all the components of a network and then roll it up all at once. That's how the Gestapo deals with the Resistance in France, and that's how MI-Five would do it in London."

"That all sounds logical. What are you suggesting?"

"Are you seeing Jordan tonight?"

"Yes."

"What time?"

"I'm meeting him at seven o'clock for dinner."

"Perfect," Neumann said. "Here's what I want you to do."

Neumann spent the next five minutes explaining in detail his plan for their escape. Catherine listened carefully, never taking her eyes off him, resisting all temptation to look at the watchers waiting outside the café. When Neumann finished he said, "Whatever you do, you must do nothing out of the ordinary. Nothing that would make them suspect that you know you're under surveillance. Stay on the move until it's time. Shop, go to a cinema, stay in the open. As long as I don't drop this film, you'll be safe. When it's time, go to your flat and get your radio. I'll be there at five o'clock—exactly five o'clock—and I'll come through the rear entrance. Do you understand?"

Catherine nodded.

"There's just one problem. Do you have any idea where I can lay my hands on a car and some extra petrol?"

Catherine laughed in spite of herself. "Actually, I know just the place. But I wouldn't suggest using my name."

Neumann left the café first. He drifted in Mayfair for half an hour, followed by at least two men—the oilskin coat and the mackintosh.

The rain fell harder, the wind picked up. He was cold, soaked to the skin, and tired. He need to go somewhere to rest, someplace where he could be warm for a while, get off his feet, and keep an eye on his friends Mackintosh and Oilskin. He walked toward Portman Square. He felt bad about involving her, but when it was over they would question her and determine she knew nothing.

He stopped outside the bookshop and peered through the glass. Sarah was on her ladder, dark hair pulled back severely. He rapped gently on the glass so as not to startle her. She turned, and her face brightened into an instant smile. She set down her books and waved enthusiastically for him to come inside. She took one look at him and said, "My God, you look terrible. What happened to you?"

Neumann hesitated; he realized he had no explanation for the bandage across his cheekbone. He mumbled something about taking a fall in the blackout, and she seemed to accept his story. She helped him off with his coat and hung it over the radiator to dry. He stayed with her for two hours, keeping her company, helping her put new books on the shelves, taking tea with her at the café next door when her break came. He noticed the old watchers leaving and new ones taking their place. He noticed a black van parked at the corner and assumed the men in the front seat were from the other side.

At four-thirty, when the last light was gone and the blackout had taken hold, he took his coat from the radiator and pulled it on. She made a playful sad face, then took him by the hand and led him into the stockroom. There, she leaned against the wall, pulled his body to hers, and kissed him. "I don't know the first thing about you, James Porter, but I like you very much. You're sad about something. I like that."

Neumann went out, knowing he would never see her again. From Portman Square he walked north to the Baker Street underground station, followed by at least two people on foot as well as the black van. He entered the station, purchased a ticket for Charing Cross, and caught the next train there. At Charing Cross he changed trains and headed for Euston Station. With two men in pursuit, he walked through the tunnel connecting the underground station to the railway terminus. Neumann waited fifteen minutes at a ticket window and then purchased a ticket for Liverpool. The train was already boarding by the time he reached the platform. The carriage was crowded. He searched for a compartment with one free seat. He finally found one, opened the door, went inside, and sat down.

He looked at his wristwatch: three minutes until departure. Outside his compartment, the corridor was rapidly filling with passengers. It was not uncommon for some unlucky travelers to spend their entire journey standing or sitting in the corridor. Neumann stood and squeezed out of the compartment, muttering about an upset stomach. He walked toward the lavatory at the end of the carriage. He knocked on the door. There was no answer. Knocking a second time, he glanced over his shoulder; the man who had followed him onto the train was cut off from view by the other passengers standing in the corridor.

Perfect. The train started to move. Neumann waited outside the lavatory as the train slowly gathered speed. It already was traveling faster than most people would consider safe to jump. Neumann waited a few more seconds, then stepped toward the door, threw it open, and leapt down onto the platform.

He landed smoothly, trotting a few steps before settling into a brisk walk. He looked up in time to spot an annoyed ticket collector pulling the door closed. He walked quickly toward the exit and headed out into the blackout.

Euston Road was crowded with the evening rush. He hailed a taxi and hopped inside. He gave the driver an address in the East End and settled in for the ride.

CHAPTER FORTY-EIGHT

HAMPTON SANDS, NORFOLK

Mary Dogherty waited alone at the cottage. She had always thought it was a sweet little place—warm, light, airy—but now it felt claustrophobic and cramped as a catacomb. She paced restlessly. Outside, the big storm that had been forecast had finally moved in over the Norfolk coast. Rain lashed against the windows, rattling the panes. The wind gusted relentlessly, moaning through the eaves. She heard the scrape of one of the tiles giving way on the roof.

Sean was away, gone to Hunstanton to collect Neumann from the train. Mary turned from the window and resumed her pacing. Snatches of their conversation of that morning played over and over in her head like a gramophone record stuck in a groove: *submarine to France . . . stay in Berlin for a while . . . passage to a third country . . . make my way back to Ireland . . . join me there when the war is over. . . .*

It was like a nightmare—as if she were listening to someone else's conversation or watching it in a film or reading it in a book. The idea was ludicrous: Sean Dogherty, derelict Norfolk-coast farmer and IRA sympathizer, was going to take a U-boat to Germany. She supposed it was the logical culmination of Sean's spying. She had been foolish to hope that everything would return to normal when the war was over. She had deluded herself. Sean was going to flee and leave her behind to face the consequences. What would the authorities do? *Just tell them you knew nothing about it, Mary.* And what if they didn't believe her? What would they do then? How could she stay in the village if everyone knew Sean had been a spy? She would be run off the Norfolk coast. She would be run out of every English village where she tried to settle. She would have to leave Hampton Sands. She would have to leave Jenny Colville. She would have to go back to Ireland, back to the barren village she had fled thirty years ago. She still had family there, family that would take her in. The thought was utterly appalling but she would have no choice—not after everyone learned that Sean had spied for the Germans.

She began to weep. She thought, Damn you, Sean Dogherty! How could you have been such a damned fool?

Mary went back to the window. On the track, in the direction of the village, she saw a pinprick of light, bobbing in the downpour. A moment later she saw the shine of a wet oilskin and the faint outline of a figure on a bicycle, body hunched forward into the wind, elbows thrust out, knees pumping. It was Jenny Colville. She dismounted at the gate and pushed the bicycle up the pathway. Mary opened the door to her. The wind gusted, hurling rain inside the cottage. Mary pulled Jenny inside and helped her out of her wet coat and hat.

"My God, Jenny, what are you doing out in weather like this?"

"Oh, Mary, it's marvelous. So windy. So beautiful."

"You've obviously lost your mind, child. Sit down by the fire. I'll make you some hot tea."

Jenny warmed herself in front of the log fire. "Where's James?" she asked.

"He's not here now," Mary called from the kitchen. "He's out with Sean somewhere."

"Oh," Jenny said, and Mary could hear the disappointment in her voice. "Will he be back soon?"

Mary stopped what she was doing and went back into the living room. She looked at Jenny and said, "Why are you so concerned about James all of a sudden?"

"I just wanted to see him. Say hello. Spend some time with him. That's all."

"That's all? What in the world has got into you, Jenny?"

"I just like him, Mary. I like him very much. And he likes me."

"You like him and he likes you? Where did you get an idea like that?"

"I know, Mary, believe me. Don't ask me how I know it, but I do."

Mary took hold of her by the shoulders. "Listen to me, Jenny." She shook Jenny once. "Are you listening to me?"

"Yes, Mary! You're hurting me!"

"Stay away from him. Forget about him."

Jenny began to cry. "I can't forget about him, Mary. I love him. And he loves me. I know he does."

"Jenny, he doesn't love you. Don't ask me to explain it all now, because I can't, my love. He's a kind man, but he's not what he appears to be. Let go of it. Forget about him! You have to trust me, little one. He's not for you."

Jenny tore herself from Mary's grasp, stood back, and wiped the tears off her face. "He *is* for me, Mary. I love him. You've been trapped here with Sean so long you've forgotten what love is."

Then she picked up her coat and dashed out the front door, slamming it behind her. Mary hurried to the window and watched Jenny pedaling away through the storm.

Rain beat against Jenny's face as she pedaled along the rolling track toward the village. She had told herself she would not cry again, but she had not been able to keep her word. Tears mixed with the rain and streamed down her face. The village was tightly shuttered, the village store and the pub closed for the night, blackout shades drawn in the cottages. Her torch was lying in her basket, its pale yellow beam aimed forward into the pitch darkness. It was barely enough light to see by. She passed through the village and started toward her cottage.

She was furious with Mary. How dare she try to come between her and James? And what did she mean by that remark about him? *He's not what he appears to be.* She was also angry with herself. She felt terrible about the insult she had hurled at Mary as she ran out the door. They had never quarreled before. In the morning, when things calmed down, Jenny would go back and apologize.

In the distance she could make out the outline of their cottage against the sky. She dismounted at the gate, pushed her bicycle up the footpath, and leaned it against the side of the cottage. Her father came out and stood in the doorway, wiping his hands on a rag. His face was still swollen from the fight. Jenny tried to push past him but he reached out and wrapped his hands around her arm in an iron grip.

"Have you been with him again?"

"No, Papa." She cried out in pain. "Please, you're hurting my arm!"

He raised his other hand to strike her, his ugly swollen face contorted with rage. "Tell me the truth, Jenny! Have you been with him again?"

"No, I swear," she cried, her arms raised about her face to ward off the blow she expected at any second. "Please, Papa, don't hit me! I'm telling you the truth!"

Martin Colville released his grip. "Go inside and make me some supper."

She wanted to scream, Make your own bloody supper for a change! But she knew where it would lead. She looked at his face and, for an instant, found herself wishing that James had killed him. This is the last time, she thought. This is the very last time. She went inside, removed her sodden coat, hung it on the wall in the kitchen, and started his dinner.

CHAPTER FORTY-NINE

LONDON

Clive Roach knew he had a problem the moment Rudolf entered the crowded carriage. Roach would be all right as long as the agent remained seated inside his compartment. But if the agent left the compartment to go to the lavatory or the restaurant car or another carriage, Roach was in trouble. The corridors were jammed with travelers, some standing, some sitting and trying vainly to doze. Moving about the train was an ordeal; one had to squeeze and push past people and constantly say "Excuse me" and "Beg your pardon." Trying to follow someone without being detected would be difficult—probably impossible if the agent was good. And everything Roach had seen thus far told him Rudolf was good.

Roach became suspicious when Rudolf, clutching his stomach, stepped from his compartment while the train was still at the platform at Euston Station and sliced forward along the crowded corridor. Rudolf was short, no more than five foot six, and his head quickly disappeared into the sea of passengers. Roach picked his way forward a few steps, earning him the grunts and groans of the other passengers. He was reluctant to get too close; Rudolf had doubled back several times during the day, and Roach feared he might have seen his face. The corridor was poorly lit because of blackout regulations and already shrouded in a fog bank of cigarette smoke. Roach stayed in the shadows and watched as Rudolf knocked twice on the lavatory door. Another passenger pushed past him, obstructing his view for just a few seconds. When he looked up again Rudolf was gone.

Roach stayed where he was for three minutes, watching the lavatory door. Another man approached, knocked, then went inside and closed the door behind him.

Alarm bells sounded inside Roach's head.

He pushed his way forward through the knot of passengers in the corridor, stopped in front of the lavatory door, and pounded on it.

"Wait your turn like everyone else," came the voice on the other side.

"Open the door—police emergency."

The man opened the door a few seconds later, buttoning his fly. Roach looked inside to make sure Rudolf was not there. *Dammit!* He threw open the door to the connecting passage and entered the next carriage. Like the other, it was dark and smoky and hopelessly crammed with passengers. It would be impossible for him to find Rudolf now without turning over the train carriage by carriage, compartment by compartment.

He thought, How did he vanish so quickly?

He hurried back to the first carriage and found the ticket collector, an old man with steel-rimmed spectacles and a club foot. Roach withdrew the surveillance photograph of Rudolf and stuck it in front of the ticket collector's face.

"Have you seen this man?"

"Short chap?"

"Yes," Roach said, his spirits sinking lower, thinking, Dammit! Dammit!

"He jumped off the train as we pulled out of Euston. Lucky he didn't break his bloody leg."

"Christ! Why didn't you say something?" He realized how ridiculous the remark must have sounded. He forced himself to speak more calmly. "Where does this train make its first stop?"

"Watford."

"When?"

"About a half hour."

"Too long. I have to get off this train now."

Roach reached up, grabbed the emergency-brake cord, and pulled. The train immediately slowed, as the brakes were applied, and began to stop.

The old ticket collector looked up at Roach, eyes blinking rapidly behind the spectacles, and said, "You're not a normal police officer, are you."

Roach said nothing as the train drew to a halt. He threw open the door, dropped down to the edge of the track, and disappeared into the darkness.

Neumann paid off the taxi a short distance from the Pope warehouse and walked the rest of the way. He switched his Mauser from the waistband of his trousers to the front pocket of his reefer coat and then turned up his collar against the driving rain. The first act had gone smoothly. The deception on the train had worked exactly as he hoped. Neumann was certain he was not followed after leaving Euston Station. That meant one thing: Mackintosh, the man who had tailed him onto the train, was almost certainly still on it and heading out of London bound for Liverpool. The watcher was not an idiot. Eventually he would realize Neumann had not returned to his compartment, and he would begin a search. He might ask questions. Neumann's escape had not gone unseen; the ticket collector had spotted him jumping from the train. When the watcher realized Neumann was no longer on the train, he would get off at the next stop and telephone his superiors in London. Neumann realized he had a very limited window of opportunity. He had to move quickly.

The warehouse was dark and appeared deserted. Neumann rang the bell and waited. There was no response. He rang the bell again and this time could hear the sound of footsteps on the other side. The door was opened a moment later by a black-haired giant in a leather coat.

"What do you want?"

"I'd like to see Mr. Pope, please," Neumann said politely. "I need a few items, and I was told this was very definitely the place to come."

"Mr. Pope is gone and we're out of business, so piss off."

The giant started to close the door. Neumann put his foot in the way.

"I'm sorry. It's really rather urgent. Perhaps you could help."

The giant looked at Neumann, a puzzled look on his face. He seemed to be trying to reconcile the public school accent with the reefer coat and bandaged face. "I suppose you didn't hear me the first time," he said. "We're out of business. Shut down." He grabbed Neumann's shoulder. "Now, fuck off."

Neumann punched the giant in the Adam's apple, then pulled out his Mauser and shot him in the foot. The man collapsed on the floor, alternately howling in pain and gasping for breath. Neumann stepped inside and closed the gate. The warehouse was just the way Catherine described it: vans, cars, motorbikes, stacks of black-market food, and several jerry cans of petrol.

Neumann leaned down and said, "If you make a move, I'll shoot you again and it won't be in the foot. Do you understand?"

The giant grunted.

Neumann selected a black van, opened the door, and started the motor. He grabbed two jerry cans of petrol and put them in the back of the van. On second thought, it was a very long drive. He took two more and put them in the back too. He climbed inside the van, drove it to the front of the warehouse, then got out and hauled open the main door.

Before leaving, he knelt beside the wounded man and said, "If I were you, I'd get straight to a hospital."

The man looked at Neumann, more confused than ever. "Who the hell are you, mate?"

Neumann smiled, knowing the truth would sound so absurd the man would never believe it.

"I'm a German spy on the run from MI-Five."

"Yeah—and I'm Adolf bloody Hitler."

Neumann climbed in the van and sped away.

Harry Dalton tore the blackout shades from the headlamps and drove dangerously fast westward across London. Transport section had offered a skilled high-speed driver, but Harry wanted to do the driving himself. He weaved in and out of traffic, one hand constantly pressing the horn. Vicary sat next to him on the front seat, nervously clutching the dash. The wipers struggled in vain to beat away the rain. Turning into the Cromwell Road, Harry accelerated so hard the rear end of the car slid on the slick tarmac. He sliced and snaked his way through the traffic, then turned south into Earl's Court Road. He entered a small side street, then raced down a narrow alley, swerving once to avoid a rubbish bin, then again to miss a cat. He slammed on the brakes behind a block of flats and brought them to a skidding halt.

Harry and Vicary got out of the car, entered the building through the rear service door, and pounded up the stairs toward the fifth floor to the surveillance flat. Vicary, ignoring the pain shooting through his knee like a knife, kept pace with Harry.

He thought, If only Boothby had let me arrest them hours ago, we wouldn't be in this mess!

It was nothing short of a disaster.

The agent code-named Rudolf had just jumped from a train at Euston Station and melted into the city. Vicary had to assume he was now attempting to flee the country. He had no choice but to arrest Catherine Blake; he needed her in custody and scared out of her wits. Then she might tell them where Rudolf was headed and how he planned to escape, whether other agents were involved, and where he kept his radio.

Vicary was not optimistic. Everything he felt about this woman told him she would not cooperate, even when faced with execution. All she had to do was hold out long enough for Rudolf to escape. If she did that, the Abwehr would possess evidence suggesting British Intelligence was engaged in a massive deception. The consequences were too awful to contemplate. All the work that had gone into Fortitude would be wasted. The Germans could deduce that the Allies were coming at Normandy. The invasion would have to be postponed and replanned; otherwise it would end in a blood-soaked catastrophe. Hitler's ironhanded occupation of western Europe would go on. Countless more would die. And all because Vicary's operation had fallen to pieces. They had one chance now: arrest her, make her talk, and stop Rudolf before he could flee the country or use his radio.

Harry pushed open the door to the surveillance flat and led them inside. The curtains were open to the street, the room in darkness. Vicary struggled to make out the figures standing in various poses all around the room like statuary in a darkened garden: a pair of bleary-eyed watchers, frozen in the window; a half-dozen tense Special Branch men leaning against one wall. The senior Special Branch officer was called Carter. He was big and bluff with a thick throat and pockmarked skin. A cigarette, extinguished for security, jutted from the corner of his generous mouth. When Harry introduced Vicary, he pumped Vicary's hand ferociously once, then led him to the window to explain the disposition of his forces. The dead cigarette flaked ash as he spoke.

"We'll go in through the front door," Carter said, a trace of North Country in his accent. "When we do, we'll seal the street at both ends and a pair of men will cover the back of the house. Once we're in the house she'll have nowhere to go."

"It's extremely important that you take her alive," Vicary said. "She's absolutely useless to us dead."

"Harry says she's good with her weapons."

"True. We have reason to believe she has a gun and is willing to use it."

"We'll take her so fast she won't know what hit her. We're ready whenever you give us the word."

Vicary turned from the window and walked across the room to the telephone. He dialed the department and waited for the operator to forward the call to Boothby's office.

"The Special Branch men are ready to move on our order," Vicary said, when Boothby came on the line. "Do we have authorization yet?"

"No. The Twenty Committee are still deliberating. And we can't move until they approve it. The ball's in their court now."

"My God! Perhaps someone should explain to the Twenty Committee that time is one thing we don't have in great abundance. If we have one chance in hell of catching Rudolf, we need to know where he's going."

"I understand your dilemma," Boothby said.

Vicary thought, Your dilemma. *My* dilemma, Sir Basil?

He said, "When are they going to decide?"

"Any moment. I'll call you back straightaway."

Vicary rang off and paced the dark room. He turned to one of the watchers and said, "How long has she been in there?"

"About fifteen minutes."

"Fifteen minutes? Why did she stay on the street so long? I don't like it."

The telephone rang. Vicary lunged for it and brought the receiver to his ear. Basil Boothby said, "We have the Twenty Committee's approval. Bring her in, Alfred. And good luck."

Vicary slammed down the receiver.

"We're on, gentlemen." He turned to Harry. "Alive. We need her alive."

Harry nodded, grim-faced, then led the Special Branch men out of the room. Vicary listened to their footfalls on the stairs gradually fading away. Then, a moment later, he spotted the tops of their heads as they stepped from the building and headed across the street toward Catherine Blake's flat.

Horst Neumann parked the van in a small quiet side street around the corner from Catherine's flat. He climbed out and softly closed the door. He walked quickly along the pavement, hands thrust deeply into his pockets, one hand wrapped around the butt of the Mauser.

The street was in pitch darkness. He came to the pile of rubble that once was the terrace behind the flat. He groped his way across broken wood, crumbled brick, and twisted pipes. The rubble ended at a wall, about six feet high. On the other side of the wall was the garden at the back of the house—Neumann had seen it from the window of her room. He tried the gate; it was locked. He would have to open it from the other side.

He placed his hands on top of the wall, thrust with his legs, and pulled with his arms. Atop the wall now, he threw one leg over the other side and turned his body. He hung that way for a few seconds, looking down. The ground below was invisible in the dark. He could fall on anything—a sleeping dog or a row of dustbins that would make a terrible clatter if he landed on them. He considered shining his torch for a second but that might attract attention. He pushed himself off the top of the wall and fell through the gloom. There were no dogs or rubbish bins, just a thorny shrub of some kind that clawed at his face and his coat.

Neumann tore himself free from the thornbush and unlatched the gate.

He crossed the garden to the back door. He tried the latch—it was locked. The door had a window. He reached in his coat pocket, withdrew the Mauser, and used it to smash the lower-left pane of glass. The noise was surprisingly loud. He reached through the shattered pane and unlocked the door, then quickly crossed the hall and ascended the stairs.

He reached Catherine's door and knocked softly.

From the other side of the door he heard her say, "Who's there?"

"It's me."

She opened the door. Neumann stepped inside and closed it. She was dressed in trousers, sweater, and leather jacket. The suitcase radio was standing next to the door. Neumann looked at her face. It was ashen.

"It could be my imagination," she said, "but I think something is going on downstairs. I've seen some men milling about on the street and sitting in parked cars."

The flat was dark, one light burning in the sitting room. Neumann crossed the room in a few quick steps and turned it off. He went to the window and lifted the edge of the blackout shade, peering out into the street. The evening traffic was moving below, throwing off just enough light for him to see four men charging from the apartment house across the street and heading their way.

Neumann turned and ripped his Mauser from his pocket.

"They're coming for us. Grab your radio and follow me down. Now!"

Harry Dalton threw open the front door and went inside, the Special Branch men behind him. He switched on the hall light in time to see Catherine Blake running out the back door, her suitcase radio swinging from her arm.

Horst Neumann had kicked open the back door and was running across the garden when he heard the shout from within the house. He rushed through the curtain of gloom, the Mauser in front of him in his outstretched hand. The gate flew open and a figure appeared there, silhouetted in the frame, gun raised. He shouted for Neumann to stop. Neumann kept running, firing twice. The first shot struck the man in the shoulder, spinning him around. The second shattered his spine, killing him instantly.

A second man stepped into his place and attempted to fire. Neumann squeezed the trigger. The Mauser bounced in his hand, emitting almost no sound, just the dull click of the firing mechanism. The man's head exploded.

Neumann raced through the gate, stepping over the bodies, and peered into the blackout. There was no one else behind the house. He turned and saw Catherine, a few feet behind him, running with the radio. Three men were chasing her. Neumann raised his gun and fired into the dark. He heard two men scream. Catherine kept running.

He turned and started across the rubble toward the van.

Harry felt the rounds whiz past his head. He heard the screams of both men behind him. She was right in front of him. He plunged through the darkness, arms outstretched before him. He realized he was at a distinct disadvantage; he was unarmed and alone. He could stop and try to find one of the Special Branch men's weapons, then chase them and try to shoot them both. But he was likely to be killed by Rudolf in the process. He could stop, turn around, go back inside, and signal the surveillance flat. But by then Catherine Blake and Rudolf would be long gone and they would have to start the damned search all over again and the spies would use their radio and tell Berlin about what they had discovered and we'd lose the fucking war, dammit!

The radio!

He thought, I may not be able to stop them now, but I can cut them off from Berlin for a while.

Harry leapt through the darkness, screaming deep in his throat, and grabbed hold of the suitcase with both hands. He tried to tear it from her grasp but she turned and pulled with surprising strength. He looked up and saw her face for the first time: red, contorted with fear, ugly with rage. He tried again to wrench the case from her, but he could not break her grasp; her fingers were clenched around the handle like a vise grip. She screamed Rudolf's real name. It sounded like Wurst.

Then Harry heard a clicking sound. He had heard it before on the streets of East London before the war, the sound of a stiletto blade snapping into place. He saw her arm rise, then swing down in a vicious arc toward his throat. If he raised his own arm he could deflect the blow. But then she would be able to pull the radio away from him. He held on with both hands and tried to avoid the stiletto by twisting his head. The tip of the blade struck the side of his face. He could feel his flesh tearing. The pain came an instant later—searing, as though molten metal had been thrown against his face. Harry screamed but held on to the bag. She raised her arm again, this time plunging the tip of the stiletto into his forearm. Harry yelled with pain again, teeth clenched, but his hands would not let go of the bag. It was as if they were acting on their own now. Nothing, no amount of pain, could make them let go.

She let go of the bag and said, "You're a brave man to die for a radio."

Then she turned and disappeared into the darkness.

Harry lay on the wet ground. When she was gone, he reached up to touch his face and was sickened when he felt the warm bone of his own jaw. He was losing consciousness; the pain was fading. He heard the wounded Special Branch men groaning nearby. He felt the rain beating against his face. He closed his eyes. He felt someone pressing something against his face. When he opened his eyes he saw Alfred Vicary leaning over him.

"I told you to be careful, Harry."

"Did she get the radio?"

"No. You kept her from taking the radio."

"Did they get away?"

"Yes. But we're chasing them."

The pain raced up on Harry very suddenly. He started to tremble and felt as though he was going to throw up. Then Vicary's face turned to water, and Harry blacked out.

CHAPTER FIFTY

LONDON

Within one hour of the disaster in Earl's Court, Alfred Vicary had orchestrated the biggest manhunt in the history of the United Kingdom. Every police station in the country—from Penzance to Dover, from Portsmouth to Inverness—was given a description of Vicary's fugitive spies. Vicary dispatched photographs by motorcycle couriers to the cities, towns, and villages close to London. Most officers involved in the search were told the fugitives were suspects in four murders dating back to 1938. A handful of very senior officers were discreetly informed it was a security matter of the utmost importance—so important the prime minister was personally monitoring the progress of the hunt.

London's Metropolitan Police responded with extraordinary speed, and within fifteen minutes of Vicary's first call roadblocks had been thrown up along all major arteries leading from the city. Vicary tried to cover every possible route of escape. MI5 and railway police prowled the main stations. The operators of the Irish ferries were given a description of the suspects as well.

Next he contacted the BBC and asked for the senior man on duty. On the main nine o'clock evening news the BBC led with the story of a shootout in Earl's Court that had left two police officers dead and three others wounded. The story contained a description of Catherine Blake and Rudolf and concluded with a telephone number citizens could call with information. Within five minutes the telephones started ringing. The typists transcribed each well-meaning call and passed them on to Vicary. Most he tossed straight into the wastepaper basket. A few he followed up. None produced a single lead.

Then he turned his attention to the escape routes only a spy would use.

He contacted the RAF and asked them to be on the lookout for light aircraft. He contacted the Admiralty and asked them to keep a careful watch for U-boats approaching the coastline. He contacted the coastguard service and asked them to keep a watch out for small craft heading out to sea. He telephoned the Y Service radio monitors and asked them to listen for suspect wireless transmissions.

Vicary stood up from his desk and stepped outside his office for the first time in two hours. The command post in West Halkin Street had been deserted, and his team had slowly streamed back to St. James's Street. They sat in the common area outside his office like dazed survivors of a natural disaster—wet, exhausted, defeated. Clive Roach sat alone, head down, hands folded. Every few moments one of the watchers would lay a hand on his shoulder, murmur encouragement into his ear, and move quietly on. Peter Jordan was pacing. Tony Blair had fixed a homicidal glare on him. The only sound was the rattle of the teleprinters and the chatter of the girls on the telephone.

The silence was broken for a few minutes at nine o'clock, when Harry Dalton walked into the room, his face and arm bandaged. Everyone stood and crowded around him—*Well done, Harry, old boy . . . deserve a medal . . . you kept us in the game, Harry . . . be all over if not for you. . . .*

Vicary pulled him into his office. "Shouldn't you be lying down resting?"

"Yeah, but I wanted to be here instead."

"How's the pain?"

"Not too bad. They gave me something for it."

"You still have any doubts about how you would react under fire on the battlefield?"

Harry managed a half smile, looked down, and shook his head. "Any breaks yet?" he asked, quickly changing the subject.

Vicary shook his head.

"What have you done?"

Vicary brought him up to date.

"Bold move, Rudolf coming back for her like that, snatching her from under our nose. He's got guts, I'll say that for him. How's Boothby taking it?"

"About as well as can be expected. He's upstairs with the director-general now. Probably planning my execution. We have an open line to the Underground War Rooms and the prime minister. The Old Man's getting minute-by-minute updates. I wish I had something to tell him."

"You've covered every possible option. Now you just have to sit and wait for something to break. They have to make a move somewhere. And when they do, we'll be on to them."

"I wish I could share your optimism."

Harry grimaced with pain and appeared suddenly very tired. "I'm going to go and lie down for a while." He walked slowly toward the door.

Vicary said, "Is Grace Clarendon on duty tonight?"

"Yeah, I think so."

The telephone rang. Basil Boothby said, "Come upstairs straightaway, Alfred."

The green light shone over Boothby's door. Vicary went inside and found Sir Basil pacing and chain smoking. He had stripped off his jacket, his waistcoat was unbuttoned, and he had loosened his tie. He angrily waved Vicary toward a chair and said, "Sit down, Alfred. Well, the lights are burning all over London tonight: Grosvenor Square, Eisenhower's personal headquarters at Hayes Lodge, the Underground War Rooms. And they all want to know one thing. Does Hitler know it's Normandy? Is the invasion dead even before we begin?"

"We obviously have no way of knowing yet."

"My God!" Boothby ground out his cigarette and immediately lit another one. "Two Special Branch officers dead, two more wounded. Thank God for Harry."

"He's downstairs now. I'm sure he'd like to hear that from you in person."

"We don't have time for pep talks, Alfred. We need to stop them and stop them quickly. I don't have to explain the stakes to you."

"No, you don't, Sir Basil."

"The prime minister wants updates every thirty minutes. Is there anything I can tell him?"

"Unfortunately, no. We've covered every possible route of escape. I wish I could say with certainty that we'll catch them, but I think it would be unwise to underestimate them. They have proven that time and time again."

Boothby resumed his pacing. "Two men dead, three wounded, and two spies possessing the knowledge to unravel our entire deception plan running loose. Needless to say, this is the worst disaster in the history of this department."

"Special Branch went in with the force they deemed necessary to arrest her. Obviously, they made a miscalculation."

Boothby stopped pacing and fixed a gunman's gaze on Vicary. "Don't at-

tempt to blame Special Branch for what happened, Alfred. You were the senior man on the scene. That aspect of Kettledrum was your responsibility."

"I realize that, Sir Basil."

"Good, because when this is all over an internal review will be convened
and I doubt your performance will be viewed in a favorable light."

Vicary stood up. "Is that all, Sir Basil?"

"Yes."

Vicary turned and walked toward the door.

The distant wail of the air-raid sirens started up while Vicary was taking
the stairs down to Registry. The rooms were in half darkness, just a couple of lights burning. Vicary, as always, noticed the smell of the place: rotting paper, dust, damp, the faint residue of Nicholas Jago's vile pipe. He
looked at Jago's glass-enclosed office. The light was out and the door was
closed tightly. He heard the sharp smack of women's shoes and recognized
the angry cadence of Grace Clarendon's brisk parade-ground march. He
saw her shock of blond hair flash past the stacks like an apparition, then
vanish. He followed her into one of the side rooms and called her name
from a long way off so as not to startle her. She turned, stared at him with
hostile green eyes, then turned away from him again and resumed her filing.

"Is this official, Professor Vicary?" she said. "If it's not, I'm going to have
to ask you to leave. You've caused enough problems for me. If I'm seen talking to you again I'll be lucky to get a job as a bloody blackout warden. Please
leave, Professor."

"I need to see a file, Grace."

"You know the procedure, Professor. Fill out a request slip. If your request is approved, you can see the file."

"I won't be given approval to see the file I need to see."

"Then you can't see it." Her voice had taken on the cold efficiency of a
headmistress. "Those are the rules."

The first bombs fell, across the river by the feel of it. Then the antiaircraft
batteries in the parks opened up. Vicary heard the drone of Heinkel
bombers overhead. Grace stopped her filing and looked up. A stick of
bombs fell nearby—too damned close, because the whole building shook
and files tumbled from the shelves. Grace looked at the mess and said,
"Bloody hell."

"I know Boothby is making you do things against your will. I heard you quarreling in his office, and I saw you getting into his car in Northumberland Avenue last night. And don't tell me you're seeing him romantically, because I know you're in love with Harry."

Vicary noticed the shine of tears in her green eyes, and the file in her hand begin to tremble.

"It's your bloody fault!" she snapped. "If you hadn't told him about the Vogel file, I wouldn't be in this mess."

"What is he making you do?"

She hesitated. "Please leave, Professor. Please."

"I'm not leaving until you tell me what Boothby wanted you to do."

"Dammit, Professor Vicary, he wanted me to spy on you! And on Harry!" She forced herself to lower her voice. "Anything Harry told me—in bed or anywhere else—I was supposed to tell him."

"What did you tell him?"

"Anything Harry mentioned to me about the case and the progress of the investigation. I also told him about the Registry search you requested." She pulled a handful of files from her cart and resumed her filing. "I heard Harry was involved in that mess at Earl's Court."

"He was indeed. In fact, he's the man of the hour."

"Was he hurt?"

Vicary nodded. "He's upstairs. The doctors couldn't keep him in bed."

"He probably did something stupid, didn't he. Trying to prove himself. God, he can be such a stupid, stubborn idiot sometimes."

"Grace, I need to see a file. Boothby's going to sack me when this business is over, and I need to know why."

She stared at him, a grave expression on her face. "You're serious, aren't you, Professor?"

"Unfortunately, yes."

She looked at him wordlessly for a moment while the building shuddered with the shock waves of the bombs.

"What's the file?" she asked.

"An operation called Kettledrum."

Grace furrowed her eyebrows in confusion. "Isn't that the code name of the operation you're involved in now?"

"Yes."

"Hold on a minute. You want me to risk my neck to show you the file on your own case?"

"Something like that," Vicary said. "Except I want you to cross-reference it with a different case officer."

"Who?"

Vicary looked directly into her green eyes and mouthed the initials *BB*.

She came back five minutes later, an empty file folder in her hand.

"Operation Kettledrum," she said. "Terminated."

"Where are the contents?"

"Either destroyed or with the case officer."

"When was the file opened?" Vicary asked.

Grace looked at the tab on the file, then at Vicary.

"That's funny," she said. "According to this, Operation Kettledrum was initiated in October 1943."

CHAPTER FIFTY-ONE

CAMBRIDGESHIRE, ENGLAND

By the time Scotland Yard responded to Alfred Vicary's demand for road-blocks, Horst Neumann had left London and was racing northward along the A10. The van had obviously been well maintained. It would do at least sixty miles per hour and the motor ran smoothly. The tires still had a decent amount of tread on them, and they gripped the wet road surprisingly well. And it had one other practical feature—a black van did not stand out from the other commercial vehicles on the road. Since petrol rationing made private motoring all but impossible, anyone driving an automobile that time of night might be stopped by the police and questioned.

The road ran straight across mostly flat terrain. Neumann hunched forward over the steering wheel as he drove, peering into the little pool of light thrown off by the shrouded headlamps. For a moment he considered removing the blackout shades but decided it was too risky. He flashed through villages with funny names—Puckeridge, Buntingford—dark, not a light burning, no one moving about. It was as if the clock had been turned back two thousand years. Neumann would scarcely have been surprised to see a Roman legion encamped along the banks of the River Cam.

More villages—Melbourn, Foxton, Newton, Hauxton. During his preparation at Vogel's farmhouse outside Berlin, Neumann had spent hours studying old Ordnance Survey maps of Britain. He suspected he knew the roads and pathways of East Anglia as well as most Englishmen, perhaps better.

Melbourn, Foxton, Newton, Hauxton.

He was approaching Cambridge.

Cambridge represented trouble. Surely MI5 had alerted police forces in the large cities and towns. Neumann reckoned the police in the villages and hamlets did not pose much of a threat. They made their rounds on foot or bicycle and rarely had cars, and communications were so poor that word might not even have been passed to them. He was flashing through the blacked-out villages so quickly a police officer would never really see them. Cities like Cambridge were different. MI5 had probably alerted the Cambridge police force. They had enough men to mount a roadblock on a large route like the A10. They had cars and could engage in a pursuit. Neumann knew the roads and was a capable driver, but he would be no match for an experienced local police officer.

Before reaching Cambridge, Neumann turned into a small side road. He skirted the base of the Gog Magog Hills and headed north along the eastern edge of the city. Even in the gloom of the blackout he could make out the spires of King's and St. John's. He passed through a village called Horningsea, crossed the Cam, and entered Waterbeach, a village that lay astride the A10. He drove slowly through the darkened streets until he found the largest one; there were no signs for the A10 but he assumed this had to be it. He turned right, headed north, and after a moment was racing through the lonely flatness of the Fens.

The miles passed very quickly. The rain eased but in the fenland the wind, with nothing in its path between here and the North Sea, battered the van like a child's toy. The road ran near the banks of the River Great Ouse, then across Southery Fens. They passed through the villages of Southery and Hilgay. The next large town was Downham Market, smaller than Cambridge but Neumann assumed it had its own police force and was therefore a threat. He repeated the same move he made in Cambridge, turning onto a smaller side road, skirting the edge of town, rejoining the A10 in the north.

Ten miles on he came to King's Lynn, the port on the southeastern base of the Wash and largest town on the Norfolk coast. Neumann turned off the A10 again and picked up a small B-road east of the city.

The road was poor—an unpaved single-lane track in many places—and the terrain turned hilly and wooded. He stopped and poured two of the jerry cans of petrol into the tank. The weather worsened the closer they moved to the coast. At times Neumann seemed to be traveling at a walking pace. He feared he had made a mistake by turning off the better road, that he was being too cautious. After more than an hour of difficult driving he reached the coastline.

He passed through Hampton Sands, crossed the sea creek, and accelerated along the track. He felt relieved—finally, a familiar road. The Dogherty cottage appeared in the distance. Neumann turned into the drive. He saw the door open and the glow of a kerosene lamp moving toward them. It was Sean Dogherty, dressed in his oilskin and sou'wester, a shotgun over his arm.

Sean Dogherty had not been worried when Neumann did not arrive in Hunstanton on the afternoon train. Neumann had warned him he might be in London longer than usual. Dogherty decided to wait for the evening train. He left the station and went into a nearby pub. He ordered a potato and carrot pie and washed it down with two glasses of ale. Then he went out and walked along the waterfront. Before the war, Hunstanton was a popular summer beach resort because its location on the eastern edge of the Wash provided remarkable sunsets over the water. On this night the old Edwardian resort hotels were mostly empty, despondent-looking in the steady rain. Sunset was nothing more than the last gray light leaking from the storm clouds. Dogherty left the waterfront and returned to the station to meet the evening train. He stood on the platform, smoking, watching the handful of passengers disembarking. When Neumann was not among them, Dogherty became alarmed.

He drove back to Hampton Sands, thinking about Neumann's words earlier that week. Neumann had said it was possible the operation might be about to end, possible that he might be leaving England and heading back to Berlin. Dogherty thought, But why wasn't he on the damned train?

He arrived at the cottage and let himself inside. Mary, sitting next to the fire, glared at him, then went upstairs. Dogherty switched on the wireless. The news bulletin caught his attention. A nationwide search was under way for two suspected killers who had taken part in a gun battle with police earlier that evening in the section of London known as Earl's Court.

Dogherty turned up the volume as the newsreader gave a description of the two suspects. The first, surprisingly, was a woman. The second was a man who matched Horst Neumann's description perfectly.

Dogherty shut off the radio. Was it possible the two suspects in the Earl's Court shooting were Neumann and the other agent? Were they now on the run from MI5 and half the police in Britain? Were they heading toward Hampton Sands or were they going to leave him behind? Then he thought, Do the British know I'm a spy too?

He went upstairs, threw a change of clothes into a small canvas bag, and came back downstairs again. He went out to the barn, found his shotgun, and loaded a pair of cartridges into the barrel.

Returning to the cottage, Dogherty sat in the window, waiting. He had almost given up hope when he spotted the shaded headlamps moving along the road toward the cottage. When the car turned into the farmyard he could see it was Neumann behind the wheel. There was a woman sitting in the passenger seat.

Dogherty stood up and pulled on his coat and hat. He lit the kerosene lamp, picked up his shotgun, and went outside into the rain.

Martin Colville examined his face in the mirror: broken nose, black eyes, swollen lips, a contusion on the right side of his face.

He went into the kitchen and poured the last precious drops of whisky from a bottle. Every instinct in Colville's body told him there was something wrong about the man named James Porter. He didn't believe he was a wounded British soldier. He didn't believe he was an old acquaintance of Sean Dogherty's. He didn't believe he had come to Hampton Sands for the ocean air.

He touched his ruined face, thinking, No one's ever done this to me in my life, and I'm not going to let that little bastard get away with it.

Colville drank the whisky in one swallow, then placed the empty bottle and the glass in the sink. Outside, he heard the grumble of a motor. He went to the door and looked out. A van swept past. Colville could see James Porter behind the wheel and a woman in the passenger seat.

He closed the door, thinking, What in the hell is he doing out driving this time of night? And where did he get the van?

He decided he would find out for himself. He went into the sitting room and took down an old twelve-gauge shotgun from over the mantel. The shells were in a kitchen drawer. He opened it and dug through the jumble inside until he found the box. He went outside and climbed on his bicycle.

A moment later Colville was pedaling through the rain, shotgun across the handlebars, toward the Doghertys' cottage.

Jenny Colville, upstairs in her bedroom, heard the front door open and close once. Then she heard the sound of a passing vehicle, unusual at this time of night. When she heard the door open and close a second time she became alarmed. She rose from her bed and crossed the room. She parted the curtain and looked down in time to see her father pedaling away through the darkness.

She pounded on the window but it was in vain. Within seconds he was gone.

Jenny was wearing nothing but a flannel nightgown. She took it off, pulled on a pair of trousers and a sweater, and went downstairs. Her Wellington boots were by the door. Pulling them onto her feet, she noticed the shotgun that usually hung over the fireplace was gone. She looked into the kitchen and saw that the drawer where the shells were kept was open. Quickly, she pulled on her coat and went outside.

Jenny groped through the darkness until she found her bicycle leaning against the side of the cottage. She pushed it down the path, climbed onto the saddle, and pedaled after her father toward the Dogherty cottage, thinking, Please God, let me stop him before someone ends up dead tonight.

Sean Dogherty pulled open the door of the barn and led them inside behind the light of the kerosene lantern. He removed his sou'wester and unbuttoned his coat, then looked at Neumann and the woman.

Neumann said, "Sean Dogherty, meet Catherine Blake. Sean used to be with an outfit called the Irish Republican Army, but he's been on loan to us for the war. Catherine works for Kurt Vogel too. She's been living in England under deep cover since 1938."

It gave Catherine a strange sensation to hear her background and work discussed so casually. After the years of hiding her identity, after all the precautions, after all the anxiety, it was difficult to imagine it was about to end.

Dogherty looked at her, then at Neumann. "The BBC's been running bulletins all night about a gun battle at Earl's Court. I suppose you were involved in that?"

Neumann nodded. "They weren't ordinary London police. MI-Five and Special Branch, I'd say. What's the radio saying?"

"You killed two of them and wounded three more. They've mounted a nationwide search for you and asked for help from the general public. Half the country's probably out beating the bushes for you right now. I'm surprised you made it this far."

"We stayed out of the big towns. It seemed to work. We haven't seen any police on the roads so far."

"Well, it won't last. You can be sure of that."

Neumann looked at his wristwatch—a few minutes after midnight. He picked up Sean's kerosene lamp and carried it to the worktable. He took down the radio from the cabinet and switched on the power.

"The submarine is on patrol in the North Sea. After receiving our signal, it will move exactly ten miles due east of Spurn Head and remain there until six A.M. If we don't appear, it turns from the coast and waits to hear from us."

Catherine said, "And how exactly are we going to get ten miles due east of Spurn Head?"

Dogherty stepped forward. "There's a fellow named Jack Kincaid. He has a small fishing boat at a quay on the River Humber." Dogherty dug out an old prewar Ordnance Survey map. "The boat's here," he said, jabbing at the map. "In a town called Cleethorpes. It's about a hundred miles up the coast. It will be hard driving on a dirty night like this with the blackout to contend with. Kincaid has a flat over a garage on the waterfront. I spoke to him yesterday. He knows we might be coming."

Neumann nodded and said, "If we leave now we have about six hours of driving time. I say we can make it tonight. The next rendezvous opportunity with the submarine is three days from now. I don't relish the idea of hiding out for three days with every policeman in Britain beating the bushes for us. I say we go tonight."

Catherine nodded. Neumann slipped on the earphones and tuned the radio to the proper frequency. He tapped out an identification signal and waited for a reply. A few seconds later the radio operator aboard the U-boat asked Neumann to proceed. Neumann drew a deep breath, carefully tapped out the message, then signed off and shut down the radio.

"Which leaves one more thing," he said, turning to Dogherty. "Are you coming with us?"

He nodded. "I've talked it over with Mary. She sees it my way. I'll come back to Germany with you; then Vogel and his friends can help me make my way back to Ireland. Mary will come across when I'm there. We've got friends and family who'll look after us until we get settled. We'll be all right."

"And how's Mary taking it?"

Dogherty's face hardened into a tight-lipped frown. Neumann knew it was quite likely he and Mary might never see each other again. He reached for the kerosene lamp, put a hand on Dogherty's shoulder, and said, "Let's go."

Martin Colville, standing astride his bicycle breathing heavily, saw a light burning inside Dogherty's barn. He laid his bicycle next to the road, then quietly crossed the meadow and crouched outside the barn. He struggled to understand the conversation taking place inside over the smack of the falling rain.

It was unbelievable.

Sean Dogherty—working for the Nazis. The man called James Porter—a German agent. A nest of German spies, operating right here in Hampton Sands!

Colville strained to hear more of the conversation. They were planning to drive up the coast to Lincolnshire and take a boat out to sea to meet a submarine. Colville felt his heart careening inside his chest and his breath coming quickly. He forced himself to be calm, to think clearly.

He had two choices: turn away, ride back to the village, and alert the authorities, or go inside the barn and take them into custody on his own. Each option had disadvantages. If he left for help, Dogherty and the spies would probably be gone by the time he returned. There were few police along the Norfolk coast, hardly enough to mount a search. If he went in alone he would be outnumbered. He could see Sean had his shotgun, and he assumed the two others were armed too. Still, he would have the advantage of surprise.

There was another reason why he liked the second option—he would enjoy personally settling the score with the German who called himself James Porter. Colville knew he had to act and act quickly. He broke open the box of shells, removed two, and snapped them into the barrel of the old twelve-gauge. He had never aimed the thing at anything more threatening than a partridge or a pheasant. He wondered whether he would have the stomach to pull the trigger on a human being.

He rose and took a step toward the door.

Jenny pedaled until her legs burned—through the village, past the church and the cemetery, over the sea creek. The air was filled with the sound of the storm and the rush of the sea. Rain lashed against her face and the wind nearly blew her over.

Jenny spotted her father's bicycle in the grass along the track and stopped next to it. Why leave it here? Why not ride it all the way to the cottage?

She thought she knew the answer. He was trying to sneak up without being seen.

It was then she heard the sound of a shotgun blast from Sean's barn. Jenny screamed, leapt from her bicycle, and let it fall next to her father's. She ran across the meadow, thinking, *Please God, don't let him be dead. Don't let him be dead.*

CHAPTER FIFTY-TWO

SCARBOROUGH, ENGLAND

Approximately one hundred miles north of Hampton Sands, Charlotte Endicott pedaled her bicycle into the small gravel compound outside the Y Service listening station at Scarborough. The ride from her digs at a cramped guesthouse in town had been brutal, wind and rain the entire way. Soaked and chilled to the bone, she dismounted and leaned her bicycle next to several others in the stand.

The wind gusted, moaning through the three huge rectangular antennas that stood atop the cliffs overlooking the North Sea. Charlotte Endicott glanced up at them, swaying visibly, as she hurried across the compound. She pulled open the door of the hut and went inside before the wind slammed it shut.

She had a few minutes before her shift began. She removed her soaking raincoat, untied her hat, and hung them both on a dilapidated coat tree in the corner. The hut was cold and drafty, built for utility, not comfort. It did have a small canteen, though. Charlotte went inside, poured herself a cup of hot tea, sat down at one of the small tables, and lit a cigarette. A filthy habit, she knew, but if she could hold a job like a man she could smoke like one. Besides, she liked the way they made her look—sexy, sophisticated, a little older than her twenty-three years. She also had become addicted to the damned things. The work was stressful, the hours brutal, and life in Scarborough was dreadfully boring. But she loved every moment of it.

There had been only one time when she truly hated it, the Battle of Britain. During the long and horrible dogfights, the Wrens at Scarborough could listen to the cockpit chatter of the British and German pilots. Once she heard an English boy screaming and crying for his mother as his crippled Spitfire fell helplessly toward the sea. When she lost contact with him,

Charlotte ran outside into the compound and threw up. She was glad those days were over.

Charlotte looked up at the clock. Nearly midnight. Time to go on duty. She stood and smoothed her damp uniform. She took one last pull at her cigarette—smoking wasn't allowed in the hole—then crushed it out in a small metal ashtray overflowing with butts. She left the canteen and walked toward the operations room. She flashed her identification badge at the guard. He scrutinized it carefully, even though he had seen it a hundred times before, then handed it back to her, smiling a little more than necessary. Charlotte knew she was an attractive girl, but there was no place for that sort of thing here. She pushed open the doors, entered the hole, and sat down at her regular spot.

It gave her a brief chill—as always.

She stared at the luminous dials of her RCA AR-88 superheterodyne communications receiver for a moment and then slipped on her earphones. The RCA's special interference-cutting crystals allowed her to monitor German Morse senders all across northern Europe. She tuned her receiver to the band of frequencies she had been assigned to patrol that night and settled in.

The German Morse senders were the fastest keyers in the world. Charlotte could immediately identify many by their distinctive keying style, or fist, and she and the other Wrens had nicknames for them: Wagner, Beethoven, Zeppelin.

Charlotte didn't have to wait long for her first action that night.

A few minutes after midnight she heard a burst of Morse in a fist she did not recognize. The cadence was poor, the pace slow and uncertain. An amateur, she thought, someone who didn't use their radio much. Certainly not one of the professionals at BdU, the Kriegsmarine headquarters. Acting quickly, she made a recording of the transmission on the oscillograph—a device that would in effect create a radio fingerprint of the signal called a *Tina*—and furiously scribbled the Morse message onto a sheet of paper. When the amateur finished, Charlotte heard another burst of code on the same frequency. This was no amateur; Charlotte and the other Wrens had heard him before. They had nicknamed him Fritz. He was a radio operator aboard a U-boat. Charlotte quickly transcribed this message as well.

Fritz's transmission was followed by another burst of sloppy Morse by the amateur, and then the communication went dead. Charlotte removed her headset, tore off the printout of the oscillograph, and marched across the room. Normally she would simply pass on the Morse transcripts of the messages to the motorcycle courier, who in turn would rush them to Bletchley Park for decoding. But there was something different about this communication—she could feel it in the fist of the radio operators: Fritz aboard a U-boat, an amateur somewhere else. She suspected she knew what it was, but she would have to make a damned convincing case. She presented herself to the night supervisor, a pale exhausted-looking man called Lowe. She dropped the transcripts and the oscillograph on his desk. He looked up at her, a quizzical expression on his face.

"I could be completely wrong, sir," Charlotte said, mustering the most authoritative voice she could, "but I think I just overheard a German spy signaling a U-boat off the coast."

Kapitänleutnant Max Hoffman would never get used to the stench of a U-boat that has been submerged too long: sweat, urine, diesel oil, potatoes, semen. The assault on his nostrils was so intense he would gladly stand a watch on the conning tower in a gale rather than stay inside.

Standing in the control room of *U-509,* he could feel the throb of its electric motors beneath his feet as they wheeled in a monotonous circle twenty miles from the British coastline. A fine mist hung inside the submarine, creating a halo around every light. Every surface was cool and wet to the touch. Hoffman liked to imagine it was dew on a spring morning, but one look at the cramped claustrophobic world he inhabited robbed him of that fantasy very quickly.

It was a tedious assignment, sitting off the coast of Britain for weeks on end, waiting for one of Canaris's spies. Of Hoffman's crew only his first officer knew the true purpose of their mission. The rest of the men probably suspected as much, since they weren't on patrol. Still, things could be worse. Given the extraordinary loss rate among the *Ubootwaffe*—nearly 90 percent—Hoffman and his crew were damned lucky to have survived this long.

The first officer came onto the bridge, face grave, a sheet of paper in his hand. Hoffman looked at the man, depressed by the notion that he probably looked just as bad: sunken eyes, hollow cheeks, the gray pallor of a submariner, the unkempt beard because there was too little fresh water to waste on shaving.

The first officer said, "Our man in Britain has finally surfaced. He'd like a lift home tonight."

Hoffman smiled, thinking, Finally. We pick him up and head back to

France for some good food and clean sheets. He said, "What's the latest weather?"

"Not good, Herr Kaleu," the first officer said, using the customary diminutive form of kapitänleutnant. "Heavy rains, winds thirty miles per hour from the northwest, seas ten to twelve."

"Jesus Christ! And he'll probably be coming in a rowboat—if we're lucky. Organize a reception party and prepare to surface. Have the radio operator inform BdU of our plans. Set a course for the rendezvous point. I'll go up top with the lookouts. I don't care how bad the weather is." Hoffman made a face. "I can't stand the fucking smell in here any longer."

"Yes, Herr Kaleu."

The first officer shouted a series of commands, echoed among the crew. Two minutes later, *U-509* punched through the stormy surface of the North Sea.

The system was known as High Frequency Direction Finding, but almost everyone involved with the project knew it as Huff Duff. It worked on the principle of triangulation. The radio fingerprint created by the oscillograph at Scarborough could be used to identify the type of transmitter and its power supply. If the Y Service stations at Flowerdown and Iceland also ran oscillographs, the three recordings could be used to establish bearing lines—known as *cuts*—which could then be used to locate the position of the transmitter. Sometimes Huff Duff could pinpoint a radio to within ten miles of its geographical location. Usually, the system was much less accurate, thirty to fifty miles.

Commander Lowe did not believe Charlotte Endicott was completely wrong. In fact, he believed she had stumbled onto something critical. Earlier that evening, a Major Vicary from MI5 had sent out an alert to the Y Service to look for this very sort of thing.

Lowe spent the next few minutes speaking with his counterparts in Flowerdown and Iceland, attempting to plot a fix on the transmitter. Unfortunately, the communication was short, the fix not terribly precise. In fact, Lowe could narrow it only to a rather large portion of eastern England—all of Norfolk and much of Suffolk, Cambridgeshire, and Lincolnshire. Probably not much of a help, but at least it was something.

Lowe dug through the papers on his desk until he found Vicary's number in London and then reached for his secure telephone.

❖

Atmospheric conditions over northern Europe made shortwave communication between the British Isles and Berlin virtually impossible. As a result, the Abwehr's radio center was housed in the basement of a large mansion in the Hamburg suburb of Wohldorf, 150 miles northwest of the German capital.

Five minutes after *U-509*'s radio operator transmitted his message to BdU in northern France, the duty officer at BdU flashed a brief message to Hamburg. The duty officer at Hamburg was an Abwehr veteran named Captain Schmidt. He recorded the message, placed a priority call to Abwehr headquarters in Berlin on the secure line, and informed Lieutenant Werner Ulbricht of the developments. Schmidt then left the mansion and walked down the street to a nearby hotel, where he booked a second call to Berlin. He did not want to make this call from the thoroughly bugged lines of the Abwehr post, for the number he gave the operator was for Brigadeführer Walter Schellenberg's office at Prinz Albrechtstrasse. Unfortunately for Schmidt, Schellenberg had discovered he was having a rather lurid affair with a sixteen-year-old boy in Hamburg. Schmidt readily agreed to go to work for Schellenberg to avoid exposure. When the call went through he spoke to one of Schellenberg's many assistants—the general was dining out that night—and informed him of the news.

Kurt Vogel had decided to spend a rare evening at his small flat a few blocks from Tirpitz Ufer. Ulbricht reached him there by telephone and informed him that Horst Neumann had contacted the submarine and was coming out. Five minutes later, Vogel was letting himself out the front door of his building and walking through the rain toward Tirpitz Ufer.

At that same moment Walter Schellenberg checked in with his office and was told of developments in Britain. He then telephoned Reichsführer Heinrich Himmler and briefed him. Himmler ordered Schellenberg to come to Prinz Albrechtstrasse; it was going to be a long night and he wanted some company. As it happened, Schellenberg and Vogel arrived at their respective offices at precisely the same moment and settled in for the wait.

The location of the Allied invasion of France.

The life of Admiral Canaris.

And it all depended on the word of a couple of spies on the run from MI5.

CHAPTER FIFTY-THREE

HAMPTON SANDS, NORFOLK

Martin Colville used the barrel of his shotgun to push back the door of the barn. Neumann, still standing next to the radio, heard the noise. He reached for his Mauser as Colville stepped inside. Colville spotted Neumann going for the gun. He turned, leveled the shotgun, and fired. Neumann leapt out of the way, hitting the floor of the barn and rolling. The roar of the shotgun blast in the confined space of the barn was deafening. The radio disintegrated.

Colville aimed the gun at Neumann a second time. Neumann rolled up onto his elbows, Mauser in his outstretched hands. Sean Dogherty stepped forward, screaming at Colville to stop. Colville turned the gun on Dogherty and squeezed the trigger. The blast struck Dogherty in the chest, lifting him off his feet and driving him backward like a rag doll. He fell on his back, blood pumping from the gaping wound in his chest, and died within a matter of seconds.

Neumann fired, hitting Colville in the shoulder and spinning him around. Catherine had by now drawn her own Mauser and, using both hands, leveled it at Colville's head. She fired twice rapidly, the silencer dampening the blasts to a dull thud. Colville's head exploded and he was dead before his body hit the floor of Dogherty's barn.

Mary Dogherty lay in an agitated half sleep upstairs in her bed when she heard the first shotgun blast. She sat bolt upright and swung her feet to the floor as the second blast shattered the night. She threw off her blanket and raced downstairs.

The cottage was in darkness, the sitting room and the kitchen deserted.

She went outside. Rain beat against her face. She realized that she was wearing only her flannel nightgown. There was silence now, only the sound of the storm. She looked out across the garden and spotted an unfamiliar black van in the drive. She turned toward the barn and saw light burning there. She called out "Sean!" and started running toward the barn.

Mary's feet were bare, the ground cold and sodden. She called Sean's name several more times as she ran. A shaft of faint light spilled from the open door of the barn, illuminating a box of shotgun shells on the ground.

Stepping inside, she gasped. A scream caught in her throat and would not come out. The first thing she saw was the body of Martin Colville lying on the floor of the barn a few feet away from her. Part of the head was missing and blood and tissue were scattered everywhere. She felt her stomach retch.

Then she turned her attention to the second body. It was on its back, arms flung wide. Somehow, in death, the ankles had become crossed, as though he were napping. Blood obscured the face. For a brief second Mary permitted herself to hope that it wasn't actually Sean lying there dead. Then she looked at the old Wellington boots and oilskin coat and knew it was him.

The scream that had been trapped in her throat came out.

Mary cried, "Oh, Sean! Oh, my God, Sean! What have you done?"

She looked up and saw Horst Neumann standing over Sean's body, a gun in his hand. Standing a few feet from Neumann was a woman, holding a pistol in her hands aimed at Mary's head.

Mary looked back at Neumann and screamed, "Did you do this? Did you?"

"It was Colville," Neumann said. "He came in here, gun blazing. Sean got in the way. I'm sorry, Mary."

"No, Horst, Martin may have pulled the trigger, but you did this to him. Make no mistake about it. You and your friends in Berlin—you're the ones who did this to him."

Neumann said nothing. Catherine still stood with the Mauser leveled at Mary's head. Neumann stepped in, took hold of the weapon, and gently lowered it toward the ground.

Jenny Colville stayed in the darkened meadow and approached the barn from the side, hidden from view. She crouched against the outside wall, rain smacking against her oilskin, and listened to the conversation taking place inside.

She heard the voice of the man she knew as James Porter, though Mary had called him something else, something that sounded like Horse. *It was Colville. . . . Sean got in the way. I'm sorry, Mary.*

Then she heard Mary's voice. It had risen in pitch and quivered with anger and grief. *You did this to him. . . . You and your friends in Berlin.*

She waited to hear her father's voice; she waited to hear Sean's voice. Nothing. She knew then they both were dead.

You and your friends in Berlin. . . .

Jenny thought, What are you saying, Mary?

And then it all came together in her mind, like pieces of a puzzle that suddenly fall in the right order: Sean on the beach that night, the sudden appearance of the man called James Porter, Mary's warning to her earlier that afternoon: *He's not what he appears to be. . . . He's not for you, Jenny. . . .*

Jenny did not understand what Mary was trying to say at the time, but now she thought she did. The man she knew as James Porter was a German spy. And that meant Sean was a spy for the Germans too. Jenny's father must have discovered the truth and confronted them. And now he was lying dead on the floor of Sean Dogherty's barn.

Jenny wanted to scream. She felt hot tears pouring from her eyes down her cheeks. She raised her hands to her mouth to smother the sound of her crying. She had fallen in love with him, but he had lied to her and used her and he was a German spy and he probably just killed her father.

There was movement inside the barn, movement and a few soft exchanges of instructions that Jenny could not hear. She heard the German spy's voice, and she heard a woman's voice that did not belong to Mary. Then she saw the spy emerge from the barn and walk down the drive, torch in hand. He was heading toward the bicycles. If he found them, he would realize she was here too.

And he would come looking for her.

Jenny forced herself to breathe slowly, evenly, to think clearly.

She was being battered by several emotions. She was frightened, she was sick with the thought of her father and Sean dead. But more than anything else she was angry. She had been lied to and betrayed. And now she was driven by one overwhelming desire: she wanted them caught and she wanted them punished.

Jenny knew she would be no use if the German found her.

But what to do? She could try to run to the village. There was a telephone at the hotel and the pub. She could contact the police, and the police could come and arrest them.

But the village was the first place the spies would look for her. There was just one way into the village from the Doghertys': across the bridge by St. John's Church. Jenny knew she could be caught very easily.

She thought of a second option. They had to be leaving soon. They had just killed two people, after all. Jenny could hide for a short time until they had left; then she could emerge and contact the police.

She thought, But what if they take Mary with them?

Mary would be better off if Jenny were free and trying to find help.

Jenny watched the spy as he moved closer to the road. She saw the beam of his torch play over the surrounding ground. She saw it settle on something for a moment, then flash in her direction.

Jenny gasped. He had found her bike. She rose and started to run.

Horst Neumann spotted the pair of bicycles lying side by side in the grass at the edge of the road. He turned his torch toward the meadow, but the weak beam illuminated only a few feet in front of him. He lifted the bicycles, took hold of them by the handlebars, and rolled them up the drive. He left them at the back of Dogherty's barn, hidden from view.

She was out there—somewhere. He tried to picture what had happened. Her father storms out of the house with a gun; Jenny follows him and arrives at the Doghertys' cottage in time to see the aftermath. Neumann guessed she was hiding, waiting for them to leave, and he thought he knew where.

For a moment he considered letting her go. But Jenny was an intelligent girl. She would find a way to contact the police. The police would throw up roadblocks all around Hampton Sands. Making it to Lincolnshire in time to meet the submarine was going to be difficult enough. Allowing Jenny to remain free and contact the police would only make it tougher.

Neumann went inside the barn. Catherine had covered the bodies with some old sacking. Mary was sitting in a chair, shaking violently. Neumann avoided her gaze.

"We have a problem," Neumann said. He gestured at the covered body of Martin Colville. "I found his daughter's bicycle. We have to assume she's here somewhere and knows what happened. We also have to assume she'll try to get help."

"Then go find her," Catherine said.

Neumann nodded. "Take Mary in the house. Tie her up, gag her. I have an idea where Jenny might be going."

Neumann went outside and hurried through the rain to the van. He started the motor, reversed down the drive, and headed toward the beach.

Catherine finished tying Mary to a wooden chair in the kitchen. She tore a tea cloth in two and wadded one half into a ball. She stuffed it into Mary's mouth, then tied the other half around her face in a tight gag. If she had her way Catherine would kill her now; she did not like leaving a trail for the police to follow. But Neumann obviously felt some attachment to the woman. Besides, it would probably be many hours before anyone found her, perhaps longer. The cottage was isolated, nearly a mile from the village; it might be a day or two before anyone noticed that Sean, Mary, Colville, and the girl were missing. Still, every survival instinct told her it was best to kill her and be done with it. Neumann would never know. She would lie to him, tell him Mary was unharmed, and he would never find out.

Catherine checked the knots one last time. Then she removed her Mauser from her coat pocket. She took hold of it, wrapped her index finger around the trigger, and touched the barrel to Mary's temple. Mary kept very still and stared defiantly at Catherine.

"Remember, Jenny is coming with us," Catherine said. "If you tell the police, we'll know. And then we'll kill her. Do you understand what I'm saying to you, Mary?"

Mary nodded once. Catherine took hold of the Mauser by the barrel, raised it into the air, and brought it down on the top of Mary's head. She slumped forward, unconscious, blood trickling through her hair toward her eyes. Catherine stood in front of the dying embers of the fire, waiting for Neumann and the girl, waiting to go home.

CHAPTER FIFTY-FOUR

LONDON

At that moment, a taxi braked to a halt in a driving rain outside a stubby, ivy-covered blockhouse beneath Admiralty Arch. The door opened and a small, rather ugly man emerged, leaning heavily on a walking stick. He did not bother with an umbrella. It was only a few feet to the doorway, where a Royal Marine guard stood watch. The guard saluted smartly, which the ugly man did not bother returning, for it would have meant switching his stick from his right hand to his left, a troublesome task. Besides, five years after being commissioned as an officer in the Royal Navy, Arthur Braithwaite still was uncomfortable with the customs and traditions of military life.

Officially, Braithwaite was not on duty for another hour. But, as was his daily habit, he arrived at the Citadel one hour early to give himself more time to prepare. Braithwaite, crippled in one leg since childhood, knew that to succeed he always had to be better prepared than those around him. It was a commitment that had paid dividends.

The Submarine Tracking Room—down a warren of narrow, winding staircases—was not easily reached by a man with a badly deformed leg. He crossed the Main Trade Plot and entered the Tracking Room through a guarded door.

The energy and excitement of the place took hold of him immediately, just as it did every night. The windowless walls were the color of clotted cream and covered with maps, charts, and photographs of U-boats and their crews. Several dozen officers and typists worked at tables around the edges of the room. In the center stood the main North Atlantic plotting table, where colored pins depicted the location of every warship, freighter, and submarine from the Baltic Sea to Cape Cod.

A large photograph of Admiral Karl Dönitz, commander of the Kriegs-marine, glowered down from one wall. Braithwaite, as he did every morn-ing, winked and said, "Good morning, Herr Admiral." Then he pushed back the door of his glass cubicle, removed his coat, and sat down at his desk.

He reached for the stack of decodes that awaited him each morning, thinking, A far cry from 1939, old son.

Back in 1939 he had degrees in law and psychology from Cambridge and Yale and was looking for something to do with them. When war broke out he tried to put his fluent German to good use by volunteering to interrogate German POWs. So impressed were his superiors they recommended a transfer to the Citadel, where he was assigned to the Submarine Tracking Room as a civilian volunteer at the height of the Battle of the Atlantic. Braithwaite's intellect and drive quickly set him apart. He threw himself into his work, volunteered for extra duty, and read every book he could find on German naval history and tactics. Equipped with near-perfect recall, he memorized the biographies of every Kapitänleutnant of the *Ubootwaffe*. Within months he developed a remarkable ability to forecast U-boat move-ments. None of this went unnoticed. He was given the rank of temporary commander and placed in charge of submarine tracking, a stunning achieve-ment for someone who had not passed through the Dartmouth Naval Col-lege.

His aide rapped on the glass door, waited for Braithwaite's nod, and let himself inside. "Good morning, sir," he said, setting down a tray with a pot of tea and biscuits.

"Morning, Patrick."

"The weather kept things fairly quiet last night, sir. No U-boat surface sightings anywhere. The storm's moved off the western approaches. The east's bearing the brunt of it now, from Yorkshire to Suffolk."

Braithwaite nodded, and the aide went out. The first items were conven-tional stuff, intercepts of routine communications between U-boats and BdU. The fifth caught his attention. It was an alert issued by a Major Alfred Vicary of the War Office. It said the authorities were pursuing two individ-uals, a man and a woman, who might be trying to leave the country. Braith-waite smiled at Vicary's guarded understatement. Vicary was obviously from MI5. The man and woman were obviously German agents of some kind and whatever they were up to must be damned important; otherwise the alert wouldn't have crossed his desk. He put Vicary's alert aside and continued reading.

After a few more routine items Braithwaite came upon something else that caught his attention. A Wren at the Scarborough Y Service station had intercepted what she believed was a communication between a U-boat and a wireless onshore. Huff Duff had pinpointed the transmitter to somewhere along the east coast—somewhere from Lincolnshire to Suffolk. Braithwaite pulled the item out of his stack and set it next to Vicary's alert.

He rose and limped out of his office into the main room, stopping at the North Atlantic plotting table. Two members of his staff were repositioning some of the colored pins to reflect overnight movements. Braithwaite seemed not to notice them. He fixed his gaze on the waters off Britain's east coast, face grave.

After a moment he said quietly, "Patrick, bring me the file on *U-509*."

CHAPTER FIFTY-FIVE

HAMPTON SANDS, NORFOLK

Jenny reached the grove of pines at the base of the dunes and collapsed with exhaustion. She had run by instinct, like a frightened animal. She had stayed off the road, keeping instead to the meadows and the marshes, flooded with rain. She had fallen more times than she could remember. She was covered with mud, smelled of rotting earth and the sea. Her face, beaten by the rain and the wind, felt as if it had been slapped. And she was cold—colder than she had ever been in her life. Her oilskin felt as if it weighed a hundred pounds. Her Wellington boots were filled with water, her feet were freezing. Then she remembered she had run from the cottage with no socks. She fell to her hands and knees, gasping for breath. Her throat was raw and tasted of rust.

She stayed that way for a moment until her breathing evened out, then forced herself to stand and enter the trees. It was pitch dark, so dark she had to walk with her hands outstretched before her like a blind person groping through an unfamiliar place. She was cross with herself for not bringing her torch.

The air was filled with the sound of the wind and the pounding of the breakers on the beach. The trees seemed to be in a familiar pattern now. Jenny walked by memory, like someone shuffling through their own home in the dark.

The trees fell away; her secret hiding place appeared before her.

She slipped down the side and sat down with her back against the large rock. Overhead the pines writhed with the wind, but Jenny was sheltered from the worst of it. She wished she could make a fire but the smoke would be visible from a long way off. She dug out her case from the bed of pine needles, took out the old woolen blanket, and wrapped herself tightly.

The warmth took hold of her. Then she started to cry. She wondered how long she would have to wait here until going for help. Ten minutes? Twenty minutes? A half hour? She wondered if Mary would still be at the cottage when she returned. She wondered if she would be hurt. A horrid vision of her father's dead body flashed before her eyes. She shook her head and tried to make it go away. She shivered, then clutched the blanket more tightly to her body.

Thirty minutes. She would wait thirty minutes. They would leave by then and it would be safe to return.

Neumann parked at the end of the track, grabbed his torch from the seat next to him, and climbed out. He switched on the light and walked quickly through the trees. He scaled the dunes and scrambled down the other side. He switched off the torch as he walked across the beach to the water's edge. When he reached the flat hard sand where the breakers met the beach he broke into a light run, head down to push through the wind.

He thought of the morning he was running on the beach and saw Jenny, emerging from the dunes. He remembered how she looked, as though she had slept on the beach that night. He felt certain she had some kind of hiding place nearby where she went when things were bad at home. She was frightened, on the run, and alone. She would flee to the place she knew best, the way children do. Neumann went to the spot on the beach that served as his imaginary finish line, then stopped and walked toward the dunes.

On the other side he switched on the torch, found a trampled footpath, and followed it. It led to a small depression, sheltered from the wind by the trees and a pair of large boulders. He shined his torch into the depression; the beam caught Jenny Colville's face.

"What's your real name?" Jenny said as they drove back to the Dohertys' cottage.

"My real name is Lieutenant Horst Neumann."

"Why do you speak English so well?"

"My father was English and I was born in London. My mother and I moved to Germany when he died."

"Are you a German spy?"

"Something like that."

"What happened to Sean and my father?"

"We were using the radio in Sean's barn when your father burst in on us. Sean tried to stop him and your father killed him. Catherine and I killed your father. I'm sorry, Jenny. It all happened very fast."

"Shut up! I don't want you to tell me you're sorry!"

Neumann said nothing.

Jenny said, "What happens now?"

"We're going on a trip up the coast to the River Humber. From there we take a small boat out to sea to meet a U-boat."

"I hope they catch you. And I hope they kill you."

"I'd say that's a very distinct possibility."

"You're a bastard! Why did you get in that fight with my father over me?"

"Because I like you very much, Jenny Colville. I've lied to you about everything else, but that's the truth. Now just do exactly as I tell you and nothing bad will happen to you. Do you understand me?"

Jenny nodded her head. Neumann turned into the Doghertys' cottage. The door opened and Catherine came outside. She walked to the van and looked inside at Jenny. Then she looked at Neumann and said in German, "Tie her up and put her in the back. We're going to take her with us. You never know when a hostage might come in handy."

Neumann shook his head, and replied in the same language. "Just leave her here. She's no use to us, and she might get hurt."

"Are you forgetting I outrank you, Lieutenant?"

"No, Major," Neumann said, his voice tinged with sarcasm.

"Good. Now tie her up and let's get the hell out of this godforsaken place."

Neumann walked back to the barn to find a length of rope. He found some, picked up the lamp, and started out. He took one last look at Sean Dogherty's body, lying on the ground, covered by the old sacking. Neumann couldn't help but feel responsible for the chain of events that led to Sean's death. If he hadn't fought with Martin, Martin wouldn't have come to the barn with a shotgun tonight. Sean would be going with them to Germany, not lying on the floor of his barn with half his chest blown away. He doused the lamp, leaving the bodies in darkness, and went out, closing the door behind him.

Jenny did not resist, nor did she speak a single word to him. Neumann bound her hands in front of her so she could sit more comfortably. He checked to make sure the knot was not too tight. Then he bound her feet.

When he finished he carried her to the rear of the van, opened the doors, and lifted her inside.

He added another jerry can of petrol to the tank and tossed the empty container into the meadow.

There was no sign of life on the track between the cottage and the village. Obviously the gunshots had gone unnoticed in Hampton Sands. They crossed the bridge, swept past the spire of St. John's, and drove along the darkened street. The place was so quiet it might have been evacuated.

Catherine sat next to him, silent, reloading her Mauser.

Neumann opened the throttle, and Hampton Sands disappeared behind them.

CHAPTER FIFTY-SIX

LONDON

Arthur Braithwaite's gaze settled on the plotting table while he waited for the file on *U-509*. Not that Braithwaite had much need for it—he thought he knew everything there was to know about the submarine's commanding officer and could probably recite every patrol the boat had ever made. He just wanted a couple of things confirmed before he telephoned MI5.

U-509's movements had been puzzling him for weeks. The boat seemed to be on an aimless patrol of the North Sea, sailing nowhere in particular, going for long periods of time without contacting BdU. When it did check in it reported a position off the British coastline near Spurn Head. It had also been spotted in aerial photographs at a U-boat pen in southern Norway. No surface sightings, no attacks on Allied warships or merchantmen.

Braithwaite thought, You're just lurking around out there up to nothing at all. Well, I don't believe it, Kapitänleutnant Hoffman.

He looked up at the dour face of Dönitz and murmured, "Why would you let a perfectly good boat and crew go to waste like that?"

The aide returned with the file a moment later. "Here we are, sir."

Braithwaite didn't take the file; instead, he began to recite the contents. "Captain's name is Max Hoffman, if I remember correctly."

"Right, sir."

"Knight's Cross in 1942. Oak Leaves a year later."

"Pinned on by the Führer himself."

"Now, here's the important part. I believe he served on Canaris's staff at the Abwehr for a brief period before the war."

The aide thumbed through the file. "Yes, here it is, sir. Hoffman was assigned to Abwehr headquarters in Berlin from thirty-eight to thirty-nine. When war broke out he was given command of *U-509*."

Braithwaite was staring at the map table again. "Patrick, if you had an important German spy who needed a lift out of Britain, wouldn't you prefer to have an old friend do the driving?"

"Indeed, sir."

"Ring Vicary at MI-Five. I think we'd better have a chat."

CHAPTER FIFTY-SEVEN

LONDON

Alfred Vicary was standing before an eight-foot-high map of the British Isles, chain smoking, drinking wretched tea, and thinking, Now I know how Adolf Hitler must feel. Based on the telephone call from Commander Lowe at the Y Service station in Scarborough, it was now safe to assume the spies were trying to slip out of England aboard a U-boat. But Vicary had one very simple yet very serious problem. He had only a vague idea of when and an even vaguer idea of where.

He assumed the spies had to meet the submarine before dawn; it would be too dangerous for a U-boat to remain on the surface near the coast after first light. It was possible the U-boat might put a landing party ashore in a rubber dinghy—that's how the Abwehr inserted many of its spies into Britain—but Vicary doubted they would attempt to do so in heavy seas. Stealing a boat was not as easy as it sounded. The Royal Navy had seized almost everything that could float. Fishing in the North Sea had dwindled because coastal waters were heavily mined. A pair of spies on the run would have a difficult time finding a seaworthy craft on short notice in a storm in the blackout.

He thought, Perhaps the spies already have a boat.

The more vexing question was where. From what point along the coastline would they put to sea? Vicary stared at the map. The Y Service could not pinpoint the exact location of the transmitter. Vicary, for argument's sake, would choose the precise center of the large area they had given him. He traced his finger along the map until he came to the Norfolk coast.

Yes, it made perfect sense. Vicary knew his railway timetables. A spy could hide in one of the villages along the coast and still be in London in three hours' time because of the direct train service from Hunstanton.

Vicary assumed they had a good vehicle and plenty of petrol. They had already traveled a substantial distance from London and, because of the heavy police presence on the railways, he was virtually certain they had not done it by train.

So how far from the Norfolk coast could they possibly travel before getting into a boat and heading out to sea?

The U-boat would probably come no closer to shore than about five miles. It would take the spies at least an hour to sail five miles out to sea, if not more. If the U-boat submerged at first light, the spies would have to set sail no later than about 6 A.M. to be on the safe side. The radio message was sent at 10 P.M. That left them eight hours of potential driving time. How far could they travel? Given the weather, the blackout, and the poor road conditions, one hundred to one hundred and fifty miles.

Vicary looked at the map, dejected. That still left a huge swath of the British coast, stretching from the Thames Estuary in the south to the River Humber in the north. It would be nearly impossible to cover it all. The coastline was dotted with small ports, fishing villages, and quays. Vicary had asked the local police forces to cover the coast with as many men as they could. RAF Coastal Command had agreed to fly search missions at first light, even though Vicary feared that was too late. Royal Navy corvettes were watching for small craft, even though it would be nearly impossible to spot them on a rainy moonless night at sea. Without another lead—a second intercepted radio signal or a sighting—there was little hope of catching them.

The telephone rang.

"Vicary."

"This is Commander Arthur Braithwaite at the Submarine Tracking Room. I saw your alert when I arrived on duty, and I think I may be of some rather serious help."

"The Submarine Tracking Room says *U-509* has been moving in and out of the waters off the Lincolnshire coast for a couple of weeks now," Vicary said. Boothby had come downstairs and joined Vicary's vigil in front of the map. "If we pour our men and resources into Lincolnshire, we stand a good chance of stopping them."

"It's still a lot of coastline to cover."

Vicary was looking at the map again.

"What's the largest town up there?"

"Grimsby, I'd say."

"How appropriate—*Grims*by. How long do you think it would take me to get up there?"

"Transport section could arrange a lift for you, but it would take hours."

Vicary grimaced. Transport maintained a few fast cars for cases just like this. There were expert drivers on standby who specialized in high-speed chases; a couple of them had even competed in professional races before the war. Vicary thought the drivers, while brilliant, were too reckless. He remembered the night he pulled the spy off the beach in Cornwall; remembered barreling through the blacked-out Cornish night in the back of a souped-up Rover, praying he would live long enough to make the arrest.

Vicary said, "How about an airplane?"

"I'm sure I could arrange a lift for you from the RAF. There's a small Fighter Command base outside Grimsby. They could have you up there in an hour or so, and you could use the base as your command post. But have you taken a look out the window lately? It's a godawful night for flying."

"I realize that, but I'm certain I could do a better job coordinating the search if I was on the ground there." Vicary turned from the map and looked at Boothby. "And there's something else that's occurred to me. If we're able to stop them before they send Berlin a message, perhaps I can send it for them."

"Devise some explanation for their decision to flee London that bolsters the belief in Kettledrum?"

"Exactly."

"Good thinking, Alfred."

"I'd like to take a couple of men with me: Roach, Dalton if he's up to it."

Boothby hesitated. "I think you should take one other person."

"Who?"

"Peter Jordan."

"Jordan!"

"Look at it from the other side of the looking glass. If Jordan has been deceived and betrayed, wouldn't he want to be there at the end to watch Catherine Blake's demise? I know I certainly would. I'd want to pull the trigger myself, if I were in his shoes. And the Germans have to think that too. We have to do anything we can to make them believe in the illusion of Kettledrum."

Vicary thought of the empty file in Registry.

The telephone rang again.

"Vicary."

It was one of the department operators.

"Professor Vicary, I have a trunk call from Chief Superintendent Perkin of the King's Lynn police in Norfolk. He says it's quite urgent."

"Put him through."

Hampton Sands was too small, too isolated, and too quiet to warrant its own police constable. It shared one constable with four other Norfolk coast villages, Holme, Thornton, Titchwell, and Brancaster. The constable was a man named Thomasson, a police veteran who had worked the Norfolk coast since the last war. Thomasson lived in a police house in Brancaster and, because of the requirements of his work, had his own telephone.

One hour earlier the telephone had rung, waking Thomasson, his wife, and his English setter, Rags. The voice at the other end of the line was Chief Superintendent Perkin from King's Lynn. The superintendent told Thomasson about the urgent telephone call he had received from the War Office in London, asking for assistance from local police forces in the search for two fugitive murder suspects.

Ten minutes after receiving Perkin's telephone call, Thomasson was letting himself out the door of the cottage, wearing a blue oilskin cape and a sou'wester knotted beneath his chin and carrying a flask of sweet tea Judith had quickly made for him. He pushed his bicycle around from the shed at the back of the house, then set off toward the center of the village. Rags, who always accompanied Thomasson on his rounds, trotted easily next to him.

Thomasson was in his mid-fifties. He never smoked, rarely touched alcohol, and thirty years of cycling the rolling coastline of Norfolk had left him fit and very strong. His thick, well-muscled legs pumped easily, propelling the heavy iron bicycle into Brancaster. As he suspected, the village was dead quiet. He could knock on a few doors, wake a few people up, but he knew everyone in the village and none of them were housing fugitive murderers. He took one pass through the silent streets, then turned onto the coast road and pedaled toward the next village, Hampton Sands.

The Colville cottage was about a quarter mile outside the village. Everyone knew about Martin Colville. He had been deserted by his wife, was a heavy drinker, and barely scratched a living from his smallholding. Thomasson knew Colville was too hard on his daughter, Jenny. He also knew Jenny spent a great deal of time in the dunes; Thomasson had found her things after one of the locals complained about tinkers living on the beach. He coasted to a stop and shined his torch toward the Colville cottage. It was dark, and there was no smoke coming from the chimney.

Thomasson pushed his bike up the drive and knocked on the door. There was no answer. Fearing Colville could be drunk or passed out, he knocked again, harder. Again, no answer. He pushed the door open and looked inside. The interior was dark. He called Colville's name one last time. Hearing no answer, he left the cottage and continued on into Hampton Sands.

Hampton Sands, like Brancaster, was quiet and blacked out. Thomasson cycled through the village, past the Arms, the village store, and St. John's Church. He crossed the bridge over the sea creek. Sean and Mary Dogherty lived about a mile outside the village. Thomasson knew that Jenny Colville practically lived with the Doghertys. It was very likely she was spending the night there. But where was Martin?

It was a difficult mile, the track rising and falling beneath him. Ahead of him, in the darkness, he could hear the click of Rags's paws on the track and the steady rhythm of his breathing. The Dogherty cottage appeared before him. He pedaled up to the drive, stopped, and shined his torch back and forth.

Something in the meadow caught his attention. He played the beam of light across the grass and—*there*—there it was again. He waded forward into the saturated meadow and reached down for the object. It was an empty jerry can. He sniffed—petrol. He turned it upside down. A thread of fuel trickled out.

Rags walked ahead of him toward the Dogherty cottage. He saw Sean Dogherty's dilapidated old van parked in the yard. Then he spotted a pair of bicycles lying in the grass beside the barn. Thomasson walked to the cottage and knocked on the door. Like the Colville cottage, there was no answer.

Thomasson didn't bother knocking a second time. He was by now thoroughly alarmed by what he had seen. He pushed back the door and called out *"Hello!"* He heard a strange sound, a muffled grunting. He shone his torch into the room and saw Mary Dogherty, tied to a chair, a gag around her mouth.

Thomasson rushed forward, Rags barking furiously, and quickly untied the cloth around her face.

"Mary! What in God's name happened here?"

Mary, hysterical, gasped for air.

"Sean—Martin—dead—barn—spies—submarine—Jenny!"

"Vicary here."

"Chief Superintendent Perkin of the King's Lynn police."

"What have you got?"

"Two dead bodies, a hysterical woman, and a missing girl."

"My God! Start from the beginning."

"After I received your call, I sent all my constables out on rounds. Police Constable Thomasson handles a handful of small villages along the north Norfolk coast. He found the trouble."

"Go on."

"It happened in a place called Hampton Sands. Unless you have a large map, you're not likely to find it. If you do, find Hunstanton on the Wash and trace your finger east along the Norfolk coast and you'll see Hampton Sands."

"I've got it." It was nearly the spot where Vicary guessed the transmitter might be.

"Thomasson found two bodies in a barn on a farm just outside Hampton Sands. The victims are both local men, Martin Colville and Sean Dogherty. Dogherty's an Irishman. Thomasson found Dogherty's wife, Mary, bound and gagged in the cottage. She'd been hit on the head and was hysterical when Thomasson discovered her. She told him quite a tale."

"Nothing will surprise me, Superintendent. Please continue."

"Mrs. Dogherty says her husband has been spying for the Germans since the beginning of the war—he was never a full-fledged IRA gunman, but he had ties to the group. She says a couple of weeks ago the Germans dropped another agent onto the beach named Horst Neumann, and Dogherty took him in. The agent has been living with them ever since and traveling regularly to London."

"What happened tonight?"

"She's not sure exactly. She heard gunshots, ran outside to the barn, and found the bodies. The German told her that Colville burst in on them, and that's when the shooting started."

"Was there a woman with Neumann?"

"Yes."

"Tell me about the missing girl."

"Colville's daughter, Jenny. She's not at home, and her bicycle was found at the Doghertys'. Thomasson speculates she followed her father, witnessed the shooting or the aftermath, and fled. Mary is afraid the Germans found the girl and took her with them."

"Does she know where they were headed?"

"No, but she says they're driving a van—black, perhaps."

"Where is she now?"

"Still at the cottage."

"Where's Constable Thomasson?"

"He's still on the line from a public house in Hampton Sands."

"Was there any sign of a radio in the cottage or the barn?"

"Hold on, let me ask him."

Vicary could hear Perkin, voice muffled, ask the question.

"He says he saw a contraption in the barn that could be a radio."

"What did it look like?"

"A suitcase filled with something that looked like a wireless. It was destroyed by a shotgun blast."

"Who else knows about this?"

"Me, Thomasson, and probably the landlord at the public house. I suspect he's standing next to Thomasson right now."

"I want you to tell absolutely no one else about what happened at the Dogherty cottage tonight. There is to be no mention of German agents in any report on this affair. This is a security matter of the utmost importance. Is that clear, Superintendent?"

"I understand."

"I'm going to send a team of my men to Norfolk to assist you. For now, leave Mary Dogherty and those bodies exactly where they are."

"Yes, sir."

Vicary was looking at the map again. "Now, Superintendent, I have information that leads me to suspect those fugitives are in all likelihood heading directly your way. We believe their ultimate destination is the Lincolnshire coast."

"I've called in all my men. We're blocking all the major roads."

"Keep this office informed of every development. And good luck."

Vicary rang off and turned to Boothby.

"They've killed two people, they probably have a hostage, and they're making a run for the Lincolnshire coast." Vicary smiled wolfishly. "And it looks as though they've just lost their second radio."

CHAPTER FIFTY-EIGHT

LINCOLNSHIRE, ENGLAND

Two hours after leaving Hampton Sands, Horst Neumann and Catherine Blake were beginning to have serious doubts about their chances of making the rendezvous with the submarine in time. To escape the Norfolk coast, Neumann retraced his course, climbing into the cluster of hills in the heart of Norfolk, then following thin ribbons of road through the heathland and the darkened villages. He skirted King's Lynn to the southeast, wound his way through a series of hamlets, and then crossed the River Great Ouse at a village called Wiggenhall St. Germans.

The journey across the southern edge of the Wash was a nightmare. Wind poured in from the North Sea and whipped over the marshes and the dikes. The rain increased. Sometimes it came in irate squalls—swirling, wind-blown, erasing the edges of the road. Neumann hunched forward mile after mile, gripping the wheel with both hands as the van raced across the flat terrain. At times he had the sensation of floating through an abyss.

Catherine sat next to him, reading Dogherty's old Ordnance Survey map by the light of her torch. They spoke in German, so that Jenny could not understand. Neumann found Catherine's German odd: flat, toneless, no regional accent. The kind of German that is a second or third language. The kind of German that has not been used in a very long time.

Neumann, with Catherine navigating, plotted his course.

Cleethorpes, where their boat was waiting for them, lay next to the port of Grimsby at the mouth of the Humber. Once they were clear of the Wash, there were no large towns standing in their way. According to the maps there was a good road—the A16—that ran several miles inland along the base of the Lincolnshire Wolds, then to the Humber. For purposes of planning, Neumann assumed the worst. He assumed that Mary would eventually be found, that MI5 would eventually be alerted, and roadblocks would be thrown up on all major roads near the coastline. He would take the A16 halfway toward Cleethorpes, then switch to a smaller road that ran closer to the coast.

Boston lay near the western shore of the Wash. It was the last large town standing between them and the Humber. Neumann left the main road, crept through quiet side streets, then rejoined the A16 north of town. He opened the throttle and pushed the van hard through the storm.

Catherine switched off the blackout torch and watched the rain swirling in the soft glow of the headlamps.

"What's it like now——in Berlin?"

Neumann kept his eyes on the road. "It's paradise. We are all happy, we work hard in the factories, we shake our fists at the American and British bombers, and everyone loves the Führer."

"You sound like one of Goebbels's propaganda films."

"The truth isn't quite so entertaining. Berlin is very bad. The Americans come with their B-Seventeens by day, and the British come with their Lancasters and Halifaxes at night. Some days it seems the city is under almost constant bombardment. Most of central Berlin is a pile of rubble."

"Having lived through the blitz myself, I'm afraid Germany deserves whatever the Americans and British can dish out. The Germans were the first to take the war to the civilian population. I can't shed many tears because Berlin is now being pounded into dust."

"You sound like a Brit yourself."

"I *am* half British. My mother was English. And I've been living among the British for six years. It's not hard to forget whose side you're supposed to be on when you're in a situation like that. But tell me more about Berlin."

"Those with money or connections manage to eat well. Those without money or connections don't. The Russians have turned the tables in the east. I suspect half of Berlin is hoping the invasion succeeds so the Americans can get to Berlin before the Ivans."

"So typically German. They elect a psychopath, give him absolute power, then cry because he's led them to the brink of destruction."

Neumann laughed. "If you were blessed with such foresight, why in the world did you volunteer to become a spy?"

"Who said anything about volunteering?"

They flashed through a pair of villages——first Stickney, then Stickford. The scent of woodsmoke from fires burning in the cottages penetrated the interior of the van. Neumann heard a dog barking, then another. He reached in his pocket, removed his cigarettes, and gave them to Catherine. She lit two, kept one for herself, and handed one back to him.

"Would you like to explain that last remark?"

She thought, Would I? It felt terribly strange, after all these years, even to be speaking in German. She had spent six years hiding every shred of truth about herself. She had *become* someone else, erased every aspect of her personality and her past. When she thought about the person she was before Hitler and before the war, it was as if she were thinking about someone else.

Anna Katarina von Steiner died in an unfortunate road accident outside Berlin.

"Well, I didn't exactly go down to the local Abwehr office and sign up," she said. "But then, I don't suppose anyone in this line of work gets their job that way, do they. *They* always come for *you*. In my case, *they* was Kurt Vogel."

She told him the story, the story she had never told another person before. The story of the summer in Spain the summer the civil war broke out. The summer at Maria's *estancia*. Her affair with Maria's father. "Just my luck, he turns out to be a Fascist and a talent spotter for the Abwehr. He sells me to Vogel, and Vogel comes looking for me."

"Why didn't you just say no?"

"Why didn't any of us just say no? In my case, he threatened the one thing in this world I care most about—my father. That's what a good case officer does. They get inside your head. They get to know how you think, how you feel. What you love and what you fear. And then they use it to make you do what they want you to do."

She smoked quietly for a moment, watching as they passed through another village.

"He knew that I lived in London when I was a child, that I spoke the language perfectly, that I already knew how to handle a weapon, and that—"

Silence for a moment. Neumann didn't press her. He just waited, fascinated.

"He knew that I had a personality suited to the assignment he had in mind. I've been in Britain nearly six years, alone, with virtually no contact with anyone from my side: no friends, no family, no contact with any other agents—nothing. It was more like a prison sentence than an assignment. I can't tell you how many times I dreamt about going back to Berlin and killing Vogel with one of the wonderful techniques he and his friends taught me."

"How did you enter the country?"

She told him—told him what Vogel made her do.

"Jesus Christ," Neumann muttered.

"Something the Gestapo would do, right? I spent the next month preparing my new identity. Then I settled in and waited. Vogel and I had a way of communicating over the wireless that didn't involve code names. So the British never looked for me. Vogel knew I was safe and in place, ready to be activated. Then the idiot gives me one assignment and sends me straight into the arms of MI-Five." She laughed quietly. "My God, I can't believe I'm actually going back there after all this time. I never thought I would see Germany again."

"You don't sound terribly thrilled about the prospect of going home."

"Home? It's hard to think of Germany as my home. It's hard to think of myself as German. Vogel erased that part of me at his wonderful little mountain retreat in Bavaria."

"What are you going to do?"

"Meet with Vogel, make certain my father is still alive, then collect my payment and leave. Vogel can create another one of his false identities for me. I can pass for about five different nationalities. That's what landed me in the game to begin with. It's all a big game, isn't it? One big game."

"Where are you going to go?"

"Back to Spain," she said. "Back to the place where it all started."

"Tell me about it," Neumann said. "I need to think about something besides this godforsaken road."

"It's in the foothills of the Pyrenees. In the morning we go hunting, and in the afternoon we ride up into the mountains. There's a wonderful stream with deep, cold pools and we stay there all afternoon, drinking icy white wine and smelling the eucalyptus trees. I used to think about it all the time when the loneliness got to me. I thought I was going to go crazy sometimes."

"It sounds wonderful. If you need a stablehand, let me know."

She looked at him and smiled. "You've been wonderful. If it weren't for you—" She hesitated. "God, I can't even imagine."

"Don't mention it. Glad I could be of assistance. I don't mean to rain on our parade, but we're not out of danger yet."

"Believe me, I realize that."

She finished her cigarette, opened the window a crack, and tossed the butt into the night. It hit the roadway and exploded into sparks. She sat back and closed her eyes. She had been running on adrenaline and fear for too long. Exhaustion stalked her. The gentle rocking of the van lulled her into a light half sleep.

Neumann said, "Vogel never told me your real name. What is it?"

"My real name was Anna Katarina von Steiner," she said, sleep creeping into her voice. "But I would prefer it if you continue to call me Catherine. You see, Kurt Vogel killed Anna before he sent her to England. I'm afraid Anna no longer exists. Anna is dead."

Neumann's voice, when he spoke again, was far away, at the end of a long tunnel.

"How did a beautiful and intelligent woman like Anna Katarina von Steiner end up here—like this?"

"That's a very good question," she said, and then fatigue overtook her and she was asleep.

The dream is her only memory of it; it was driven benevolently from her conscious thoughts long ago. She sees it now in flash bursts—stolen glimpses. Sometimes she sees it with her own eyes, as though she is reliving it, and sometimes the dream makes her watch it again like a spectator in a grandstand.

Tonight she is reliving it.

She is lying beside the lake; Papa lets her go alone. He knows she will not go near the water—it is too chilly for swimming—and he knows she likes to be by herself to think about her mother.

It is autumn. She has brought a blanket. The tall grass at the edge of the lake is damp with the morning's rain. The wind moves in the trees. A flock of rooks scatter and wheel noisily overhead. The trees weep flaming leaves of orange and red. She watches the leaves float gently downward, like tiny hot air balloons, and settle on the rippled surface of the lake.

It is then, as her eye follows the descent of the leaves, that she sees the man, standing in the trees across the lake.

He is very still for a long time, watching her; then he moves toward her. He is wearing knee-high boots and a thigh-length coat. A shotgun, broken at the breech, is cradled over his right arm. His hair and beard are too long, his eyes are red and damp. As he moves closer she can see something hanging from his belt. She realizes it is a pair of bloody rabbits. Limp with death, they seem absurdly long and thin.

Papa has a word for men like him: poachers. They come onto other people's land and kill the animals—deer and rabbit and pheasant. She thinks it is a funny word, poachers. It sounds like someone who prepares eggs in the morning. She thinks about that now as he approaches, and it makes her smile.

The poacher asks if he can sit next to her and she tells him yes.

He squats and lays the shotgun in the grass.

"Are you here alone?" he asks.

"Yes. My father says it's all right."

"Where is your father now?"

"He's in the house."

"And he's not coming here?"

"No."

"I want to show you something," he says. "Something that will make you feel wonderful."

His eyes are very damp now. He is smiling; his teeth are black and rotten. She becomes frightened for the first time. She tries to stand up but he grabs her by the shoulders and forces her down onto the blanket. She tries to scream but he smothers the sound with a big, hairy hand. Suddenly he is on top of her; she is paralyzed beneath the weight of him. He is reaching up her dress and pulling at her underwear.

The pain is like nothing she has ever felt. She feels she is being ripped apart. He pins her arms behind her head with one hand and covers her mouth with the other so no one will hear her scream. She feels the still-warm bodies of the dead rabbits pressing against her leg. Then the poacher's face becomes contorted, as if he is in pain, and it stops as suddenly as it began.

He is talking to her again.

"You saw the rabbits? You saw what I did to the rabbits?"

She tries to nod, but the hand over her mouth is pressing so hard she cannot move her head.

"If you ever tell anyone about what happened here today, I'll do the same to you. And then I'll do it to your father. I'll shoot you both, and then I'll hang your heads from my belt. Do you hear me, girl?"

She starts to cry.

"You're a very bad girl," he says. "Oh, yes, I can see that. I think you actually liked it."

Then he does it to her again.

The shaking starts. She has never dreamed it this way before. Someone is calling her name, Catherine . . . Catherine . . . wake up. Why is he calling me Catherine? My name is Anna. . . .

Horst Neumann shook her once more, violently, and shouted, "Catherine, dammit! Wake up! We're in trouble!"

CHAPTER FIFTY-NINE

LINCOLNSHIRE, ENGLAND

It was 3 A.M. when the Lysander broke through the thick clouds and bumped to a landing at the small RAF base two miles outside the town of Grimsby. Alfred Vicary had never flown in an airplane, and it was not an experience he wished to repeat soon. The heavy weather tossed the plane during the entire flight from London, and as they taxied toward the small operations hut Vicary was never so glad to see any place in all his life.

The pilot shut down the engine while a crewman opened the cabin door. Vicary, Harry Dalton, Clive Roach, and Peter Jordan quickly climbed down. Two men were waiting for them, a young square-shouldered RAF officer and a bluff pockmarked man in a dilapidated raincoat.

The RAF man stuck out his hand and handled the introductions. "Squadron Leader Edmund Hughes. This is Chief Superintendent Roger Lockwood of the Lincolnshire County Constabulary. Come inside the operations hut. It's crude but dry, and we've set up a makeshift command post for you."

They went inside. The RAF officer said, "I suppose it's not as nice as your digs in London."

"You'd be surprised," Vicary said. It was a small room with a window overlooking the airfield. A large-scale map of Lincolnshire was tacked up on one wall, a desk with a pair of battered telephones opposite. "It will do just fine."

"We have a wireless and a teleprinter," Hughes said. "We even can manage some tea and cheese sandwiches. You look as though you could use something to eat."

"Thank you," Vicary said. "It's been a long day."

Hughes went out and Chief Superintendent Lockwood stepped forward.

"We've got men on every major road between here and the Wash," Lock-wood said, his thick finger jabbing at the map. "In the smallest villages, they're just constables on bicycles, so I'm afraid they won't be able to do much if they spot them. But as they move closer to the coast, they'll be in trouble. Roadblocks here, here, here, and here. My best men, patrol cars, vans, and weapons."

"Very good. What about the coastline itself?"

"I've got a man on every dock and quay along the Lincolnshire coast and the Humber. If they try to steal a boat, I'll know about it."

"What about the open beaches?"

"That's another story. I don't have unlimited resources. I lost a lot of my good lads to the army, same as everybody else. I know these waters. I'm an amateur seaman myself. And I wouldn't want to head out to sea tonight in any boat I could launch from a beach."

"This weather may be the best friend we've got."

"Aye. One other thing, Major Vicary. Do we still need to pretend these are just a pair of ordinary criminals you're after?"

"Actually, Chief Superintendent, we do indeed."

The junction of the A16 and a smaller B-road lay just outside the town of Louth. Neumann had planned to leave the A16 at that point, take the B-road to the coast, turn onto another secondary road, and head north to Clee-thorpes. There was just one problem. Half the police in Louth were stand-ing in the junction. Neumann could see at least four men. As he approached, they shone their torches in his direction and waved for him to stop.

Catherine was awake now, startled. "What's going on?"

"End of the line, I'm afraid," Neumann said, bringing the van to a halt. "They've obviously been waiting for us. No talking our way out of this."

Catherine picked up her Mauser. "Who said anything about talking?"

One of the constables stepped forward, carrying a shotgun, and rapped on Neumann's window.

Neumann wound down the window and said, "Good evening. What's the problem?"

"Mind stepping out of the van, sir?"

"Actually, I do. It's late, I'm tired, the weather's dreadful, and I want to get where I'm going."

"And where would that be, sir?"

"Kingston," Neumann said, though he could see the constable was already doubting his story. Another constable appeared at Catherine's window. Two more took up positions behind the van.

The policeman pulled open Neumann's door, leveled the shotgun at his face, and said, "All right. Put your hands up where I can see them and get out of the van. Nice and slow."

Jenny Colville sat in the back of the darkened van, hands and feet bound, mouth gagged. Her wrists hurt. So did her neck and her back. She had been sitting on the floor of the van for how long? Two hours? Three hours? Maybe four? When the van slowed, she allowed herself a brief flash of hope. She thought, Maybe this will all be over soon and I can go back to Hampton Sands and Mary and Sean and Dad will be there and things will be like they used to be before he came and it will all turn out to be a bad dream and— She stopped herself. Better to be realistic. Better to think about what was really possible.

She watched them in the front seat. They had spoken softly in German for a long time, then the woman fell asleep, and now Neumann was shaking her and trying to wake her up. Ahead, through the windscreen, she saw light— beams of light—bouncing back and forth, like torches. She thought, Police officers would carry torches if they were blocking the road. Was it possible? Did they know that they were German spies and that she had been kidnapped? Were they looking for her?

The van stopped. She could see two policemen in front of the van and outside, near the back of the van, she could hear the footfalls and voices of at least two more. She heard the policeman tap on the glass. She saw Neumann wind down his window. She saw that he had a gun in his hand. Jenny looked at the woman. She had a gun in her hand too.

Then she remembered what happened in the barn. Two people got in their way—her father and Sean Dogherty—and they had killed them both. It was possible they had killed Mary too. They weren't going to surrender just because some country policemen told them to. They would kill the policemen too, just like they killed her father and Sean.

Jenny heard the door open, heard the police officer yelling at them to get out. She knew what was about to happen. Instead of getting out they would start shooting. Then the policemen would all be dead and Jenny would be alone with them again.

She had to warn them.

But how?

She couldn't speak because Neumann had gagged her mouth so tightly.
She could do only one thing.
She raised her legs and kicked the side of the van as hard as she could.

If Jenny Colville's action did not have its intended effect, it did grant at least one of the officers—the one standing nearest Catherine Blake's door—a more benevolent death. When he turned his head toward the sound, Catherine raised her Mauser and shot him. The Mauser's superb silencer damped the explosion of the round so that the gun emitted only a tense burst. The bullet smashed through the window, struck the constable at the hinge of his jaw, then ricocheted into the base of his brain. He collapsed onto the muddy apron of the road, dead.

The second to die was the constable at Neumann's door, though Neumann did not fire the shot that killed him. Neumann knocked the shotgun away with a sweep of his right hand; Catherine turned and fired through the open door. The bullet struck the constable in the center of the forehead and exited at the back of his skull. He fell back onto the roadway.

Neumann tumbled from the door and landed in the road. One of the officers at the rear of the van fired over his head, shattering the half-open window. Neumann quickly squeezed the trigger twice. The first shot struck the constable in the shoulder, spinning him around. The second pierced his heart.

Catherine stepped from the van, the gun in her outstretched hands aimed into the darkness. On the other side of the van, Neumann was doing the same thing, only he was still lying flat on his stomach. Both waited, making no sound, listening.

The fourth constable thought it best to flee for help. He turned and started running into the darkness. After a few steps he came into Neumann's range. Neumann took careful aim and fired twice. The running stopped, the shotgun clattered on the tarmac, and the last of the four men fell to the rainy roadway, dead.

Neumann collected the bodies and stacked them at the back of the van. Catherine opened the rear doors. Jenny, eyes wide with terror, raised her hands to cover her head. Catherine lifted the gun into the air and struck Jenny's face. A deep gash opened over her eye. Catherine said, "Unless you want to end up like them, don't ever try anything like that again."

Neumann lifted Jenny and laid her on the apron of the road. Then, together with Catherine, he placed the bodies of the dead constables in the back of the van. The idea had come to him immediately. The police officers had traveled to this spot in their own van; it was parked a few yards away on the side of the road. Neumann would hide the bodies and the stolen van out of sight in the trees and use the police van to drive to the coast. It might be hours before any other policeman came here and discovered the constables were missing. By then he and Catherine would be heading back to Germany aboard the U-boat.

Neumann carried Jenny and placed her in the back of the police van. Catherine climbed into the driver's seat and started the motor. Neumann walked back to the other van and got inside. The engine was running. He reversed and turned around, then sped down the road, Catherine following. He tried not to think about the four dead bodies lying just inches from him.

Two minutes later Neumann turned into a small track leading off the road. He drove about two hundred yards, stopped, and shut down the motor. Then he climbed out and ran back to the road. Catherine had turned the van around and was sitting in the passenger seat when Neumann returned. He climbed in, slammed the door, and sped away.

They passed the spot where the roadblock had been and turned onto the smaller B-road. According to the map it was about ten miles to the coast road, then another twenty miles to Cleethorpes. Neumann opened the throttle and pushed the van hard. For the first time since spotting the MI5 men in London, he allowed himself to imagine they just might make it after all.

Alfred Vicary paced in his room at the RAF base outside Grimsby. Harry Dalton and Peter Jordan sat at the desk, smoking. Superintendent Lockwood sat next to them, arranging matches into geometric shapes.

Vicary said, "I don't like it. Someone should have spotted them by now."

Harry said, "All the major roads are sealed. They have to hit one of the roadblocks at some point."

"Maybe they're not coming this way after all. Maybe I've made a dreadful miscalculation. Maybe they went south from Hampton Sands. Maybe the signal to the U-boat was a ploy and they're heading to Ireland on a ferry."

"They're coming this way."

"Maybe they've gone to ground, called it off. Maybe they're holed up in another remote village, waiting for it all to blow over before they make their move."

"They've signaled the submarine. They have to go."

"They don't *have* to do anything. It's possible they've spotted the roadblocks and the extra police about and decided to wait. They can signal the submarine at the next opportunity and try again when things have quieted down."

"You're forgetting one thing. They don't have a radio."

"We *think* they don't have a radio. You took one from them, and Thomasson found a destroyed radio in Hampton Sands. But we don't know for certain they don't have a third."

"We don't know *anything* for certain, Alfred. We make educated guesses."

Vicary paced, looking at the telephone, thinking, Ring, dammit, ring!

Desperate to do something, he picked up the receiver and asked the operator to connect him to the Submarine Tracking Room in London. Arthur Braithwaite, when he finally came on the line, sounded like he was inside a torpedo tube.

Vicary asked, "Anything, Commander?"

"I've spoken with the Royal Navy and the local coastguard. The Royal Navy is moving a pair of corvettes into the area as we speak—numbers 745 and 128. They'll be off Spurn Head within the hour and will commence search operations immediately. The coastguard is handling things closer to shore. The RAF is putting up planes at first light."

"When is that?"

"Around seven A.M. Maybe a little later because of the dense cloud cover."

"That may be too late."

"It won't do them any good to go up before then. They need light to see. They'd be as good as blind if they went up now. There *is* some good news. We expect a break in the weather shortly before dawn. The cloud cover will remain, but the rain is expected to ease and the winds diminish. That will make it easier to conduct search operations."

"I'm not sure that's such good news after all. We were counting on the storm to bottle up the coast. And better weather will make it easier for the agents and the U-boat to operate as well."

"Point well taken."

"Instruct the Royal Navy and the RAF to conduct the search as discreetly as possible. I know it sounds farfetched, but try to make it all look *routine*. And tell everyone to mind what they say on their radios. The Germans listen to us too. I'm sorry I can't be more forthcoming, Commander Braithwaite."

"I understand. I'll pass it up the line."

"Thank you."

"And try to relax, Major Vicary. If your spies try to reach that submarine tonight, we'll stop them."

Police constables Gardner and Sullivan pedaled side by side through the dark streets of Louth, Gardner big, bluff, and middle-aged, Sullivan thin and fit and barely twenty years old. Chief Superintendent Lockwood had ordered them to ride to a roadblock just south of the village and relieve two of the constables there. Gardner complained as he cycled. "Why do London's criminals always manage to end up here in the middle of a rainstorm, would you tell me that?" Sullivan was thoroughly excited. This was his first big manhunt. It was also the first time he had carried a weapon while on duty— a thirty-year-old bolt-action rifle from the weapons room at the station was slung over his shoulder.

Five minutes later they arrived at the junction where the roadblock was supposed to be. The place was deserted. Gardner stood, legs astride the frame of his bike. Sullivan laid down his bike, broke out his torch, and shined it over the area. First he saw the tire marks, then the shattered glass.

Sullivan shouted, "Over here! Quick!"

Gardner climbed off his bike and pushed it over to where Sullivan was standing.

"Christ almighty!"

"Look at the tracks. Two vehicles, the one they were driving and ours. When they turned around, the tires were muddied on the apron of the road. They've left us a nice set of tracks to follow."

"Aye. You see where they lead. I'll ride back to the station and alert Lockwood. And for heaven's sake, be careful."

Sullivan pedaled along the road, holding his torch in one hand, watching the tracks gradually fade away. One hundred yards after leaving the site of the roadblock, the trail was gone. Sullivan rode for another quarter mile, looking for any sign of the police van.

He rode a little farther and then spotted another set of tire tracks. These were different. The tracks became more clear and defined the farther he pedaled. The vehicle that made them had obviously come from the other direction.

He followed the tracks to their point of origin and found the small path leading into the trees. He turned his torch down the path and saw the pair of fresh tire tracks. He turned the beam horizontally down the tunnel of trees, but the light was not powerful enough to penetrate the darkness. He looked at the track—too rutted and muddy to handle his bike. He climbed off, leaned the bike against a tree, and started walking.

Two minutes later, he spotted the back of the van. He called out but there was no reply. He looked more closely. It was not the police vehicle; it had London plates and was a different model. Sullivan moved forward slowly. He approached the front of the van from the passenger side and shone his torch inside. The front seat was empty. He turned the beam toward the storage area at the back.

It was then he spotted the bodies.

Sullivan left the van in the trees and rode back to Louth, pedaling as fast as he could. He arrived at the police station and quickly raised Chief Superintendent Lockwood at the RAF base.

"All four of them are dead," he said, out of breath from the ride. "They're lying in the back of a van, but it's not theirs. The fugitives appear to have taken the police van. Based on the tracks on the road, I'd say they came back toward Louth."

Lockwood said, "Where are the bodies now?"

"I left them in the wood, sir."

"Go back and wait with them until help arrives."

"Yes, sir."

Lockwood rang off. "Four dead men. My God!"

"I'm sorry, Chief Superintendent. So much for my theories about them going to ground. They're obviously here and they'll do anything to escape, including murder four of your men in cold blood."

"We have another problem—they're driving a police vehicle. To get word to the officers manning the roadblocks is going to take time. Meanwhile, your spies are dangerously close to the coast." Lockwood walked to the map. "Louth is here, just to the south of us. They can now take any number of secondary roads to the sea."

"Redeploy your men. Throw everything between Louth and the coast."

"Indeed, but it's going to take time. And your spies have a jump on us."

"One other thing," Vicary said. "Bring those dead men back here as quietly as possible. When this is all over, it may be necessary to concoct another explanation for their deaths."

"What do I tell their families?" Lockwood snapped and stormed out.

Vicary picked up the telephone. The operator connected him with MI5 headquarters in London. A department operator answered. Vicary asked for Boothby and waited for him to come on the line.

"Hello, Sir Basil. I'm afraid we've got big trouble up here."

A stiff wind drove rain across the Cleethorpes waterfront as Neumann slowed and turned into a row of warehouses and garages. He stopped and shut down the motor. Dawn was not far off. In the faint light he could see a small quay, with several fishing boats tied up there and additional boats bobbing at their moorings in the black water. They had made excellent time up the coast. Twice they had approached roadblocks and twice they were waved through with no question, thanks to the van they were driving.

Jack Kincaid's flat was supposed to be over a garage. There was a wooden exterior staircase with a door at the top. Neumann climbed out and walked up the stairs, reflexively pulling out his Mauser as he approached the door. He rapped softly but there was no answer. He tried the latch; it was unlocked. He opened the door and walked inside.

He was immediately struck by the stench of the place: rotting rubbish, stale cigarettes, unwashed bodies, an overwhelming smell of alcohol. He tried the light switch but nothing happened. He removed his torch from his pocket and switched it on. The beam caught the figure of a large man sleeping on a bare mattress. Neumann picked his way across the filthy room and nudged the man with the toe of his boot.

"You Jack Kincaid?"

"Yeah. Who are you?"

"My name is James Porter. You're supposed to give me a lift in your boat."

"Oh, yes, yes." Kincaid tried to sit up but couldn't. Neumann shone the light directly into his face. He was at least sixty years old, and his craggy face showed the signs of heavy drinking.

"Have a little bit to drink last night, Jack?" Neumann asked.

"A little."

"Which boat is yours, Jack?"

"The *Camilla*."

"Where is she, exactly?"

"Down at the quay. You can't miss her."

Kincaid was passing out again.

"You won't mind if I just borrow her for a bit, do you, Jack?"

Kincaid didn't answer, just started snoring heavily.

"Thanks awfully, Jack."

Neumann went out and got back inside the van.

"Our captain is in no condition to sail. Drunk out of his mind."

"The boat?"

"The *Camilla*. He says it's right down there on the quay."

"There's something else down there."

"What's that?"

"You'll see in just a minute."

Neumann watched as a constable stepped into view.

"They must be watching the entire coast," Neumann said.

"It's a shame. Another needless casualty."

"Let's get it over with. I've killed more people tonight than I did in all the time I was in the *Fallschirmjäger*."

"Why do you think Vogel sent you here?"

Neumann didn't respond. "What about Jenny?"

"She comes with us."

"I want to leave her here. She's no use to us now."

"I disagree. If they find her she can tell them a great deal. And besides, if they know we have a hostage on board they'll think twice about what steps they take to stop us."

"If you're suggesting they'll hesitate to fire on us because we have a British civilian on board, you're mistaken. There's too much at stake for that. They'll kill us all if need be."

"So be it, then. She comes with us. When we get to the submarine, we'll leave her behind on the boat. The British will rescue her and she won't be harmed."

Neumann understood that to continue arguing would be a waste of time. Catherine turned around and, in English, said to Jenny, "No more heroics. If you make one move, I'll shoot you in the face."

Neumann shook his head. He started the motor, dropped the van into gear, and drove down to the quay.

The constable at quayside heard the sound of a motor, stopped pacing, and looked up. He spotted the police van driving toward him. Odd, he thought, since his relief was not due to arrive until eight o'clock. He watched the van draw to a halt and saw two people getting out. He struggled to make them out in the darkness, but after a few seconds he realized they were not police officers. It was a man and a woman, very probably the fugitives!

He then had a terrible sinking feeling. He was armed with only a prewar revolver that jammed frequently. The woman was walking toward him. Her arm swung up and there was a flash but almost no sound, just a muffled thump. He felt the bullet tear through his chest, was aware of losing his balance.

His last sight was the dirty water of the Humber rushing toward him.

Ian McMann was a fisherman who believed the pure Celtic blood flowing through his veins gave him powers mere mortals did not possess. During his sixty years living near the North Sea, he claimed to have heard distress calls *before* they went out. He claimed to see the ghosts of men lost at sea floating over the quays and the harbors. He claimed to know that some vessels were haunted and would never go near them. Everyone in Cleethorpes accepted all this as truth but in private suggested Ian McMann had spent far too many nights at sea.

McMann had risen as usual at five o'clock, even though the dismal forecast promised conditions that would keep all boats off the water that day. He was eating a breakfast of porridge at the kitchen table when he heard a noise outside on the quay.

The smack of the rain made it difficult to detect any other sound, but McMann could have sworn he heard someone or something falling into the water. He knew there was a constable outside—he had taken him tea and a wedge of cake before turning in last night—and he knew why he was there. The police were looking for a pair of murder suspects from London. McMann guessed these were not ordinary murder suspects. He had lived in

Cleethorpes for twenty years, and never had he heard of the local police guarding the waterfront.

The kitchen window of McMann's cottage provided an excellent view of the quay and the mouth of the Humber beyond. McMann rose, parted the curtains, and looked out. There was no sign of the constable. McMann threw on an oilskin and sou'wester, took his torch from the table beside the door, and went out.

He switched on his torch and started walking. After a few steps he heard the sound of a boat's diesel motor firing and sputtering into life. He walked faster until he could see which boat it was: the *Camilla,* Jack Kincaid's boat.

McMann thought, Is he daft heading out in a storm like this?

He started running, yelling, "Jack, Jack! Stop! Where do you think you're going?"

Then he realized the man untying the *Camilla* from the quay and jumping onto the aft deck was not Jack Kincaid. Someone was stealing his boat. He looked around for the constable, but he was gone. The man stepped into the wheelhouse and opened the throttle, and the *Camilla* nosed away from the quay.

McMann ran forward and shouted, "Come back, you!"

Then a second person stepped from the wheelhouse. McMann saw a muzzle flash but heard no sound. He felt the round whiz past his head, dangerously close. He hit the ground behind a pair of empty drums. Two more shots struck the quay; then the gunfire ended.

He stood up and saw the stern of the *Camilla,* running out to sea.

Only then did McMann see something floating in the oily water off the quay.

"I think you need to hear this for yourself, Major Vicary."

Vicary took the telephone receiver Lockwood handed to him. Ian McMann was on the line from Cleethorpes.

Lockwood said, "Start from the beginning, Ian."

"Two people just stole Jack Kincaid's fishing boat and are making for open water."

Vicary snapped, "My God! Where are you calling from?"

"Cleethorpes."

Vicary squinted to see the map. "Cleethorpes? Didn't we have a man there?"

"You did," McMann said. "He's floating in the water right now with a bullet through his heart."

Vicary swore softly, then said, "How many were there?"

"At least two that I saw."

"A man and a woman?"

"Too far away and too dark. Besides, when they started shooting at me I hit the dirt."

"You didn't see a young girl with them?"

"No."

Vicary covered the mouthpiece with the palm of his hand. "Maybe she's still in that van. Get a man out there as quickly as you can."

Lockwood nodded.

Vicary removed his hand and said, "Tell me about the boat they stole."

"The *Camilla,* a fishing vessel. The boat's in bad shape. I wouldn't want to be aboard the *Camilla* heading out in a blow like this."

"One other question. Does the *Camilla* have a radio?"

"No, not that I know of."

Vicary thought, Thank God. He said, "Thank you for your help."

Vicary rang off. Lockwood was standing before the map. "Well, the good news is we know exactly where they are now. They have to slip through the mouth of the Humber before they can reach open water. That's only about a mile from the quay. There's no way we can stop them from doing that. But get those Royal Navy corvettes into position off Spurn Head, and they'll never make it through. That fishing boat they're in will be no match for them."

"I'd feel better if we had our own boat in the water."

"Actually, that can be arranged."

"Really?"

"The Lincolnshire County Constabulary keeps a small police boat on the river—the *Rebecca*. She's in Grimsby now. She's not built for the open sea, but she'll do in a pinch. She's also quite a bit faster than that old fishing boat. If we get under way immediately, we should be able to overtake them before too long."

"Does the *Rebecca* have a radio?"

"Aye. We'll be able to talk to you right here."

"How about weapons?"

"I can pick up a couple of old rifles from the lockup in the Grimsby police station. They'll do the trick."

"Now all you need is a crew. Take my men with you. I'll stay here so I can remain in contact with London. The last thing you need is *me* on board a boat in weather like this."

Lockwood managed a smile, clapped Vicary on the back, and went out. Clive Roach, Harry Dalton, and Peter Jordan followed him. Vicary picked up the telephone to break the news to Boothby in London.

Neumann stayed between the channel markers as the *Camilla* sliced through the choppy waters of the mouth of the Humber. She was about forty feet, broad in the beam and desperately in need of paint. There was a small cabin aft, where Neumann had left Jenny. Catherine stood next to him in the wheelhouse. The sky was beginning to lighten slightly in the east. Rain drummed against the window. Off the port side he could see waves breaking over Spurn Head. Spurn Light was blacked out. A compass was set in the dash next to the wheel. Neumann put the boat on a heading due east, opened the throttle full, and headed out to sea.

CHAPTER SIXTY

THE NORTH SEA, OFF SPURN HEAD

U-509 hovered just below the surface. It was 5:30 A.M. Kapitänleutnant Max Hoffman stood in the control room, peering though the periscope, drinking coffee. His eyes hurt from spending the entire night staring at the black seas. His head ached. He badly needed a few hours of sleep.

His first officer came to the bridge. "The window closes in thirty minutes, Herr Kaleu."

"I am aware of the time, Number One."

"We have had no further communication from the Abwehr agents, Herr Kaleu. I think we must consider the possibility that they have been captured or killed."

"I have considered that possibility, Number One."

"It will be light soon, Herr Kaleu."

"Yes. It is a phenomenon that takes place at this time every day. Even in Britain, Number One."

"My point is that it will not be safe for us to remain so close to the English coast for much longer. The depth here is not great enough for us to escape the British *wabos*," the first officer said, using the slang common among German submariners for depth charges.

"I am perfectly aware of the dangers involved in the situation, Number One. But we are going to remain here at the rendezvous point until the window is closed. And then, if I believe it is still safe, we will stay a little longer."

"But, Herr Kaleu—"

"They have sent us a proper radio signal alerting us that they are coming. We must assume they are traveling in a stolen vessel, probably barely seaworthy, and we must also assume they are exhausted or even hurt. We will stay here until they arrive or I am convinced beyond doubt that they are not coming. Is that clear?"

"Yes, Herr Kaleu."

The first officer walked away. Hoffman thought, What a pain in the ass.

The *Rebecca* was about thirty feet in length with a shallow draft, an inboard motor, and a small open wheelhouse amidships barely big enough for two men to stand shoulder to shoulder. Lockwood had telephoned ahead, and the *Rebecca*'s engine was idling by the time they arrived.

The four men clambered on board: Lockwood, Harry, Jordan, and Roach. A dock boy untied the last line, and Lockwood guided the craft into the channel.

He opened the throttle full. The engine note rose; the slender prow lifted out of the water and sliced through the wind-driven chop. Night was draining from the eastern sky. The silhouette of Spurn Light was visible off the port side. The sea was empty before them.

Harry leaned down, snatched the handset of the radio, and raised Vicary in Grimsby to bring him up to date.

Five miles due east of the *Rebecca,* corvette Number 745 was maneuvering on a tedious crisscross pattern through rough seas. The captain and the first officer stood on the bridge, glasses raised to their eyes, peering into the curtain of rain. It was useless. Along with the dark and the rain, a fog had rolled in and reduced visibility even further. In conditions like these they could pass within a hundred yards of a U-boat and never see it. The captain moved to the chart table, where the navigator was plotting the next course change. On the captain's order, the corvette made a 90-degree starboard turn and pushed farther out to sea. Then he instructed the radio operator to inform the Submarine Tracking Room of their new heading.

In London, Arthur Braithwaite stood over the map table, leaning heavily on his cane. He had made certain that all Royal Navy and RAF updates crossed his desk as soon as they came in. He knew the odds of finding a U-boat in weather and light conditions like these were remote, even if the craft was on the surface. If the submarine was lurking just below the surface, it would be almost impossible.

His aide handed him a signal flimsy. Corvette Number 745 had just changed course and was on an easterly heading. A second corvette, Number 128, was two miles away and moving south. Braithwaite leaned down over the table, closed his eyes, and tried to picture the search in his mind. He thought, Damn you, Max Hoffman! Where the hell are you?

The *Camilla,* though Horst Neumann did not realize it, was precisely seven miles due east of Spurn Head. Conditions seemed to be worsening by the minute. Rain fell in a blinding curtain and hammered against the window of the wheelhouse, obscuring the view. The wind and the current, both beating down from the north, kept nudging the boat off course. Neumann, using the dashboard compass, struggled to keep them on an easterly heading.

The biggest problem was the sea. The past half hour had been a relentless repetition of the same sickening cycle. The boat would climb one roller, teeter for an instant on the top, then plunge down into the next trough. At the bottom it always seemed as if the vessel were about to be swallowed by a gray-green canyon of seawater. The decks were constantly awash. Neumann could no longer feel his feet. He looked down for the first time and noticed he was standing in several inches of icy water.

Still, miraculously, he thought they might actually make it. The boat seemed to be absorbing all the punishment the sea could dish out. It was 5:30 A.M.—they still had thirty minutes left before the window closed and the U-boat turned away. He had been able to keep the boat on a constant heading and felt confident they were approaching the right spot. And there was no sign of the opposition.

There was just one problem: they had no radio. They had lost Catherine's in London, and they had lost the second to Martin Colville's shotgun blast in Hampton Sands. Neumann had hoped the boat would have a radio, but it didn't. Which left them no means of signaling the U-boat.

Neumann had only one option: to switch on the boat's running lights.

It was a gamble but a necessary one. The only way the U-boat would know they were at the rendezvous position was if it could see them. And the only way the *Camilla* could be spotted in conditions like these was to be illuminated. But if the U-boat could see them, so could any British warships or coastguard vessels in the vicinity.

Neumann reckoned he was a couple of miles from the rendezvous point. He pressed on for five more minutes, then reached down and threw a switch, and the *Camilla* came alive with light.

Jenny Colville leaned over the bucket and threw up in it for the third time. She wondered how there was anything left to come out of her stomach. She tried to remember the last time she'd had food. She had not eaten dinner last night because she was angry with her father, and she had not eaten any lunch either. Breakfast, maybe, and that was nothing more than a biscuit and tea.

Her stomach convulsed again, but this time nothing came out. She had lived next to the sea her entire life but she had been on a boat just once—a day sail around the Wash with the father of a friend from school—and never had she experienced anything like this.

She was absolutely paralyzed with seasickness. She wanted to die. She was desperate for fresh air. She was helpless against the constant pitching and rocking of the vessel. Her arms and legs were bruised from the battering. And then there was the noise—the constant deafening rumble and clatter of the boat's engine.

It felt as if it were just beneath her.

She wanted nothing more in the world than to get off the boat and be back on land. She told herself over and over again that if she survived this night she would never get on a boat again, ever. And then she thought, What happens when they get where they're going? What are they going to do with me? Surely they weren't going to take this boat all the way to Germany. They would probably meet another boat. *Then what happens?* Would they take her with them again or leave her on the boat alone? If they left her alone she might never be found. She could die out on the North Sea alone in a storm like this.

The boat skidded down the slope of another enormous wave. Jenny was thrown forward in the cabin, striking her head.

There were two portholes on either side of the cabin. With her bound hands, she rubbed away the condensation in the starboard porthole and looked out. The sea was terrifying, rolling green mountains of seawater.

There was something else. The sea boiled and something dark and shiny punctured the surface from below. Then the sea was in turmoil and a giant gray thing like a sea monster in a child's tale floated to the surface, seawater slipping from its skin.

❖

Kapitänleutnant Max Hoffman, tired of holding at the ten-mile mark, had decided to take a chance and creep a mile or two closer to shore. He had waited at the eight-mile mark, peering into the gloom, when he suddenly spotted the running lights of a small fishing vessel. Hoffman shouted an order to surface and two minutes later he was standing on the bridge in the driving rain, breathing the cold clean air, Zeiss glasses pressed to his eyes.

Neumann thought it might be a hallucination at first. The glimpse had been brief—just an instant before the boat plunged downward into yet another trough of seawater and everything was obliterated once again.

The prow dug deeply into the sea, like a shovel into dirt, and for a few seconds the entire foredeck was swamped. But somehow the boat climbed out of the trough and scaled the next peak. At the top of the next roller, a squall of windblown rain obscured all view.

The boat fell, then rose again. Then, as the *Camilla* teetered atop a mountain of seawater, Horst Neumann spotted the unmistakable silhouette of a German U-boat.

It was Peter Jordan, on the pitching aft deck of the *Rebecca,* who spotted the U-boat first. Lockwood saw it a few seconds later and then spotted the running lights of the *Camilla,* about four hundred yards off the U-boat's starboard side and closing quickly. Lockwood brought the *Rebecca* hard to port, set it on a collision course with the *Camilla,* and picked up the handset to raise Alfred Vicary.

Vicary snatched up the receiver of the open phone line to the Submarine Tracking Room.

"Commander Braithwaite, are you there?"

"Yes. I'm here, and I could hear the entire thing over the line."

"Well?"

"I'm afraid we've got a serious problem. Corvette 745 is a mile due south of the U-boat's position. I've radioed the captain and he's making for the scene now. But if the *Camilla* is really only four hundred yards away from the submarine, they're going to get there first."

"Dammit!"

"You do have one other asset, Mr. Vicary—the *Rebecca.* I suggest you use it. Your men have got to do something to slow that boat down until the corvette can intervene."

Vicary set down the telephone and picked up the handset of the radio.

"Superintendent Lockwood, this is Grimsby, over."

"Lockwood here, over."

"Superintendent, listen carefully. Help is on the way, but in the meantime I want you to ram that fishing boat."

All of them heard it—Lockwood, Harry, Roach, and Jordan—for they were all pressed around the cabin, sheltering from the weather.

Lockwood, shouting above the wind and the roar of the *Rebecca*'s engines, said, "Is he out of his mind?"

"No," Harry said, "just desperate. Can you get there in time?"

"Sure—but we'll be staring right down the barrels of that U-boat's deck guns."

They all looked at one another, saying nothing. Finally, Lockwood said, "There are life jackets in that locker behind you. And bring out the rifles. I have a feeling we may need them."

Lockwood looked back at the sea and found the *Camilla*. He made a minor course correction and opened the throttle as far as it would go.

Max Hoffman, standing on the bridge of *U-509,* spotted the *Rebecca* approaching fast.

"We've got company, Number One. Civilian craft, three or four men on board."

"I see them, Herr Kaleu."

"Judging from their speed and heading, I'd say they're the opposition."

"They appear to be unarmed, Herr Kaleu."

"Yes. Give them a warning shot from the foredeck gun. Shoot across their bow. I don't want needless bloodshed. If they persist, fire directly on the craft. But at the waterline, Number One, not the cabin."

"Yes, Herr Kaleu," the first officer snapped. Hoffman heard shouted orders, and within thirty seconds the first shot from *U-509*'s forward *bootskanone* deck gun was arching across the prow of the *Rebecca*.

Though U-boats rarely engaged in surface artillery battles, the 10.5-centimeter shell of the forward deck gun was capable of inflicting lethal damage, even on large vessels. The first shot sailed well off the *Rebecca*'s prow. The second, fired ten seconds later, came much closer.

Lockwood turned to Harry and shouted, "I'd say that's the last warning we get. The next one is going to blow us right out of the water. It's your call, but we're no help to anyone if we're dead."

Harry shouted, "Turn away!"

Lockwood turned the *Rebecca* hard to port and circled around. Harry looked back toward the U-boat. The *Camilla* was two hundred yards away and closing, and there wasn't a damn thing they could do about it. He thought, Goddammit! Where's that corvette?

Then he picked up the handset and told Vicary there was nothing they could do to stop them.

Jenny heard the boom of the U-boat's deck gun and saw the shell flash along the waterline toward a second boat. She thought, Thank God! I'm not alone after all. But the U-boat fired again, and a few seconds later she saw the little boat turn away and her spirits sank.

Then she steeled herself and thought. They're German agents. They've killed my father and six other people tonight and they're about to get away with it. I have to do something to stop them.

But what could she do? She was alone, and her hands and feet were tied. She considered trying to free herself, sneak up on deck, and hit them with something. But if they saw her they wouldn't hesitate to kill her. Perhaps she could start a fire, but then she would be trapped with the smoke and the flames and she would be the only one to die. . . .

Think, Jenny! Think!

It was hard to think with the constant roar of the boat's motor. It was driving her crazy.

And then she thought, Yes, that's it!

If she could somehow disable the engine—even just for a moment—it might help. If there was one boat chasing them, there might be others—perhaps bigger boats that could shoot back at the German submarine.

The engine sounded as if it was just below her, the noise was so loud. She struggled to her feet and pushed away the coiled lines and tarpaulins she had been sitting on. And there it was—a door, built into the floor of the hold.

She managed to open it and was immediately overwhelmed by the thunderous noise and heat of the *Camilla*'s engine.

She looked at it. Jenny knew nothing of engines. Once, Sean tried to explain to her the repairs he was making on his rattletrap old van. There was always something going wrong with the blessed thing, but what was it then? Something to do with the fuel lines and the fuel pump. Surely this engine was different from the engine in Sean's van. It was a diesel engine, for one thing; Sean's van ran on petrol. But she knew one thing: no matter what kind of engine it was, it needed fuel to run. Cut the fuel supply and it would die.

But how? She looked closely at the motor. Several black metal lines ran across the top and converged at a single point on the side of the motor. Could those be the fuel lines? Was the point where they met the fuel pump?

She looked around. She needed tools. Sailors always carry tools with them. After all, what happens if the engine breaks down at sea? She spotted a metal toolbox at the end of the cabin and crawled forward. She looked out the porthole. The U-boat filled her field of vision. They were very close now. She saw the other boat. It had moved off. She opened the box and found it filled with greasy, filthy tools.

She removed two, a pair of bladed pliers and a large hammer.

She took the pliers in her hands, turned the nose toward her wrists, and started hacking through the rope. It took about a minute to free her hands. Then she used the pliers to cut away the rope around her ankles.

She crawled back to the motor.

She put the pliers on the floor and hid them beneath a coiled line. Then she reached down, picked up the hammer, and smashed the first of the fuel lines. It severed, leaking diesel. Quickly, she brought down the hammer several more times until the last fuel line was ruptured.

The engine died.

With the noise gone, Jenny could finally hear the roar of the sea and the wind. She closed the door over the crippled engine and sat down. The hammer was next to her right hand.

She knew that Neumann or the woman would come down in a matter of seconds to investigate. And when they did they would realize that Jenny had sabotaged the motor.

The door flew open and Neumann stormed down the companionway. His face was wild, the way it had been that morning when she saw him racing along the beach. He looked at Jenny and noticed her hands and feet were no longer tied. He looked down and noticed the loose gear had been cleared away.

He shouted, "Jenny, what have you done?"

The boat, now powerless, skidded helplessly down the side of a wave.

Neumann leaned down and opened the hatch.

Jenny grabbed the hammer and rose to her knees. She raised it high into the air and hit him in the back of the head as hard as she could. Neumann fell to the floor, blood pouring from his split scalp.

Jenny turned away and threw up.

Kapitänleutnant Max Hoffman saw the *Camilla* begin to wobble helplessly in the rough seas and realized at once that it had lost power. He knew he had to act quickly. With no propulsion, the boat would founder. It might even turn turtle. If the agents were thrown into the icy North Sea, they would be dead in a matter of minutes.

"Number One! Take us forward toward the craft and prepare to board."

"Yes, Herr Kaleu!"

Hoffman felt the throb of the U-boat's diesel screws turning beneath his feet as the submarine crept slowly forward.

Jenny was afraid she had killed him. He lay very still for a moment; then he stirred and somehow forced himself to stand. He was very unsteady. She could easily have hit him with the hammer again, but she couldn't summon the courage or the will to do it. He was helpless, holding on to the side of the cabin. Blood poured from the wound, into his face, down his neck. He reached up and wiped the blood out of his eyes. He said, "Stay down here. If you come up onto the deck, she'll kill you. Do as I say, Jenny."

Neumann struggled up the companionway. Catherine looked at him, alarm on her face.

"I fell and hit my head when the boat pitched. The motor's dead."

His torch was next to the wheel. He picked it up and walked out onto the deck. He aimed the light at the conning tower of the U-boat and flashed a distress signal. The submarine was coming toward them with agonizing slowness. He turned and waved at Catherine to join him on the foredeck. The rain washed the blood off his face. He looked up, feeling it beat down on him, and waved his arms at the U-boat.

Catherine joined him on the deck. She couldn't quite believe it. The previous afternoon they were sitting in a Mayfair café surrounded by MI5 men and now, miraculously, they were about to step onto the deck of a U-boat and sail away. Six long, painfully lonely years—over at last. She never believed she would see this day. Never really dared imagine it. The emotion of the moment overtook her. She let out a joyous, childlike scream and, like Neumann, turned her face to the rain, waving her arms at the U-boat.

The steel nose of the submarine nudged against the prow of the *Camilla.* A boarding party scrambled down the U-boat's deck toward them. She put her arms around Neumann and held him very tightly.

"We did it," she said. "We made it. We're going home."

Harry Dalton, standing in the wheelhouse of the *Rebecca,* described the scene to Vicary in Grimsby. Vicary, in turn, described it to Arthur Braithwaite in the Submarine Tracking Room.

"Dammit, Commander! Where's that corvette?"

"She's right there. She just can't see because of the weather."

"Well, tell her captain to do something! My men are powerless to stop them."

"What should I instruct the captain to do?"

"Fire on the boat and kill those spies."

"Major Vicary, may I remind you there is an innocent girl on board."

"God help me for saying this, but I'm afraid we can't be concerned about her at a time like this, Commander Braithwaite. Order the captain of that corvette to hit the *Camilla* with everything he has."

"Understood."

Vicary set down the telephone, thinking, God, but I've become a perfect bastard.

The wind tore a momentary hole through the curtain of rain and fog. The captain of corvette 745, standing on the bridge, spotted *U-509* and the *Camilla* one hundred and fifty yards off his bow. Through his glasses he could see two people standing on the foredeck of the *Camilla* and a rescue party on the deck of the German submarine. He immediately gave the order to fire. Seconds later the corvette's machine guns opened up.

Neumann heard the shots. The first rounds sailed overhead. The second burst clattered against the side of the U-boat. The rescue party fell flat on the deck to avoid the fire as the rounds moved from the U-boat to the

Camilla. There was nowhere on the foredeck of the fishing boat to take cover. The gunfire found Catherine. Her body was instantly shredded, her head exploding in a flash of blood and brain.

Neumann scrambled forward and tried to reach the U-boat. The first round that hit him cut off his leg at the knee. He screamed and crawled forward. A second round hit, severing his spine. He felt nothing. The last shot hit him in the head, and there was darkness.

Max Hoffman, watching from the conning tower, ordered his first officer to engage the diesel engines full and dive as quickly as possible. Within a matter of seconds, *U-509* was racing away from the scene. Two minutes later it submerged beneath the surface of the North Sea and was gone.

The *Camilla,* alone on the sea, her decks awash with blood, foundered.

The mood aboard the *Rebecca* was euphoric. The four men embraced as they watched the U-boat turn and steam away. Harry Dalton raised Vicary and told him the news. Vicary made two calls, the first to the Submarine Tracking Room to thank Arthur Brathwaite, the second to Sir Basil Boothby to tell him that it was finally over.

Jenny Colville felt the *Camilla* shudder. She had fallen flat on her stomach and covered her head with her hands. The shooting stopped as suddenly as it started. She was too terrified to move. The boat pitched about wildly. She guessed it had something to do with the dead motor. With no engine to push the boat forward, it was defenseless against the onslaught of the sea. She had to get on her feet and get outside and signal the other boats that she was there and she was alive.

She willed herself to stand, was immediately knocked down by the bucking of the boat, then stood again. Climbing the companionway was nearly impossible. Finally, she reached the deck. The wind was tremendous. The rain slashed sideways. The boat seemed to be going several directions at once: up and down, back and forth, and rolling from side to side. Standing was impossible. She looked toward the prow and saw the bodies. They hadn't just been shot to death. They had been mangled, torn to bits, by the gunfire. The decks ran pink with all the blood. Jenny retched and looked away. She saw the U-boat, diving in the distance, disappearing below the surface of the sea. On the other side of the boat she saw a warship, gray, not too large, coming toward her. A second boat—the one she had seen through the porthole earlier—was approaching fast.

She waved and yelled and started to cry. She wanted to tell them that *she* had done it. *She* was the one who disabled the motor so the boat stopped and the spies couldn't make it to the U-boat. She was filled with an enormous, fierce pride.

The *Camilla* rose on a gigantic roller. As the wave passed beneath the boat, it pitched wildly to the port side. Then it fell downward into the trough and, at the same time, righted itself and rolled over on its starboard side. Jenny was unable to keep her grip on the top of the companionway. She was thrown across the deck and into the sea.

The cold was like nothing she had ever felt: shocking, numbing, paralyzing cold. She fought her way to the surface and tried to gasp for air but she swallowed a mouthful of seawater instead. She sank below the surface, gagging, choking, taking more water into her stomach and her lungs. She kicked to the surface and was able to take a small breath before the sea pulled her down again. Then she was falling, sinking slowly, pleasantly, effortlessly. She was no longer cold. She felt nothing, saw nothing. Only an impenetrable darkness.

The *Rebecca* arrived first, Lockwood and Roach in the wheelhouse, Harry and Peter Jordan on the foredeck. Harry tied a line to the life ring, tied off the other end in a cleat on the prow, and threw the ring overboard. They had seen Jenny come up for air a second time and disappear below the surface. Now there was nothing, no sign of her at all. Lockwood brought the *Rebecca* in hard and straight; then, a few yards from the *Camilla*, he reversed the engine, bringing the boat to a shuddering halt.

Jordan leaned over the prow, looking for any sign of the girl. Then he stood and, with no warning, dived into the water. Harry shouted back to Lockwood, "Jordan's in the water! Don't get any closer!"

Jordan surfaced and removed his life vest. Harry screamed, "What are you doing?"

"I can't get deep enough with this damned thing on!"

Jordan filled his lungs with air and was gone for what seemed to Harry like a minute. The sea was beating against the port side of the *Camilla*, forcing it to roll from side to side and driving it toward the *Rebecca*. Harry turned over his shoulder and waved his arms at Lockwood in the wheelhouse.

"Back off a few feet! The *Camilla*'s right on top of us!"

Jordan finally surfaced, Jenny in his arms. She was unconscious, her head to one side. Jordan untied the line from the life ring and tied it around Jenny beneath her arms. He gave Harry a thumbs-up sign, and Harry pulled her through the water toward the *Rebecca*. Clive Roach helped Harry lift her onto the deck.

Jordan was furiously treading water, waves washing over his face, and he looked exhausted from the cold. Harry quickly untied the line from Jenny and threw it overboard toward him—just as the *Camilla* finally capsized and dragged Peter Jordan under the sea.

PART
FIVE

CHAPTER SIXTY-ONE

BERLIN: APRIL 1944

Kurt Vogel was cooling his heels in Walter Schellenberg's luxuriously appointed anteroom, watching the squadron of young assistants scurrying feverishly in and out of the office. Blond, blue-eyed, they looked as though they had just leapt from a Nazi propaganda poster. It had been three hours since Schellenberg had summoned Vogel for an urgent consultation about "that unfortunate business in Britain," as he habitually referred to Vogel's blown operation. Vogel didn't mind the wait; he didn't really have anything better to do. Since Canaris had been sacked and the Abwehr absorbed by the SS, German military intelligence had become a ship without a rudder, just when Hitler needed it most. The old town houses along Tirpitz Ufer had taken on the despondent air of an aging resort out of season. Morale was so low, many officers were volunteering for the Russian front.

Vogel had other plans.

One of Schellenberg's aides came out, jabbed an accusing finger at Vogel, and wordlessly waved him inside. The office was as big as a Gothic cathedral, with magnificent oil paintings and tapestries hanging on the walls, a far cry from Canaris's understated Fox's Lair at Tirpitz Ufer. Sunlight slanted through the tall windows. Vogel looked out. Fires from the morning's air raid smoldered along Unter den Linden, and a fine soot drifted over the Tiergarten like black snow.

Schellenberg smiled warmly, pumped Vogel's bony hand, and gestured for him to sit down. Vogel knew about the machine guns in Schellenberg's desk, so he kept very still and left his hands in plain sight. The doors closed, and they were alone in the cavernous office. Vogel felt Schellenberg feeding on him with his eyes.

Though Schellenberg and Himmler had been plotting against Canaris for years, a chain of unfortunate events had finally done in the Old Fox: his failure to predict Argentina's decision to sever all ties with Germany; the loss of a vital Abwehr intelligence-gathering post in Spanish Morocco; the defections of several key Abwehr officers in Turkey, Casablanca, Lisbon, and Stockholm. But the final straw was the disastrous conclusion of Vogel's operation in London. Two Abwehr agents—Horst Neumann and Catherine Blake—had been killed within sight of the U-boat. They had been unable to transmit a final message explaining why they had decided to flee England, leaving Vogel with no way to judge the authenticity of the information Catherine Blake had stolen on Operation Mulberry. Hitler exploded when he heard the news. He immediately fired Canaris and placed the Abwehr and its sixteen thousand agents in the hands of Schellenberg.

Somehow, Vogel survived. Schellenberg and Himmler suspected the operation had been compromised by Canaris. Vogel—like Catherine Blake and Horst Neumann—was an innocent victim of the Old Fox's treachery.

Vogel had another theory. He suspected all the information stolen by Catherine Blake had been planted by British Intelligence. He suspected she and Neumann attempted to flee Britain when Neumann discovered she was being watched by the opposition. He suspected Operation Mulberry was not an antiaircraft complex destined for the Pas de Calais but an artificial harbor bound for the beaches of Normandy. He also suspected all the other agents sent to Britain were bad—that they had been captured and forced to cooperate with British Intelligence, probably from the outset of the war.

Vogel, however, lacked the evidence to substantiate any of this—good lawyer that he was, he did not intend to bring charges he could not prove. Besides, even if he had the proof in his possession, he wasn't sure he would have given it to the likes of Schellenberg and Himmler.

One of the telephones on Schellenberg's desk rang. It was a call he had to take. He grunted and spoke in a guarded code for five minutes while Vogel waited. The snowstorm of soot had diminished. The ruins of Berlin shone in the April sun. Shattered glass sparkled like ice crystals.

Remaining at the Abwehr and cooperating with the new regime had its advantages. Vogel had quietly slipped Gertrude, Nicole, and Lizbet from Bavaria to Switzerland. Like a good agent runner, he had financed the operation with an elaborate shell game, moving funds from secret Abwehr accounts in Switzerland to Gertrude's personal account, then covering the exchange with his own money in Germany. He had moved enough money out of the country to enable them to live comfortably for a couple of years after the war. He had another asset, the information he possessed in his mind. The British and Americans, he felt certain, would pay handsomely in money and protection.

Schellenberg rang off and made a face as though he had a sour stomach.

"So," he said. "The reason I asked you to come today, Captain Vogel. Some exciting news from London."

"Oh?" Vogel said, raising an eyebrow.

"Yes. Our source inside MI-Five has some very interesting information."

Schellenberg produced a signal flimsy with a flourish and presented it to Vogel. Reading it, Vogel thought, Remarkable, the subtlety of the manipulation. He finished and handed the flimsy across the desk to Schellenberg.

Schellenberg said, "For MI-Five to take disciplinary action against a man who is a personal friend and confidant of Winston Churchill is extraordinary. And the source is impeccable. I recruited him personally. He's not one of Canaris's flunkies. I believe it proves the information stolen by your agent was genuine, Captain Vogel."

"Yes, I believe you're right, Herr Brigadeführer."

"The Führer needs to be told of this right away. He's meeting with the Japanese ambassador at Berchtesgaden tonight to brief him on preparations for the invasion. I'm sure he'll want to pass this along."

Vogel nodded.

"I'm leaving on a plane from Tempelhof in one hour. I'd like you to come with me and personally brief the Führer. After all, it was your operation to begin with. And besides, the man has taken a liking to you. You have a very bright future, Captain Vogel."

"Thank you for the offer, Herr Brigadeführer, but I think *you* should tell the Führer about the news."

"Are you certain, Captain Vogel?"

"Yes, Herr Brigadeführer, I'm quite certain."

CHAPTER SIXTY-TWO

OYSTER BAY, NEW YORK

It was the first fine day of spring—warm sunshine, a soft wind from the Sound. The day before had been cold and damp. Dorothy Lauterbach had worried that the memorial service and reception would be ruined by the cold. She made certain all the fireplaces in the house were laid with wood and ordered the caterer to have plenty of hot coffee ready for when the guests arrived. But by midmorning the sun had burned away the last of the clouds, and the island sparkled. Dorothy quickly moved the reception from the house to the lawn overlooking the Sound.

Shepherd Ramsey had brought Peter's things from London: his clothes, his books, his letters, the personal papers that the security men had not seized. Ramsey, sitting on the transport plane from London, had leafed through the letters to make certain there was no mention of the woman Peter was seeing in London before his death.

The graveside ceremony was packed. There was no body to bury, but they laid a small headstone next to Margaret's. All of Bratton's bank attended, as did most of the staff of the Northeast Bridge Company. The North Shore crowd came too—the Blakemores and the Brandenbergs, the Carlisles and the Duttons, the Robinsons and the Tetlingers. Billy stood next to Jane, and Jane leaned against Walker Hardegen. Bratton accepted the American flag from a representative of the navy. The wind tore blossoms from the trees and tossed them on the crowd like confetti.

One man stood slightly apart from the rest, hands clasped behind his back, head bowed respectfully. He was tall and thin, and his double-breasted suit of gray wool was a little too heavy for the warm spring weather.

Walker Hardegen was the only person present who recognized him. Hardegen did not know the man's real name. He always used a pseudonym that was so ridiculous Hardegen had trouble saying it without laughing.

The man was Hardegen's control officer, and the pseudonym he used was Broome.

Shepherd Ramsey carried the letter from the man in London. Dorothy and Bratton slipped into the library and read it during the reception. Dorothy read it first, hands trembling. She was older now, older and grayer. A fall on the icy steps of the Manhattan house in December had left her with a broken hip. The resulting limp had robbed her of her old physical presence. Her eyes were damp when she finished reading, but she did not cry. Dorothy always did things in moderation. She handed the letter to Bratton, who wept as he read.

> *Dear Billy,*
>
> *It is with great sadness that I write this letter. I had the pleasure of working with your father for only a very brief period, but I found him to be one of the most remarkable men I have ever met. He was involved in one of the most vital projects of the war. Because of the requirements of security, however, there is a strong possibility you may never be told exactly what your father did.*
>
> *I can tell you this—the work done by your father will save countless lives and make it possible for the people of Europe to be rid of Hitler and the Nazis once and for all. Your father truly gave his life so that others may live. He was a hero.*
>
> *But nothing your father accomplished gave him as much pleasure and satisfaction as you, Billy. When your father spoke of you his face changed. His eyes brightened and he smiled, no matter how tired he might be. I was never fortunate enough to be blessed with a son. Listening to your father talk about you, I realized the depth of my misfortune.*
>
> *Sincerely,*
> *Alfred Vicary*

Bratton handed the letter back to Dorothy. She folded it, put it back in its envelope, and placed it in the top drawer of Bratton's desk. She went to the window and looked out.

Everyone was eating and drinking and seemed to be having a good time. Beyond the crowd she could see Billy, Jane, and Walker sitting on the grass down by the dock. Jane and Walker had become more than friends. They had started to see each other romantically, and Jane was actually talking about marriage. She thought, Wouldn't it be perfect. Billy would have a real family again.

There was a neatness to it, a closure about the whole thing that Dorothy found comforting. It was warm again, and soon it would be summer. The houses would all be opening soon, and the parties would begin. Life goes on, she told herself. Margaret and Peter are gone, but life most definitely goes on.

CHAPTER SIXTY-THREE

GLOUCESTERSHIRE, ENGLAND: SEPTEMBER 1944

Even Alfred Vicary was surprised at the speed with which he was able to drop out. Technically, it was an administrative leave pending the findings of the internal inquiry. Vicary understood that was gobbledygook for a sacking.

Perversely he took Basil Boothby's advice and fled to his Aunt Matilda's house—he could never get used to the notion it was his—to sort himself out. The first days of his exile were appalling. He missed the camaraderie of MI5. He missed his wretched little office. He even found himself missing his camp bed, for he had lost the gift of sound sleep. He blamed it on Matilda's sagging double bed—too soft, too much room to wrestle with his troubled thoughts. In a rare flash of inspiration, he went to the village store and purchased a new camp bed. He erected it in the drawing room next to the fire, an odd location, he knew, but he had no plans for guests. From that night on he slept as well as could be expected.

He endured a long blue period of inactivity. But in the spring, when the weather warmed, he focused his boundless wasted energy on his new home. The watchers who paid the occasional visit looked on in horror as Vicary attacked his garden with pruning shears, a sickle, and his half-moon eyeglasses. They watched in amazement as he repainted the interior of the cottage. Considerable debate erupted over his choice of color, a bright institutional white. Did it mean his mood was improving, or was he making a hospital of his home and checking in for an extended stay?

There was also a good deal of concern in the village. Poole, the man from the general shop, diagnosed Vicary's mood as one of bereavement. "Not possible," said Plenderleith, the man from the nursery who advised Vicary on his garden. "Never been married, never been in love apparently." Miss Lazenby from the dress shop declared them both wrong. "Poor man's in love, any fool can see that. And by the looks of him the object of his devotion isn't returning the favor."

Vicary, even had he known of the debate, could not have settled it, for he was as much a stranger to his own emotions as those who witnessed them. The head of his department at University College sent him a letter. He had heard Vicary was no longer working at the War Office and was wondering when he might be coming back. Vicary tore the letter in half and burned it in the fireplace.

London held nothing for him—only bad memories—so he stayed away. He went just once, a morning in the first week of June, when Sir Basil summoned him to hear the results of the internal review.

"Hello, Alfred!" Sir Basil called out as Vicary was shown into Boothby's office. The room was ablaze in a fine orange light. Boothby was standing at the precise center of the floor, as though he wanted room to maneuver in all directions. He wore a perfectly cut gray suit and seemed taller than Vicary remembered. The director-general was sitting on the handsome couch, fingers interlaced as if in prayer, eyes fixed on some spot in the Persian carpet. Boothby thrust out his right hand like a bayonet and advanced on Vicary. By the chaotic smile on Boothby's face, Vicary wasn't sure if he was planning to embrace him or assault him. And he wasn't sure which he feared more.

What Boothby *did* do was shake Vicary's hand a little too affectionately and lay a big paw on Vicary's shoulder. It was hot and damp, as though he had just finished a set of tennis. He personally served Vicary tea and made small talk while Vicary smoked a last cigarette. Then, with considerable ceremony, he removed the review board's final report from his desk and laid it on the table. Vicary refused to look at it directly.

Boothby took too much pleasure in explaining to Vicary that he was not permitted to read the review of his own operation. Instead, Boothby showed Vicary a sanitized single-page letter purporting to "condense and summarize" the contents of the report. Vicary held it in both hands, the paper tight as a drum, so it would not shake while he read it. It was a vile, obscene document, but challenging it now would do no good. He handed it back to Boothby, shook his hand and then the director-general's, and went out.

Vicary walked downstairs. Someone else was in his office. Harry was there, an ugly scar along his jaw. Vicary was not one for long farewells. He told Harry he had been sacked, thanked him for everything, and said goodbye.

It was raining again and cold for June. The head of Transport offered Vicary a car. Vicary politely refused. He put up his umbrella and drifted back to Chelsea through the pouring rain.

He spent the night at his house in Chelsea. He awakened at dawn, rain rattling against the windows. It was June 6. He switched on the BBC to listen to the news and heard that the invasion was on.

Vicary went out at midday expecting to see nervous crowds and anxious chatter, but London was dead quiet. A few people ventured out to shop; a few went into churches to pray. Taxis cruised the empty streets in search of fares.

Vicary watched Londoners as they went about their day. He wanted to run up and shake them and say, Don't you know what's happening? Don't you realize what it took? Don't you know the clever, wicked things we did to deceive them? *Don't you know what they did to me?*

He took his supper at the corner pub and listened to the upbeat bulletins on the wireless. That night, alone again, he listened to the King's address to the nation; then he went to bed. In the morning he took a taxi to Paddington Station and caught the first train back to Gloucestershire.

Gradually, by summer, his days took on a careful routine.

He rose early and read until lunch, which he took each day in the village at the Eight Bells: vegetable pie, beer, meat when it was on the menu. From the Eight Bells he would set off for his daily forced march over the breezy footpaths around the village. Each day it took a little less time for the cobwebs to clear from his ruined knee, and by August he was walking ten miles each afternoon. He gave up cigarettes and took up a pipe. The rituals of the pipe—the loading, the cleaning, the lighting, and the relighting—fitted his new life perfectly.

He was not aware of the exact day it happened—the day it all faded from his conscious thoughts: his cramped office, the clatter of the teleprinters, the vile food in the canteen, the crazy lexicon of the place: Double Cross . . . Mulberry . . . Phoenix . . . Kettledrum. Even Helen receded to a sealed chamber of his memory where she could do no more harm. Alice Simpson started coming on weekends and stayed for an entire week in early August.

On the last day of summer he was overcome by the gentle melancholia that afflicts country people when the warm weather is ending. It was a glorious dusk, the horizon streaked in purple and orange, the first bite of autumn in the air. The primroses and bluebells were long gone. He remembered an evening like this half a lifetime ago when Brendan Evans taught him to ride a motorcycle along the pathways of the Fens. It was not quite cold enough for fires, but from his hilltop perch he could see the chimneys of the village gently smoking and taste the sharp scent of green wood on the air.

He saw it then, played out on the hillsides, like the solution of a chess problem. He could see the lines of attack, the preparation, the deception. Nothing had been as it seemed.

Vicary rushed back to the cottage, telephoned the office, and asked for Boothby. Then he realized it was late and it was a Friday—the days of the week meant nothing to him any longer—but by some miracle Boothby was still there, and he answered his own telephone.

Vicary identified himself. Boothby expressed genuine pleasure at hearing his voice. Vicary assured him he was fine.

"I want to talk to you," Vicary said, "about Kettledrum."

There was silence on the line, but Vicary knew Boothby had not abruptly hung up because he could hear him fidgeting in his chair.

"You can't come here any longer, Alfred. You're persona non grata. So I suppose I'll have to come to you."

"Fine. And don't pretend you don't know how to find me because I see your watchers stalking me."

"Tomorrow, midday," Boothby said and rang off.

Boothby arrived promptly at noon in an official Humber, dressed for the country in tweeds, a shirt open at the neck, and a comfortable cardigan sweater. It had rained overnight. Vicary dug out a pair of extra-large Wellingtons from the cellar for Boothby, and they walked like old chums around a meadow dotted with shorn sheep. Boothby chatted about department gossip and Vicary, with considerable effort, feigned interest.

After a while Vicary stopped walking and gazed into the middle distance. "None of it was real, was it," he said. "Jordan, Catherine Blake—it was all bad right from the beginning."

Boothby smiled seductively. "Not quite, Alfred. But something like that."

He turned and continued walking, his long body a vertical line against the horizon. Then he paused and gestured for Vicary to join him. Vicary broke into his stiff-jointed mechanized limp, chasing after Boothby, beating his pockets for his half-moon glasses.

❖

"It was the nature of Operation Mulberry that presented us with the problem," Boothby began, without warning. "Tens of thousands of people were involved. Of course, the vast majority had no idea what they were working on. Still, the potential for security leaks was tremendous. The components were so large they had to be built right out in the open. The sites were scattered around the country, but some of it was built right at the London docks. As soon as we were told of the project, we knew we had a problem. We knew the Germans would be able to photograph the sites from the air. We knew one decent spy poking around the construction sites could probably figure out what we were up to. We sent one of our men to Selsey to test out the security. He was having tea in the canteen with some of the workers before anyone bothered to ask him for identification."

Boothby laughed mildly. Vicary watched him as he spoke. All the bombast, all the fidgeting, was gone. Sir Basil was calm and collected and pleasant. Vicary thought under different circumstances he might actually have liked him. He had the sickening realization he had underestimated Boothby's intelligence from the beginning. He was also struck by his use of the words *we* and *us*. Boothby was a member of the club; Vicary had only been allowed to press his nose against the glass for a brief interval.

"The biggest problem was that Mulberry betrayed our intentions," Boothby resumed. "If the Germans discovered we were building artificial harbors, they might very well have concluded that we intended to avoid the heavily fortified ports of Calais by striking at Normandy. Because the project was so large and difficult to conceal, we had to assume that the Germans would eventually find out what we were up to. Our solution was to steal the secret of Mulberry for them and try to control the game." Boothby looked at Vicary. "All right, Alfred, let's hear it. I want to know how much you've really figured out."

"Walker Hardegen," Vicary said. "I'd say it all started with Walker Hardegen."

"Very good, Alfred. But how?"

"Walker Hardegen was a wealthy banker and businessman, ultraconservative, anticommunist, and probably a little anti-Semitic. He was Ivy League, and he knew half the people in Washington. Went to school with them. The Americans aren't so unlike us in that respect. His business regularly took him to Berlin. When men like Hardegen went to Berlin, they attended embassy dinners and parties. They dined with the heads of

Germany's biggest companies and with Nazi officials from the party and the ministries. Hardegen spoke perfect German. He probably admired some of the things the Nazis were doing. He believed Hitler and the Nazis were an important buffer between the Bolsheviks and the rest of Europe. I'd say during one of his visits he came to the attention of the Abwehr or the SD."

"Bravo, Alfred. It was the Abwehr, actually, and the man whose attention he captured was Paul Müller, head of Abwehr operations in America."

"Okay, Müller recruited him. Oh, I suppose he probably soft-pedaled it. Said Hardegen wouldn't really be working for the Nazis. He'd be helping in the struggle against international communism. He asked Hardegen for information on American industrial production, the mood in Washington, things like that. Hardegen said yes and became an agent. I have one question. Was Hardegen already an American agent at this point?"

"No," Boothby said, and smiled. "Remember, this is very early in the game, 1937. The Americans weren't terribly sophisticated then. They *did* know, however, that the Abwehr was active in the United States, especially in New York. The year before, the plans for the Norden bombsight walked out of the country in the briefcase of an Abwehr spy named Nikolaus Ritter. Roosevelt had ordered Hoover to crack down. In 1939, Hardegen was photographed meeting in New York with a known Abwehr agent. Two months later, they saw him again, meeting with another Abwehr agent in Panama City. Hoover wanted to arrest him and put him on trial. God, but the Americans were such plods at the game. Luckily, MI-Six had set up its office in New York by then. They stepped in and convinced Hoover that Hardegen was more use to us still in the game than sitting in some prison cell."

"So who ran him, us or the Americans?"

"It was a joint project really. We fed the Germans a steady stream of excellent material through Hardegen, top-grade stuff. Hardegen's stock soared in Berlin. In the meantime, every aspect of Walker Hardegen's life was placed under a microscope, including his relationship with the Lauterbach family and with a brilliant engineer named Peter Jordan."

"So in 1943, when the decision was made to stage the cross-channel attack at Normandy with the help of an artificial harbor, British and American intelligence approached Peter Jordan and asked him to go to work for us."

"Yes. October 1943, to be precise."

"He was perfect," Vicary said. "He was exactly the type of engineer needed for the project, and he was well known and well respected in his field. All the Nazis had to do was go to the library to read about his accomplishments. The death of his wife also made him personally vulnerable. So late in 1943, you had Hardegen meet with his Abwehr control officer and tell him all about Peter Jordan. How much did you tell them then?"

"Only that Jordan was working on a large construction project connected with the invasion. We also hinted about his vulnerability, as you put it. The Abwehr bit. Müller sold it to Canaris, and Canaris passed it on to Vogel."

"So the entire thing was an elaborate ruse to foist false documents on the Abwehr. And Peter Jordan was the proverbial tethered goat."

"Exactly. The first documents were ambiguous by design. They were open to interpretation and debate. The Phoenix units could be components of an artificial harbor or they could be an antiaircraft complex. We wanted them to fight, to squabble, to tear themselves to bits. Remember your Sun-tzu?"

" 'Undermine your enemy, subvert him, sow discord among his leaders.' "

"Exactly. We wanted to encourage the friction between the SD and the Abwehr. We also didn't want to make it too easy for them. Gradually, the Kettledrum documents painted a clear picture, and that picture was passed directly to Hitler."

"But why go to so much trouble? Why not just use one of the agents that had already been turned? Or one of the fictitious agents? Why use a live engineer? Why not just create one out of whole cloth?"

"Two reasons," Boothby said. "Number one, that's too easy. We wanted to make them work for it. We wanted to influence their thinking subtly. We wanted them to think *they* were the ones making the decision to target Jordan. Remember the mantra of a Double Cross officer: Intelligence easily obtained is easily discarded. There was a long chain of evidence, so to speak: Hardegen to Müller, Müller to Canaris, Canaris to Vogel, and Vogel to Catherine Blake."

"Impressive," Vicary said. "The second reason?"

"The second reason is that we became aware late in 1943 that we had not accounted for all the German spies operating in Britain. We learned about Kurt Vogel, we learned about his network, and we learned one of his agents was a woman. But we had a serious problem. Vogel had taken such care in burying his agents in Britain that we couldn't locate them unless we brought them into the open. Remember, Bodyguard was about to go into full gear. We were going to bombard the Germans with a blizzard of false intelligence. But we couldn't feel comfortable knowing there were live active agents operating in the country. All of them had to be accounted for. Otherwise, we could never be certain the Germans weren't receiving intelligence that contradicted Bodyguard."

"How did you know about Vogel's network?"

"We were told about it."

"By whom?"

Boothby walked a few paces in silence, contemplating the muddy toes of his Wellington boots. "We were told about the network by Wilhelm Canaris," he said finally.

"Canaris?"

"Through one of his emissaries, actually. In 1943, late summer. This probably will come as a shock to you, but Canaris was a leader of the *Schwarze Kapelle*. He wanted support from Menzies and the Intelligence Service to help him overthrow Hitler and end the war. In a gesture of goodwill, he told Menzies about the existence of Vogel's network. Menzies informed the Security Service, and together we concocted a scheme called Kettledrum."

"Hitler's chief spy, a traitor. Remarkable. And you knew all this, of course. You knew it the night I was assigned the case. That briefing on the invasion and deception plans. . . . It was designed to ensure my blind loyalty. To motivate me, to manipulate me."

"I'm afraid so, yes."

"So the operation had two goals: deceive them about Mulberry and at the same time draw Vogel's agents into the open so we could neutralize them."

"Yes," Boothby said. "And one other thing—give Canaris a coup to keep his head off the block until the invasion. The last thing we wanted was Schellenberg and Himmler in control. The Abwehr was totally paralyzed and manipulated. We knew that if Schellenberg took over he would question everything Canaris had done. We didn't succeed there, of course. Canaris was fired, and Schellenberg finally got hold of the Abwehr."

"So why didn't Double Cross and Bodyguard collapse with the fall of Canaris?"

"Oh, Schellenberg was more interested in consolidating his empire than running a new crop of agents into England. There was an impressive bureaucratic reorganization—offices moved, files changing hands, that sort of thing. Overseas, he threw out experienced intelligence officers loyal to Canaris and replaced them with unseasoned bloodhounds loyal to the SS and the party. In the meantime, the case officers at Abwehr headquarters went to great lengths to prove the agents operating inside Britain were genuine and productive. Quite simply, it was a matter of life and death for those case officers. If they admitted their agents were under British control, they would have been on the first train east. Or worse."

They walked in silence for a time while Vicary absorbed all he had been told. His head was spinning. He had a thousand questions. He feared Boothby might shut down at any time. He arranged them in order of importance, setting aside his seething emotions. A cloud passed in front of the sun, and it became cold.

"Did it all work?" Vicary asked.

"Yes, it worked brilliantly."

"What about the Lord Haw-Haw broadcast?" Vicary had heard it himself, sitting in the drawing room of Matilda's cottage, and it had sent a shiver through him. *We know exactly what you intend to do with those concrete units. You think you are going to sink them on our coasts in the assault. Well, we're going to help you boys. . . .*

"It sent panic through the Supreme Allied Command. At least on the surface," Boothby added smugly. "A very small group of officers knew of the Kettledrum deception and realized this was just the last act. Eisenhower cabled Washington and requested fifty picket ships to rescue the crews in case the Mulberries were sunk during the journey across the Channel. We made sure the Germans knew this. Tate, our double with a fictitious source inside SHAEF, transmitted a report of Eisenhower's request to his Abwehr controller. Several days later, the Japanese ambassador toured the coastal defenses and was briefed by Rundstedt. Rundstedt told him about the existence of the Mulberries and explained that an Abwehr agent had discovered they were antiaircraft gun towers. The ambassador cabled this information to his masters in Tokyo. That message, like all his other communications, was intercepted and decoded. At that moment, we knew Kettledrum had worked."

"Who ran the overall operation?"

"MI-Six, actually. They started it, they conceived it, we let them run it."

"Who knew inside the department?"

"Myself, the DG, and Masterman from the Double Cross Committee."

"Who was the control officer?"

Boothby looked at Vicary. "Broome, of course."

"Who's Broome?"

"Broome is *Broome,* Alfred."

"There's just one thing I don't understand. Why was it necessary to deceive the case officer?"

Boothby smiled weakly, as though troubled by a mildly unpleasant memory. A pair of pheasant broke from the hedgerow and shot across the pewter-gray sky. Boothby stopped walking and stared at the clouds.

"Looks like rain," he said. "Perhaps we should start heading back."

They turned around and started walking.

"We deceived you, Alfred, because we wanted it all to feel real to the other side. We wanted you to take the same steps you might take in a normal case. You also had no need to know Jordan was working for us the entire time. It wasn't necessary."

"My God!" Vicary snapped. "So you ran me, just like any other agent. You *ran* me."

"You might say that, yes."

"Why was I chosen? Why not someone else?"

"Because you, like Peter Jordan, were perfect."

"Would you like to explain that?"

"We chose you because you were intelligent and resourceful and under normal circumstances you would have given them a run for their money. My God, you almost saw through the deception while the operation was under way. We also chose you because the tension between us was legendary." Boothby paused and looked down at Vicary. "You weren't exactly discreet in the way you ran me down to the rest of the staff. But most importantly, we chose you because you were a friend of the prime minister and the Abwehr realized this."

"And when you sacked me, you told the Germans about it through Hawke and Pelican. You hoped that the sacrifice of a personal friend of Winston Churchill's would bolster their belief in the Kettledrum material."

"Exactly. It was all part of the script. And it worked, by the way."

"And Churchill knew?"

"Yes, he knew. He personally approved it. Your old friend betrayed you. He loves black arts, our Winston. If he wasn't the prime minister, I think he would have been a deception officer. I think he rather enjoyed it all. I heard that little pep talk he gave you in the Underground War Rooms was a classic."

"Bastards," Vicary muttered. "Manipulative bastards. But then, I suppose I should consider myself lucky. I could be dead like the others. My God! Do you realize how many people died for the sake of your little game? Pope, his girl, Rose Morely, the two Special Branch men at Earl's Court, the four police officers at Louth and another one at Cleethorpes, Sean Dogherty, Martin Colville."

"You're forgetting Peter Jordan."

"For God's sake, you killed your own agent."

"No Alfred, *you* killed him. You're the one who sent him out on that boat. I rather liked it, I must admit. The man whose personal carelessness almost cost us the war dies saving the life of a young girl and atones for his sins. That's how Hollywood would have done it. And that's what the Germans think really happened. And besides, the number of lives lost pales in comparison to the slaughter that would have taken place if Rommel had been waiting for us at Normandy."

"It's just credits and debits? Is that how you look at it? Like one giant accounting sheet? I'm glad I'm out! I don't want any part of it! Not if it means doing things like that. God, but we should have burned people like you at the stake a long time ago."

They crested a last hill. Vicary's house appeared before them in the distance. Matilda's flowering vines spilled over the protective limestone wall. He wanted to be back there—to slam his door and sit by the fire and never think of any of it again. He knew that was impossible now. He wanted to be rid of Boothby. He quickened his pace, pounding down the hill, nearly losing his balance. Boothby, with his long body and athletic legs, struggled to keep pace.

"You don't really feel that way, do you, Alfred? You liked it. You were seduced by it. You liked the manipulation and the deception. Your college wants you back, and you're not sure you want to go because you realize everything you've ever believed in is a lie and my world, this world, is the real world."

"You're not the real world. I'm not sure what you are, but you're not real."

"You can say that now, but I know you miss it all desperately. It's rather like a mistress, the kind of work we do. Sometimes you don't like her very much. You don't like yourself when you're with her. The moments when it feels good are fleeting. But when you try to leave her, something always pulls you back."

"I'm afraid the metaphor is lost on me, Sir Basil."

"There you go again, pretending to be superior, better than the rest of us. I would have thought you'd have learned your lesson by now. You need people like us. The country needs us."

They passed through the gate and into the drive. The gravel crunched beneath their feet. It reminded Vicary of the afternoon he was summoned to Chartwell and given the job at MI5. He remembered the morning at the Underground War Rooms, Churchill's words: *You must set aside whatever morals you still have, set aside whatever feelings of human kindness you still possess, and do whatever it takes to win.*

At least someone had been honest with him, even if it was a lie at the time.

They stopped at Boothby's Humber.

"You'll understand if I don't invite you in for refreshment," Vicary said. "I'd like to go wash the blood off my hands."

"That's the beauty of it, Alfred." Boothby held up his big paws for Vicary to see. "The blood is on my hands too. But I can't see it and no else can either. It's a secret stain."

The car's engine fired as Boothby opened the door.

"Who's Broome?" Vicary asked one last time.

Boothby's face darkened, as though a cloud had passed over it.

"Broome is Brendan Evans, your old friend from Cambridge. He told us about that stunt you pulled to get into the Intelligence Corps in the First War. He also told us what happened to you in France. We knew what drove you and what motivated you. We had to—we were running you, after all."

Vicary felt his head beginning to throb.

"I have one more question."

"You want to know if Helen was part of it or whether she came to you on her own."

Vicary stood very still, waiting for an answer.

"Why don't you go find her and ask her for yourself?"

Then Boothby disappeared into his car and was gone.

CHAPTER SIXTY-FOUR

LONDON: MAY 1945

At six o'clock that evening, Lillian Walford cleared her throat, knocked gently on the office door, and let herself inside without waiting for an answer. The professor was there, sitting in the window overlooking Gordon Square, his little body folded over an old manuscript.

"I'll be leaving now, Professor, if you've nothing else for me," she said, beginning the ritualistic closing of books and straightening of papers that always seemed to accompany their Friday evening conversations.

"No, I'll be fine, thank you."

She looked at him, thinking, No, somehow I doubt that very much, Professor. Something about him had changed. Oh, he was never the talkative sort, mind you; never one to strike up a conversation, unless it was completely necessary. But he seemed more withdrawn than ever, poor lamb. And it had grown worse as the term progressed, not better, as she had hoped. There was talk round the college, idle speculation. Some said he had sent men to their death, or ordered men killed. Hard to imagine the professor doing such things, but it made some sense, she had to admit. *Something* had made him take a vow of silence.

"You'd better be leaving soon, Professor, if you want to make your train."

"I rather thought I'd stay in London for the weekend," he said, without looking up from his work. "I'm interested in seeing what the place looks like at night, now that the lights are back on again."

"That's certainly one thing I hope I never see again, the bloody blackout."

"Something tells me you won't."

She removed his mackintosh from the hook on the back of the door and placed it on the chair next to his desk. He laid down his pencil and looked up at her. Her next action took them both by surprise. Her hand seemed to go to his cheek on its own, by reflex, the way it would reach out for a small child who had just been hurt.

"Are you all right, Professor?"

He drew away sharply and returned his gaze to the manuscript. "Yes, I'm fine," he said. There was a tone in his voice, an edge, she had never heard before. Then he mumbled something under his breath that sounded like "never better."

She turned and walked toward the door. "Have a pleasant weekend," she said.

"I intend to, thank you."

"Good night, Professor Vicary."

"Good night, Miss Walford."

The evening was warm, and by the time he crossed Leicester Square he had removed his mackintosh and folded it over his arm. The dusk was dying, the lights of London slowly coming up. Imagine Lillian Walford, touching his face like that. He had always thought of himself as an adequate dissembler. He wondered if it was that obvious.

He crossed Hyde Park. To his left, a band of Americans played softball in the faint light. To his right, British and Canadians played a noisy game of rugby. He passed a spot where only days before an antiaircraft gun had stood. The gun was gone; only the sandbags remained, like the stones of ancient ruins.

He entered Belgravia, and by instinct he walked toward Helen's house.

I hope you change your mind, and soon.

The blackout shades were up, and the house was ablaze with light. There were two other couples with them. David was wearing his uniform. Helen hung on his arm. Vicary wondered how long he had been standing there, watching them, watching her. Much to his surprise—or was it relief, perhaps—he felt nothing for her. Her ghost had finally left him, this time for good.

He walked away. The King's Road turned to Sloane Square, and Sloane Square to quiet side streets of Chelsea. He looked at his watch; there was still time to make the train. He found a taxi, asked the driver to take him to Paddington Station, and climbed inside. He pulled down the window and felt the warm wind in his face. For the first time in many months, he felt something like contentment, something like peace.

He telephoned Alice Simpson from a phone box at the station, and she agreed to come to the country the next morning. He rang off and had to rush for his train. The carriage was crowded, but he found a seat next to the window in a compartment with two old women and a boyish-faced soldier clutching a cane.

He looked at the soldier and noticed he was wearing the insignia of the 2nd East York Regiment. Vicary knew the boy had been at Normandy—Sword Beach, to be precise—and he was lucky to be alive. The East Yorks had suffered heavy casualties during the first minutes of the invasion.

The soldier noticed Vicary looking at him, and he managed a brief smile.

"Happened at Normandy. Barely made it out of the landing craft." He held up the cane. "Doctors say I'll need to use this for the rest of my life. How'd you get yours—the limp, that is?"

"The First War, France," Vicary said distantly.

"They bring you back for this lot?"

Vicary nodded. "A desk job in a very dull department of the War Office. Nothing important, really."

After a while the soldier slept. Once, in the passing fields, Vicary saw her face, smiling at him, just for an instant. Then he saw Boothby's. Then, as the darkness gathered, his own reflection, riding silently next to him in the glass.

ABOUT THE AUTHOR

DANIEL SILVA, a veteran newspaper and television journalist, is the executive producer of CNN's Washington-based public affairs programming, including such popular series as *Crossfire, The Capital Gang, Inside Politics Weekend, Late Edition,* and *Evans & Novak. The Unlikely Spy,* his first novel, has been translated into more than a dozen languages. He lives in Washington, D.C., with his wife, NBC *Today* show correspondent Jamie Gangel, and their two children. He is currently at work on his second novel.